DUEL AT GOLDEN CITY

Gilish cut at Gustave's head.

Instead of ducking out of the way, the hero stepped *into* it, and reversed his grip on the blade so it lay braced along his left forearm. With his metal-reinforced arm, he parried the saber with a simple sweep. He then brought up his right fist and punched the pirate's ugly face, busting his lip and three intertwined emerald snakes.

A snarl spread across Gilish's features. Rather than stepping back and using his sword properly, he grabbed Gustave's wrist, twisting his thumb and index finger into a painful lock.

Gustave smiled. He was now inside the reach of Gilish's saber with a proper close-fighting weapon. With a twist of his free hand, he reversed the blade that lay against his forearm, and skewered the pirate's throat, impaling a lovely tattoo of a slave girl bound in chains.

The green pirate turned white, dropped his saber, and fell to the floor . . .

D1150313

Also by Eric S. Nylund in New English Library paperback

Pawn's Dream

About the author

Eric S. Nylund was born in Los Angeles, California in 1964, and was raised in the alpine mountains near Lake Tahoe and, later, in the wind-swept Mojave desert. He obtained his Master's degree in chemical physics from the University of California, San Diego. He uses science fiction and fantasy as a palette to explore the human psyche and soul, and to tell the stories of his life.

Nylund currently resides in the spirit-filled woods of the Pacific Northwest.

A Game of
Universe

Eric S. Nylund

NEW ENGLISH LIBRARY
Hodder and Stoughton

Copyright © 1997 by Eric S. Nylund

First published in Great Britain in 1997
by Hodder and Stoughton
A division of Hodder Headline PLC

A New English Library paperback

The right of Eric S. Nylund to be identified as the Author of
the Work has been asserted by him in accordance with the
Copyright, Designs and Patents Act 1988.

10 9 8 7 6 5 4 3 2 1

British Library Cataloguing in Publication Data

A CIP catalogue record for this title is available from the
British Library

ISBN 0 340 64949 6

Typeset by Avon Dataset Ltd, Bidford-on-Avon, Warks

Printed and bound in Great Britain by
Cox & Wyman, Reading, Berks

Hodder and Stoughton
A division of Hodder Headline PLC
338 Euston Road
London NW1 3BH

To Joseph Campbell who led me to the lair of the
Dragon of Not.

To Joan Wrin who set my feet on the path to
Mount Purgatorio.

And to the Lady who was at the end of my
journey – Syne.

Chapter One

Cheaters were burned here. It happened the last time we came to Golden City. Two bouncers stopped the floor show and dragged the guy on stage. Right there with spotlights reflecting off their metallic skins, and the genetically modified feather girls watching, they torched him. It might happen to me tonight. The gambler was cheating – and with borrowed money.

He made my head look up from his cards, and massaged the aching neck muscles we shared. A column covered with triangular tiles of silver and onyx stood to my right. Eight reflected faces regarded me. It was a face that had been altered so many times I didn't recognize the long black hair, nor the splash of freckles across a wide nose, nor the green eyes dilated in the darkness. It was a face I did not command. There were others within me, parasites. No, to be fair, their existence was my doing. I absorbed their souls.

You did not absorb their souls, the persona I called the psychologist remarked. *Mysticism has little to do with what I have diagnosed as a self-induced multiple personalities disorder; however, since you have duplicated eight neural matrices into a non-fragmentary hierarchy, I am uncertain precisely how to treat your condition.*

Then don't try, I said.

I assure you it is no trouble. Your case intrigues me. It is yet another example of what barbarians believe to be magic, but in reality is an amazingly sophisticated piece of psychology.

Fantastic. But you're in no position to write me up in The Journal of Clinical Psychology. *You're dead, remember?*

He ignored my comment and said, *Had you been taught proper mental control rather than this . . . this occultism, I am certain your mind would be coherent. But first, tell me how long it has been since you last possessed your body?*

It had been seven days, but I said nothing. The psychologist became unbearably smug when he analyzed me. Instead, I returned to my vigil, and waited for an opportunity to seize my body back.

Normally, my ego had the strength to withstand my extra personas. There were times, however, when their fascinations lent them the strength to wrest control from me.

My body stood up from the velvet stool and stretched. We had been here for six hours, long enough for the smell of the place, sweat, exotic perfume, and expensive rum, to get under my skin.

Smoke drifted through the casino in ever-changing currents, around columns, over the Universe tables, churned by the spinning roulette spheres – vortices in mid-air – that were sucked in, then exhaled by the crowds of tourists determined to lose their money.

The gambler had my body tonight. His compulsion to wager, and cheat, gave him the stamina to stand up to the rest of us, and maintain his count of the one hundred twenty-eight-card Universe deck. No one knew what he was up to, yet.

Across the casino floor, the bone pit caught his attention. It was a high-stake game by the size of the crowd. The pitcher shook three dice in his hand. He heaved the cubes with all his strength, then watched them bounce at crazy angles through the uneven gravity field. One came up a blank and his face collapsed. The other two rolled into a jackpot orbit! Lights exploded and sirens wailed. The cocktail waitresses on either side kissed him.

My most recent persona, Omar, thought the gambler sufficiently distracted and extended his will. He had a vested interest at Golden City, too.

They struggled, ego grappled with ego, but the gambler's addiction crushed Omar's ambition. The gambler kept my body.

Omar, like me, was a muse, what some called a sorcerer – what the psychologist called a primitive. And like me, Omar killed for a living.

You should have taken my deal, Omar said.

I think not. The Corporation sent me to check on your free-lancing. If I had accepted, they would have sent two operatives. One for you and one for me.

Destiny knocks but a single time. You pass up the contract of a lifetime. The man who owns this place will pay us a fortune. My offer of a sixty–forty split is still open.

Omar hadn't quite figured out he was dead. *Who said I was passing it up?*

What do you mean? he demanded.

I have your invitation. I know the code. I'll take your place.

That's illegal.

So it is.

A week ago, I stole Omar's mind for the mnemonic lore within. His ambitions caught me off guard. He had a freelancing job that would make him a rich man, or so he thought. He hijacked my body, brought it here, and went about his business. Practical man, that Omar.

He almost got away with it too; a single mistake he made: strolling though the casino . . . past the Universe tables. That's when the gambler woke up and took control from *him*.

A cocktail waitress came and left a frosty glass filled with a fluorescing yellow liquid and pink paper umbrella for the gambler. He took a sip: tequila, slushy ice, lime, and the tang of sea salt. The gambler set it aside, squeezed the bridge on my nose, and pretended to be as stoned as the other tourists.

Omar struggled again for control, a futile gesture. The gambler squashed the attempt. *Just a few more hands*, he insisted. *I'm almost to the end of the deck.*

He commanded my body to sit, rubbed his sweaty palms on the green felt of the table, then smiled apologetically at the dealer. Her glare told him to forget any ideas of drinks together later, which was a shame, for she had lovely brown eyes. She was a handsome girl with high cheekbones and fingers nimble enough to cheat the tourists. On the outer corner of either eye were triangle-cut sapphires, the mark of a full-apprentice card dealer. The gambler specifically sought a dealer of her rank, since a master-dealer would have immediately known what he was up to, and the junior apprentices were monitored too closely.

We had the table to ourselves.

There was one more nova in this deck, and that worried the gambler because he held two of them already. Two novas were a good hand, three nearly unbeatable, so he discarded both exploding stars, increased his bet by five, and told her, 'Two please'.

She flicked her wrist and a pair of magnetically repelled cards skimmed to his waiting fingers. He picked them up with great care: a fragment of the celestial dragon, all gold and ebony scales, and a brilliant quasar wearing a halo of silver (that card was hot to the touch). These he added to the remainder of his hand: an ice comet with diamond dust tail, a gas giant, and two moons, one volcanic, sulfurous yellow, the other covered with ivory clouds, lustrous like a pearl. The gambler did a quick count and determined the odds to be greatly in the house's favor. Precisely what he wanted.

'When do you finish your shift?' he asked her. 'There's a game of non-linear roulette tonight in the Fantastica Lounge. Maybe you and I could go as a team?'

'I'm sorry, sir,' she replied, 'but fraternization with our customers is prohibited. It compromises the integrity of the game.' She didn't even flash him one of those fake smiles the staff had to give when propositioned. Then again, with a line like that, what did he expect?

Celeste whispered to me, *Shall I suggest a line to our clumsy friend so he can seduce her?* Celeste had been an imperial geisha to the Tun Mi Lung Empire, mistress-class, and a spy. There was a time when I cared for her. I wanted to believe her loyalty to her emperor had forced her hand when she had tried to murder me. No so. When I absorbed her soul I learned what she truly was: treachery and lust unsatisfied.

We have enough problems without an unscheduled orgy, I warned her. *Be good.*

'Is that your bet, sir?' the dealer inquired.

'Yes,' the gambler answered. 'I call.'

The dealer reversed the magnetic field of the table and our card plates turned over. She had a stellar cluster: two red giants and a white dwarf, plus three planets. It easily beat his incomplete system.

The endgame tone sounded, and the winning cards came to life. Three stars blazed above the table; the red giants smoldered as embers would, lumbering about one another, while the white dwarf traced a figure-eight orbit between them – a lady dancing with her clumsy brothers. The image stayed just long enough for me to feel the suns' warmth upon my face, then they collapsed back into cards.

The gambler sighed, pretending to be surprised at yet another loss. Now, if he counted correctly (never an absolute certainly with a deck of one hundred and twenty-eight cards), there were twenty-three left in the deck. Twelve of which were dragons, and two the elusive head-biting-tail segments.

You have had enough opportunity, Omar said. *Let me take over. The job I have will profit us more than this game.*

Have patience, the gambler told him. *The next hand is the one.*

To win, the gambler needed the co-operation of our dealer. She did have the option to reshuffle and ruin everything. But would she? Maybe not. He had been careful to lose all evening, careful to look like one unlucky tourist among thousands. I had to admit he was good at it, too. He kept my face molded in the appropriate hopeful expression, and placed the minimum wager in the betting circle, a single, then pretended to count his pathetic stack of chips.

The dealer didn't reshuffle, bless her heart.

Six card plates glided over the felt to him: three sections of the dragon, a head-eating-tail piece, all curved teeth and one eye, a supernova with explosions of white brilliance and ruby, and a vacuum, frigid empty black (and cold to the touch).

He pulled the supernova and vacuum from his hand and set them aside.

'Cards, sir?' the dealer inquired.

'Yes, I'll take . . .'

Wait! the psychologist cried. *She suspects.*

Impossible, the gambler thought. *How could she?*

Unknown. I predict, however, she will use the table's reader to view our discards. Exercise caution.

If she saw his discards, she might as well see his hand, for no one threw away a supernova on the first pass unless they were collecting dragons. She might even guess he had been counting cards.

The gambler frowned, this time for real, then added one of his dragons to the supernova and vacuum – there was no other way to fool her. Apprehension flooded my stomach, burning acid and adrenaline.

'Three cards,' he said.

'And the dealer takes . . .' She peered into the table's reader, scanning the cards just as the psychologist had predicted. She chewed on her lower lip, puzzled by the supernova and the dragon together, but she didn't figure it out. 'The dealer takes two,' she said, then collected his discards and tossed them down the disposal slot. 'Bets before cards, please.'

It was time. From his tuxedo vest, he removed an iridium chip the shape of the casino's seal, a seven-pointed star. He set his fortune into the betting circle.

'One hundred thousand is my wager.'

Her brown eyes went wide and her eyebrows arched in surprise. It was too late, though. Once she eliminated the discards from the table, the hand had to continue; it was a rule. Her wide eyes narrowed to slits, angry, then relaxed. She passed her hand over the comlink, summoning the pit boss, and said, 'If you don't mind, sir, I must take a fifteen-minute break. Casino regulations.'

'I understand completely,' the gambler said. Her replacement would be a master dealer, one of the best in the joint. The game began for real.

The master dealer came immediately, materializing from the shadows and smoke that filled this corner of the casino. His forehead was scarred by worry lines, the skin under his eyes ringed black, and when he saw the hundred thousand chip, he wrinkled his lipless mouth into a scowl. His insignia was a single diamond, about three carats' worth, implanted in the outer corner of his left eye. Built into the jewel were thermal sensors that detected the blush response of a liar, a link to the casino's computer to track the cards in a working deck, and other technologies I could only guess at to enhance his skills.

Our first dealer stepped aside and whispered to him. His glare never moved from me as she explained.

'Who are you?' he asked, neither demanding nor being polite.

We answered, 'Germain,' and casually set my right hand on the table. About my wrist wound a copper band designed to scramble probes and divinations. It would counter his diamond.

He stared off into blank space for a moment – a quick scan for illegal devices on my body – and his frown deepened. He had detected nothing. 'I'm afraid,' he said, 'that this must be your last hand at the Golden City tonight, Mister Germain.'

'One game is all I have time for. I'm expected in the Turquoise Room soon.'

The master dealer reappraised the gambler, then nodded. 'The Turquoise Room, of course . . .'

Why did you speak? Omar demanded. *Now everyone will know of our job.*

Including the dealer and the casino manager, the gambler replied. *If we are the owner's guest, they may play this hand without stacking the deck. And odds are I'll be able to keep my winnings. A rare event.*

That's how the gambler originally met his demise. He won too much, too many times, from the same source. Hit a jackpot once, and a casino chalks it off to good public relations. The tourists loved to see it – usually doubled the profits for the evening – but win over and over, or worse, win big without giving the casino a chance to recoup, and someone like me gets hired.

'I believe you owe me three cards?'

'So I do,' he admitted. With his index finger, he slid the top cards from the deck and pushed them to the gambler.

There was a minuscule wobble to the gliding cards when they came close to his right hand, the hand with the obscuring bracelet. The gambler hastily scooped them up: a crimson nebula and two more sections of the dragon. He thought, *Allowing the chance of the dealer to get dragons from the deck, and if my count is accurate, then three of the remaining six cards are dragons. Even money to make the wyrm.*

The master dealer looked at his hand, gave a sideways glance to the remaining cards in the deck, pondered a moment, then his mouth cracked into a ghoulish grin. 'The dealer takes six,' he said.

Six cards finished the deck and took our dragons! He'd need a new deck to finish our hand. The gambler's odds suddenly dropped from an even split to less than one in seven (assuming this dealer didn't try to deal off the bottom).

It complicated matters because the gambler had to win. It

wasn't my money he bet with. He had borrowed the sum from a group of unsavory individuals (at a stiff rate of interest), and if not repaid within twelve hours, they'd extract the balance from his flesh – my flesh. For this amount, I estimated an arm or a few teeth might be left for the Corporation to find. Maybe.

The dealer waved his hand over the call pad and summoned a fresh deck. A glitter of stars, then a gold-leaf package faded into reality, never before touched, and with all its random probabilities intact beneath the certified seal, a black seven-pointed star.

'Bets before cards, please,' he announced, appearing quite happy with himself.

The gambler quickly composed his thoughts, removed the second, and last, iridium chip from my vest, and set it atop the other in the betting circle. 'One hundred thousand,' he answered in a deadpan voice.

The dealer's smile vanished, replaced by more wrinkles on his forehead. 'I am sorry, sir, but to place a wager of that magnitude I must obtain permission from the manager.'

'Why?' the gambler demanded, raising my voice to everyone within five tables heard. 'That's the maximum legal bet, isn't it? Or do you have one set of rules for the losers and another for the winners?'

'There is no need to shout sir, I only wish to—'

'—You'll accept my bet, or I will withdraw from the game and take my money elsewhere.' Only then did I notice that all the games within earshot had stopped, and a crowd had gathered around our table, tourists eager to see the casino lose big. The gambler saw them too, and held his cards closer, fearing Golden City spies.

The master dealer glanced at the display on his left and saw a blinking green light. 'Very well, Mister Germain, the house approves this transaction. It is your money to throw away.' He grabbed the new deck.

'Wait!' the gambler said before he snapped the seal. 'I double my wager.'

'Double?'

'Yes, I may double my bet if a new deck is used to finish a hand, and do so on credit. It's in the rules, number seventeen, section three. Look it up if you wish.'

The master-dealer called up the dictionary of rules on his display, and did just that.

This rule is for suckers, the gambler explained to us. *It tempts the tourists with dreams of wealth, tempts them into serious debt. The odds favor the house – more so with their professional dealers. They ordinarily make money on it . . . but not always, and not tonight.*

The dealer halted his scan, pausing to read what the gambler knew was there. He nodded to me, and said, 'You are correct, sir. You do have the option to double . . . on credit. I salute your knowledge of the game.'

The crowd buzzed with excitement. No one had won, or lost, such a sum for a long time.

Besides, the gambler reasoned, *if I'm going to risk your neck for money, it should be an astronomical amount, right?* He threw the nebula away, and said, 'One card.'

The dealer snapped the seal.

When shuffling, a dealer will cut the one hundred twenty-eight-card Universe deck into two or three sections that are manageable. Not this time. The master dealer made them waltz for him, layers of spinning cards, cut, and cut again with one hand, then arched, fanned into a circle, and repeated even faster. He offered us a cut. The gambler took it, but what was the point?

He tossed the top card. It skimmed slowly over the felt, and came to rest in his hand, the first from the supposedly random-ized deck, face down. A billion stars gleamed on its reverse side, stars that determined my fate: riches or ruin.

'The dealer takes two,' he said.

I didn't hear him. My entire concentration was on the card, still floating a hairsbreadth above the table. The gambler touched it: ice cold, so I knew it wasn't a star, but maybe all the cards from a new deck were this cold.

Beneath the stars, he turned to find . . .

Vacuum, black and empty as his luck,

'*I fold*,' the gambler whispered to us and left my body.

Omar hesitated, frustrated by the souring of our fortune.

I moved in quickly before anyone else took control. Like emerging from a tunnel, my full senses returned to me. The cool metallic surfaces of the card plates, the scent of my own perspiration, the whisperings of the crowd, the thumping of my heart – all sensations I'd never take for granted again.

Not a twitch betrayed my emotions; neither a frown nor a sigh marred my expression of stone. I kept my eyes upon the unwanted card, however, so no one saw the panic in them.

There were few options. If I continued to play, I'd lose. Without the last piece of the dragon, this hand was worthless. A single pair of moons beat me. Could I escape? Possibly. Melt into the crowd, sprint to the spaceport, and forget Omar's meeting? No, that wouldn't work. For this kind of money, they'd come looking for me. An example would be made of me.

As a muse I had mental constructs. That was cheating – not that I had any objections at this point – but the casino tortured to death the muses they found cheating at their tables. Six engrams of power were mine to use, three of my own, and three stolen.

'Additional bets?' the dealer inquired.

My mental constructs were impractical in this situation: *The Theorem of Malleability* softened metals; the ocular enhancer enabled me to see in absolute darkness; and the ritual of borrowing gave me the power to absorb my extra personas – all useless in a game of chance.

The dealer cleared his throat and again asked: 'Mister Germain, are you betting?'

Three of my extra personalities contained mnemonic lore. These were priceless to me because I could use them only once. Each had originally required years of laborious study from their former owners. Forcing that knowledge unwound their intellect like threads from a tapestry.

In Omar's mind was the *Abridged Manifoldification*. I had only to visualize another place, and I appeared there, exchanging my mass with another of equal value. It made escape trivial. But again, it would buy me only a brief respite, then the casino and the gambler's money lenders would track me down.

Next: *Aaron's Air Attraction*, held within the persona of an alien king. For the span of three heartbeats, it condensed a large volume of gas into liquid. When the surrounding air rushed in to fill this void it added enough thermal energy to the liquified air to flash-vaporize it, and explode. Using it within the confines of the casino would kill me. And I had never been suicidal.

Finally, my Master's mnemonic construct, the *Enchantment of Time Lost*, reversed time for seven seconds, to replay, hopefully, with an alternate outcome. Seven seconds would change nothing now. I had spent longer than that just thinking this through.

Pandemonium erupted in my mind as my personas offered their advice: *We don't have a chance!* the gambler cried. *Don't panic*, whispered the psychologist. *I am certain if you explain your situation to the authorities they would be reasonable.* Omar hissed, *You deserve what they're going to do to you. Keep your chin up, Honey*, Celeste cooed. *You'll figure a way out.* And Fifty-five said, *Five security men at your back, watch it.*

I answered them all: *Why don't you go to Hell?* They couldn't, of course. They were motionless within my mind, insects petrified in resin. Motionless? Motion implied movement, a shift from one place to another? – or a switch! Yes, a switch.

How many cards covered the gambler's first discard, the dragon? There were the dealer's six, then his two, for a total of eight. Add one for the nebula he just threw away, so nine. Nine cards were ahead of the one I wanted in the disposal chute. There was no time to go over it again. I held the vacuum card in my left hand, concentrated, and released the *Abridged Manifoldification*.

Omar struggled, and held onto his memories.

I knew that if I didn't pull this off, we'd all be tortured for the gambler's crime. Omar's will was no match for that. I ripped the engrams free; they drained from his intellect, and the last moments of his life passed before my eyes – a disturbing image of my own face leering above his while I strangled him.

Please, he begged, but his voice faded. Omar's soul unraveled, then was gone.

The power to travel light-years through space made my ears buzz and my eyes water; yet I only exchanged two cards about a meter apart. Mentally counting through the card plates in the discard chute, top to bottom, I grabbed the tenth and held it firmly in my imagination.

But as I grabbed the card, something grabbed me. A spike of white-hot metal shattered my thoughts.

That would be the casino's psychologist probing for illegal constructs, my psychologist informed me. *He will confirm who you are, determine precisely what you are doing, then scramble your mind.*

How do I stop him?

You cannot.

Like hell I can't.

A glowing sapphire seven-pointed star appeared. It was transparent with hundreds of veins zigzagging to the center, pulsing with energy and life.

That is his construct, the psychologist said. *Quite impenetrable. He is protected in the center.*

I entered. Inside, the pathways intersected, pulled apart, pinched closed, and opened at random. I took the first right. I guessed left next, then right, then found myself trapped in an infinitely decreasing spiral.

This has a pattern, whispered the psychologist.

I recognized it: Hadrain's Law of Diminishing Returns. The exit had to be straight up. I took it. Behind me the path I had been on snapped shut.

The tunnel narrowed. I moved faster like a liquid forced into a smaller pipe. Omar's *Abridged Manifoldification* trailed behind me, brushed the sides of the maze, and sent sparks into the ether.

Right and left corkscrew tunnels, and I emerged in the center. The casino's psychologist turned, startled.

Mental probes link mind to mind, I said, *which is risky not knowing whom you face.*

Who are you?

We are many.

I snuffed him.

A flash of light—

—then my perspective flickered. I again sat at the Universe table.

The card in my hand blurred, almost imperceptibly, as if I waved it rapidly back and forth (but I did not). In the blank blackness that was once a vacuum, hundreds of shimmering golden scales appeared. I had the gambler's original dragon back.

I exhaled and looked up from my card. Had anyone seen the switch? No, the dealer, his face was still wrinkled with concern, not filled with the joy I'd expect if he caught my deceit. I glanced to the first dealer, the girl. Her eyes locked with mine. There was something in her stare, a glimmer of understanding. She knew.

'Last call for bets sir,' the master dealer announced.

Why hasn't she said anything?

I sense, the psychologist replied, *that she derives pleasure from the casino's ill fortune.*

'Sir?' the master dealer asked. 'Stand pat or raise?'

'I double my bet *again*.'

'Double? Again, sir?'

'Double and call,' I stated flatly.

He swallowed, and the diamond in the corner of his eye flashed blue, reflecting the overhead lights, then he reversed the magnetic field of the table. His cards turned first: a cluster of three binary stars, two quasars, and a black hole – an excellent hand, for which I privately admired his skill at cheating.

Then my cards flipped.

The six spun apart and came to rest in a hexagon pattern, the sections of the celestial dragon melding in one seamless circle, joined by the head-eating-tail, a ring of gold.

'Universe!' I cried.

The master dealer hung his head, and an appreciative 'Ahhh' rolled through the crowd, along with a smattering of applause.

The endgame tone sounded thrice, and my winning cards animated. The dragon leapt off the cards and into the air, a serpentine circle. It twisted and growled and consumed itself in a contorted toroidal Möbius, head devouring tail, shrinking until it was no more than a golden ball over the betting circle, then compressed to a point of light. A roar, primeval, part reptile, part earthquake, came from every direction. And while the echoes still lingered, the compressed dragon detonated. Scales, ivory teeth, and talons erupted from the point, each one transforming into a glistening galaxy, motes of brilliance that spun with celestial grace.

It was a beautiful sight to behold. I was rich and alive.

The stars revolved about the table clockwise, spiraling in ever larger circles, every cluster of galaxies rotating at a different angle, some spinning fast, others globs of star dust with no perceivable gyrations. They slowed, and when the universe spanned five tables in diameter and touched the chandeliers overhead, it halted. With a scarcely detectable motion, it reversed course, counterclockwise, into the center, increasing speed, galaxies colliding, faster and faster, a million stars exploding, still faster, blurring into a single mass, the light compressing into solid scales and teeth and talons, a dragon again! He winked his single eye at me, and back into the cards he slithered.

The master dealer, without meeting my eyes, said, 'Pardon me, Mister Germain, we have insufficient funds at this table to settle our wager.' His display flashed amber. He glanced into it, and hastily added, 'However, I have been authorized to open an account at the casino bank and deposit your winnings there, if that is acceptable.'

'Eminently acceptable,' I said.

He offered me a receipt ring, which I slipped on. I allowed it to imprint my DNA pattern, then handed it back to him.

'Thank you for the game. Now, if you will excuse me.' I quickly left the Universe table before questions were asked, loans requested, or someone bothered to count the dragons in either deck.

Stay a while, Celeste urged. *There were ladies and boys, delectable young things, itching to meet you back there. Spend some cash. Buy them a few drinks. Pleasure yourself. Why don't we? You never relax.*

My dear, I said, *that's why I'm still alive.*

I crossed the sparkling, smoke-filled arena, past one-armed machines that glittered prismatic and bleeped cheerfully while they ate money, past dealers who carefully milked the tourists, and past cocktail waitresses who wore only sequins and veils and offered an endless supply of pleasures. A plaque of gold above an indigo curtain on the far wall proclaimed, TURQUOISE ROOM – RESTRICTED, in clear black letters. Twin guards, part human and part mechanized tank, bristling with armor and weapon implants, blocked the entrance.

For a moment, I almost played it safe and left, but the late Omar believed there was money in this, enough to risk the wrath of Umbra Corp by freelancing. How much could it hurt to hear the wealthy man out? I handed his invitation chip to the guard on the left and spoke the code phrase: 'Life is precious.'

The cyborg scanned the chip with a reader in its thumb, then snapped it in half. With a voice that might have been female once, it replied, 'Please go in, sir. You are expected.'

I entered an antechamber and a wall formed behind me. A faint hum emanated from all sides, a scan for weapons and offensive mental devices. I had nothing detectable on my person. The door facing me dissolved open, and I walked through.

The chamber had seven sides paved with turquoise squares set in silver. Arcane mnemonic runes of inlaid moonstones were set into every seventh stone. Some of them I understood – *Isolation, the Void, Stability* – but most were beyond my comprehension. Whatever the enchantment was, I sensed it. The hairs on my arms stood tall, and the back of my neck tingled.

Five rows of plush seats had been arranged in concentric circles around a central projection pad, maybe forty seats in all. Filling a third of them were an odd assemblage. There were several I recognized with outstanding reputations. Better than mine.

Standing in the corner was E'kerta, a collection of insects, a small self-contained hive that I knew well from my Corporation. Each of his ten arms, composed of hundreds of beetles, was equally deadly and silent. He was a strange creature to watch, for his shape shifted periodically, limbs that stretched to long and frail, or compressed to fat tentacles. He appeared fluid, but I had seen him kill, and when organized the overlapping carapaces of his hive were as strong as adamant steel.

In the second row, I spotted Gilish the Green. Our paths had crossed before and I was fortunate to have escaped with my life. My features were different now. He didn't recognize me. The pirate covered his body with green animated tattoos, one for each of his legendary conquests. Tiny starships burned, women were ravaged, and men were slain across his flesh.

And there were heroes. Gustave Barbaroux, who single-handedly smashed the invasion plans of the Spartan Conglomerate and saved countless lives on the world of Colonus, sat with his hands politely folded in his lap. He ignored the riff-raff about him, brushed back his thick blond hair, and waited for the show to begin. He was young, perhaps twenty-two, skinny, and human. I judged him no threat to my abilities.

But there was an old woman who sat alone, far from the others, Sister Olivia of the Order of the Burning Cross. Give me a fire worshipper, a priest of Shiva the Destroyer, an acolyte of Bloody Elisa, the patron saint of vacuum, or even a scholar of Thoth, but not someone who believed they ate their own god's flesh and drank his blood once a week. Barbarians. I wouldn't have minded so much, but Sister Olivia was said to possess holy powers – exorcism, walking on water, pillars of fire – and that I did mind.

I counted twelve heads in all, thirteen including myself. What did we have in common? Why would the owner of Golden City bring cutthroats and saints, heroes and villains together?

The lights dimmed, and I took the closest empty chair, just making it before the center lit up with a virtual image. The waves of static solidified into an elderly man. His black eyes were what I noticed first, large, dilated, bottomless. His silver hair draped behind his shoulders, loose but still neat. He wore a smartly tailored suit and stood two meters tall. Although the image could have been programmed to look like anything, I perceived this man to be exactly as he showed himself. The way he stood and held his head high, he was absolute in his confidence. I appreciated that.

'I am Erybus Alexander,' he said. His voice was soft, but powerful, like the rumble after a crack of thunder. 'My gratitude for responding to my summons.'

Someone came in late, passed in front of me, and took the seat on my left. 'So, he invited you too,' this person whispered from the dark. 'Rumor has it your luck is as strong as ever, and the casino is poorer for it. That is a good omen.'

The voice was familiar, slick and deep, like a reptile in human form. I keyed the mnemonic constructs on my right hand and released the ocular enhancer. My vision pierced the shadows and showed me what I suspected. It was Omar – the man whose mind I had absorbed and erased moments ago, the man I had strangled seven days ago with my bare hands.

Chapter Two

'I have an offer I would like you to consider,' Omar whispered to me.

I nodded. 'Later. I would hear our host first.'

There were two possibilities. Either it was not the real Omar I had strangled and buried a week ago, or the man I sat next to was an impostor. Yet he appeared as he always had, clean shaven, short gray hair, and an infectious smile. Even his cologne was the same clean citrus scent.

One more possibility, junior, the persona I called Fifty-five said. Fifty-five was both his rank and his name. He was also an assassin, the one who led me to this career. He was paranoid in the extreme, but his advice had often saved my life. Dying tends to make one cautious.

Tell me.

Cloned. The practice is forbidden by Corporate law. It messes up our ranking system – not that any regulation would stop Omar. He'd kill, blackmail, and cheat to advance himself.

How did he get in? I have his coded invitation chip.

We've got bigger things to worry about, Fifty-five said. *This is a secret meeting, invitation only, right? The man you're supposed to be is sitting next to you. How long do you think it will take them to figure that out? You better leave.*

He was correct. I could be silenced in a number of extremely unpleasant ways if caught. Looking for the door I came through, I saw only turquoise tiles and moonstones . . . and no exit.

The psychologist whispered, *No one has noticed. Remain calm. Do nothing to draw attention to yourself. Perhaps we may yet walk out unscathed.*

If we're lucky.

The virtual Erybus continued, 'My time is limited, so I shall dispense with formalities. You are here because of your reputations, your resourcefulness, and because you exist outside the influential spheres of my corporations.

'First, your compensation.' He snapped his fingers and faded from view. 'If you find it compelling, you may remain so we may discuss the assignment.'

A new image appeared on the projection pad, two balls of light, a binary star, shining in the center of the room. A golden orb cradled a smaller blue-white companion; fingers of plasma writhed between them. The inlaid moonstones on the walls glowed in this new sunlight like pale stars in the night sky.

'The binary system, Erato, contains seven planets,' Erybus's disembodied voice explained. 'Two are gas giants rich in industrial fluorocarbons, three are balls of ice, but two, the second and third worlds, are special.'

A sphere of cobalt replaced the blazing stars. It had a cap of ice on either pole and pink clouds finger-painted upon its surface. One continent, a jigsaw of rivers and mountains, floated among a thousand islands in a mirror-dark seas. 'This planet has been terraformed to a prime rating and is ready for immediate colonization.'

Another globe materialized. Streaks of black and orange, clouds from its active volcanoes, smeared a third of the sky with veils of ash. 'This planet possesses only a tertiary rating, but yields an annual treasure-trove of gems, heavy metals, and rare Philosopher Stones.'

The worlds winked out of existence, and Erybus reappeared center stage, his raven eyes inspecting the shadows we sat in. 'In exchange for your co-operation, the title to the seven worlds and both stars is yours.'

'No man has such wealth to proffer,' Omar said to me.

'Indeed.' I grew up mining Philosopher Stones. A perfect specimen was worth a fortune. How much would a planetful be worth? A sum beyond my reckoning.

Not mine, remarked the gambler.

Gilish the Green jumped to his feet and cried, 'Rocks? What do I care for rocks? You own Morning Star. You offer me more or I leave. You offer me more or I order my ships to destroy Golden City!'

The tattooed pirate's greed was legendary. I admired him for it because you always knew where you stood with Gilish – at the business end of his saber. He wore his sword openly. Curious that he had been allowed to keep it in his secure room; then again, I couldn't imagine anyone foolhardy enough to try and take it from him.

A smile rippled across Erybus's lips, then withered. 'I value your bravado, Mister Gilish. Feel free to attack my Golden City. The diversion would prove amusing. You have, however, anticipated my generosity. My Morning Star Cartel has many facets, rewards to suit every appetite . . . even yours.'

His virtual image shattered: glittering bits upon the projection pad. Octahedral crystals of gold packed into ebony chests, coffers filled with Indigo-Fire diamonds and bipolar Star Emeralds and pink pearls the size of goose eggs, bolts of Iridescene silk, embroidered with roses, lilies, and chrysanthemum, cut crystal vials of bioluminescent life-extending elixir, idols of jade, a throne of lapis, and countless silver coins spilled across the stage, surged forward, then vanished before they touched the floor.

Erybus returned. No smile. 'Sufficient?'

Gilish's face split in two – a grin of crooked teeth the dividing line – and he sat down.

His wealth appealed to me, but even more appealing was that Erybus owned the Morning Star Cartel. That was real power and wealth.

The Cartel was on Earth before the First and Second Expansions. They were the first to get a firm financial hold on Mars, Alpha Centauri, and the rest of the colonies. When the Second Expansion hit, they were *everywhere* at once. Only a handful of corporations made the transition to a galactic market. Morning Star led them. Among the governments, cults, and corporate entities that swam the choppy sea of changing political boundaries and fiscal opportunity, Morning Star Cartel was a shark that went out of its way to gobble up the competition. If Erybus owned the cartel, then he could offer a reward to make my winnings in the casino seem like dropped change . . . too small to pick up.

'With extraordinary compensation,' Erybus continued, 'comes an equally extraordinary task. Some have claimed it impossible.'

'Pardon me,' the young hero Gustave said and politely raised his hand. 'If, sir, you are wealthy as you claim, then why not undertake this task yourself? Surely you are better equipped and have more resources than any one of us.'

Watch this one, Fifty-five said. *He doesn't fit in with the rest of this bunch. Something stinks about him.*

'If I could use my resources in this affair,' Erybus said, the rumble underlying his voice crackling like thunder, 'I would. I am, however, bound by contractual obligations to follow an exact set of rules. These rules . . . the contract which binds me, has insured my long life, my success in business, and my delight for centuries. But like all contracts of its type, it has a limited duration. When it expires, my life and my immortal soul are forfeit.'

Sister Olivia rose from her seat, her bones popping and crackling. She pointed a trembling finger at him, and hissed, 'You sold your soul to the devil? How dare you beg for God's mercy.'

Erybus's dark eyes twinkled. 'Sold my soul to the devil? That is a simplistic analysis of an intricate business transaction, but yes, technically, if you wish to describe it in such terms, I did precisely that.'

'And what makes you think I would help undo your folly?' she demanded.

'Daughter of God, I appreciate your apprehension.' His eyes found her in the shadows, and fixed upon her. They simultaneously sparkled and absorbed the light around them. 'Seventeen hundred years ago I condemned my soul. Since then I have changed. The man who I was, the man who craved only power, is not the one who stands before you this evening. You know of my charitable record, the private trusts, my donations to worthy charities . . . as I recall, even your own Order of the Burning Cross.'

Sister Olivia wavered under his stare. 'Gold cannot purchase redemption from God,' she said, and sunk back into her seat. She made the sign of the cross, prayed a moment, then added, 'Nevertheless, if you have truly repented the Lord may see fit to forgive you.'

Her Order of the Burning Cross was popular, perhaps because it offered its followers a rigid code of rules in an unruly universe. Some people needed rules. And no matter what Sister Olivia said about gold and God and redemption, she needed money. Her order had political muscle, but when things got nasty, she used armies, thugs, and inquisitions to force their enlightened ways upon others. That required cash.

'I am not ashamed of anything I have done,' Erybus said. 'I did what I had to. Now I seek a solution to my quandary. If any feel uneasy with the spiritual nature of this, you are free to go. I would not fault you.'

That was my cue to leave.

And what are the odds of staying alive? the gambler asked. *You better stand pat. One word about his deal with the devil, and his stock loses half its value. Don't think he won't fold you if you walk out.*

But how much longer could I stay and remain undiscovered? I was dead either way.

Aren't you curious to see what his game is?

I'd rather be alive than curious.

A moment passed, and no one got up to leave, including me.

'Perfect,' Erybus said. 'I shall divulge to you what this impossible task of mine is. Lights, please.' Overhead illumination, amber in colour, filled the turquoise room with a warm glow, making the blue stone darken and the moonstones blush.

'When I negotiated the contract to exchange my soul for power,' he explained, 'I bartered for the inclusion of an escape clause. A standard year before my contract expires, I may summon thirteen champions to risk their lives and souls in place of mine. He or she,' Erybus paused while E'kerta stretched its collective body, 'or it, must do so freely and with full knowledge of the consequences.'

'No task is impossible,' snorted Gilish. 'Show me what you want. I get it.'

Erybus became shadows and faded. In his place appeared a bowl of gilt silver with eight panels, each engraved with a leering face. There were disjoined arms and legs carved upon it too, and on the inside rim sculpted cavalry and armies marched.

'This is one incarnation of what I seek,' Erybus's voice whispered.

A second vision appeared: A silver cup, polished to a mirror shine. It had a wide mouth, short stem, and fat base inscribed with crosses and angels and inlaid with a mosaic of garnet and ivory. Within was a stagnant liquor. Sister Olivia gasped. It too then vanished.

And a third image: A drinking horn of beaten gold. About the mouth was fastened a crown of five points, and along its lengthy were fashioned the faces of a hundred kings.

'What I seek changes through myth and time and place, but the core of what it is remains constant. You will know it when you find it.'

He spoke of the Grail. When I was younger, much younger, and beginning my apprenticeship, my Master made me read Chrétien de Troyes, *Le Conte del Graal*, and all the other Grail myths. Only one pure of heart could claim the relic. It almost made me laugh that Erybus thought anyone in this room had a chance.

'Almost,' because the laughter froze in my mouth. I tried to swallow, but my muscles would not respond. A smothering veil clouded my perceptions. I listened from the inside of a sea shell, peered through a foggy lens, and only sensed my flesh through a dozen quilted blankets. I had lost control of my body.

Who possessed me? I demanded.

Silence.

Then who's not in control?

It's not me, honey, Celeste purred. *I'm right here next to you.* Her thoughts mingled with mine, erotic, and tempting, but I gently pushed her away.

Perhaps you had a seizure, offered the psychologist.

My personas of Aaron and Medea gave me a mental nod. Aaron was an alien king, a creature of stone whose mind was indecipherable. Like an oyster coats an irritating grain of sand, so did I surround Aaron's crystalized thoughts with a blanket of obliviousness.

Medea rarely had anything to say. She preferred action to words.

The gambler said: *I'm not even dealt in on this hand.*

That only leaves one unaccounted for, said Fifty-five, *your Master.*

That's not possible, I replied. There was too little left of my Master. The mnemonic lore I stole from his mind was intricate and huge; it left no room for his intellect. The power was there, a shred of his feelings, but no awareness. At least, that was what I had assumed. Could he have been there, mute, all these years?

Master? Are you the one who possesses me? I'm sorry for what happened. Believe me. I never meant you harm.

My body stood, moved without my permission, then I spoke: 'You make reference to the Holy Grail. The first image was a pre-Christian Celtic artefact, the Gundestrop Cauldron. The second is a classical reconstruction from the early French legends of the cup of Christ. And the last is the vessel of the Celestial Dragons' Blood, discovered in deep space, and according to myth, containing the souls of the hundred wisest kings yet to be born.'

Thirteen heads turned toward me.

Get control back, Fifty-five hissed. *The last thing we want is attention.*

Stop! I screamed at whoever directed my body. *You are going to get us killed.* I wrestled with the mind dominating my body, but it was titanic, alien, a blank black wall that I could not see through, a will so powerful it couldn't be human.

'We have an educated man among us,' Erybus said and fixed his somber gaze upon me. He studied me, perplexed.

He had to realize I was not on his guest list, not one of his thirteen hand-picked champions. I wanted to shrink back into my chair, slither under it to avoid his gaze, but whoever controlled my body stood tall and stared back without so much as a blink.

'Yes,' Erybus answered, 'it is the Holy Grail I seek. If found and submitted to me, then and only then shall I be spared, and my rewards disbursed.'

I spoke more words that were not mine: 'Why would the issuers of your contract, apparently agents of evil, wish to possess a relic that has traditionally been associated with virtue? It puzzles me.'

'My underwriters knew how well the Grail is hidden,' Erybus said, his gaze hardening. 'They knew only one hero in a million has the qualities necessary to find it. It makes my escape clause, at best, improbable. Does that answer your question?'

'Yes, quite. Thank you.' The mysterious persona who controlled my body rippled with satisfaction. Without warning the presence vanished.

I possessed myself again.

My eyes peered directly into Erybus's eyes, two holes in space that seemed to contain the stars themselves. I had to look away and sit down.

Master? Was that you? Can you help me?

Find the Grail, said a faint voice. *Do not allow . . .*

Yes? Do not allow what?

No one answered.

Why, my Master, have you returned after twenty years of silence? To satisfy your curiosity? Forgive me. Speak to me, please.

Erybus relaxed his gaze. He did not call for his bouncers and have me removed.

Instead, he continued, 'Whatever the *reason* for my escape clause, I have one. And while I have not been allowed to actively seek the Grail, I have compiled every legend and fact pertaining to it. An army of historians and theologians toiled for two hundred years to complete this work, and their efforts I shall give you to aid you. Yet, even with this collection of lore, the location of the relic remains a mystery. You will be taking a grave risk, speculating on your abilities to interpret this data, and testing your luck.'

'And our souls will be lost if we fail?' Omar asked.

'Precisely,' Erybus answered. 'If you fail to satisfy the terms of the contract within the standard year, a devil called Nefarious will collect your soul and it will burn forever in Hell.'

Why not do it? urged the gambler. *What is the risk? Your soul? Call a spade a spade – we all know where yours is going anyway. There is nothing to lose.*

Only thirteen champions allowed, remember? I'd be the fourteenth.

Still, it was the only way I'd be walking out of here alive. I had to eliminate one of the people here – and quickly. How?

Gilish. His greed was the key. I silently recited a mantra to calm my fear, gathered my nerve, and again spoke: 'Thirteen to take the risk. But only one can be rewarded. The rest die. Is that correct?'

Before Erybus replied, Gilish stood and cried. 'What?'

The hero Gustave cleared his throat, and announced, 'I shall partake of your challenge, sir. But I request a binding agreement of my own to ensure full payment when I return with the Grail.'

Gilish shouted, 'No young punk'll take what's my treasure.' He held a plasma tube in his hand. It was aimed at Gustave's chest. The weapon expelled a cone of xenon dimers that instantly decayed, incinerating anything that got in their way. I had used one before, flashy, and a trifle messy, but highly effective at close range. Pirates and pilots liked them because they worked well in vacuum. It would probably kill everyone on that side of the room.

E'kerta's body scattered, and the others leapt out of their seats.

Gilish fired. Nothing happened.

'You will find that your equipment has been rendered temporarily inoperative,' Erybus said.

'Perhaps this will work, then,' Gustave said and pulled a knife free from his belt. The blade was slim and slight curved, a half-meter in length, and had a golden mirror shine.

Gilish unsheathed his saber, a sword with twice the reach of his opponent's, the metal dull, nicked, and covered with old blood.

Gustave moved to the center of the room, onto the projection pad, causing the image of Erybus to distort.

The pirate kicked over a chair and joined him.

This is wrong, Fifty-five said. *Erybus neutralized his plasma tube, but let him keep the saber. Why? And why haven't those bouncers come in here to break it up? He could stop this if he wanted to.*

The image of Erybus's face blurred and smeared above the two champions like a ghost, watching but not interfering.

Maybe, I replied, *he wants to weed out the weaklings before he commits to picking his thirteen champions. So much the better for us.*

Gustave slashed at Gilish, scoring the pirate's forearm with a deep cut (and destroying the tattoo of a starship in flames). The young hero was fast.

The pirate growled and took a pace back, bringing his own blade in line with his opponent's breastbone. He lunged at Gustave, but his blow was parried by the smaller blade with a motion so swift it was only a blur of gold. Then a quick riposte that nicked the pirate's hand and scarred a leering skull of green ink.

Gilish stepped back to reassess his opponent.

A traditional opening sequence to test one another, Medea commented. My persona of Medea knew more about blades and combat than I could learn in a lifetime. *The younger one is more proficient than the pirate.*

Unlikely, I told her. *Gilish has twice his years and twice the skill. He's toying with him.*

Gilish cut at Gustave's head.

Instead of ducking out of the way, the hero stepped *into* it, and reversed his grip on the blade so it lay braced along his left forearm. With his metal-reinforced arm, he parried the saber with a simple sweep. He then brought up his right fist and punched the pirate's ugly face, busting his lip and three intertwined emerald snakes.

A snarl spread across Gilish's features. Rather than stepping back and using his sword properly, he grabbed Gustave's wrist, twisting his thumb and index finger into a painful lock.

Gustave smiled. He was now inside the reach of Gilish's saber with a proper close-fighting weapon. With a twist of his free hand, he reversed the blade that lay against his forearm, and skewered the pirate's throat, impaling a lovely tattoo of a slave girl bound in chains.

The green pirate turned white, dropped his saber, and fell to the floor.

We should kill this hero Gustave from a distance, Medea whispered.

Gustave's smile vanished. He took two steps back and allowed the virtual Erybus to resolve on the projection pad (now tinged red with spilled blood).

'Well fought, Mister Barbaroux,' Erybus said, 'but that shall be enough violence for one evening. I suggest the remainder of you direct your energies to finding the Grail.' He stared directly at the hero, who bowed his head and retreated to his seat.

'There is one last condition to this transaction. When you find the Grail, you must not drink from it. Doing so will ruin its pristine state. The wording of my release clause specifies that this incarnation of the Grail must remain untainted. Drink from it and there shall be no reward – and a most unpleasant penalty.

'Now, if you have questions of a legal nature, feel free to consult with my solicitor.' He pointed to the back of the room. A middle-aged man with a pointed beard stood there, holding an alligator-skin briefcase. The solicitor gave a nod to his boss, then opened the case and removed an armful of scrolls. Each one was tied with a black ribbon. He handed one to me.

Omar whispered: 'Listen, my friend. I offer you the opportunity to join me and others here. We have agreed to unite our efforts and increase our prospects to find this relic. We can cover more territory in less time. And should any of the others cross our path, they could be taken care of.'

'Including me?'

He shrugged.

'What of the tiny matter of your immortal soul?'

'You surprise me, Germain, being deluded by such superstitious nonsense.'

'I shall consider, my colleague.'

I untied the scroll, and inspected the screen of the disposable computer. It was a replication of parchment, yellowed, and the calligraphy characters were familiar to me, blood dried to a crimson dark sheen. The index tab along the side listed thirteen sections, containing over a thousand pages of legal-speak. I thumbed to the escape clause, a blur of words and riders and paragraphs.

Wait, the psychologist whispered. *Go back, page five hundred three, please.*

I did.

There, he said. '*The party of the first part has the option to release the party of the second part from all obligations herewithin, provided the mortgage on the party of the second part's soul is negotiated in good faith.*'

This is highly unusual, the psychologist said. *Usually, two contractually joined parties can agree to waive the contract if they so desire. Placing this in writing indicates an erroneous motive, I believe.*

So the devil is sitting in on this hand, the gambler said. *That doesn't alter the odds.*

It made a difference. Taking on a freelance assignment for a wealthy eccentric man was one thing; taking on an assignment for a liar was another. Omar might not take his immortal soul seriously. I did.

I scrolled to the escape clause. In plain words it explained that in one Earth year hence, if the undersigned returned with the Grail (subject to tests of authenticity and its untainted state), he should be rewarded with the title to the Erato system, and – there followed a long list of documents verifying the quality of gems, the deeds to a hundred of slaves, and thirty escrow accounts scattered on a dozen worlds in triple-A rated banks. But if the undersigned failed, his soul became the property of the first party. Simple. Erybus Alexander's signature was scrawled in blood at the bottom of the page; the capital 'A' of his last name stood tall and pointed above the others. Three runes of *Absoluteness* glowed brilliant white at the very bottom of the contract. They made it unbreakable. In the lower right-hand corner was a blank line for my mark.

A year. That worried me. I had never been comfortable with time limits. My assignments rarely had them. I preferred to oversee every detail, study my subjects, and get it right the first time. But a single year? It grated against my better judgment and professional training.

Omar's alliance had appeal. He was correct that we would cover more territory. But he was wrong: there could be only one winner. The contract indicated that clearly enough. In the end, we would have to kill one another. And I had already killed him once. I'd pass on his offer.

Erybus's solicitor distributed quills, albino peacock feathers with their tips sharpened. The ink we'd have to provide ourselves. Omar wasted no time. He impaled the tip of his finger, drew his blood into the quill's tip, and made his mark. Goose flesh crawled across the arm that was next to him.

I glanced up and saw Erybus's solicitor speaking to him. I read his lips. He said: 'Sir, we must find another champion to replace the pirate. His death was poorly timed.'

'Yes,' Erybus replied and looked among us, 'possibly . . . wait.'

I lowered my head and pretended to examine the contract.

Sign, insisted the gambler. *Do it before we lose out!*

I held the quill firmly in my right hand, poised over the meaty pad of my left hand . . . and I faltered. The door the solicitor came through was wide open. I had a chance to escape. Did I need Erybus's money? No. With my casino winnings I could live an extravagant life for a decade, or, if properly invested, I could retire and live comfortably for the rest of my days. I wasn't greedy.

Nothing justified this level of risk. Failure equaled death and eternal damnation in a year. I wasn't willing to chance that.

E'kerta disassembled his collective self. Each of the ten-legged scarab beetles in his body-hive made their mark upon the pact, a character and identifying scent that spelled his full name. Even Sister Olivia had signed and gently blew the ink dry on her contract.

So why was I stalling? I should sneak out.

You're stalling because it's a trap, Fifty-five said. *That open door is Erybus's way to see who's going to chicken out. He'd be a fool to let anyone go who wasn't under his thumb.*

He won't kill you if you're legitimately one of his thirteen, the gambler whispered.

You were smart enough to take a second look at that contract, junior, Fifty-five continued, *but not smart enough to know that the instant you stepped inside this room, you signed up.*

I felt like a tourist in the casino, out of my element in a rigged game, hoping to get lucky and hit the big jackpot. They were right. The only way I'd walk out of here alive was as one of Erybus's champions.

Looking over the contract one last time, and finding no hidden or misleading clauses, I drove the quill's point into my hand and released my well-guarded life fluid.

The quill's reservoir filled and I signed.

My stomach twisted into a knot, and a fever flashed across my skin, then a chill turned it cold and clammy – dead man's flesh. The ink congealed in an instant. My name froze upon the contract, permanently proclaiming my foolishness . . . and it was a done deal.

Chapter Three

I had not been challenged when I turned in the escape clause. Erybus had to know I was not invited, not one of his thirteen chosen. Why had he let me sign?

I regretted it. I should have snuck out. All night I studied his Grail database. Jam-packed on a disposable computer was more information than I could read in a year.

My spray-on timepiece was in countdown mode, flashing the deadline into my eye whenever I looked at it. Three hundred sixty-four days and four hours remained. And after twenty hours and scanning ten thousand alphabetized entries in the database, I had no clue where the Grail was. There had to be a better way, some way to cheat.

Omar had tried to contact me three times, twice by messenger, and once personally at my door. I ignored him . . . no, not entirely. I had seen to it that Umbra Corp was brought up to date on his freelancing activities, E'kerta too. Maybe they would eliminate them for me. I had also informed the Corporation of my plans to pursue them. That gave me a cover for my own ventures.

My venture – where to start? A random investigation of the legends in the database was useless. There was a common theme in the stories: a Grail quest and a Grail King. The King was a symbol of the land, and if he was healthy, then the land was too. All standard stuff. But how did Erybus fit in? The Grail King? And what was I? A knight in shining armor? Or court jester?

I shifted the suite's display to scenic, and gazed at the Melbourne cluster. It looked like so many pearls scattered upon black silk. There were several hundred thousand million stars in the Milky Way, and basking in their light were millions of democracies, corporations, monarchies, dictatorships, bureaucracies, colonies, and free trade ports where the Grail could be. So many diverse societies trading, making alliances and war. They evolved with exponential ferocity.

Change fluxed through the galaxy: technological and psychological advancements, revolutions, nanoplagues, war, corporate takeovers, natural disasters, and the fall of empires. It made it nothing less than enigmatic. Irreparably fragmented.

The alien civilizations were no less ferocious. We were xenophobes all, and those that were not were conquered and enslaved or eradicated.

The psychologist interrupted my thoughts. *I believe I know why your former Master possessed you last evening.*

The psychologist always had a theory for everything. *OK. Let's hear it.*

He was a subconscious representation of your guilt. Identification of the Grail triggered a cascade emotional response: your Master, his murder, your guilt. Your feelings remain unresolved. Until you face them and—

—Thanks for the free analysis. Why don't you get lost?

The psychologist sighed, then said, *If you are unable to take my expert advice, then listen to a suggestion to enhance your search. Necatane.*

Out of the question.

The man who trained me is a master psychologist. He can see into the future or the past as easily as you see across this room. If anyone can divine the location of the Grail, it is he.

I know who he is, and I know what he can do, but there are two minor snags. First, he lives on his own world. Getting there may prove difficult. And second, he vowed if our paths ever crossed, he'd kill me. I'll stick with Erybus's data and blind luck.

Your mind was blank when you came to kill me, the psychologist said. *Can you not repeat this?*

The device I used burned out, I replied, *and the man who made it is probably dead. Besides, I was after you that time, not Necatane. I doubt any psychic shield will screen me from him.*

With my skills, I can hide your intentions, and make your thoughts transparent.

This was a tricky point. When I absorbed my extra personas, I had to choose which fragments to preserve, and which to discard. There was no room in my mind for all of them intact. This made their thoughts polarized, and their recollections partial. It made the psychologist interested only in analysis, and forgetful of his past loyalties. Still, I had no guarantee how he would react in the presence of his guru.

I'll have to think about it, I told him. I didn't want to say it, but it *was* a better idea than just sitting here and reading the database.

Why are you wasting your time with that egghead? the gambler asked. *There are places to go. Lost civilizations to sift through. Let the game begin.*

I commanded the Grail database: 'Reset to novice mode. Show me the legend of Parzival, verbosity level two, then the biography of Wolfram von Eschenbach.' The disposable computer complied, and as I read the first sentence, the door chimed.

With a flick of my eyes, I shifted the display to the hall. Standing there was the handsome dealer who saw me switch cards. A black metallic dress clung to the curves of her body, and revealed a figure that no dealer needed. She could have been a model, tall, lean, and muscular, but her face was a bit too angular, too serious. Her hair was different than when I last saw her, now curled in luxurious spirals, and the color of honey. I knew her from somewhere, somewhere other than the Universe tables, but I couldn't put my finger on it.

Take a close look, Fifty-five whispered, *just above her hip*.

A slim chain and plastic souvenir four-leafed clover dangled there.

Not that, he hissed. *Underneath*.

A slight cylindrical bulge. *A weapon?*

You better believe it, junior. Watch yourself.

I couldn't ignore her. She had seen me exchange cards – and could make trouble if she wanted to. I got up and opened the door. At least it would be entertaining to see how she intended to blackmail me.

'Good evening,' I said and managed a warm smile.

'Technically it is morning,' she told me. 'May I come in?' She wobbled slightly in her heels.

Walking in heels takes practice, Celeste said. *She's unskilled, but still attractive in an earthy sort of way. Why don't we make love to her? Dally a while and enjoy yourself. Let me enjoy myself also*.

Under normal circumstances, I'd agree. We could both use the diversion, but not now. I couldn't afford to become distracted. Not with a dozen competitors close.

It's unfair, Celeste said, pouting.

I stepped aside, wary of that concealed weapon, and let her in.

She pointed a finger at me. 'Let me be straight with you, Mister Germain. I know you performed an illegal action in that last hand of Universe – with the final card. I don't know exactly what, but you can bet the management will freeze your account while they investigate the matter.'

She wasn't bluffing. It was an approach I hadn't encountered in years: honesty. I sealed the door behind her and said, 'I never caught your name.'

'Virginia, pilot second-class.'

'A pilot? Why would a pilot be working the tables?'

She crossed her arms. 'Mister Germain, have you lost money

at the Golden City? I mean lost more money than you had?' Her eyes darted around my opulent suite, landing on the thick hand-knotted rugs, the hammered gold trim of the furniture, and the dark Dutch landscapes adorning the walls. 'No,' she said, 'you probably haven't. Well, they give you three options. They turn you over to their police so you can rot in jail, they let you work off your debt, or they make you disappear.'

I wandered into the living room and sat on one of the two divans there. 'You're a full-apprentice card plate dealer,' I said. 'From what little I know of the game, that takes two years. You must have lost quite a sum.'

'Only two hundred,' she replied and followed me, wobbling, into the living room. Her dress made a crisp metal-on-metal tinkling with every step. I offered her a seat. She declined with a shake of her head.

'Two hundred thousand?'

'No, two hundred.'

I leaned forward, intrigued. 'It shouldn't have taken more than a week to work that off. Are you a compulsive gambler, Miss Virginia?'

Her eyes narrowed. 'Living here costs money, eating in this dump costs money, they even charge you for the water flushed down your toilet.' She chewed her lower lip, then said, 'After eighteen months of double shifts, I owe the casino two hundred and seventeen.'

I understood. This con had many names: debtor's prison, indentured servitude, the democratic middle class. Whatever you called it, it had one thing in common, a poor worker forced to spend more than he had. I saluted Erybus's business savvy.

'So what do you think I can do for you?'

'You can pay my debt and buy me passage off this rock. You won over four million, so it shouldn't be too much to ask.'

'Only that? If what you claim is true, certainly your silence is worth more.'

'I'm a hard worker. I'm honest. I just want to get out of this snake pit, get back to my Guild, and do what I do best – pilot.'

Her hand drifted closer to that hidden weapon, and she added, 'I know you're some sort of sanctioned assassin. I don't want trouble. I just want out of here. If I disappear, the casino will investigate. Probably not as thoroughly as if I told them about that card, but the way I see it, you're better off paying me.'

I looked appropriately shocked at her accusation. 'What makes you think I'm an assassin?'

'I hear things,' she whispered. 'Things like the owner hired a bunch of licensed killers. You said you were going to the Turquoise Room. I can put two and two together.'

She had made a shrewd guess or she knew more than she was telling. Either way I didn't like it. 'Yes, I heard that rumour too, but it was mercenaries and war heroes your owner hired, not assassins.'

She looked me over once, and remarked, 'You're no war hero, Mr Germain.'

'No. I'm not.'

Maybe it would be better to pay her off, yet another option occurred to me. Nothing along the lines of what Celeste might enjoy. This girl had integrity. I knew how hard Golden City worked its dealers. With a body like hers, she must have been offered other ways to settle her debt.

'You said you were a first-class pilot?'

'Second,' she corrected.

'I can settle your account, but if you're interested I have a different proposition, one you might find more appealing.'

She sat on the divan opposite me and carefully crossed her legs. 'If you're thinking about sex, forget it.'

She doesn't mean it, Celeste whispered.

'My ego is bruised,' I said, 'but that's not what I had in mind. I have a better use for your talents. May I offer you a drink?'

She glanced to the well-stocked bar across the suite. 'Quantum ice, please.'

I used the pad on the coffee table and watched her drink dissolve in reverse; a blue crane materialized, the ceramic cup upon which it was painted came next, then the steaming liquor within appeared.

Quantum ice was a mixture of solvents that boiled at room temperature. It got you very drunk, very quick. She tossed the cup back, blushed, and blew a smoke ring straight up. Her full lips made a perfect 'O.' Very sexy.

'As I was saying, I am engaged in what you might call a scavenger hunt. I have a computer full of clues to search through, but that will take far too long for my purposes.'

She summoned another drink and sipped it as I explained.

'There is one man, however, who can help me find what I seek. He values his privacy, so normal means of communication are impossible. I must see him in person.'

'So take a commercial flight. Charter a private ship. You have the money.'

'This individual has his own planet, outside the normal commercial zones, and private charters have . . . disadvantages.' Disadvantages like Omar probably had all the available pilots staked out. He wasn't a complete idiot, neither were the other Grail champions.

She frowned at my less than informative reply. 'I don't see what good I can do you. I don't own a ship.'

'Let *me* be straight with *you*,' I said. 'I must find a particular item in less than a year and return with it to Golden City. To increase my flexibility, I intend to purchase my own ship. Therefore, I require a pilot, a pilot who won't ask questions or make a fuss about flight plans and other legalities. In exchange for this pilot's services, after the year I will sign the ship over to her. Understand?'

She raised one eyebrow and the triangle-cut sapphire in the

corner of her eye sparkled. 'And if this pilot was in debt?'

'I'd pay that off, of course.'

'My own ship?' She considered, then asked, 'Just how dangerous is this scavenger hunt of yours?'

'Extremely,' I answered.

I liked this Virginia, despite her compulsive honesty, but if
she wouldn't work with me, I'd have to eliminate her. She knew
too much, too much about the card game, too much about my
mission, and too much about me. Her hand rested on her lap, close
to that weapon. I recalled how nimble her hands were in our card
game, so I readied myself to move quickly if she declined.

She studied me for a moment. 'I think I'm going to regret this,'
she said, 'but OK. You got yourself a deal.' She drained the cup,
stood, and offered me her hand.

I shook it. It was warm and soft and strong. 'Excellent, we
should leave immediately.'

'There are a few things I'll need from my room.'

'Very well, I'll clear your debt and meet you in the lobby in,
say, five minutes?' I kept her hand in mine, so she wouldn't trip
in her heels, and walked her to the door.

She lingered in the entry as if she had something else to say,
then drew closer, and pressed her body against my chest. Her eyes
sparkled brighter than the jewels framing them. She kissed me.
It was warm, wet, lasting too long to be a polite good-bye . . .
but too short to be an invitation. She withdrew, flashed me a quick
smile, and jogged down the corridor. Her heels – she left those
behind.

I had been with this woman before. One doesn't forget a kiss
like that. The smell of jasmine in her hair, and the way she yielded
slightly in my arms, it was all familiar . . . and frustrating that I
couldn't recall where or when I knew her.

You should have killed her, Fifty-five said. *Absorb her personality if you need a pilot. She knows our plans. And giving her
a ship! Are you out of your mind?*

It's not as crazy as it sounds. If I am successful, then we'll be rich enough to buy a fleet of ships, and if not, we won't be around to worry about it.

I packed my equipment into two large suitcases that were shielded from the casino's sensors. Then, using the suite's terminal, I linked to the bank and squared my debts. For the two hundred thousand the gambler borrowed, I paid twice that for a day's accumulated interest. Next, I located Virginia's account, hidden in a file marked 'Golden eggs.' There were thousands of similar accounts. So much for Erybus being a reformed man. Half the Golden City staff was slave labor.

Before you rescue our pilot, Fifty-five said, *shouldn't you take some precautions? I can think of a dozen people who would like to see you dead.*

I stripped off my tuxedo, and slid into a shadow skin. It analyzed the ambient light, and canceled it with an identical but inverted wave pattern, making me a non-reflective piece of darkness. Over this, I slipped into a pair of gray slacks and a white shirt that were thin enough to let it function properly. The shadow skin was no cloak of invisibility. If I moved too fast, its tiny brain couldn't process the data fast enough, and I 'blurred.' And in strong light, the batteries got sucked up quickly. There were better models, but this was what Fifty-five packed for me when we left to hunt Omar.

Don't complain, junior. We didn't have time to learn new technology. Stick with what I know.

I deposited two hundred and seventeen into Virginia's account, then grabbed the Grail database, folded it twice, and stuffed it in my vest pocket. Herding my luggage in front of me, I left the suite, entered the lift, and descended into the lobby of the hotel.

Virginia waited for me, and she neither looked like a casino dealer, nor the attractive young woman who had kissed me minutes ago. She wore a pilot's suit: layers of tubes, armor, life-support micromodules, and combat boots. I preferred her in a cocktail dress and heels. Her long hair was drawn back into a tail then stuck down her collar. And upon her forehead was a double silver star, the insignia of a pilot of the second rank. It linked the bioware inside her skull to a starship's computer.

'Congratulations,' I told her. 'You're a free woman.'

'Thank you,' she said, then immediately asked, 'What model ship do you want?'

I thought I'd at least get another kiss for settling her debt, but nothing, hardly a smile.

A professional pilot cannot become involved with her employer, Celeste told me. *It's a rule within their guild. No sex on the job.*

You might have told me that before.

'I'll leave the choice of the vessel up to you,' I replied. 'All I require is speed, but nothing that produces relativistic effects. I'd rather not worry about time dilatation when I'm working with a deadline.'

'They all have relativistic effects,' she told me. 'Diminishing the temporal dilatation narrows our choices quite a bit. A space-cutter or a mass-folding generator would be best, assuming the impound yard has one. It'll be a crap shoot.'

'You've been to the casino's impound yard before?'

She nodded. 'They mainly sell scrap, old ships seized from long-time losers, but now and then a rich guy will hit a streak of bad luck. He either sells his yacht or gets sold on the slave blocks. I know the mechanics, so we should be able to get a decent price. How much do you want to spend?'

'Will three million suffice?'

Virginia whistled low, and her eyes glazed over in thought. 'That's a lot of money.'

'Then, please,' I said with a sweep of my hand, 'lead the way and let us spend it.'

We marched together through the Golden City, through casinos full of tourists who had forgotten the time, lost in losing their money, submerged in clouds of smoke and flashing lights, mesmerized. Virginia took a short cut through the red-light level, past the sensual mud pits, the chamber of horrors, and a medieval castle, complete with princesses waiting to be rescued or captured.

You've picked up a tail, whispered Fifty-five.

We caught an escalator to the next level, where cheap hotels, black plastic rectangles three storeys tall, stood one after the other in perfect rows. They reminded me of dominoes, balanced and ready to topple with the slightest push. This was where the unlucky ended their tour of the Golden City. They were too broke to stay anywhere else, and too desperate to recoup their losses to leave.

I glanced over my shoulder and spotted my tail. Indeed, they were obvious. Four gigantic men, more oxen than human, pushed their way up the escalator to get closer. Their muscles bulged and flexed under their tight shirts – so large they had to be implants.

We stepped off the walkway, and I ushered Virginia into the nearest glass elevator and punched the button marked 'S' for spaceport. Below, I saw my four friends pile in the next available lift and continue their pursuit.

We were about thirty seconds ahead of them.

Up three levels, through twenty meters of foamed concrete, then the doors dissolved and we walked onto the spotless white tiled floor of the spaceport. Clusters of bank terminals, instant-win machines, souvenir vendors, and fast-food joints were strategically placed so the tourists couldn't help stopping to spend their money. The place was packed with a crowd of fresh arrivals all heading in the opposite direction to the one we wanted to go.

Overhead, through the clear dome, ships propelled by waves of gravitons or mystic sails effervescent with wizardry drifted lazily by, all with different trajectories like motes of dust. It always fascinated me to watch them.

'There,' Virginia said, and pointed to a hangar on the far end of the ever-plastarmac, 'that's the impound yard.'

'Why don't you go ahead of me?' I suggested. 'There are a few things I have to take care of before we leave. I'll catch up to you in one hour.'

'One hour,' she said, 'you got it.' Then she marched into the crowd and disappeared.

I must caution you about this pilot, said the psychologist.

Dragging my luggage with me, I ducked into a restroom to change clothes and arm myself. The bathroom had four stalls for privacy, a locker area, six urinals, and a smiling attendant.

I smiled back and said, 'Beat it.'

'I beg your pardon, sir?' His grin vanished.

I dug an orange token out of my pocket, flipped it to him, and said, 'Leave.'

The attendant's smile returned. He left.

The psychologist continued, *I sense from her an unusual loyalty for you. This is common for a woman who is rescued from an unpleasant situation; however, you should be aware of certain emotional dangers—*

Later, snapped Fifty-five. *We've got work to do. Did you see? Your pursuers wore gold crosses, crucifixes with a single eye in the center.*

The Order of the Burning Cross, I said. *Sister Olivia's men.*

My former Master had lousy timing. I was happy to know he lived, in some fashion, but his appearance at Erybus's meeting put me in a precarious position. The others thought I was an expert on the Grail. If I were in their shoes, that's what I'd think too, and I'd either pump me for information, or eliminate me, or both. Probably both.

I doublechecked my shadow suit's batteries: full. Good.

My favorite blade was under my sleeve in an ejector sheath. Why bother to carry a knife, when I had an arsenal of modern weapons? It was the best close-fitting weapon. It couldn't be dampened (as Gilish's plasma tube in the Turquoise Room had been), it couldn't jam, or run out of ammunition, but most of all, there's nothing like a length of steel in your hand, its weight, edge, and balance a natural extension of your arm. Besides, with the persona of Medea to help me, I was one of the best swordsmen alive.

This particular weapon had a self-stick grip inlaid with black opal, and a straight double-edged blade enchanted to slice through normal metals like paper, but never to cut its wielder.

Next, I took a recoilless accelerator pistol from my bag. While it occasionally did malfunction, and run out of ammunition, it handled most trouble before I had to use a blade. No larger than my hand, it was easy to hide and easy to use. With a brush of my thumb I could adjust the power from the lowest setting, which welded metal, to the highest, an overload discharge, without moving my finger from the trigger. Into its grip went a bar of depleted uranium that was ionized then accelerated to a fraction of light speed. These jewels of kinetic energy ripped through stone like tissue paper, not to mention what it did to human flesh.

I sensed Medea close. She knew what was about to happen.

Your rings, she reminded me.

Thanks. I fished two rings from my bag and slipped one onto each hand. They were emerald green, but when held up to a bright light, they shimmered with rainbows. Inside was a core of high explosive, and about that was wrapped a hollow wire filled with nerve toxin. The blast didn't do much damage, but the cloud of poisoned wire fragments made for an effective anti-personnel weapon.

Last, I gave the copper band on my wrist a twist for luck. That made the gambler happy. Without its obscuring properties to confuse the spaceport's sensors, I'd never be able to carry the tools of my trade.

I left the bathroom and returned to the crowds surging through the terminal like salmon swimming upstream. A bellhop slid up to me and offered to carry my luggage. I hefted my suitcases onto

its flatbed and ordered it to the impound yard. Then, as it left, I
snapped the antenna off. This would mean a trip to the repair shop
for the robot, but only after my bags were dropped off. I'd be long
gone before anyone traced my luggage or me.

My escorts were still with me, milling about, reading maga-
zines, and trying to be inconspicuous. There was little chance
of that. They were two and a half meters tall, and followed me
with obvious bovine eyes. All very unprofessional.

I went to the ticket counter and booked passage for Virginia
and me to the middle of nowhere, then sat and watched my tails
watching me, hoping to give her enough time to find a decent
ship. Half an hour, then I stood, stretched, and strolled back to
the bathroom. This time, my muscular friends decided to go in
with me. It appeared an ambush was in order . . . for one of us.

One stall was occupied.

You'll have to eliminate him, said Fifty-five. *No witnesses.*

Dialing the accelerator pistol to its lowest setting, I welded
the stall's latch in place. By the time the fellow inside pulled up
his pants and crawled out, it would be over.

I moved my fingers, thumb to pinkie, first, followed by three
other rapid mnemonics that released the ocular enhancer from
my memory. The blue-tiled room turned brilliant in my boosted
vision, and I saw everything, every scrap of toilet paper stuck
on the floor, every character of graffiti etched into the mirrors,
and the thousands of fingerprints smeared on the aluminum
condom dispenser.

I shot the lights out.

The man inside the stall cursed at the darkness, cursed again
when he jiggled the hot latch, and cursed a third time with scalded
fingers stuffed in his mouth.

Witness eliminated, I informed Fifty-five.

Someone entered, then hesitated, uncertain what lurked here
in the dark, and quickly closed the door. It opened a crack. A
grenade was tossed in, and the door slammed shut again.

I ducked, rolled into the corner, and covered my head . . . but there came no explosion, only a whisper of gas from the device. Good, they wanted me alive. That gave me an edge. The room started to spin, my tongue went dry, and vision blurred. I had to get out, and quick.

They wanted me to make a run for it. I would, but not in the direction they thought.

I picked a wall, dialed the pistol to full power, and fired. A shower of white ceramic chips, foamed concrete, and metal sparks filled the air where I blasted a hole. Water erupted from the wall, dousing me, and steaming where it touched the molten stone. I stuck my hand into the opening, past ruptured water pipes. It was a hair too small for me to get through. I could have made it larger, but water was everywhere. Shooting now would just get me a face full of steam. Gritting my teeth, I dislocated my shoulder, held my breath, and squirmed into the newly-made hole, through the rushing water, and brushed against scalding stone. It hurt like hell.

I fell into a narrow access corridor stuffed with valves, pipes, and air conduits. The air was noticeably clearer. So was my head. It wouldn't be long before they figured what had happened, so I removed one explosive ring filled with poison, set its proximity fuse, and ran.

At the first intersection, I took the descending path and jogged for ten meters before I reset my shoulder. I had done this so many times you'd think I'd be used to it by now. No such luck. The bone ground back into the socket and sent excruciating lances down my arm and across my heart. That was my right shoulder. Had I thought about it, I should have dislocated my left. I was right-handed.

Behind me I heard crumbling stone, and squealing metal echoed in the tunnel. My muscular friends were widening the hole. There was a dull thump, my ring exploding, followed by a pair of screams. Good.

Hearing footfalls, I activated my shadow skin and flattened against a wall. In these cramped quarters, however, they might hear me, and they were large enough so they might scrape against me if they came too close.

Two men appeared in my branch of the tunnel. They bled from a dozen cuts, wore green glowing low-light goggles, and carried lethal-looking side arms. They didn't appear to happy either.

Rest your arm, Medea said. *Let me take care of this. I am left-handed.*

I thought you'd never ask.

Chapter Four

Medea pressed my body against the wall, tensed my muscles, and with her left hand unsheathed my blade in one smooth motion, savoring the gesture. She was rated an expert with most firearms, possessed three black belts, but her real passion was for swords and knives – anything with an edge. She was one of the most dangerous people I ever had to kill.

The two men trotted down the tunnel. Up close, they were two hundred kilos of angular muscle, square jaws, and crewcuts that revealed their low foreheads. They didn't need the pistols they carried; they could tear me apart with their bare hands. The one on the right stopped and waved a scanner in front of him.

Medea crouched into a ball and waited.

I find a hint of cowardice in your actions, the psychologist whispered. *Every time there is barbarity to be done, you release her.*

What do you mean?

Killing without guilt. It must be convenient for someone in your line of work.

I might have argued, but why? He was right. I didn't enjoy killing people. It was just what I did for a living.

The muscle boy with the scanner whispered to his partner, 'He's close. I'm not picking up a heat trail, but his footprints end here.' They both looked up, thinking maybe that I crawled into the network of pipes overhead. No such luck.

Medea moved then, a shadow in the shadows. She kicked low

– knocked the one closest to her off his feet.

The other one shot at her. A sticky net expanded and hit the wall, sounding like a wet towel snapped. It stayed there, aimed too high to touch Medea.

She lunged up and caught the gunman in the soft underparts. Beneath his skin was a layer of armor, a weave of metal and carbon fibers, but my enchanted blade easily slid through, up into his guts, and pierced his heart. A single convulsive cough and he died.

She had time to shoot his partner while he got to his feet; instead, she kicked his pistol out of reach and flicked off the shadow skin. She wanted to take him up close and personal. She wanted him to try to kill her.

When he saw Medea step from her personal shadow, he charged.

It startled me how fast he moved, but Medea was ready. She stepped out of the way, grabbed his arm, and twisted. Something popped. Using his tremendous momentum, she directed him into the concrete wall. The crack of skull on stone, and he fell stunned to the floor. Medea finished him there, once across the throat and again in his back to sever the spine.

'Is that all?' she asked, disappointed, and glanced down the tunnel for more playthings. There were none in sight, so she released control of my body.

I immediately caught the scent of blood, thick in the air, and felt my muscles burning with her leftover adrenaline.

Medea was a homicidal psychopath (the psychologist confirmed this diagnosis). She lived for the thrill of murder. That was all there was to her, all that I absorbed from her soul. Ironically, this made her the best behaved of all my personas, because she never wore my flesh too long. She stayed only to kill, then departed, unable to understand any other aspect of consciousness.

There were probably more of Olivia's men around, so I ran.

A dozen twists and turns, and I found a passage that doubled back under itself, back under the runway and out to the hangar where I hoped my escape waited. Stenciled over the entrance were the words: ABANDONED #A-11. DO NOT ENTER.

I ignored it, entered, and sunk knee-high into the foul-smelling sewer.

It was familiar terrain. After the death of my Master, it was in the sewers I hid. A shadow of guilt entered my mind, which I banished before the psychologist had a chance to dissect it. Unfortunately, like the smells rising from these murky waters, the incident would not go away.

Excellent, cried the psychologist. *Such a rare pleasure to examine your early memories. Continue, please.*

Sixteen years ago, my Master died by my hand. He was a popular man with powerful friends, so no expense would be spared to locate his murderer. I had to flee.

There were two options: leave the planet, which cost more money than I had, or go underground, literally. Only meters of stone would screen the divinations and probes the police used to locate criminals such as myself. The logical decision was the sewers. I had the ocular enhancer to see in the dark, and if I could stand the smell I might have a chance.

The sewer was a maze of tunnels, drains, concrete and earth that mingled with civilization's water: pungent urine and excrement. I wandered there for ten weeks, all that time afraid of the police finding me, and afraid of my Master's spirit rising from the water to avenge his death. But those things never happened. The only phantoms that roamed the wormholes were my own feelings of guilt.

That didn't mean I was alone.

The sewer was alive with predator and prey. There were insects with white bodies, long antennae and stingers. There were leeches to suck the blood from my legs. There were floating colonies of microbes that glowed faintly red and dissolved any organic matter they happened upon. Also here were mole-like creatures, no eyes, with whiskers longer than their body, inoffensive except for their taste. They were hunted by the king of the underground, the Lermix.

Lermix swam and slithered faster than I ran. They weren't worms, nor reptiles, but something of both with translucent segmented bodies that stretched for a dozen meters. Tiny mouths covered their tentacles that touched, tasted, and dragged them through the darkness. And they stank, stank like nothing else in the damp rotting place, of rotten eggs and month-old milk. I learned to run whenever I caught that odor.

I might have stayed there forever, forgetting my life on the surface, had not Fifty-five crossed my path. Most of the time, I didn't need to see. I heard everything I needed to amidst the continual dripping of water, and that's how I detected him. His heavy strides and rhythmic sloshings echoed ahead of him.

I backed away from the source of that noise, and released my ocular enhancer.

The sloshing stopped.

With the veil of darkness lifted from my eyes, I saw a man, ten meters away, wearing green phosphorescent bug-eyed goggles. He turned that unnatural gaze my way, grinned, then started towards me, sending a wave of filth in my direction.

He must be the police. In a way, I was relieved to see him. At last, I'd have a chance to explain what I did and why. Explain that it was an accident. But he didn't look like a policeman, no uniform, no partner . . . although he did have a gun strapped on his shoulder.

I ran.

Plowing through the waist-length water, I heard him laugh behind me.

I sprinted, given new energy from my fear.

Usually, I took care not to run. It stirred up the stuff that had settled on the bottom. I gagged on the stench – ammonia, vomit, and rancid table scraps – coughing while I struggled to keep ahead of him. Spending the last seven years in libraries didn't help, either. I was in lousy shape.

His sloshing got closer and closer.

I had to hide. And the only thing to conceal myself in was the water. To drink a drop of it, however, was to endure cramps and diarrhea for days. I had to be careful. I ducked around a corner and saw what I wanted, a deep pool where the stone of the tunnel sagged. I plunged in.

The cold water was full of floating *things* that I didn't care to identify. With one hand pinching my nose shut, the other only partially sealing my mouth, I went down to the slimy bottom. Above, I felt the vibrations of his boots on the stone. His steps got louder until I though this next one would fall on my head. A pause. Then he ran, down another passage.

My breath was gone, but I waited until black dots danced inside my lids before I surfaced. Eyes still shut, I cleared my mouth of the poisonous water, spit the putrid taste out quietly, then looked.

He was there waiting for me.

I hesitated only for a second, but that was long enough for him to draw his gun. A strange sound, a polite cough, and halfway between my hip and knee, my leg exploded. I reeled from the impact and collapsed into the swampy liquid. My shattered bones ground together. Pain flooded my mind.

'Gotcha!' he cried and sloshed over to me.

I crawled to the side of the passage, half in and half out of the water, in a daze, not really certain what had happened. I knew I had to get out. The blood in the water, the Lermix would smell it. They would come searching with their tentacles for breakfast . . . Breakfast, which meant fat sausages floating down the sewer, scrambled eggs, pancake boats, and orange juice . . . I drifted for a moment, not awake, but neither asleep, in a dream state, peaceful, calm . . . then the stench of reality pierced my delirium. I saw the man tinkering with a device on my leg, a box of blinking lights and small mechanical arms.

'There,' he said, 'that should keep you alive while we talk.'

'What?'

'No, no,' he wagged his finger in front of me, 'I'll ask the questions. Who sent you? The Red Guard, or has Sixty-two decided to take me on again?'

'I was just here,' I whimpered. 'I wasn't sent by anyone.'

He punched my mangled leg and knives of fire flashed along every nerve. I didn't scream, though; the Lermix had good ears.

'No one is *just* anywhere, junior. You have guts, though, I'll give you credit. It's not every person who'd take a dunk in this stiff. But why make your death a messy thing? I have drugs that can make it easier. Tell me what I want to know, and I'll give you one final dream.'

The pain sharpened my mind. I was beyond fight or flight – this was when the fox chews his leg off to escape the trap – so I stared into his solid green glowing eyes and told him what he wanted to hear. 'OK, it was Sixty-two. He sent me here to track you down.' I had no idea if what I said meant anything, but from the man's reaction, the nodding of his head, I knew it did.

'And he knows about my assignment?'

'I guess so,' I said.

He frowned and thought about that for a moment. Past the dripping water, past the ringing in my ears, I heard them come, the near-silent ripples and the vile stench that always accompanied the Lermix.

The man made a face at this new aroma, but dismissed it and asked, 'Where is he now?'

'Not on this world. He said he was going to . . .'

The Lermix were close. I saw their probing tentacles in the dark, reaching forward, touching, mouths opening, and leaving trails of slime. Maybe I'd get lucky and they would surprise my assailant, give me the opportunity to crawl away while they ate him.

He followed the motion of my eyes as they tracked the monsters' approach. Turning, he didn't even panic at the sight of the three massive worms. He carefully drew his pistol and fired. A dull thump, and one of the titanic worms thrashed about in convulsions. A second shot and it stopped.

He spared a glance at me, but my head was tilted back in the water, eyes shut, not in pain (although there was enough of that to occupy my thoughts), but in concentration. I prepared the mental construct I swore only ten weeks ago I'd never use, the borrowing ritual.

Underwater, I made the gestures that keyed the mnemonics. It was complex, hideously so. A mistake would destroy my intellect and leave me an empty shell.

Four more shots, and a final fifth, then he turned back to me. 'Now, Junior, you were about to tell me where I could find Sixty-two?'

The sorcery bloomed before me, full in its strength. It snared him in a steel web, penetrated his brain, and forced our minds to touch.

He was astonished, not expecting an attack from me, and certainly not psychology of this magnitude. The man, however, managed to slowly bring up his pistol and aimed it at me with his remaining willpower.

I had an edge. I had used this ritual against a mind greater than his, that of my former Master, and survived. Still, this man's desire to live was great, and he struggled like a fish tangled in my net. I let him think he was winning, allowed my concentration to flag for a moment – long enough to remove the weapon from his grasp – then I clamped down on his mind and broke his will.

His stray thoughts came to me. I learned he had been awake for two days planning a murder, and that took its toll on his determination.

Sleep, I told him. *Rest, and I'll give you one last dream to send you on your way.* I entered his soul. 'Knowledge,' I commanded as required by the ritual. 'Give me your life.'

He taught me, unfolded his life for me as a rose would open in the sun. Those inner layers, his childhood, the center that influenced the shape of the outer petals, poured from his mind. Each memory I tore out by the roots. Gone was the family who took care of him with their wealth and love. He wasted it. I took his education in art history, which he only used to cheat his clients with sophisticated lies. Then to the outer petals, the recent recollections, which I discovered were as blood-red as mine.

Tiring of simple cons, he purchased an audience with Umbra Corp. They heard of him and his schemes and were impressed with the moderate wealth he'd accumulated. They took him in, trained him, and made him one of their own.

This Sixty-two he mentioned wanted to kill him. While it was illegal to murder their ranked counterparts, it happened. Attrition meant advancement. The man before me was ranked Fifty-fifth out of one hundred and twenty-eight active members. With his death, Sixty-two moved up one notch to become Sixty-one, as did all the others ranked Fifty-sixth or less.

I took the names of Fifty-five's contacts, the names of his victims, and the secrets of the Corporation he was privy to. Those were buried deep, shielded from probes, and protected from unwanted intrusion. I tore through his mind, cracked it open like an egg, not caring what spilled out, only wanting that golden yolk: information. And it came, as I knew it would.

I stopped the ritual and let out a sob, not from the pain, or remorse, but the tender sweet sob of rapture. It was not like the first time, when I destroyed my Master's mind; this was pure pleasure, the tasting of forbidden fruit. I would have continued, but there was nothing left. His mind was devoid of memory. With no thoughts to command his body, his breath became erratic, bowels loosened, and spasms jangled his body.

Pain snapped me out of the trance, sharp throbbing from my leg. Whatever drugs Fifty-five had given me were wearing off. I knew what to do, though. The device on my leg was a small robot doctor, a blue shield. It could heal me.

'I have to move,' I told it. 'Override safety protocol, no sedatives, highest priority to reconstructing bone tissue, then take care of the infection.' The robot bleeped, and injected a leg full of medicine, then went to work on my bones; I smelled something burning.

I removed Fifty-five's goggles, his clothes, and found a transport ticket. Satisfied, I got up and limped away, defying the squeals of protest of the blue shield.

I left the mindless man for the Lermix.

To his Umbra Corp I went. My application to their academy was accepted with the second-highest score ever. Every record of my existence was wiped clean, and my DNA was subtly altered. My name and face were lost. I disappeared from the police, from everyone. I was given a new life. I was reborn.

It was after the indoctrination ceremony that Fifty-five whispered to me, first in my dreams, then with growing regularity as he emerged in my thoughts. He coached me, and suggested ways to advance my career.

I thought I had gone mad.

Hardly mad, remarked the psychologist. *A bit disoriented, but not insane. Now, if you wish to share additional recollections with me, I am certain I could ease your suffering.*

You mean find out what makes me tick? I'll pass.

I shuffled through water that was half as deep, walked among odors half as pungent, yet the memory was as sharp as ever. Time does not heal all wounds, especially when you carry the people you've murdered inside your head.

The passage split: one branch descending, one ascending. I took the one up and that emptied into an access tunnel, filled

with air conduits, blinking optical cables, and the dust of decades.
I stopped and listened to make sure no one followed me.

Silence.

I was under the landing fields and close to the hangar Virginia
had pointed out. Above me a ventilation duct snaked up, marked
STORAGE HEATING. A quick burst from my pistol and I had
a hole large enough to get in. The tube wasn't big, about half a
meter in diameter, but I fit and started climbing. My shoulder
ached.

I squirmed inside the cylinder until I came to a filter and grate.
This I burned off, and found a deserted office. Half a cup of coffee
sat on a white plastic desk. I got out, stretched, drank the coffee
(it was cold), and noticed a sign flashing on the door that said:
'With customer, back in one hour.' Outside was the impound
hangar.

I released the tension in my muscles, took two deep breaths
of fresh air, and assessed my position. Sister Olivia had played
her hand early. Obviously. Omar and E'kerta would be more
subtle. A bomb. Poison. Perhaps a nanoassassin. The hero Gustave
worried me. A nagging feeling about him festered in my thoughts.
I calmed my mind, shuffled and then stacked my personas. I
placed Fifty-five on top. I needed his keen eyes and paranoia.
The psychologist came next with his intellect and capability for
analysis. Then Medea, in case I needed her. The gambler and
Celeste for company, my silent Master, and last Aaron, the alien
king, whose thoughts were so different from human they pained
me to focus upon.

Overhead, the artificial sun dipped behind a bank of equally
artificial pink clouds and made the shadows fade. Casually, I
strolled out and heard Virginia arguing with a man inside: 'It's
too much and you know it.'

'The drive has only thirty hours logged on it,' he retorted. 'It's
practically new!'

There were rows of yachts parked, polished and gleaming with chrome and gold details. All their prices were clearly labeled. The ones in the back, however, looked a little neglected. I smiled insincerely at the plaid-jacketed salesman, then asked Virginia, 'Have you found something?'

She wrinkled her nose at me. 'Maybe.' Then she cast a frigid glance to the salesman, 'But there's nothing here that's worth half the asking price.'

'Can you give us a few moments to discuss this?' I asked him. Then to Virginia I whispered, 'Show me.'

She led me to a sleek ship, low to the ground, a compressed oval of emerald superalloy with twin insect eyes bulging forward. Its price tag read four and a half million.

'This one,' she said, 'is the best among the bunch, a custom sloop. It has a space-cutting turbine, but unfortunately little room inside. With the two of us, and all that baggage you're lugging around, we'll barely fit. She's the fastest thing here, though.'

I noticed my bags were stacked to the side of the craft.

'It's impractical,' I remarked.

'The man who owns this won't need practicality. He could afford to have his baggage sent ahead of him.'

'It won't do.'

She sighed. I could tell she had her heart set on this one.

'Are there any others?' I asked.

'One other,' she said, frowned, then admitted, 'no, two.'

'Is there a problem with the second one?'

'Let's look at the first one, maybe you'll like it.' She turned without answering my question and walked to a larger craft, enameled red and chromium yellow. Written in bold gold letters on her tail was *The Sun Dancer*. It bristled with antennae, and arrays, fingers of alloy that reached forward, a blackened nose, and twin drone racks mounted fore and aft.

'She's a sturdy vessel,' Virginia explained, 'decent weapons, excellent communications, but the computer is a little small for its mass-folding drive. It is slower than the first one, but it is large.

Room and quarters for twelve. It's probably an older corporate model. You want to take a look inside?'

'It requires a larger computer?'

'Faster,' she corrected. 'The mathematics involved in folding the ship's mass into higher dimensions are tricky. We might be able to refit her, but that will take a day, at least.'

'What about this last one?'

She said in a hushed voice, 'You don't want that one. It's bad luck.'

'Show me,' I insisted.

Shaking her head, she nonetheless took me to the back of the hangar. Here the older models were mothballed, covered in grime, and lonely for someone to fire up their engines and take them away from this boneyard. Tucked behind the ion engines of a rusting tanker was Virginia's third ship. I felt something about this one, a cold tightening in my stomach, a sense of déjà vu. I had seen this ship before . . . been a passenger on it. But when?

The psychologist informed me: *Déjà vu is an illusion brought on by the mind's ability to jump to associative conclusions. It has no basis in reality.*

The ship, despite my misgivings, was gorgeous. Three wings arched back like the fins of an angelfish, black and wispy. Each contained a recessed oval, bulging slightly through the metal skin, placed midway along its length, three mass-folding generators. I'd never seen a ship with three before. The body was a teardrop of black metal with recessed X-ray lasers, and a magic circle of silver runes inscribed on her nose to ward off attacks.

She looked fast just sitting there.

That feeling of familiarity wouldn't go away. I knew this ship. On the other side was a painted mascot, I knew without looking, an angel. Only this angel didn't have white wings and a golden halo. She was a lascivious nymph, nude, wings like a parrot's, long and rainbow-colored, and a silver crown upon her head.

I strode to the prow, and sensed the static pull of the magic circle. On the port side, indeed, the mascot was; her wings were spread wide, and wind blew through a long mane of blood-red hair. Her name was etched in calligraphy: *Grail Angel*. Normally, I abhorred happy coincidences like this. They usually turn out to be neither happy, nor coincidental.

What do you think now? I asked the psychologist. *Déjà vu still unreal?*

Remarkable, he whispered. *Perhaps your mind, despite its corruption by primitive beliefs, has become clairvoyant.*

At least take a look at what you've been dealt, insisted the gambler. *To throw away an inside straight, the namesake of our mission, would be spitting in Lady Luck's eye!*

Virginia saw me staring at the thing, and whispered, 'It's haunted. Can't you feel it? I put the screws to the dealer and he told me it showed up here, drifting in orbit, without a crew.'

'Is the computer large enough to run three mass-folding generators?'

'There was never a computer large enough or fast enough to handle the interactions of three mass-folding fields. I've seen some theoretical papers on two fields – folding already folded masses – but three fields is an intractable problem.'

'We don't have to run all three, do we? Can't we use one at a time?'

'Well, I suppose—'

'You said it was found without a crew? Where did they go?'

She shrugged.

'And how long has it been here?' I asked.

'Thirty-four years. Like I said, the casino found her in orbit and towed her in. The mechanics say there's nothing wrong with her, but all things considered, no one wants to touch the thing. She could be a military unit, a spy ship, maybe? Who knows?'

'Let's see the inside,' I said, and keyed the outer hatch.

Virginia sighed, but followed me in.

No one had been in here for a while. It was dusty. Everything was made from a lustrous gray metal inlaid with panels of briarwood that was in need of a good polishing. There were three separate sections, apart from the bridge, which we wandered through from the back to the front. In the aft was a storage room. Racks and securing webs ran along every wall, the floor and the ceiling, holding nothing but a cargo of dust bunnies.

The next section must have been the crew's quarters. There was a triple bunk bed (each with its own built-in virtual units), and a table made from the armor plate of a battleship with 'P-7' stenciled on top. It looked like a good place to play cards.

The last room was the captain's quarters. It was larger than the other two put together. The carpet was thick wool and embroidered upon it was a replica of the ceiling of the Sistine Chapel. I trod lightly upon the host of heaven. In one corner was a set of shelves (alas, empty), a red leather reading chair, and a small table for setting one's pipe or drink upon. A bed with a satin comforter the color of blood and a cracked headboard sat along the far wall. The walnut headpiece had been carved into a skull and crossbones. I tested the mattress: firm.

In the captain's bathroom was a marble tub that sat on four cast-iron gargoyle feet, with a water recycler underneath. Three people could sit in it without bumping into each other. Sculpted upon its outer rim were porpoises, whales, sharks, even a few mermaids swimming together, and galleons being tossed about like so many toy ships. I ran my hand along the inside of the tub, enjoying the luxury of the cool, smooth stone.

'All very nice,' Virginia said a bit sarcastically, 'but let's take a look at the important parts, like the mass-folding generators, and the bridge, before you buy a bathtub with wings.'

I reluctantly agreed and we continued our tour.

Unlike the captain's frilly quarters, the cockpit had a practical design. Systems and displays easily within reach and clearly labeled. On the right was the pilot's form-fitting wraparound, and

Virginia tried it on for size. To her left was a seat for the co-pilot, and behind that a third terminal.

Virginia examined the systems, then told me, 'She has triple back-up for the life-support, weapons, communications, computers and, as you saw outside, propulsion. The computer has an advanced architecture, rated at double prime, which is more than enough to handle the equations for one mass-folding generator.'

I asked, 'Is that a trace of approval I hear?'

'It's a fine vessel,' she said carefully. 'I can't believe she is thirty-four years old.'

The salesman poked his head through the hatch, 'She's a gem, isn't she? And only four hundred thousand.'

Virginia looked at me, shocked, and whispered. 'Something has to be wrong. That's a tenth of what she should be worth.'

'I want to see the generators working,' I told the salesman, 'and I want every system double-checked before I even consider buying this scrap heap. And then, I don't think I could offer you more than three hundred fifty.'

'Yes, sir,' he said, and scrambled across the hangar to rouse his mechanics.

'And get someone in here to clean her up,' I shouted after him.

'You're not seriously going to buy this Flying Dutchman, are you?' Virginia asked.

'Let's get my bags.'

Chapter Five

Virginia went through her checklist. The cockpit came alive with virtual displays; scattered stars and dusky blue nebulae floated in mid-air, then a miniature *Grail Angel* appeared with overlapping circles of probability, ripples on a pond. She sat centred in this miniature galaxy, one hand on a trackball, the other manipulating a matrix of crystals. The real activity, however, took place inside her head. From her double-star insignia shone a beam that linked her bioware to the ship's computer. It flashed across the instruments, touched the displays, gathered data, and gave commands.

While the *Grail Angel* was being cleaned, Virginia had turned the ship upside-down searching for some reason not to buy her. Everything worked perfectly. She claimed all the components looked new, even though the ship was thirty-four years old, and warned me not to buy it, calling it a 'ghost ship.' To ward off evil spirits, she hung her plastic four-leaf clover on the console.

'All ready,' she declared. 'Destination?'

'The Needles free trade colony.'

She fetched the coordinates, muttering, 'Out of one scum hole and right back into another. You never said anything about smuggling contraband. I could lose my rating.'

'Smuggling is not our purpose,' I assured her. 'I'm going to visit a colleague.'

The man who constructed the thought shield? the psychologist inquired.

Yes, I replied. *His name is Quilp. If he is alive, I believe I can persuade him to manufacture me another. Then we shall pay a visit to your master-psychic, Necatane, and see if he knows the location of the Grail.*

The Golden City tower gave us clearance, and the *Grail Angel* rose, like a bubble through champagne, through the artificial sunset and past the atmospheric barrier. On the other side of the field that kept the air clinging to Golden City, the warm sky instantly turned black and filled with stars.

'Why are we traveling so slow?' I asked.

'Mass-folding generators are touchy,' she said, 'especially near gravimetric potentials.'

'You mean planets?'

'Planets, suns, moons, even Golden City back there can scatter out low-mass wave functions.'

The aft display projected the artificial planetoid, a ball of glitter and neon, silver and gold and sparkling diamonds. Virginia then initiated the number one mass-folding generator. Our mass dwindled (although I felt nothing); the *Grail Angel* unfurled her sails, caught a quantum wind, and plunged into icy waters of indigo ink. Golden City vanished.

It was good to be underway, and better that I had some distance between myself and my deadly competition.

'ETA to Needles colony: twenty-four days, seven hours,' Virginia told me. 'Relativistic time: twelve hours, forty-seven min—' The beam of light from her insignia froze on the display. She jerked her head away.

'Is there a problem?'

'Maybe. An irregular code in the secondary memory core,' she said. 'It's growing.' She reconnected. 'It is a single file, no passwords, no customized shells . . . and this is curious, the system log indicates it's new, created fourteen seconds ago.'

Smells like a virus to me, Fifty-five said. *Someone sabotages our navigation, and we drift in space, or end up in a different galaxy.*

Pure speculation. Our pilot checked the ship before we left.
'What is it?' I asked her.

'It's nothing I've seen before,' she said and broke the connection. 'If I had to guess, I'd say a virus. I'll purge it before it's done expanding.'

Like I told you, said Fifty-five. *Whoever planted it knew you'd buy this ship. You shook the tail to the impound yard, but our girl here is another story. Or she could work for the competition. There might be a clue in the code, the real date of creation, or a locus of insertion.*

He had a point, a paranoid point, but a point nonetheless. 'Let it be,' I told Virginia. 'I want you to isolate it from the operating system.'

She chewed on her lower lip, then said, 'I can secure the core, but it would be safer to get rid—'

'—No.'

A furious burst of light discharged from her insignia. It pierced the displays, flickered through the spectrum, cold ultramarine to smoldering crimson. 'Done.' She glared at me. 'Computer control transferred to you. If the virus gets out of hand, you alone have the authority to erase the secondary core. Dump the entire system and we can reboot from back-up. You have eight minutes before the code turns viable.'

I examined the mysterious virus. It displaced the entire secondary memory core. How did Virginia miss it when she inspected the ship? My suspicions germinated.

'Make certain,' she said, 'to place the purge command in the super-user's shell.' She leaned over to show me. Her breast pressed against my arm.

Celeste whispered into my ear, *This spunky one desires you. There was no need to throw herself into your lap to show you. She wants to touch you.* Celeste drew my attention to Virginia's flesh pressing mine (albeit through the intervening layers of plastic and metal of her pilot's suit), and she flooded my mind with fantasies of dragging her aft, and making love under the skull and crossbones headboard. Hunger simmered inside Celeste; it boiled over, and I became aroused. Indeed, to be with Virginia . . . what would it take to win her favor?

Favor? A loaf of bread, a jug of wine, and thou? Celeste smirked. *You were never the romantic. Take her! She is begging for it. Twelve hours to kill. Don't you want her?*

More images from Celeste: silk cords and bound limbs, the flick of a riding crop, ice, electric current, and candle wax, bodies sliding over one another.

'Leave it alone, Celeste.'

I installed the purge command, concentrating solely on that task; otherwise, Celeste might possess me. Not only had Omar and the gambler run my body ragged, but I had stayed up the previous evening reading the Grail database. I was dead tired. Celeste had a weak will, but this was her area of expertise. That gave her an advantage I was unwilling to test.

Virginia returned to her wraparound seat. With her touch gone, the passion in my blood cooled.

I told her, 'To access the computer use the password Osiris.' There was a second password that locked Virginia out and gave me control of the ship. Fifty-five was right. How far could I trust her?

Upon the center console, a new display materialized: a hollow cube of faint black lines. Tiny shapes animated in one corner, triangles, squares, and pentagons, and they filled with shades of green, and blue, and yellow. A diffuse glow appeared in the center of the cube and made it look like stained glass.

Virginia probed this display with her beam of light. 'It's a visual of our mystery program,' she said. 'It's compiling itself. Complex. I can't tell what it is, or what it's up to.'

The expansion of colors in the cube accelerated. A mosaic of turquoise and jade covered half its surface. I rotated the display and saw the inside crowded with volumes of glowing color, too;

they quivered as if alive; pulsed with a heartbeat.

I'd seen this before . . . in a dream perhaps. In its luminous patterns I saw radiation and biohazard and nanoplague warning symbols, and trouble. 'Very well. I have changed my mind. Show me how to purge the secondary core.'

'Too late,' she said. Her eyes were glazed over, staring deep into the computer system with her bioware. 'It's in the folding subroutines.'

'I thought you isolated it?'

'I did. Something *inside* our computer bypassed my isolation procedure, maybe a second virus. Whoever installed this knew what they were doing.'

'Then we'll dump the entire system.'

'Not with this code inside the folding subroutines. Without the proper unfold cycle, our wave function will scatter. We never resolve. We die.'

The cube drew more lines, faster. I held my breath and watched. Colors of grass and dandelions and robin's egg saturated the air.

Fifty-five hissed, *Dump the core, quick! Take your chances with this unfolding cycle. This virus could set our course to edge of the universe and lock us out. It might shut down life support. We could be dead either way.*

The last line on the cube connected; it flared neon red; it exploded.

The spectrum of colors bleached to brilliant white, dividing the cockpit into splinters of hard shadow and dazzling light. For several seconds I saw nothing but dots swimming before me, then my sight returned. The cube sat there, quiet and pulsing with abstract patterns.

Virginia whispered, 'It's not doing anything I can detect. We're still on course.'

The cube startled me. It spoke: a male contralto voice that demanded, 'Whom do I have the honor of addressing?' Its words made four green hexagons shift upon its surface like the tiles of a puzzle.

'I am Germain, owner of this vessel,' I said. 'What are you?'

'Forgive me, Master,' it humbly replied, 'but my courtesy subroutines were only now accessed. I am Setebos, an artificial intelligence, and your faithful servant.'

'No AI unpacks, compiles, and initiates itself,' Virginia said. 'I don't believe it.'

'Yes, madam. I assume you are the pilot of the *Grail Angel*? Do you prefer to be addressed as madam, madam captain, or miss?'

'Captain will do,' she said curtly. 'Explain how you got in our secondary core.'

'My records indicate I have always been here,' he replied, 'nested in directory two-zero-seven. When the mass-folding generator engaged, I woke up. It is my duty to refold the fields for optimum performance, and, naturally, any other duties you command.'

'That directory didn't exist a moment ago,' she whispered to me.

Erase it, urged Fifty-five.

I thought you were the one who wanted to find out who put it here? I asked the cube, 'What happened to this ship's last crew?'

'I'm sorry, Master, but that information is unavailable to me. This is the first time the mass-folding generators have been engaged in a non-test mode. I was just born.'

'But you claim you will do anything I ask?'

'If it is within my ability, yes, Master,' Setebos replied. 'I am here to serve.'

'What if I told you to erase yourself?'

A cluster of blue rhombuses broke apart, rotated ninety degrees, then settled into a starburst pattern on the cube's surface. 'I regret that I cannot. I have a directive that prevents self-annihilation. However, I shall be delighted to give you complete instructions, so you may erase me yourself.'

'AIs don't talk like this,' Virginia said, 'not the ones I've heard before, anyway. I don't trust it. I suggest you turn it off. The mass-folding fields run perfectly without it.'

The light inside Setebos's cube dimmed and quivered like a flickering candle. 'Madam captain,' he said in a small voice, 'I have taken the liberty of reconfiguring the mass-folding fields. Please, if you would care to inspect them, I can prove my worthiness to you.'

'You can't do that with the generators running! We'll be ripped apart! Who told you to take control of my ship?'

'A thousand apologies,' he squeaked. 'I shall install a command chain in my action path. Do you desire me to return the fields to their previous state?'

Without answering, she summoned the schematic of the wave function surrounding the *Grail Angel*. Previously, the ship had looked like a stone in a stream, ripples of probability stretching to infinity fore and aft. Now one end didn't radiate into space; instead, it was a whirlpool that vanished into nothingness. It had been folded, twisted to a point.

'Velocity is the wrong term. Our mass is . . . is close to non-existent.' The beam from her insignia flashed into the main computer. She frowned, then said, 'I've recalculated thrice. Our ETA to Needles is now five hours and three minutes.'

'Setebos,' I inquired. 'Are you using one field or two?'

'Two, O wise Master. I have computed a crease for the locus of—'

'Can you use all three simultaneously?'

The puzzle cube shifted rapidly, simple figures fragmented and collected into smaller asymmetric bodies; specks of yellow swelled in the mosaic of light, and a few grains of blood-red emerged, then Setebos halted and returned to his normal soothing blues and greens.

'Forgive me, Master. I am unable to solve the necessary equations. Shall I try again?'

I asked Virginia, 'Is it safe to run the ship at this speed?'

'Like I said, it's not a question of speed,' she replied. 'The ship can handle it. But this AI has me worried. It shouldn't be able to solve the mathematics of a twice-folded field.'

'Are there any dangers? Complications or relativistic effects?'

'None that I can detect.'

'This AI makes the *Grail Angel* more efficient, faster. It stays. If you detect any anomalies notify me immediately. Until that time, I would appreciate your cooperation with Setebos.'

'I don't think that's a good—'

'— I'm not paying you to think. I am paying you to pilot this ship. Now do as I wish.'

Her lips tightened. Her left hand balled into a fist. 'You're the boss.' She glanced at her hanging lucky four-leaf clover, then glared at me. 'I hope you know what you're doing.'

I was suddenly uncomfortable with Virginia, suspicious of her honesty and good intentions. She had showed up precisely when I needed a pilot, and I didn't believe in coincidences. Fifty-five's seeds of doubt sprouted like weeds. She could be a spy for Omar, maybe even for Sister Olivia. Although I saw no crucifix on her person, she was superstitious. I had to learn more about her.

'How, exactly,' I asked her, 'did you know about that last card? In the Universe game.'

'No one bets like you did against a master dealer without a nova up his sleeve.' She was silent a moment, then looked up, licked her lips, and whispered, 'You're not supposed to know this, but pilots above third-class have special implants.'

'Your implants I know about. Every pilot has them.'

'These are different. They enhance our reactions in ship-to-ship combat. They extrapolate the future based on a present data set. And there is an additional augmentation in one out of ten of us, precognitive powers, what you might call good guesses. That's how I knew you were going to cheat. I couldn't prove anything, so I kept my eyes glued on your cards.'

'And?'

'I saw one card blur on the last deal.'

'How can that be?' I inquired. 'Cards don't move by themselves.'

'That has me stumped. I thought it might be sleight of hand, but when I reviewed the recording of the game, it didn't show up.' A coolant warning for the magic circle diverted her attention. She tapped the blinking amber light and it went dark, then she snapped her fingers and said, 'Magic! It had to be magic. You're a muse.'

Her guesses were getting better and better. She knew I was an assassin, now this. It made me uneasy. 'I'm no muse,' I lied and left it at that.

'Now, if you have everything under control,' I said, 'I must clean up and rest.'

'But the card. How did—'

'Trade secret.'

She pursed her lips, unsatisfied with my explanation, then turned her attention back to the ship's wave function. 'Impossible,' she whispered to herself.

In the captain's quarters, I unpacked a new shadow skin, an armored vest, slacks, and a silk shirt. I removed the Grail database from my pocket, crumpled my old clothes into a ball and threw them into the corner. My eye caught a glowing cube on the reading desk.

It said: 'Master, shall I have those cleaned for you?'

'My name is Germain, not Master.' I sat in the chair next to it, enjoying the sensation of the leather sticking to my back. 'Summon me a glass of brandy, please.'

A snifter materialized next to the cube, smelling of century-old cherries and pungent alcohol. I took a sip of the ruby liquid. It warmed me from the inside out.

'Shall I draw a bath for you, Master Germain? My olfactory sensors detect an unacceptable level of volatile amines and hydrogen sulfide on your person.'

I reeked of the sewers. 'Please.' If I couldn't have a sexual adventure with my pilot, I'd settle for a drink and a hot bath.

Celeste whispered, *The least you can do for me is masturbate. You have withheld pleasure too long. It's dangerous to your health.*

I didn't dare. Even that slight indulgence would give Celeste the opportunity to slip into my flesh. *Sorry, my dear, but you're going to have to wait.*

'Germain,' Setebos humbly said, 'I offer you my most sincere gratitude for not erasing me. If there is anything I can do for you, please do not hesitate to ask.'

I took the Grail database and set it on the table. 'You can upload this.'

Three blue triangles in the cube flashed, then it replied, 'Done.'

'Scan the words, correlate them, and give me your best guess of the present location of the Grail.'

'I shall require one day and six hours to correlate a rudimentary "best guess" based on the quantity of data. I apologize for the lengthy time, but I was designed more for mathematics than literature. Do you wish me to continue?'

'Proceed.'

I peeled myself off the chair and went into the bathroom. The marble tub was two-thirds full of steaming water, bubbles, and scented with lilacs. I eased in. It was two degrees above a comfortable temperature, which was perfect. A smaller version of the cube appeared at the foot of the tub, cradled between the breasts of an erotic mermaid.

'Show me the database, please.'

From the whale's mouth near my head flashed the information, painting the inner surface of my eye with an illuminated text. The database had opened at random, page four thousand thirty-five: an Earth legend of the origins of the Grail.

When Lucifer revolted against heaven, one-third of the divine host remained loyal to God, while one-third of the angels fell with their leader. The last third, however, remained neutral in this conflict. They were the ones who took the Grail to the mortal world.

The story was severely annotated; a footnote graced every line. One of the asides was T. S. Eliot's *The Waste Land*, complete with its own set of footnotes. Erybus was crazy if he thought anyone could decipher this.

'Let's start with something simple,' I told Setebos. 'Give me the story of how the Grail quest began in King Arthur's court. Suppress the annotation.'

A new tale flashed from the whale's mouth.

I remembered reading of the Round Table when I was young. My Master was researching an incantation to summon spirits of nature, and believed a reference might be found therein. The epics captured my imagination, and I read as many of the stories as he had – a world of dragons and jousts, black knights and captive princesses.

The Grail quest began when Arthur's knights assembled for a feast. Before any eating occurred, however, there had to be an adventure. It was the King's custom. The Grail then appeared, a floating chalice, covered by a cloth. His knights swore to see the Grail unveiled, and the quest commenced.

But that wasn't the way I remembered it. Close, but something was missing. 'Setebos, run a difference map. Compare this legend to all versions in the database.'

Characters danced a mazurka in my eye while the AI shuffled through the sagas. I blocked the transmission so I wouldn't get seasick.

'Finished,' Setebos said. 'In the Old French translation of the tale, the knights specifically declared they must go on the Grail quest *alone*. To go in a group on the quest was considered dishonorable.'

I laughed. I'd never be alone – not with my collection of personalities. And even if I could go by myself, I wouldn't. I needed Virginia, and I needed the little man on Needles colony, who called himself Quilp, to make my thoughts invisible from the master psychic.

Needles, like Golden City, was a free-trade colony stuck between the borders of several empires. But unlike Golden City, it serviced another vice: drugs. Quilp took advantage of his tax-free, lawless home, both as a trader of technology and as an addict. He collected technology from all parts of the galaxy, then sold it off to support his one true love, stimulants. He stayed high and awake for weeks at a time, tinkering with his computers, building bombs for revolutionaries (as long as they could afford his price), and playing mathematical games with himself. 'Forget sleep,' he once told me, 'it's the biggest evolutionary blunder Mother Nature ever made.' The last time I paid him, he went on a binge and remained sleepless for nearly a month. I figured he had about a one in three chance of still being alive.

As for sleep, Quilp might not need it, but I had been up for thirty hours. My edge was dull. 'Wake me fifteen minutes before we get to Needles,' I told Setebos.

Soft music resonated through the tub, Tchaikovsky's *Dance of the Sugar Plum Fairy*. Setebos whispered to me, 'Pleasant dreams, Master.'

My muscles unknotted. I relaxed my recently dislocated shoulder, then drifted. Worries stilled like the liquid in a cup, a blue stone goblet filled to the brim with the purest water. I slept.

Stuffed pigeon, roast lamb, and tender venison weighed the tables, making them groan nearly as loud as my stomach. Waiting for an adventure, what a ridiculous custom. A man could starve before adventure found him! Fresh off the spit, a roasted wild boar was set in front of me, its skin a cracked golden brown. The odor made my stomach roar with frustration.

The feasting-hall doors parted and our candles dimmed. No, a light outside flooded the hall. It made our candles and braziers pale in comparison. In the center of this luminosity floated phantom hands that held a chalice aloft. The image was bright as the sun, yet blue like lapis, and covered with a delicate veil. I could not bear to watch it, but neither could I look away.

It hovered, while a thousand angels sang its praises – then it vanished.

The hall immediately went cold and dark. Our light seemed inadequate now to drive the shadows away. Only a blurred red after-image remained to remember the beauty of this vision, then this too faded.

'The Grail!' Someone cried.

The cup of Christ? Had God chosen us to see it?

The members of the fellowship stood, and one by one pledged to find the sacred chalice, each going alone. The adventure had begun! I started to stand, compelled also to go and find glory, then stopped. I realized I could not, for I was King.

'Fifteen minutes,' Setebos chimed.

I was submerged to my lower lip, still tired but clean. I yawned and pulled myself out of the water. By the side of the tub was a thick cotton towel for my wrinkled body, and a mug of black coffee for my groggy mind.

I staggered into the bedroom, pulled on my clothes and armored vest, then selected my weapons. There would be no need for subtlety on Needles. So in addition to my blade, explosive ring, and side arm, I chose a rifle version of my accelerator pistol. The weapon weighed five kilos, and could cut through three meters of steel in seconds, or spray a small army of men into oblivion. On full auto its charge lasted over a minute. I felt very safe carrying it.

Also I grabbed a blue shield, and slipped it into my pocket. Under the sapphire corporate caduceus logo the little robot surgeon had tentacles, probes, lasers, and drugs of all varieties to repair human flesh. I never depended on them, having heard stories of malfunctions – accidentally rerouting an artery through a lung – especially when their monthly premiums weren't paid.

I drained my coffee and stepped onto the bridge. Virginia's hand danced over the controls, adding mass to the *Grail Angel*, bringing us back under the influence of Newtonian physics and into a black sparkling sea.

Needles colony floated in our displays, a silver orb in orbit about a planet with olive and coral clouds, an abstract of ribbons, curls, and whirlpools. The illusion of the colony's smooth edges vanished when we approached. Docking gear and cannons stuck out at odd angles. A swarm of insects gathered here to sip dark nectar, a hundred ships buying contraband, smuggling it elsewhere, and multiplying their profits. There was no port authority, or if there was they didn't bother to hail us.

Everyone kept their noses out of each other's business here.

The *Grail Angel* glided into an open bay and settled in an empty slot.

'Still think this ship is haunted?' I asked Virginia.

She ran a hand over the inlaid briarwood. 'One trip isn't long enough to shake the bugs out of her. The mass-folding generators are impressive. I've never seen the likes of them before.'

'Is that a hint of approval I hear?'

'No. I'd prefer to see the AI purged. This ship is plenty fast without it.'

'Setebos is quirky for an AI, I admit, but it stays. I need the extra speed.'

'I don't trust it.'

'Learn to.'

'It's your ship.' She disentangled herself from the wraparound pilot's chair. 'It's your life.'

'Setebos,' I said, 'we'll be gone for a few hours. Don't let anyone in the ship except Virginia or me.'

'Yes, sir: security procedures active. Magic circle energized and enhanced. Identification required for all functions.'

'Excellent.' Then I asked Virginia, 'Are you armed?'

She removed a plasma cannon (just like the one Gilish tried on Gustave) from a pocket in her pilot's suit. Her lucky four-leaf clover dangled on a chain from its handle. 'I have a spare, if you need one.'

I wasn't sure if she meant the weapon or the charm, but I hefted the accelerator rifle and said, 'This should cover me.'

Virginia double-checked the ship's systems, then we disembarked.

A warm breeze blew through the hangar, bringing with it the scent of grease, ozone, and the smokes of opium and marijuana. Merchants loitered by the entrance of the colony, waiting for customers. Three of them immediately approached the *Grail Angel*. I shifted my rifle into a more threatening position.

'Dream?' inquired the first and waved a vial of viscous liquid before me.

'Perhaps some Samber juice, O worthy one?' queried the second. His lips and fingers were stained black from the hallucinogen, and his breath was the stuff of nightmares.

'Freeze?' the third asked, his eyes darting to Virginia then back to me.

Virginia kept walking, ignoring them. I halted. 'You have Freeze? How much? What else do you have?'

'Metadexidrene, chlorozeneatol, Lightning, and Shazam,' the merchant said, digging through his backpack. His hands shook uncontrollably.

Virginia turned and came back to me.

'I'll take a dozen hits of each,' I told him.

'You're not—' she said.

'Kit,' I insisted.

The merchant removed a tester so I might gauge the purity of his goods.

'This is sixty-three per cent. Do I look like a tourist?'

'A thousand pardons, benevolent sir.' He dug deeper into his pack.

I tested again. 'Ninety-three per cent. Good enough.' I transferred funds on his disposable from the Golden City bank to his account. In return, he dropped sixty thimble-sized capsules into my hand. 'May your visit be filled with delight,' he said, and moved on.

'I can't believe you ingest that poison,' Virginia said and crossed her arms.

'I'm not. It's for a friend here.'

'A friend?'

'Not really,' I admitted. 'He has something I need.' I didn't explain further. I could almost see her bioware churning away, trying to guess what I was up to.

Others approached me, but I turned them down. I had enough stimulants to keep one man awake for months, and that might do Quilp for the time I needed him.

We entered the marketplace, packed with a crowd of vendors and beggars, the air rich with voices haggling, blooming with the odors of fried food, perspiration, and urine. Bald slavers paraded their living wares and gave appreciative glances to Virginia.

She held her plasma tube a bit higher, and clicked the safety off.

They gave her no trouble.

There were plenty of customers for flesh today: necromancers with tarnished silver nose rings who searched for bodies to fuel their rituals, lonely men who looked for beauty, and industrialists who preferred human hands to expensive mechanical ones. Flesh to match every desire was on the auction block today, top-of-the-line pleasure constructs that lived for three centuries, enchanted to provide their master with delight. They were ridiculously expensive, hard to make, and I found myself scrutinizing a flame-haired obalisque.

Celeste filled my head with her fantasies, the things I could do with my own personal harem, but I gritted my teeth and moved on.

Everyone was sold here – even small girls and boys with hopeless pleading stares. My childhood was much the same, chattel to my father and brother, no friends, tortures that the psychologist would love to dissect. The other slaves, they deserved to be here, in debt or to pay for their crimes, but the children were just unlucky. Unlucky to be born into a cruel family and sold off, or unlucky to trust the wrong stranger at the wrong time. I knew about that.

There was money left in my account. I could buy their freedom. Give them a second chance.

We don't have time to rescue slaves, hissed Fifty-five. *And you can't drag a hundred screaming brats along on your mission. Keep moving.*

The logic of his words was undeniable. I turned my back on them, grabbed Virginia's arm, and continued. Their desperate faces lingered in my memory, reminding me what a coward I was.

Why don't you stand up to that bully? the psychologist demanded. *You possess the willpower.*

I had no answer.

There were more drugs to be had. And as we ventured deeper into the colony, they grew in strength and selection: pink antibiotics, powdered tiger-penis aphrodisiacs, eerier glowing green mutagens to change the color of your eyes or alter your sex, sparkling black psychotropics to expand your consciousness, lift your soul to paradise or drag it to hell, and, naturally, prescriptions simply to make you forget. There were countless shoppers, not only merchants buying in bulk but tourists who came to get higher than they'd ever been. Many stayed, spent all they had, then were recycled as slaves or medical surplus. Nothing went to waste on Needles.

The further away from the central market we wandered, the more trash accumulated on the sides of the streets, both people and physical refuse. Long stares were cast our way, lean looks of hate.

This was where the locals hung out, where the hard-core remained to keep their high as long as they could – anyway they could. I set my rifle into warm mode. Its tip hummed with power and glowed with an evil red eye. That was all the warning I intended to give.

The buildings were boarded up, paint crumbling off, and covered with layers of faded graffiti. Figures moved in the shadows. Street lights were dim infrequent pools of illumination, islands in the murky avenues. On our left stood a five-storey office, its walls blackened by fire and its smoked-glass windows busted out and boarded up. This was Quilp's home. The metal entrance was battered and the intercom smashed. I knocked hard on the door with the butt of my rifle. The booms echoed beyond, then silence.

Across the street, four teenagers watched us with interest and whispered to one another. I didn't like the way they looked. They were alert, eyes clear and calm, not drugged like everyone else. They started toward us.

'Trouble,' Virginia whispered and gripped her plasma tube tighter.

I took a step back, set the rifle to a narrow aperture and fired at the door. The beam sliced it cleanly in half, and it fell with a loud clatter. I turned to see if these punks wanted any. They ran away.

They'll be back, said Fifty-five. *They aren't what they appear to be.*

I went in, feeling the danger rise about us like a tide. Virginia followed me down the hallway to an antiquated lift. We got in, the door slid shut, and the car jerked up.

We stopped on the top floor and stepped into a studio apartment crowded with trash, benches overflowing with scopes, computers, smoldering components, tiny robots struggling to move through the filth, and broken glass. Fast-food wrappers were piled in the center (a good month's worth), the home for a tribe of cockroaches. In back was the bedroom, a wad of torn sheets, empty Chinese food cartons, pizza boxes, and a wall of virtual projectors, their images melting into one unintelligible jumble. The sound from them blended into a symphony of voices, crashes, lovemaking grunts, and music. Pure chaos.

In the furthest corner lay a naked Quilp. He didn't move when we plowed a path through the dump to get to him. His pale right hand clutched four remotes, and in his left was an injector, empty.

Virginia knelt by his side, scattered roaches, and touched the side of his neck. 'There's no pulse,' she told me. 'He's dead.'

Chapter Six

I handed her my blue shield and said, 'Feel the back of his head.'

She set her hand there and quickly withdrew it. 'It's hot.'

'Then he's alive.'

She attached the robot doctor to his arm and touched it with a beam of light from her double-star insignia. 'I'm reading no pulse,' she told me, 'and a zero heart rate.'

'There are tetraoxide crystals embedded in his skull. When his heart seizes, the crystals release oxygen for his brain. The reaction is exothermic.'

'The kit says there are massive amounts of amphetamines in him.'

'I know. He overdosed on purpose. He'll pull through.'

She touched his hairless white chest. 'He's so cold, and his heart . . .'

'It will start again. He has a pacemaker to reset his cardiac rhythm. He would have replaced it with a synthetic, but he says it interferes with his rush.'

Virginia took the remotes from Quilp's hand and turned off the wall of virtual projectors. One by one the images of violence, pornography, news and commercials faded. 'Why does he do it?'

'To stimulate his thinking,' I said. 'When Quilp has a problem to solve, he overloads his mind with drugs. He's brilliant when he's high, otherwise he can't even count straight. It's a shame really.'

A roach scurried across a nearby mountain of food cartons,

navigating its way across a treacherous slope of dried teriyaki and slimy vegetables. It paused, ten legs twitched, then it tested the air with a feathery antenna. I brought my rifle butt down on top of it. It popped quite nicely.

The blue shield beeped.

'His heart is beating,' Virginia said. 'Pulse rising, blood pressure still below normal. Shall I instruct it to filter the stimulants out of his system?'

'No.' Then I thought better of it, and said, 'Perhaps half, so he doesn't lapse into a coma.'

She made the adjustments; we waited for three minutes, then Quilp stirred. His hand clutched for the remotes that weren't there, and he shook with dry heaves. He shivered. I noticed his feet were blue.

Virginia touched his shoulder.

He jerked away, suddenly more alive than either of us thought. His eyes were wide open, and stared at us with petite pupils. 'Who are you?' He covered his private parts with one hand, then, 'Where are my remotes?'

I cleared my throat.

He turned. 'Yeah, buddy? I'm still waiting for an answer. I got a gun around here somewhere, and I know how to use it.' His face was more weathered than I remembered, dried leather creased in all the wrong places. He was three years younger than me, but had the tired look of a great-grandfather, hunched over: only a half-circle of fine white hair capped his head, and deep lines etched a permanent scowl around his mouth.

'You are pathetic, Quilp. Get dressed. We're leaving soon.'

He stood, and stuck a trembling finger in my face. 'You can't order me around. Why don't you go trip and crash?'

'I am Germain,' I told him. 'I am disappointed you don't recognize me.' I picked up a soiled sheet and offered it.

He withdrew the finger from my face, grabbed the sheet, and wrapped it about his naked body. He smiled, cracking his frown lines. 'Got your face changed again, huh? Looks like they did a decent job on the nose this time. I should have guessed.'

His grin evaporated. 'Wait a second, I gotta finish something.' He placed one hand on his head (which was assuredly splitting apart), and staggered to a display that filled the air with equations and graphs of imaginary spaces only he could decipher. It was the problem he overdosed to solve.

'Are you certain you want him to come with us?' Virginia asked.

'He is merely hungover,' I whispered back.

'How long will he be like this?'

'He's always like this.'

'He seems a bit . . .' She couldn't find the word.

'Unstable?' I offered. 'He may be, but he's the only one who can build—'

Let's not go telling the hired help more than they need to know, said Fifty-five.

Quilp shouted into his display, 'No! This is all wrong.' He shook uncontrollably and pulled a handful of hair from his head.

'Can you link with the blue shield?' I asked Virginia.

It clung to his arm, blinking red warning lights. Virginia's beam flashed across the room. 'It's in range.'

'Filter the rest of the amphetamines out. He may be more stoned than I thought.' For a moment, Quilp's life was linked to mine. Without him, there was no thought shield, no master psychic, Necatane, and no Grail. It wouldn't do to let him have a stroke.

Quilp attacked the equations, and tried to make sense of the army of symbols that scattered in retreat across the display. He chased after them, expanded some into long series, approximated a heap of Greek letters into transcendental functions, and dropped others completely. I had no idea what any of it meant. The symbols marched themselves into orderly rows and columns, and simplified. These surviving variables he herded together, then collected them into a single line. The solution hovered in midair, pistachio green numbers as tall as Quilp: $0 = 1$.

He cursed profusely for several seconds.

Quilp noticed the blue shield on his arm. 'What's this? I don't remember . . .' His pale face flushed. He turned to me and hissed, 'You blew my high! I had this problem licked. The answer was right in front of me. Now it's gone! Two days wasted!'

'I need your assistance, Quilp.'

'Oh, I bet you do. You still owe me from the last job. 12 K if I remember right. You think I enjoy living in this low-rent cesspool?'

I did, but I reserved my comments. 'I can settle our debt now if you wish.' I reached into my shirt pocket. He tensed. Unfolding the wrinkled piece of electronics, I asked, 'What account?'

Quilp relaxed when he saw it wasn't a weapon. '3471-KAPPA, the Swiss defense fund, Earth.'

'Let's make it a nice round 20 K then, call it interest.'

He forgot the mathematical battlefield behind him, and remarked, 'You're not known for your generosity . . .' He mulled this over for a second, then came over and sat on a pile of pizza boxes, crushing the greasy cardboard. 'You must have something big going this time. OK, I'll bite. What is it?'

'A routine mission,' I lied.

'And my cut?' he inquired, casting a suspicious look at Virginia.

'If we are successful, I will be in a position to support you full time, a lab, drugs, and let's say a salary of 30 K per year?'

His glassy little eyes, points for pupils, stared into mine (no doubt trying to calculate ways to soak me for more money). '30 K? And if we're not successful?'

'The majority of the danger is mine. I can give you 5 K as a retainer fee. The rest you must earn. It shouldn't be any more difficult than the last two missions.'

He snorted a laugh and stood. 'What's that mean? We all get

to die if you fail? No, I think I'm gonna have to pass this time, buddy. All that violence, I'm just not cut out for it. Thanks for thinking of me, though – you know the way out.'

'Make it 40 K a year then,' I said, my voice a touch less friendly. 'I wouldn't want you to starve.'

He went back to his display and said, 'I'll have to think about it. Why don't you come back tomorrow? I have a few things to wrap up here, debts to settle, and people to talk to.'

'I'm sorry, Quilp, but we depart now. I am working with a deadline. I need your answer immediately.'

'Who you going to kill this time?'

To Virginia I said, 'Excuse us a moment, would you?' I grabbed Quilp's arm and escorted him to the far side of his studio. 'It's not that kind of job'

'Something illegal, then? I can't get caught doing anything that'll louse up my credit rating. I've gotta think about my future.'

'It's nothing illegal. I have to find something.'

Quilp crossed his arms. 'I know all about your routine missions: two assassinations, one coup d'état, and a little industrial espionage. You're gonna have to fill in more of the blanks before I risk my butt.'

'Very well.'

Wait, Fifty-five said. *You're not going to tell this worm about our mission. He'd sell us out in the blink of an eye.*

I know. And he knows that I know it, too. That's how I shall trap him.

'How much do you know about ancient Earth?' I asked.

He shook his head. 'Nothing.'

'I have been hired to locate an antique, a relic of the old Christian mythologies.'

'—And you want me to make a duplicate so you can pawn it off as the real one?'

'Not exactly,' I said. 'It cannot be duplicated. It is supposed to be magic.'

'Magic?' Quilp made a face like he'd swallowed a bitter pill. 'There's magic involved? You didn't tell me that! That's all I need, demons, genies, and spirits. Count me out. I'll stick with what I know.'

'Most unfortunate,' I replied and unslung the accelerator rifle, letting it rest level with his groin. Quilp took a startled step back – as if he had only now noticed the weapon. 'There are other competitors in this search, and I cannot allow anyone to know I've been this way, nor the nature of my mission. My ship could be traced and my safety compromised. And I know you wouldn't want that.'

Quilp shifted from side to side. He loathed magic, even hated me slightly for the tiny amount I practiced. It bothered him even more that I was a muse. To him that was one part knowledge, one part faith, and two parts mystery. Anything he couldn't isolate in a stasis field or reduce mathematically he hated . . . or feared. But he also knew I had killed before to keep things quiet. It was a good thing he didn't know how badly I needed him.

He swallowed, and asked, 'What is it you want?'

Good, he was curious. I had him halfway hooked. 'Do you recall the mental shield you constructed three years ago? I need you to build me another one, a better one.'

'Gonna bump off another shrink, huh? I hate those suckers almost as much as you muses.' He spotted something under a box of empty beer bottles and pulled it out – a pair of wrinkled pants that he stepped into. 'What happened to the last one?'

'Burned out,' I told him. 'Fortunately, I completed my mission before it failed.'

'It won't be easy,' he said and buttoned his pants. 'Your brain pattern is . . . unusual.' He focused on the distant wall a moment while he thought the problem through, then he said, 'I think it could be done, but I want 80 K a year plus expenses, and don't expect me to read any goat entrails or chant mantras.'

'I can offer you 50 K, no more.'

'Deal!' he said. 'Let me grab a few things, then we can go.' He dug around, finding two sneakers that didn't match, and a pale green sweatshirt with the corporate logo of the Californian Empire, DNA helix coiled about a sword, stitched on the front. He emptied a duffel bag of glass eyes onto the floor, let them roll away like marbles, then went from bench to bench gathering tools, meters, storage cubes, a small wandering robot, and other components I couldn't identify. 'I'll need to visit a few of my buddies here before we leave. I'm missing a few tools.'

'Very well, if you need them.'

'You need to secure your apartment,' Virginia told him. 'We cut the outer door when we came in. It was an emergency.'

'My door? Just as well. The way I see it, in a week I'll either be stranded on an alien world, dead, or set up in a new lab. The stuff here is all junk anyway.' He stopped, then asked, 'What kind of emergency?'

'Street punks,' I told him, 'they wanted a piece of us. Nothing serious.'

'And you were carrying that rifle? Then they weren't street punks. Come to think of it, I've seen a bunch of people hanging around since this morning. People trying awfully hard to blend in and look like locals. They weren't high, not even trying to score, just waiting . . . maybe for you?'

'Maybe.' It was impossible we had been followed here. The Grail Angel was too fast.

It wouldn't hurt to take precautions, Fifty-five said.

'Is there another way out of this building?'

'The elevator to the roof,' Quilp said, 'then down a fire escape to the back alley.'

'Perfect. We can take a look while we're up there.' I asked him, 'Do you have everything?'

'Yeah,' he said. '—Wait, there's one more thing.' He rummaged through a locker and pulled out a twisted alloy gear. He hefted it, then chucked it into the display he had been working on. The emitters shattered, and his problem melted into static, then vanished.

'OK, now I'm ready.'

We got into his antique elevator, and Quilp pressed both the up and down buttons together. We were jerked up to the roof. The view from five storeys high showed a colony that might look like any town: buildings lined up one after another in the residential section, tall towers of glass in the business district, and panels of white and lavender, the tents of the marketplace. I guess you had to take a close look to see what this place was really made of.

I did a quick check of the alley. It was filled with overflowing trash cans, and the only occupant was a dog nosing about for dinner. The fire escape was a zigzag of folded ladders.

Check the street side, Fifty-five suggested. *Better paranoid, than sorry.*

I walked to the street-side edge – dropped flat when I saw what was there. Two dozen men, all with chest-mounted cannons, were on the street. And with them was E'kerta, bristly black arms and antenna, looking ugly even from up here.

How did they get here so fast? cried Fifty-five. *Bug-man must have left right after Erybus's meeting.*

That doesn't make sense, I said. *Did he know we were coming here?*

I crawled back to Quilp and Virginia. 'We have company,' I told them. 'The alley is out. We'd be stuck in a dead end and spattered before we hit the street.' I glanced to my right. Another building was close, slightly lower than this one with a flat aluminum roof, and a crumbling brick fringe. 'How far a jump to that structure?' I asked Virginia.

She flashed a beam across the distance from the double star on her forehead and told me, 'Five meters with an angle of declination of point two radians.'

'Then we jump.'

'Jump?' cried Quilp. 'No sir, not me. I'd never make it with my equipment.'

'Our choices are limited at this point,' I said. 'Come with us . . . or stay and explain to my friends how you were just an innocent bystander.'

Quilp didn't look too happy with my suggestion and bit his nails.

'Virginia, can you make it?'

'No problem,' she said, then pulled a thin braided line from her pilot's suit. 'We use these for vacuum work.'

'Don't worry about me,' I assured her, 'I've jumped further before.'

'Maybe you have. Doesn't mean *I* have to risk the fall.' She clipped the line about my waist, then pulled about eight more meters.

'Go,' I told her, 'and secure the area. I'll come last, after Quilp.'

She sprinted across the roof, leapt the distance, and landed on the slippery aluminum surface.

I went back to the street and ventured another glance. The mercenaries were gone (probably inside Quilp's building), but scaling the walls were E'kerta's insects, giant cockroaches with ten arms and four antennae each, slimy-looking bastards. Behind me, the elevator's doors shut, and the motor made a low-pitched growl while the car descended.

I ran back to Quilp, hauled him up by his arm, and said, 'Make up your mind. We're about to be paid a visit.'

He handed me his bag full of equipment. 'OK, I'm in. You brought supplies for me? Dex, maybe?'

I fished through my pocket, and found the Metadexidrene he wanted, then handed him a single hit.

His eyes tracked the bulb as I passed it to him. He held it up to the artificial sun and appraised the clear fluid within. 'Ah,' he purred, 'the good stuff. I knew I could count on you, buddy.' Quilp pressed it to the artery on his neck, closed his eyes, and squeezed. There was a crisp snap as the drug hypercompressed into his bloodstream. He took a deep breath, exhaled, and his pale skin flushed. Without saying a word, he ran to the edge, jumped, and made it.

The elevator halted, stayed on the ground for ten seconds, then began squealing and jerking its way up. I let it get about halfway, then fired the rifle. The motor and cables turned red, then yellow, then melted into a gelatin blob and snapped. The elevator fell.

I swung Quilp's bag twice to build up momentum, and threw it across to Virginia. It landed on the slick roof and skimmed to the edge. Quilp caught it before it went over and shot me a glare for abusing his equipment.

Virginia looped the safety line around an air duct.

I slung my rifle, ran, and jumped.

Halfway across, in mid-air, a blast of pain kicked me square in the spine, forced the wind from me, and snapped my head back. I pawed for the edge – grabbed nothing.

I fell.

Virginia's line snapped taut around my waist. I bounced twice against the wall of the building, once on my face, once on my back. There was a sizzling sound and the scent of my own burnt flesh.

I dangled, stunned, twisting, listening to my ears ring.

Move! Fifty-five screamed. *We've been shot.* He started to take over, filling my flesh with his presence, but I stopped him and regained control.

I can do it. I hauled myself up the line, every movement tearing the wound on my backside open a little more. It hurt like hell.

I pulled myself up and saw Virginia struggling with the line, braced against the air duct which was twisting off. Quilp crouched behind her, not helping, but pointing to the other rooftop. Virginia let go of the line as soon as I had one hand on the edge, then grabbed her plasma tube. She aimed it my way.

'Duck,' she cried.

A cone of Xenon plasma spewed from the tube, sparkling amethyst. It thundered over my head (the ultraviolet radiation bathing my back with new agony). The aluminum roof I clung to got scalding hot.

I glanced over my shoulder. Half-assembled on the roof of Quilp's building was E'kerta. His individual beetles, spiky mandibles and leg-spider limbs, held each other to make his legs, parts of his torso, and one arm. In that one arm he held a pistol – but only for a second. The billowing purple cloud engulfed him. E'kerta flared with brilliant blue flames, then fell apart, charred black, and shells cracked.

Quickly, I pulled myself up. The roof was too hot to touch.

'Man, you're lucky,' Quilp said. 'That thing must have missed you.'

I ripped off my smoldering armored vest and showed him the hole burned through.

'Oh.' He looked to the next building and declared, 'We better get to that next one. There might be more of them.' Without pause he ran and leapt across. The Metadexidrene must be kicking in full force, influencing his normal gutless self.

'Thanks,' I said to Virginia as she placed the blue shield on my wound. 'He's right, you know. We have to move. There are more where they came from.'

'Cancel anesthesia,' she ordered the robot doctor. 'Administer topical nerve block instead, please.' It bleeped in compliance. 'That should take care of the pain until we get back to the ship.'

I wanted to say more to her, thank her again for saving my life, but Fifty-five urged me. *Go! Or there will be no one left to thank.*

I grabbed her hand and we jumped across, following Quilp. There were no more buildings, at least none within reasonable jumping distance. Even Quilp, on one hit of Metadexidrene, wasn't crazy enough to try and vault all the way across the street.

'Down,' I said and led the way into the shadowy stairwell of this building. The place wasn't as accommodating as Quilp's. It was a shell with only an occasional wall separating the stairwell from corridors, rooms, exposed supports, and broken windows. I caught a glimpse of the tenants as we descended; people sprawled on the floor, gazing into other realms of drugged delight (or the spray-painted walls). Others rocked back and forth, scratched themselves, paced, and stared hotly at us as we invaded their domain and passed through. The floors were covered in filth, human excrement, an endless collection of spent drug capsules, and strips of faded paisley carpet. Someone screamed close by, followed by sobbing. I ignored a cry for help and quickly spiraled down five flights, occasionally stepping over bodies, living and dead and various states in between.

Once on the ground floor, I jogged to the back door and burst through without listening first, just relieved to be outside in the cleaner-smelling air.

'We can lose whoever is after us in the marketplace,' Quilp said. 'Come on.'

'Slow down,' I said and grabbed his shoulder. 'We're not wired like you.'

'Why don't you give it a try?' he asked. 'Sure would speed things along.'

'Forget it,' I said, then set my rifle to maximum power, adjusted the field to a medium spray, and held it before me. 'I'll be leading the way.'

We went quickly through the evening, through the crowds. There were just as many people on the streets at night as there were this afternoon, maybe more. Dealers, slavers, prostitutes, all emerged like vampires to suck the life (what little there was) from the inhabitants of Needles colony. They gave me and my rifle a wide berth as we strode toward the docks.

One merchant, however, approached me. 'Samber juice, friend?' He stepped forward and sloshed the contents of his bottle.

'No, thanks, we—' His hands were clean, and a closer look at his smile revealed perfect, white, square teeth, not rotten as they ought to be. He was no Samber peddler.

I shot him.

From the accelerator rifle a blast of golden ions struck his midsection. He wore armor beneath his robes, the good kind, a thousand layers of synthetic sapphire (that only professionals wore). It only gave him a moment to feel the pain, but not enough time to scream.

We ran. Quilp led the way on with his enhanced reactions, through the metallic womb where huge traders' ships bobbed in their gravity wells, and men scrambled over their surfaces looking like small fish scrubbing the giants free of parasites. There was the thick scent of grease in the air. We passed through unnoticed into the smaller bays where our ship was.

I halted at the *Grail Angel* and started to key open the hatch when Virginia said, 'Not that one,' and dashed ahead of me, five slots up.

There was another vessel there, identical to this one – another *Grail Angel* – but turned about so her nose pointed toward the exit. One of the mass-folding generators hummed with power. It was warmed up and ready to depart.

But the one I stood next to had three wispy fins, three mass-folding generators, and even a silver magic circle inscribed upon her prow. There were two *Grail Angels*? The model couldn't be mass-produced. Virginia seemed to think it was a one-of-a-kind vessel.

I wanted to walk around, inspect this second ship and see if it maybe had a different name etched on her port side, but instead, I decided to trust Virginia's intuition. I ran to the *Grail Angel* she thought was ours.

Quilp whistled in appreciation and said, 'She has three mass-folders? I didn't think it was possible to balance three fields simultaneously.'

'This is a very special ship,' Virginia replied.

Two hemispherical depressions marred the metal floor close to the ship, a meter in diameter each. Coating these dimples was a black tar that smelled of rotten eggs left in the sun to bake. The scent triggered another feeling of déjà vu. Somewhere before I had caught this odor. The memory was strong, but the specifics obscure. It was beginning to bother me, these recurring recollections.

The voice of Setebos inquired, 'Proper identification of ownership is required, please.'

'Setebos, what happened here?'

'Proper identification is required,' it repeated in a threatening tone.

'Germain,' I answered in a neùtral voice.

'Voice print match within specified tolerances. Please place your hand on the entrance plate for DNA match.'

'Setebos, what's going on here?'

Silence.

I swore under my breath but did as the thing asked.

'Verification complete,' it said. Then the hatch opened and we boarded.

'A thousand regrets for delaying your entrance, Master,' Setebos said apologetically, 'but two attempts were made to compromise my structure. I had to resort to drastic actions or the integrity of the hull would have been breached.'

'The stains outside?' I asked.

'Remains of the individuals who attempted to penetrate my defenses. I focused a mass-folding field on their spatial coordinates and reversed polarity.'

'You *added* mass to them?' Virginia asked amazed.

'Approximately fourteen hundred metric tons, Madam Captain,' Setebos replied. 'Additionally, there have been attempts to probe my files from external sources. The protective circle has been drained to forty per cent of its maximum rated capacity. I took the liberty of turning the ship about and readying the systems for takeoff.'

'What kinda AI you got running this ship?' Quilp asked.

'Take a look for yourself,' I said, and pointed to the terminal aft of the copilot's seat.

Virginia hopped into the pilot's wraparound and flashed her beam about the panel, checking everything. 'Ready to go.' She frowned and added, 'But we're getting a hold signal from the port authority.'

'That's a load of garbage,' Quilp said. 'This is a smugglers' port. No one is ever stopped from leaving. Go, before they can bring up the outer doors.'

We skimmed past the small mass field that prevented the atmosphere from leaking out, and back out into the cool dark desert of space.

'This AI is something,' Quilp said to me, 'very advanced architecture.' I noticed he had already bypassed the first password I had installed.

'Where to?' Virginia asked.

'Where? Nowhere for now,' I said, 'just out into space. Let's get some distance between us and Needles.'

'Course plotted and the navigation – you better take a look at this, Germain.' Her voice was icy cold. 'Setebos, ready the forward weapons, full auxiliary power to the protective circle.'

Four warships were on the tactical display, ugly things bristling with weapons and fat with layers of alloy plating. They lumbered toward us, the tips of their particle cannons glowing, ready to cut us to pieces.

'Can you activate the mass-folding generator?'

'Too dangerous,' she said. 'This close to the planet's gravity well, our wave function would scatter.'

Fifty-five whispered, *We've been set up, junior.*

Chapter Seven

Four octopi swam through the night, metal-plated bodies with tentacles pointed toward us, aglow with radiation, prepared to fire.

'Four Sedition-class war cruisers confirmed,' Virginia said. 'They have us in a classic tetrahedral formation.'

'Why haven't they shot us?' Quilp cried.

'They want something,' I said, 'probably me. Quilp, try to establish communications.'

One of the metallic squids fired. A razor of lightning flashed, traced a line against the velvet dark of space, and struck. The *Grail Angel* shimmered in a haze of charged particles. Static danced across my skin, the displays in the cockpit flickered, and the temperature jumped ten degrees, making the burn on my back flare with pain.

'Protective circle operating at seventeen per cent of rated capacity,' Setebos said.

'Can we outmaneuver them?' I asked Virginia.

'They have us surrounded. If we attempt to flee on any vector, three can close and triangulate their fire.'

Another lightning bolt flashed, and phosphorescent ghosts played on the inside of the hull. Perspiration collected in the small of my back. We couldn't just sit here and let them destroy us. 'Damage?'

'Protective circle inoperative,' Setebos reported. 'Primary atmospheric system has failed. Switching to backup.'

On the nose of the *Grail Angel*, the runes of the magic circle blazed white-hot. It would take hours before they cooled down enough to absorb another blast.

'I'm getting a signal from them,' Quilp said. 'You want me to put it on?'

'Unless you enjoy being used for target practice.'

Quilp muttered something about my ancestry as he dumped the signal onto a working display.

Omar and his infectious grin appeared. His smile was wider than usual because he knew he had me.

'Friend Omar,' I said, trying to look like I expected him. 'What brings you here? Do you think the Grail is on Needles?'

He examined me with his hazel eyes, then took a sip of wine from a crystal flute. 'I don't know, friend. Is it?'

'No.'

'Most disappointing. I heard a rumor you were here. I thought it only civil to drop by and say hallo.'

'Heard? From whom?'

His smile grew even wider. 'I followed a trail of omens like bread crumbs to you . . . friend.'

Omens and bread crumbs, my ass, junior, said Fifty-five. *Someone tipped him off that we were coming to Needles, unless he cast a spell to see the future.*

Unlikely. Even my Master's most powerful mnemonic construct only affects seven seconds of time. To see hours into the future is beyond any lore I know of. That's why I need the psychologist, Necatane.

'It has also come to my attention,' Omar said, his grin fading, 'that you and I had a parting of the ways three weeks ago.'

Then he knew I had murdered his previous clone. I said nothing.

He swirled his wine and took another sip. 'But no matter now. You should have taken the deal I offered you on Golden City.'

'I suppose it's too late to join you?'

'Much too late.'

'You and E'kerta were working together,' I said. 'Those were his mercenaries down there, but whose ships are you commanding? You never had the capital to buy four warships and crew.'

'My thanks for eliminating E'kerta. He had a logical mind, but was far too dangerous. Unpredictable. And the ownership of these fine vessels is none of your concern.

'Now,' he said, 'let us do business. I have a new deal for you. One that you cannot afford to decline. In exchange for your life, I demand your expert services to help me find the Grail. Do not tell me you know nothing. You demonstrated your knowledge quite adequately at Erybus's meeting.'

'I may know something,' I lied to Omar. 'But why should I tell you?' I stood with my arms akimbo, trying to look like I had a firmer bargaining position than I did. 'True, you could destroy my ship, but you'd gain nothing.'

'Not true, friend. There would be one less in the race, one whom I consider serious competition. On the other hand, if you cooperate with me, I'll merely take your ship and strand you on Needles.' That smile of his returned. 'I shall even allow you to keep your casino winnings. I wouldn't want anyone to say I was ill-mannered.'

'Thanks,' I replied. 'In fifty weeks I'll still be dead.'

You're a fool, said Fifty-five, *if you think he'll let you live a second longer than he has to*.

Omar shrugged. 'A year on Needles with money to spend is better than an immediate death, is it not?' He took a large gulp of his wine, finishing it, then asked, 'What shall it be?'

I glanced to Virginia and Quilp. Maybe it would be best to give up. Omar might cut a deal with Virginia, hire her, or let her go unharmed. Quilp? He'd probably kill him.

Virginia had no fear in her eyes; she was ready to fight. And Quilp, it was hard to tell what he was thinking. All I saw were his pupils constricted to the extreme.

I had to buy us time.

'Very well, Omar, I know when I've been beaten. I shall tell you what I know.' In a whisper, I added, 'However, if anyone is to win this competition other than me, I would rather it were a fellow member of the Corporation. How far do you trust your business partners? Wouldn't it be better if we spoke face to face? These ship-to-ship transmissions are notoriously unsecure.'

He stroked his chin. 'True. Hold your position and prepare to be boarded. And let me remind you that I have four warships with their weapons ready to cancel you. Let us not have any tricks.'

'No tricks. You have my word.'

'Omar out.' His Cheshire-cat smile faded from the display.

'Virginia, what is that planet like?' I asked. 'Can we make an emergency landing?'

Information flashed into her double-star insignia, and she reported, 'Hydrogen sulfide atmosphere of seventeen thousand kilopascals, mean temperature over six hundred degrees Kelvin, winds at five hundred kilometers per hour – not what I'd call a picnic spot.'

'Setebos, give me your Grail database analysis. Do we have anything to barter with?'

'My study is only twenty-three per cent complete, Master; however, I have three locations with high correlations: Bebin in the Lydia system, Lesser Byzantia in the Melbourne cluster, and New Jerusalem on Earth, with respective probabilities of twelve, eight, and five per cent. There are others, but they fall well below these levels of certainty.'

'Great.'

'So give Omar those locations,' Quilp suggested, 'and up the percentages.'

'Omar likes to be told the truth,' I said. 'He'll use a verifier or something worse to check the accuracy of our claims.' I didn't need to tell Quilp that Omar had several psychological means at his disposal to extract the truth. He was close to panicking already.

Quilp slammed his fist into the terminal. 'Man! I knew this was a mistake. I gotta get out of here.' He suddenly composed himself and asked, 'Wait, pilot, we can't use mass-folding generators close to the planet because we'll get scattered, right?'

'Correct,' she replied. 'If our mass falls below the light-neutrino mass limit, virtually any potential scatters our wave function. We degenerate into non-coherent plane waves, unable to resolve, and drift forever.'

'But what if we didn't go below the LNM limit? What if we retained a finite mass?'

'Can't,' Virginia said. 'All the folding subroutines are designed to make our mass as small as possible, to go below the LNM limit.'

'And at finite masses,' Setebos interjected, 'the *Grail Angel* is restricted to sub-light velocities. The warships will detect our motion and destroy us. Additionally, all finite-mass folded wave functions are inherently unstable.'

There was a gleam in Quilp's eyes, the hint of a solution. I'd seen him like this before, excited, on the verge of a breakthrough. 'Let's tackle the warship problem first,' he said. 'Assuming we retain a finite but extremely small mass, above the LNM limit, we remain in the domain of normal quantum mechanics. Low-mass particles like electrons have a probability of tunneling through potential barriers as a function of their energy and the height of the barrier.'

Omar's ship rearranged, and one ship broke ranks to swim towards us, distorting the tetrahedral formation, leaving a tilted triangle behind. All their weapons were still armed, aglow with radiation, and looking like angry little octopi.

'We tunnel through the planet,' Quilp declared and thrust a finger through the circle of his forefinger and thumb to demonstrate.

Virginia shook her head. 'Tunneling only works with very light mass, and small potentials. You're talking about a planet. Seven thousand kilometers of molten rock!'

'It'll work,' he assured her. 'But we gotta keep ourselves exactly at the LNM limit.'

'Impossible,' Setebos declared.

'No. It's impossible for you,' he said, 'because you're programmed for efficiency, to make us go as far below that mass as possible. If I let you use one mass-folding generator to do that, and unfold a portion of your folds with a second mass-folding generator, then I can manually adjust our mass, make it resonate at the LNM limit.'

'Manual alteration of the field parameters is inadvisable,' Setebos declared.

'Keep your shirt on,' Quilp told the AI. 'I'll use you. I'm just gonna be tweaking a few off-diagonal elements on the field matrix.'

'It might work,' Virginia said, and stared out from the display to the churning green and scarlet clouds of the planet below. 'But we'd have to keep our mass resonating exactly at the light neutrino mass limit. If we go below it, we leave the domain of normal quantum mechanics and get scattered into plane waves, and if we go too far above it, we won't tunnel through.'

'Won't tunnel through?' I said.

'There are two possibilities,' Quilp answered, 'we either never leave our starting point or we end up parked inside the planet.'

'Since we'll be fine-tuning our energy,' Virginia said to Quilp, 'there might be a problem with uncertainty. But we really don't have a choice. What do I do?'

Quilp didn't like women, and he didn't like strangers. He pursed his lips and prepared some insult. Then he surprised me. 'The second mass-folding field will diverge when we enter the upper atmosphere,' he said, 'and again as we enter the planet's crust. You'll need to find a way to dampen that effect.'

'I can use power from the atmospheric system.'

'That might work,' he replied, 'as long as we don't mind breathing stale air for a few minutes.'

Virginia turned to me. 'There's only one problem: the warships will detect our generators when they power up. They'll blast us to atoms before we move. We need a way to distract them – just for a second.'

'We have weapons,' I said.

'No power,' she answered. 'We need it all for the generators.'

I sighed and considered.

One of my personas had neutralized a similar threat before. Usually, I ignored the strange symbols and indecipherable thoughts residing within Aaron, the alien king. When ships attacked his home world, he dispatched them with the mnemonic lore I stole from him. Those vessels were primitive compared to Omar's, but, in theory, the strategy was sound. If it wasn't, Omar would be extremely upset. And we'd be dead.

Aaron had been a creature of stone, with organs of metal, and wore only raw gems and crystals for ornamentation. He and his people lived a peaceful life deep within the molten core of their world, never bothering anyone, until they met Rhodes Industries Intergalactical.

The cartel wanted to mine his planet; actually, they wanted to blast it to pieces and extract the rare metals. Aaron's race refused to cooperate. They refused to be relocated. They even had the audacity to fight back – even had the nerve to win. That's why I was hired.

Immediately, I called for a peace conference. The earth creatures never intended to harm anyone; they just wanted to be left alone, so they accepted my offer to negotiate in good faith. That's when I met Aaron. That's when I froze his body, drank his mind, and scattered his soul to the void.

'You'll have your distraction,' I told her. 'Ready the ship. I can destroy Omar's vessel when he closes.'

'Destroy?' Quilp cried. 'What do you mean, destroy his ship? You heard the girl.'

Virginia narrowed her eyes at him.

'We have no weapons! What are you going to do, throw a rock at it?'

'You tend to your equations and let me do what I have to do.' There was no need to distract Quilp by telling him I would be using what he believed to be magic. He had enough on his mind. I fumbled through my pocket and handed him five capsules.

He grabbed them, muttered something, then threw himself into the co-pilot's seat. A jumbled matrix appeared before him, rotating slowly, the colors of its elements changing from cool, safe green, to orange, then red. He and Virginia debated certain mathematical operators while Omar's warship approached.

The smooth motion of the ship was deceptive. Sedition-class vessels were enormous, lumbering things, with plenty of fire-power, but short on speed and grace. For what I wanted to do, the bigger his ship was, the better.

Two crisp snaps caught my attention. Quilp removed a pair of spent capsules from his neck. Good. The little addict would be in peak stimulated form.

Omar's ship was very close now; she filled our displays, and all illusions of her being a sleek sea creature vanished, replaced by obvious patches of armor plate, blemished with blackened scars, and tentacles that were really cannons.

'Incoming communication,' Setebos announced.

'Germain,' Omar said, giddy with satisfaction, 'prepare to surrender your ship and be boarded.'

He was within range. I released my precious stolen memo-ries, including the one Aaron called his 'air attraction', summoned the energies and wove them into patterns I had never learned. I could do this but once, then the alien king would unravel from my mind.

Aaron never spoke, which was fine with me. His mind was

different from the others, and I doubted if he was ever friendly towards me, with or without the enchantment placed upon him. His memories flooded my thoughts, memories of how he constructed the air attraction to save his race. In the span of three heartbeats, it condensed all gaseous elements within an enormous volume into liquid. When it was done, the liquefied air flash-vaporized back to its original state.

More memories surfaced: a dozen bejeweled offspring of amazing grace and beauty, a world full of warm fluid, crystalline caves, thermal plumes to play in, and a joy I would never know. It was little wonder he fought so hard to keep it.

Regret filled my heart, guilt over his death, over the annihilation of his race. I tried to ignore it and concentrated on the air attraction, concentrated on saving my own skin.

'You ready?' I whispered.

'Whenever you are,' Virginia said.

Quilp was too high to say anything; his mind polarized to solve the equations before him.

I released the mnemonic lore. Aaron screamed as the energies coursed through me, through the blank void of space, directed into the warship. He screamed as his soul unraveled, along with the air attraction, from my mind.

First heartbeat: the air within Omar's ship condensed into liquid, making a vacuum on board. This wouldn't damage the hull. It was designed to withstand such changes in pressure (although the crew might not fare as well). The sensors would detect the change in pressure and report a hull breach to the computer.

Second heartbeat: the computer automatically sealed the corridors and rooms, compartments and passages (a sensible procedure), then repressurized them. With any luck the liquefied air was trapped in a single sealed section.

'Now,' I said to Virginia. 'Go!'

The generators throbbed with power, straining against one

another, one wrinkling our mass, the other smoothing it out. Quilp moved his hands through a virtual matrix, adjusting the glowing field values, making us hover on the edge of existence.

Third heartbeat: the liquid atmosphere flash-vaporized. In a compartment never designed to withstand such pressure, a hundred thousand cubic meters of air were suddenly present, pushing against the hull, tearing it apart like an over-inflated balloon. Even Aaron's mental construct couldn't fool thermodynamics for long.

Omar's ship bulged, seemed to pause mid-flight, then exploded. Tentacled weapons spun in space, wriggling as if they had a life of their own, and armored plates were thrown into the night sky like confetti in celebration.

'Maximal probability of wave function in upper atmosphere now at point oh three,' Virginia informed Quilp.

He grunted an acknowledgment, and his equations flashed a violet warning. He compensated with a flick of his hands, fine-tuning our mass.

The displays were a jumble of simultaneous images: warship fragments shooting through space, clouds of hydrogen sulfide, wind-carved red rocks, and all spaces in between. Our existence was reduced to its pure quantum mechanical components, and we were no longer in any one place at any one time. Position had no meaning. We were only an envelope of probability smeared across space.

'Maximum probability entering planetary crust,' Setebos announced.

Quilp and Virginia were too engrossed in keeping our mass adjusted to respond. Quilp wasn't even breathing. His tetraoxide reserves would keep him healthy for the few minutes, so I didn't worry about him.

The displays revealed the interior of the planet. Liquid stone surrounded the *Grail Angel*, and I felt strangely comfortable among the heat and pressure, despite the burn on my back. The air turned thick and stale.

'What's going on?' I asked.

Neither of them answered.

'Setebos? Why is it so hot?'

'Atmospheric systems off-line and power rerouted to compensate for a divergent secondary field,' he told me.

The psychologist remarked, *The heat you feel is primarily based on the perception that we are inside the planet. There exist several examples of such an induced . . .*

His voice faded away. It was just as well; I wasn't listening. Instead, I sat and watched the displays, watched as our probability shifted through the molten core. There were currents and eddies out there, and I knew exactly what it would feel like to ride them, to swim through the convection rolls, to explore the caves of liquid crystals deeper than any surface dweller could imagine. My sexmate and offspring were here, too. Their names, so long since I had heard them, echoed for kilometers in the dense hot sea.

'Warning,' Setebos said in a formal tone, 'path integral not bounded in non-diagonalized matrix. Please reconfigure.'

Quilp cursed and raced through the tangle of symbols to find his error.

In my haze of Aaron's reminiscence, I heard Virginia say, 'Exponential decay of wave function approaching critical level. Boosting power to the second mass-folding field.' Her voice was a squeaky thing to me, not the slow melodies of my sexmate.

Quilp hissed, 'It's not working, we're gonna have to bring the third mass-folding generator on-line.'

This was all wrong. I was cold and too solid. I should be out there, surrounded by warm fluidity, my body melding with my world's minerals, not confined within this bubble of air and frozen metal. I went to the hatch, and my hand fumbled with the control pad.

'Master,' asked Setebos, 'may I inquire what you are doing?'

'Going home,' I answered. 'My family waits for me. Cannot

you hear their songs? Cannot you see my offspring sheathed in liquid gold, their lovely flames? They are waiting for me. They have been waiting too long . . .'

'Master, if you release the hatch, our wave function will become asymmetric. The core temperature is twenty-two thousand degrees Kelvin, and while the *Grail Angel* is designed to withstand these extremes, your flesh is not. I beg you to reconsider.'

'But my family, they need me, my protection.'

So faint I barely heard him, the psychologist whispered, *They are dead, long dead. You are not King Aaron. You are Germain of Umbra Incorporated. These are not your memories.*

Germain, his name I knew. He was the surface dweller who called us to speak of peace, the man who wished to speak to me alone in the meeting cave, the man who had trapped me, froze me solid, immobile, then he—

I was he.

I removed my hand from the control pad. I was not the noble Aaron, but the cold killer, the professional assassin.

This had never happened before. When one of my personas took over, I knew what was happening, I sensed in a limited fashion what they did from the background of my mind. I always retained my identity. This time was different. For a moment, I had been Aaron. My ego had been washed completely away.

I warned you this would eventually happen, the psychologist said.

'Energy spike!' cried Virginia. 'They've fired on our initial position. It's disrupting the tail end of our wave function, and propagating through our extended field. Intersecting our maximal probability in six seconds.'

'I'm bringing the third mass-folding generator on-line,' Quilp said. 'It'll boost our resolution, and – what in blazes?'

My vision blurred. The ship seemed to be drifting apart in all directions at once.

'Confirm that I have thirty-three distinct wave functions,' Quilp asked Virginia.

Virginia's insignia flashed continuously, a single unbroken stream of data, then she said, 'Confirmed. Thirty-three identical overlapping wave functions. Increase power to the number two generator. Give us some mass before we scatter apart.'

Images of clouds poured from the displays, a swirl of green mist, then the dark coolness of space. The blurring sensation vanished.

'Exiting probability increasing to point eight nine,' Virginia said. 'Field arrays powering down, resolution of wave function imminent.'

'Look!' Quilp cried.

Ahead of us, another *Grail Angel* popped into reality, then another, then a dozen more, all identical to our ship. The displays aft showed more *Grail Angels*. An explosion bloomed there, engulfed one of them, white fire, then red, then only a dot of black smoke that was swept away by the raging winds of the planet.

The other *Grail Angels* veered away and, one by one, faded from our displays.

Quilp released the equations he so tightly controlled, then slumped over in his chair and started breathing again. There were no pupils in his eyes that I could discern and all his muscles twitched from over-stimulation. It was a wonder his heart hadn't burst.

'Did you see that?' he wheezed. 'Our wave function split when I brought the last generator on-line. They resolved, too. Weird. I'm gonna have to run a few simulations to figure out how it happened.'

'What course?' Virginia asked. 'I'd like to put some distance between us and your friends on the other side of the planet.'

Since Setebos hadn't found the location of the Grail, there was no choice but to pay a visit to the master psychologist, Necatane.

'Set course for the Delphid system,' I said.

Virginia turned her attention to the navigation display. Setebos balanced our mass-folding fields, and we left what remained of the cloned Omar far behind. Did a clone even have a soul?

'Estimated arrival in eleven days, twenty hours, sixteen minutes, non-relative time,' Setebos said. 'Six hours, fourteen minutes, relative time.'

I took another look back and pondered the sea of liquid metal we sailed through . . . thought of Aaron and his people . . . considered my role in their extinction.

Would you care to discuss your feelings? the psychologist inquired.

There's no time to dig through the past, Fifty-five said. *What happened back there with those other ships?*

I asked Quilp, 'Those other *Grail Angels*, what were they? An optical distortion?'

'They were no distortion,' he replied. 'They were us.'

'How can that be?'

'You know the uncertainty principle?' he asked.

'You can't measure a quantum object's position and momentum simultaneously.'

'Yeah, but there's another version of the principle that applies to energy and time. When we tried to smooth out that energy spike, and keep our wave function resonating at the light neutrino mass limit, we forced our energy into an extremely narrow range.'

'Correspondingly,' Virginia said, 'our wave function was scattered through time. For a brief instant there were thirty-three *Grail Angels*.'

'But they vanished,' I said.

'That's because only one of us can exist in the same temporal frame,' Quilp explained, seeming slightly annoyed that I didn't know. 'The exclusion principle? Only one set of quantum numbers per customer? Those other wave functions had to collapse.'

'It was curious they lasted so long, though,' Virginia added, then she got up. 'If you two don't mind, I'm going aft to make sure the ship is intact.'

Setebos said, 'Madam Captain, I have performed three checks of the hull integrity, and tested all the—'

'I'd feel better, Setebos, if I took a look for myself.' She left us.

Quilp seemed certain those other *Grail Angels* disappeared. I wasn't so sure. I definitely saw another *Grail Angel* in the hangar on Needles. Could it have been one of the shadows we cast in time? And the déjà vu I felt since this mission started, that remained unexplained. Maybe there were other Germains out there now. Would we all be saved if one of us found the Grail, or could there be only one winner? It might explain how Omar found me. Another Germain, projected back in time, might tip him off to eliminate the competition from his other selves. Yet, if Omar had killed me on Needles, wouldn't that wipe out my other selves? I'd never have left Needles, never have tunneled through the planet, and never have split myself through time. Paradox.

I could go crazy working out all the implications.

Quilp interrupted my thoughts, 'Why are we headed to the Delphid system? There's nothing there but a brewery. Kinda off the beaten path.'

'Not a brewery,' I corrected him, 'a winery. But that's not why we are going there. We're going there to see a man.'

'You gonna ask him where this thing is you're looking for?'

'No,' I said. 'I'm going to kill him.'

Chapter Eight

Half of Quilp's money was mine. The rest was Virginia's. Six stacks of ivory chips were piled neatly in front of her. For the last five hours, I hadn't been able to consistently beat her, even with the gambler's advice. She wore a nonchalant mask, which made it impossible to tell when she bluffed.

I was Quilp's deal. His shaking hands threw me two blank vacuums, a pair of planets, a gas giant, and a binary star, which gave me the beginnings of a system.

'You're both cheating,' he hissed after scrutinizing his cards.

'There's no need,' I said. 'You're doing a fine job of losing without our help. Maybe if you gave your mind a rest from those stimulants, you'd win a hand or two.'

The corner of his eye twitched. 'They don't affect my game.'

Virginia sipped her shot of boiling quantum ice, ignored our debate, and opened with a cautious bet of twelve.

'Both of you will see,' he mumbled. 'I've gotta sure-fire method. The cards just need to catch up to the statistics. I'll win everything back.'

I laughed. Poor Quilp sounded like he believed himself.

Discarding my pair of vacuums, I hoped for another planet, a comet, or even an asteroid to complete my system. Instead, I got a black hole and a section of the celestial dragon for my wishful thinking. That left a single pair of planets – a lousy hand – but that wouldn't stop me from bluffing. Another round of betting and cards remained. I felt lucky.

The gambler said, *Your pilot is a good guesser. She'll know a bluff.*

Care to play this hand out? I asked.

Sorry, I couldn't sit in for less than ten thousand. I am a professional, after all.

I tossed forty into the pot. 'Your twelve and twenty-eight more.' I let a fake smile crack my poker face, then turned to Quilp. 'That's forty to you. And how's our little project coming along? Shouldn't you be tinkering with that rather than losing your shirt?'

'It'll be ready,' he said and tugged thoughtfully at one of the few hairs on his head. 'Setebos is compiling the code for me and etching it into crystal. Some fine-tuning after that, and we'll be in business.' He stared at his cards, then, 'Forty, huh? You wouldn't want to extend me a line of credit, would you?'

'Not a chance.'

'I can cover you,' Virginia volunteered. She pushed a stack of chips (that were recently his) toward him.

'Who are you,' he sneered, 'my mother?' He pocketed his remaining seven chips, and threw his cards across the crew's quarters. 'I'm gonna go see what's taking that AI so long. We'll finish this later.' He sulked back into the cargo bay where he had set up his equipment.

Virginia picked up his cards, inspected them, then placed them on the discard pile.

Now that you two are secluded, Celeste whispered, *steal another delectable kiss.*

You said a pilot cannot get involved with her employer.

So discharge her.

I just might do that. My thoughts wandered from the game, and my eyes became more concerned with the shades of gold, platinum, and copper in her hair, than with how many planets I held. Virginia was better at Universe than I, which indicated intelligence, intuition and luck, all traits I admired, yet there was still that feeling that we had met before, not as strong as when we kissed at Golden City, but there nonetheless. It bothered me.

'Cards?' she asked.

I dropped the black hole (which was heavier than the other cards) and the freezing vacuum. 'Please, two.' She flicked a pair of card plates to me.

I'll tell you what's bothering you, said Fifty-five. *She's a traitor. Who else could have tipped Omar and E'kerta off? She was the only one who knew we were going to Needles.*

If she signaled them while we were en route, I said, *they would have arrived hours after we did. Those Sedition-class warships couldn't be faster than the* Grail Angel. *They had to leave for Needles before we did. Any bright ideas how that happened?*

My cards: a third planet, newly formed, its crust cracked with lines of glowing magma, and a comet. I had my system, not a great one, but it had to be better than her hand. Last round she picked up four cards. Unless she was phenomenally lucky, I had her.

'Twenty more,' she said, and slid her chips between the 'P' and the '7' stenciled in the center of the table.

'Your twenty and a hundred,' I answered with a stone face, and tossed a stack of chips into the pot.

She raised an eyebrow. 'One hundred . . . and three hundred more.'

Now we're talking, the gambler said.

'You're bluffing.'

She shrugged. 'We'll see.'

Consider the possibility of her being a spy, Fifty-five said.

I asked the psychologist, *You told me Virginia was loyal.*

You want my professional opinion? he said. *I must make note of this occasion. Yes, I did. And since you shared a near-fatal experience, I sense the bond even stronger than before. I might add that your feelings toward her are also—*

Enough professional opinion, Fifty-five interrupted. *So she's loyal to you. She might be brainwashed and acting on a subcon-*

scious level. The Corporation does it all the time.

'Tell me,' Virginia said and leaned across the table. 'At Golden City you used magic to change your last card, didn't you?'

'Why do you ask?'

'Just curious,' she answered and traced the edge of the stenciled 'P' on the table with her finger. 'I've never seen real magic before. They have magicians at the casino, but they use holograms, sleight of hand, and mirrors. It's not real. Not like what you did.'

'What I did was nothing, really.'

'Then it *was* magic.' Her brown eyes widened. 'Can you teach me? Do you have to be born with the ability? Is there some dark ritual to perform?' She glanced at her pile of chips, then whispered, 'I've heard muses sell their souls for power.'

'No selling of souls,' I told her. 'And there is no magic or rituals. Just years spent with your nose in books.'

Tell her the truth, the psychologist said. *Your so-called magic is merely a low-grade, undisciplined psychic talent cloaked in superstition.*

I didn't let him bait me into the argument we had had a thousand times before.

'So anyone could learn it?' Virginia squared her cards and set them down. 'Show me exactly what you did.'

My mental constructs were precious. Using it to impress her seemed wasteful; yet, I wanted to impress her. I wanted her to like me. But I couldn't switch the cards as I did before, that mnemonic lore was Omar's, and it was gone . . . he was gone. I'd have to do something else.

After I said nothing for several seconds, she spoke: 'Or maybe it's asking too much.' She scooped up her cards, fanned them, then, 'It's three hundred to you. Are you betting or folding?'

In plain sight, so she could see, I squeezed my thumb and pinkie together, the first of the seventeen mnemonics that unlocked the *Theorem of Malleability* from my mind. Memories and power unwound together, flooding my thoughts: Einstein oscillators and blackbody radiation and energy bands.

Virginia watched as pale blue light spread across my right hand, watched as sparks dripped from my fingers and mist collected in my palm, but did not see the three stacks of chips I secreted under the table with my other hand.

'I am betting,' I whispered.

More memories uncoiled; energy took form and erupted into a lavender flame, a ghostly fire that did not consume my hand. It was hot and cold. While flames licked my palm, frost crystallized on the tips of my fingers, and water vapor condensed, beading at my wrist and trickling down my arm. I set my burning hand flat on the table, and the metal turned soft beneath. My fingers sank into it.

On the underside of the table, the metal there softened too. With one smooth motion, I pushed the stacks of chips through, and removed my hands. The mnemonic construct vanished. The metal hardened.

Virginia gasped. 'How did—'

'Magic,' I lied, then blew the flames dripping from my fingers out.

She carefully probed the table with one finger. It was solid. 'The '7-P' stenciled on the surface, however, was slightly distorted. The tail end of the '7' curled around, making it look like a hybrid between a '6' and a backwards '5'.

'If I hadn't seen it with my own eyes.' She stared at my stack of chips, then asked, 'This your bet?'

'I suppose.'

'Then I call,' she said. 'What have you got?'

She wasn't amazed. Or if she was, she had recovered quickly enough to take advantage of me. We flipped our cards. She gave an appreciative nod to my three-planet system, but that was nothing compared to her black cluster, fourth-order no less: three stars, a nebula, and a black hole.

Her winning hand sprang to life; a virtual projection radiated from each card. The nebula engulfed our table in a blood-tinged hydrogen mist. And in its center, three suns spun about a point of darkness. From those stars, tails of plasma spiraled into the center, heated to white brilliance, and vanished forever (like the money I had just lost).

The image faded.

She collected the cards, and her chips, then asked with a wry smile, 'Another hand?'

This woman was clever. Anyone who could outfox me was worth knowing. I picked up my chair and moved next to her. I then took her hands into mine, and answered, 'The only hands I desire are these.' I kissed them, her palms, the inside of her wrist, moving up along her arm, then her neck. She didn't seem to mind.

She ran her fingers through my hair. My pulse jumped – the blood pumping hot through my body. I detected a faint fragrance from her: cinnamon and musk. Virginia drew me to her face, and kissed me like she had before in my suite, sensual, wet, only longer, increasing in passion, not diminishing.

I sensed Celeste close, waiting for me to relax my guard so she could step in. I had to stop now or abandon myself altogether to her.

Let yourself go, the imperial geisha whispered. *I promise you ecstasy beyond your wildest dreams.*

'Hey,' Quilp said and stepped into the room, 'I need you for a few—' He did an about face when he saw us intertwined. The interruption gave me time to realize what was about to happen. I pulled away from Virginia.

'Wait,' I said. 'What is it?'

He poked his head back in. 'Sorry to bother you,' he said unapologetically, 'but this mental shield of yours needs adjusting.' He held up a baseball cap with the words *Unico Robotics* stitched along the brim.

Virginia turned away from me, her face burning, and said, 'I better check the navigation systems.' She got up and left quickly, brushing past Quilp.

'Look, Germain,' he said and took a step back, 'you're not mad, are you? All I was gonna do was fine-tune the shield.'

I was mad, but not at Quilp. I wanted companionship, normal physical contact. How could I have that with ghouls in my mind watching, waiting to take control when I was vulnerable?

Celeste was the worst. She had eclectic tastes when it came to intimacy. If I allowed her to have her way with Virginia she was capable of anything, sadistic torture, masochism, rape, just as easily as tenderness and submission – whatever struck her fancy. More than once I awoke in the arms of strangers, both men and women, sometimes animals, or machines, having performed acts both horrific and wonderful to satisfy her urges.

It's only sex, she sighed. *You don't have to marry her. What do you care?*

Let's just say I'm partial to this one.

You're not falling for this trollop-spy, I hope, Fifty-five said.

I didn't answer him.

'Let's get on with it,' I told Quilp.

He handed me the baseball cap. Inside was a sheath of flexible crystalline material, blinking with soft pastel colors. I set it atop my head.

'Not like that,' he told me and smashed it down tight enough to give me a headache. 'The contact has to be snug. It would be better if you shaved your head. But maybe then our pilot wouldn't find you so attractive?'

I cast a deadly look at him.

'I don't blame you, though, she's a knockout.' He waved a scanner in front of me. 'OK, think kinky thoughts.'

I thought about killing the little maggot.

Quilp removed the cap, swapped one of the crystals, and we tried it again, and again, and finally a third time, then he declared, 'Nothing, the scanner reads zero mental emissions. You're technically brain dead. When do I get paid?'

Fifty-five whispered, *Has it occurred to you that the creep is expendable? He's done his job. Who would care if he disappeared?*

'Approaching Delphid system,' Setebos chimed (possibly saving Quilp's life).

I grabbed my winnings, not trusting Quilp alone with them, and went forward to the bridge.

'The fifth planet,' I told Virginia.

A ruby giant burned on the ship's displays and filled my eyes with its dreary dim light. A star in the last years of its expansion, it would soon dwindle to a tiny white dwarf, only slightly brighter than the rest of the stars in the night. This was where Necatane made his home. This was where he taught his pupils, and grew his famous silver grapes that only thrived in the light of a dying star. The wine he fermented from them was renowned for making the drinker relive forgotten memories. Some vintages brought only pleasant memories to the surface: one's first love, long summer days, or swimming in a warm ocean.

'Coordinates?' Virginia asked me.

'Sector fourteen north, thirty-eight east,' I told her. Then to Setebos I commanded, 'Full power to the magic circle. If there is a detection net, I want to absorb the energies and slip in unnoticed.'

'Yes, Master,' Setebos replied. 'Magic circle operating at ninety-seven per cent of rated capacity.' The blue and green cube grew brighter on the console, then spoke: 'Warning: magic circle drained to seventy-two per cent by multiplexed radar and solid-state augur forces.'

'Solid-state what?' Quilp asked.

'A crystal ball,' I told him. 'Virginia, take us down quick. There is a canyon at those coordinates. It should partially screen us before the magic circle fails.'

'Strap yourselves in,' she said.

I hopped into the co-pilot's chair and let it wrap around me. When we hit the upper atmosphere, the *Grail Angel* shuddered.

'Setebos, what was that vibration?' Virginia demanded.

'Diagnostic running, Madam Captain.'

'It was just a little shake,' Quilp said. 'Nothing to worry about.'

Virginia pored over the engine schematics. 'Here,' she said, pointing to the mass-folding generator, 'what's this low reading?'

Setebos answered: 'That is the primary vortex circuit. I'm afraid it is nonfunctional.'

Virginia said to herself, 'It must have burned out with that maneuver we pulled tunneling through the planet.'

'Is it serious?' I asked.

'Yes.' Through her double-star insignia information flashed, then she told me, 'I can keep us flying for about thirty seconds, then the back-ups burn out too. Hang on.'

'Wait!' Quilp shouted. 'I'm not—'

To the far side of the planet we arced, then dove with dizzying velocity. I heard Quilp go bouncing to the back of the bridge. Infrared images spilled from the displays: a film of clouds, then the earth rushed to merge with us. Virginia twisted into a barrel roll an instant before we crashed. The acceleration pushed me deep into the seat, made my face sag, and my arms too heavy to lift.

The *Grail Angel* skimmed over treetops, then dropped to a lower altitude and shot out across a smooth lake, flying alongside a smeared orange moon reflected in its dark water. We slowed only when we entered the canyon. Its walls were strips of eroded stone, and a river twisted through it. A distressing whine came from the generator. The ship drifted over a sandy shoal, then, with a sudden drop, we landed.

Virginia frowned as she examined the display. The damaged circuits glowing red.

I asked Setebos, 'Are we still being probed?'

'Yes, Master, although the energy being absorbed is substantially lower. Magic circle integrity can be maintained for seven hours at current power consumption.'

'How long to repair the ship?' I asked Virginia.

'It shouldn't take me more than a few hours,' she said, 'then we can get what you came here for.'

What's this 'we' stuff? Fifty-five inquired.

'I must go alone,' I told her. 'You and Quilp stay here and ready the ship. I should be back before sunrise.'

Quilp pulled himself off the floor, rubbed his head, and remarked, 'Suits me fine. Hey, while you're out there, grab me a bottle of that booze, too.'

Virginia however, did not look fine. Her brows bunched together, frustrated or concerned maybe. Usually, no one cared about the details of my missions – if I went alone or not – and I was unsure how to approach this.

'Don't worry,' I assured her, 'this is what I am trained to do.'

This did not reassure her. Her brows stayed bunched together. 'Quilp or Setebos can fix this,' she said with a wave of her hand. 'Let me go with you.'

I'd almost have welcomed her company; a stroll through the evening with a beautiful woman on my arm. It was impossible. Too dangerous. I shook my head. 'There is a village five kilometers north of this canyon. I need you to stay here. If I am not back in six hours, I want you to come looking for me.' What I didn't mention was that if I wasn't back in six hours, I'd be dead.

'OK,' she replied and her brows relaxed. 'I'll get the generator fixed right away, in case we need to leave in a hurry.' She got up, gave me a kiss on the cheek, for luck I suppose, then keyed open the outer hatch and went to inspect the generators.

'Help her if you can, Quilp.'

'Sure,' he said, rubbing the bruises on his arm, 'no problem. You want a smooch from me too?'

I ignored his obnoxious comment and went to my quarters. Stretching, I found the blue shield had done its usual thorough job on my burn and knitted the tissue together too tightly. On the red satin comforter, I laid out my accelerator pistol, my blade, then unpacked a case containing the parts of a rifle.

The leering skull and crossbones on the headboard watched as I assembled the weapon. Motion-damping stock connected to a non-linear accelerator, and on top of this, a fine Swiss imager – the whole thing no longer than my arm. Out of a block of foam I picked three wasp-like darts that were each black iridescent wings, eight bulging eyes, and a hypodermic stinger. I had only to site the target and the wasps programmed themselves with an uncanny accuracy. They would even circle around for a few minutes, if you desired, while you established an alibi. Within their sleek bodies were different cartridges for different occasions: poisons, high explosives, but tonight, a narcotic to freeze the voluntary muscles and dull the mind.

It was an old, simple technology, but Fifty-five liked it.

This would have been easier if I hadn't needed Necatane alive. But only a living man could have his mind stolen. I intended to rob his power of prophecy with my borrowing ritual and use it to find the Grail. I had to be careful, though, to immobilize him first and from a distance. Necatane had many powers, telekinesis, pyrokinesis, telepathy, and others I couldn't guess at.

Even If I managed to knock him out, there were still risks. There was no guarantee I would win the contest of wills in the borrowing ritual. I was counting on the drug to weaken his resolve. If I won, I'd have to be careful to take only the parts of his intellect associated with his prophetic visions. The idea of having *his* persona in my head filled me with apprehension. The psychologist was bad enough.

I knew Necatane. We had met before, once, after I had murdered his pupil.

It had been six years ago, and the psychologist in my mind had been alive and influencing the senators of his government. He saw to it that laws were passed to stop pollution, reverse unfair trade agreements, and secure civil rights. It was the trade agreements that got him into trouble.

One of the conglomerates to lose in the new deal hired me to discover why. The rulers of a world government do not forget their greed overnight. A week of undercover work, and I found the connection. The therapist of forty senators was the same man. His business always picked up before a critical vote. Additionally, this psychologist was a member of the Free-Thinkers Society. What more proof did I need?

I found him and stole his mind.

The senators became greedy again. The conglomerate went back into business. I was paid a bonus. Everyone was happy.

It was then that Necatane tried to contact his student, not physically but with his mind. He found me instead. First, he was curious, then shocked, then outraged that I had destroyed the intellect of his pupil. We had a colorful conversation, exchanged threats, and left it at that. I had never had any intention of seeking the man out, until now.

I stepped out into the cool night; the only illumination was a band of stars that hugged the edge of the canyon walls. My fingers moved, mnemonics released, and the ocular enhancer uncoiled from my memory. I saw through the eyes of a magical cat. About me were layers of sedimentary rock, and red and gray clays, and ribbons of gold dust, every grain of sand, every black pebble visible in the canyon. Mist rose from the river like cigarette smoke, wispy curls in the air, and a million more suns crowded the brilliant evening. It was all clear to me.

But something else I saw made the breath catch in my throat: me.

There were six other Germains scrutinizing the canyon: two already marched ahead on different paths, one had a limp, and one talked to Virginia while she worked on the mass-folding generator. She ignored the phantom.

These other Germains faded. Like the after-image of a bright light, their color inverted, then bleached away entirely. Were they real or was I hallucinating?

Real, the psychologist remarked. *I sensed from these images memories and intelligence. They are you, or rather were you, before they vanished.*

When we tunneled through the planet our existence split. We cast thirty-three shadows in time. Were these other Germains distributed along other time lines? And if so, why did they appear as ghosts? Quilp, however, claimed our degenerate wave functions could not exist. So what were they?

They're gone, that's what they are, Fifty-five said. *Concentrate on our mission.*

It frustrated me not knowing, but Fifty-five was correct. I had to do my job and get out quickly. *Which way?* I asked.

The path ahead, the psychologist replied, *will take us out of this canyon and to Necatane's temple.*

I walked away from the *Grail Angel*, and forgot my duplicates for the time being. Later, I'd ask Quilp what they might be. My thoughts instead wandered to Virginia. I admired her cool head, and her honesty (somewhat), but what did I really think was going to happen? That after this, we'd settle down, raise a few kids, and live happily ever after? It wasn't in the cards. Celeste would never stand for monogamy; Fifty-five would never allow me to leave Umbra Corp (even if that were possible); and the psychologist would never let me forget my guilt. Why did I feel so strongly for her? A few kisses didn't mean anything.

When I reached the top of the canyon, I looked back. The ship was well hidden from up here, which was good. I had no idea how many guards Necatane employed.

None, answered the psychologist. *He has never had need of any.*

That information did not comfort me. I'd rather he surrounded himself with bodyguards and force fields – things I knew how to counter. I pulled Quilp's mental shield tighter on my head, and tried to think of nothing.

I trekked over hills of worn sandstone, wind- and water-carved fingers of rock, sharp and full of shadows in the amplified starlight. A Bristlecone Pine grew in the cracks. Its limbs and trunk twisted many times, channels and grooves of smooth white woods. I kept my eyes peeled for any more visions of myself, but I remained alone. Three more hills I marched over, then down into a valley.

Surrounding Necatane's village were groves of olive trees and nurtured vines, silver grapes that glowed in the light of the moon looking like ball bearings on the branches. The largest building in the village was an acropolis perched on a grassy hill. It had rows of scalloped Ionic columns and, above them, a relief of gods, a scene I recognized from the *Iliad* of mortals dying and immortals bickering outside the walls of Troy.

Inside, a glow of fire cast rectangular patches of darkness upon the marble pillars, their edges flickering. With the ocular enhancer upon my sight it was as bright as a sun. I turned on my shadow-skin, carefully looked about and, when I saw no one, I entered.

You're just going to sneak in there and shoot him? Fifty-five asked. *Where's the finesse in that?*

No time for finesse, I answered. *The last mental shield I had burned out. I cannot risk that occurring again. We must hazard being conspicuous.*

Keeping in the shadows, I mounted the steps and entered his home. I felt eyes watching everywhere. The light was strongest to my left, so I followed it through wide corridors lined with heavy black curtains until it brought me to a courtyard. A circle of rose bushes made an outer ring, broken in four places to allow passage; their blossoms were dark and wilted. Four statues stood to greet anyone bold enough to enter. The first was Mars, his spear and shield upraised in challenge; the second could only be Venus with a flawless body and a smile that knew the inner thoughts of men; the third was a great serpent, coiled and ready to strike; and the last was a blindfolded man, his back turned to me.

In the center of this was a circular pit with a wide basalt rim. A fire blazed in it, tended by an old man, Necatane. He was blind. His eyes had been torn out of his head, obviously, for no cloth covered them. A thick ribbon of scar tissue made his forehead sunken and disfigured.

I stepped back and held my breath.

He was here, alone and unprotected? He gave no indication that he detected my presence, but I couldn't believe it. It was too easy. To be on the safe side, I whispered to the psychologist, *Quiet my thoughts.*

I am uncertain of the moral correctness of this situation.

He must have remembered more of his past than I gave him credit for. *All our lives are at stake. I'm your client. Your inaction places me in jeopardy. Where is your professionalism?*

I sensed his struggle, his inability to link his missing past together. *Very well*, he sighed. *Visualize a pond, rippling in a breeze. Smooth the ripples. Hold the water as quiet as your thoughts, placid, still, and like a mirror.*

I did as he said. My thoughts turned silent, and I unshouldered the rifle.

Unthinking, I aimed – a clean shot. The optics gathered the required data and transferred it to the three wasps. A silent pulse from the grip signalled me it was ready. All I had to do was fire.

The master psychologist sat beside his fire; the twisted wood crackled and popped. His bare feet rested close to the flames, toasting. In the firelight, his white beard was tinged red, making him seem more vital and alive than a man his age should be. He prodded the coals with a stick and sent a shower of sparks into the heavens.

I squeezed the trigger.

Three darts, whisper-quiet, accelerated out of the barrel, only a slight 'snik' as their wings snapped into place. The first curved between the legs of mighty Mars; the second took a hyperbolic route, arced up, stalled, then dove straight down; and the last flew in a straight line. They hit together, pierced his neck, stomach, and arm. The old man slumped over.

Too easy, hissed Fifty-five.

Are you certain this was Necatane? I asked.

Quite certain, whispered the psychologist.

I listened, but no alarms rang. Even the crickets did not pause in their evening song. I inched forward, still wary, kept within the shadow of Mars, and when I was within six paces of him, I saw what was amiss. His breaths were regular, steady and strong, not slowed as in a man who had just been injected with a triple dose of narcotics.

I grabbed my pistol, aimed it, and—

—from his body the three darts withdrew, turned, and flew towards me. I tracked one, shot it, the ions from the accelerator pistol leaving a gold trail in the air, but the other two struck me, one in the chest, the other in the thigh, and injected their contents.

I dropped.

'Kind of you to join me this evening,' Necatane said and strolled over. 'It is exactly halfway through your life's journey, and the end of mine. I find a pleasing symmetry in that, don't you, killer?'

He found me, ripped the cap off my head, and dragged me closer to the fire. I couldn't feel a thing. My eyes stared at the same spot in space, frozen open.

Necatane ran his fingers across the inside of the cap, and remarked, 'A brilliant piece of engineering. It might have worked too, had not I known you would be here tonight. I knew before you were born, killer.'

How did my wasps miss?

'They hit,' he said, answering my silent question, 'all well and good. Stung like the devil, too. It was a simple matter to freeze their injection mechanisms. I can move this entire building with the power of my mind. Did you think your insects would seriously threaten me? You are a brash young man indeed, brave, but extremely foolish. No, that's not quite right: not foolish, desperate.'

He stroked my face with his weathered hands, then in a soft voice added, 'Oh, I don't expect to cheat fate this evening. I have seen that you are the one to cause my death, and I dare not interfere with the designs of the great ones, but I shall have my way with them before I am done. I'll break the universe into three pieces: a scrap for darkness, a bone for the light, and the lion's share for nature to devour. Socrates could not have had a better death!'

He was crazy.

'Not crazy,' he whispered. 'Inspired. Some men compose poetry before they die, I shall do something far more lasting – something to you.'

You told Omar and E'kerta where I was! You knew I'd be going to Needles. You were the only one who could have.

'An excellent bit of reasoning,' he said, 'but incorrect. You are very close to the truth, though, closer than you will ever know.'

He rubbed his hands over the fire, then, 'It is a pity you came to kill me. Under different circumstances, I feel you would have made a fine student. You have a strong mind, well-developed, disciplined. If our positions were reversed, if my immortal soul was at stake, I suppose I would have attempted the same.' He turned his attention to his toes and scraped a bit of crust out between them. 'However, I do not intend to have my mind savaged by you because you cannot find the Grail. You must earn that prize yourself.

'Does any of this seem familiar to you, killer? It should. You have been here sixteen times before. Perhaps this time will turn out differently.'

Warmth poured into my mind, then withdrew. 'I see my pupil is with you tonight. The poor soul, you didn't even leave him his name. It is a mockery to all life to bottle his soul within you thusly,' he declared, outraged. 'He is a mere fraction of what he was alive, but you shall need him on your quest, and as distasteful as I find this, I must allow you to keep all your extra personalities.'

The warmth returned to my thoughts. Necatane spoke again, but his lips remained sealed. The bastard was inside my mind. *Let us go then, you and I, my etherized friend, into the evening, and into those twisty passages to examine your half-forgotten memories.*

Get out! I screamed. *This is my mind, my thoughts. You have no right to do this.*

No right? I have just as much right as the victims of your borrowing ritual, just as much right because this is what you planned to do to me. But do not worry, assassin, I shall be insidiously kind. You shall recall everything in perfect detail. You shall retain all your memories, skills, and thoughts . . . although you may not want to by the time we are done.

Chapter Nine

Necatane shuffled through my recollections with blinding speed – like cards in a deck – blurred fragments of images and feelings, nightmares and dreams.

Your childhood is the place to begin, he said.

I know what happened when I was a kid.

Of course you do, but that knowledge has been distorted by emotion. Tonight, you and I shall see with the clarity of experience, and without the fogging influence of time.

Why are you doing this, Necatane?

He laughed, then said, *Ask your gambler what 'Go Fish' means.*

A snap of his fingers and we stood in a different place, a different world: Hades. The sky was opaque with ash, and it glowed red in spots, lit up beneath by distant volcanoes. We must have been ghosts here, because I could breathe. Normally, you had to wear a breather to protect your lungs from the heat and acid in the air. I remember always having a sore throat and coughing. It started to snow ash, little flakes of chalky gray and smoldering orange that passed through us. We had to wear heat suits to protect us from getting burned. The three layers of asbestos padding trapped all the sweat inside – made you stink.

Hades was a young planet, its crust unstable, and no life except the restless ground and the miners. Sometimes, the sun broke through the dense atmosphere and charged it with luster, a golden shaft that pierced the ash. Whenever that happened, I dropped my tools and ran toward it. Once, I got to stand in the middle of

the glorious radiance for a few seconds, then caught hell from
Dad for leaving the fields.

Not a pleasant environment, Necatane remarked.

It was a place of hard work, that's mostly what I remember.

It is *a place of hard work*, he corrected me. *The past is the
present. Your father mines for Philosopher Stones. A tough life,
scraping the skins of new worlds for magical rocks. Is he rich?
Does he have his own land, or does he work for a company?*

*You're the psychologist. Why don't you drag the information
out of me?*

*This way is better, and, in the long run, more painful and more
useful to you. Think of it as therapy.*

All I can remember was eating cans and cans of refried beans.

A company man, then. Most interesting, Necatane mused. *You
have a deeply suppressed hatred for your father. Let us look closer.*

The world moved. Layers of stone and magma engulfed our
phantom bodies. We went underground through solid rock,
pockets of steam, then a tunnel, and an air lock that isolated the
caves beyond from the harsh outer world. It was my home.

A man paced the living room, wearing a track between the
kitchen and sofa on the bare stone floor. There too, watching him
march back and forth, was a woman. Her face was worn from
work, bags under her dull eyes, but it wasn't that she was tired
of the work, it looked like she was tired of life. She was eight
months pregnant.

Your happy family, Necatane said. *That's you inside her, killer.*

*Impossible. I can't remember things before I was born. You
show me only illusions, lies to torment me.*

*Torment? Yes, you deserve to suffer a bit, but that is not my
aim. All these scenes are real, killer. To bring you here I drain
the very life from my body. Pay attention, lest I resort to stimula-
ting the pain centers of your mind.*

I watched.

They argued about water. My father, I recognized his voice,

that threatening dangerous tone, waved his fists at her. 'There's not enough water for you to take a damn bath,' he thundered.

The woman mustered what defiance she could, sat straighter, and said, 'It's the only thing that makes me feel decent in this pit. I'll keep doing it.' It was not much, not loud, but she *did* stand up to him. That was something I never could do, and I admired her courage.

His eyes narrowed and he took a step closer to her. 'You can't even work any more, you're so fat. All you do around here is take and take and take. I'm sick of it.'

'How do you expect me to work with this?' She placed a hand on her stomach. 'That's your doing.'

'Is it?' he asked with a snort.

'What do you care? It's the only reason you wanted me. So you could have another pair of goddamned hands to help to haul those rocks!'

Dad's teeth ground together, I heard them. He slapped her hard, knocking her off her feet.

She is right, Necatane said. *Your father only wanted her for breeding stock. Oh, that's not what he said to steal her away from her pimp. He promised her a life together, a life of luxury, of safety, and he promised he'd care for her. Lies on all counts.*

My father didn't stop. He kept beating her, even though she was on the floor, screaming for mercy.

I closed my eyes. *Please, Necatane, make him stop.*

I cannot, he said softly, then took my hand and led me away. *We shall leave your father to his own devices and look in on your brother, Mike. He had as much a role in your development as your father, perhaps more.*

The woman shrieked, but her cries muffled as we passed through the rock wall and into my brother's bedroom.

Mike hid under his bed. He had his eyes squeezed shut and his hands over his ears. Necatane opened his mind to me. He was scared of my father, what he was capable of doing when he got mad, and terrified what might happen to his mother.

He knows she is not his real mother, Necatane explained. *It does not matter to him. She was the only one to show him kindness. She was the only one to tuck him in, and the only one who read him bedtime stories. He loved her.*

The door swung open, and in tramped my father, blood spattered on his arms to his elbows. 'Mike!' he yelled. 'Where the hell are you, boy? I need you. Right now!'

Mike first wiped his tears away, then he crawled from under the bed, and asked, 'Mom? Is she OK?'

My father hauled him up with one red hand and said, 'She's fine. But I need you to run to get the Doc from the settlement.'

'Wh – Wh – What did you do to her?' he asked and tears welled up in his eyes.

'Nothing. She fell and your brother inside decided it was time to come out. He's a little early. That's why we need the Doc. You tell him that we've got a new baby – that you've got a new brother.'

Mike stared at the dried blood on my father's arms. He panicked and twisted out of his grip, only to be snatched up again before he got away. 'Is she hurt?'

'You better run,' my father whispered in a deadly serious tone, 'or else the baby's gonna die. You want that?' He dragged Mike out by the arm, through the living room (that had on the floor an obvious smear of blood leading to the kitchen) and shooed him into the air lock, slammed it shut, and locked him out.

'Do I sense a modicum of discomfort from you, killer? Does the sight of blood suddenly bother you?'

What kind of man was he? I asked. *To kill a pregnant woman?*

He was a man like you, I think, able to justify anything to do his job.

Necatane led me into the kitchen.

The woman who was supposedly my mother was on the floor, not moving, and not breathing. I looked away and heard my father struggling with her body, then a sucking sound, and the cries of a baby. He cut the umbilical cord, then set the infant, swaddled in a dishrag, into the sink. This creature was covered in blood, born too soon. He was blue, and with his first breath his chest reddened, then his face and extremities. He was so tiny and wrinkled . . . he was me.

My father dragged her body outside. The heat, acid and ash would consume it.

If only we had time, Necatane said, *we could go back to see what drove your father to do this. I surmise that his father was as much a monster as he. These behaviors tend to get passed down from generation to generation.*

He came back and poured himself two shots of booze, drank those, and two more. Into the cellar he then marched, pulled up the sonic disrupter we used to cut through rock, and took the top layer off the floor. Not a speck of my mother's blood remained.

Humming to himself, he turned up the heat, and went back to look at the infant in the sink. There was no love in his eyes, only a calculating gaze. With one hand resting on the faucet, he figured the additional expenses of raising another child and the profits another pair of hands might produce in the long run. He was deciding if I should live or die – which was more profitable.

My fate was determined on a balance sheet?

Nothing novel about that, is there, killer? Most of your missions are motivated by profit – my own students, Aaron the alien king, the gambler, and so many others – do not forget them.

There was a banging on the air lock. Mike was back with the doctor. My brother was in such a hurry to get help he forgot his heat suit and only wore a breather. Tiny blisters, ash burns, covered his shoulders and back. He didn't seem to notice – all he could do was look for his mother.

The doctor spoke briefly with my father, then shuffled into the kitchen.

'Mike,' my father said, kneeling down beside him, 'I have some bad news for you, but you're a big enough boy now, so I'm gonna tell you the truth.'

'She's dead, isn't she?' he said, his chin quivering.

Dad shook his head. 'I almost wish it were so, but she just up and left after your brother came out. She told me that she couldn't stand taking care of two brats. She wanted to see the city. She wanted things we couldn't afford yet.'

The monster even looked sincere.

Mike stood trembling. My mother was his world. She was the only source of kindness in his otherwise weary existence. 'She left because of me?' he whispered.

'Yep,' Dad said, 'you and your brother. It's just gonna be the three of us from now on. We've got to stick together and make the best of it.' He embraced Mike who, having nothing left in his world, hugged him back and burst into tears.

Happy birthday, killer. I pity you, having the misfortune to be born into this – I cannot even call it a family. We must learn more. You shall be sent back to relive certain events. It will be most unpleasant, I assure you.

What do you mean, sent back? I thought we were in the past?

Yes, but merely as observers. You are going back to when you were a child. You are six years old, no longer a professional killer, only a little boy. You are the same age that Mike was when your dear mother departed. For brothers, the two of you were very close. You shared everything, and that is unusual for brothers separated by six years.

Necatane vanished.

I was six and on Hades. The memories of the future were dim in my thoughts. My body was not powerful, efficient and disciplined; I was small, and had a child's body, clumsy, and ever afraid to touch anything for fear of breaking it. I always broke things.

I sat on the living room sofa, a dusty piece of foam covered with a rotting green and orange tweed. Next to me was Mike.

He was twelve years old, and had big muscles from all the digging we did. In the kitchen, my father spoke and drank with another miner, Rebux. And sitting across from us, in my father's chair, was Rebux's daughter.

Rebux had a dozen or so such girls who traveled with him from camp to camp. For a few fragments of Philosopher Stone, the miners got them for an evening.

I had the impression she was bored. She shifted in the chair, seeming never to get comfortable, glancing at Mike, or me, or the ceiling, but no one thing for too long. Mike asked her name, but she didn't answer him. She wore a skimpy white top, no sleeves, and her arms were covered with pinprick blisters. She was clean, too. Her eyes darted to the kitchen, then back to us.

My father and Rebux staggered into the living room. Their faces were flushed and they stank of booze.

She smiled, and no longer looked bored.

'You boys have the day off,' Dad slurred to us. 'Make our guest at home, and don't get into any trouble. I'm gonna be busy this afternoon, so don't come crying to me if you burn your pinkie.'

'Yes, sir,' answered Mike. That's what he always said to him: anything else would catch you a face full of fist.

My father grabbed the girl by her hand and hauled her off the bedroom. She gave us a strange look when she left, a look of pity almost, maybe compassion. The door then slammed shut, and that was the last I ever saw of her.

Rebux sat on the sofa's arm next to Mike, making the whole thing sag under his weight. He leaned over and said, 'So, I hear you boys are hard workers.' His breath was so foul I could almost see the vapors of tequila come out of his mouth. 'Your pa is proud of you both. Says that on your day off you go to the fields and do a little diggin' on your own. You ever find anything?'

'No, sir,' Mike fibbed.

'Well, if you do, you just let me know. Maybe one day I'll introduce one of my daughters to you.' He made a clicking sound and scratched his rough face. He then looked about the room and his eyes found the basement door. 'That your cellar, boy?' he asked.

Mike nodded.

Necatane interrupted the memory.

There is something down there, he whispered. *It terrifies you. What?*

I hesitated, then admitted, *Mom had all these peach preserves, at least, that's what Mike told me.*

You fear fruit?

It's the jars. They're two liters and real thick green glass – full of rotten peaches. Sometimes one'll explode, and glass goes everywhere. I've seen shards embedded in the stone walls. Think what could happen if you were close to one when it went.

That, Necatane said, *is not your entire fear. We shall soon learn what, however.*

The memory continued.

'Come on,' Rebux said to Mike, 'I want to show you something. But just us two. Your brother is too young . . . I think.'

'I am not,' I said.

'What is it?' Mike asked, 'a porn?'

'Something like that, but better.'

Mike's eye slit up. When Dad went to the market once a month, we snuck a peak at the porns he hid in his room. They had men and women touching each other. It seemed exciting enough for the characters in the virtuals, all that squealing and panting, but I could never see what all the fuss was about. Mike was more impressed, however, and sometimes he'd kick me out and watch them by himself. He did something in there. I hadn't quite figured out what.

Mike followed Rebux into the cellar. They closed the door on me, and I stuck my ear to the warm metal surface, hoping at least to hear some of the virtuals. I wasn't too young!

A couple of seconds went by, then Mike screamed, 'No!'

Boxes overturned, and the familiar sound of a backhand to the face, then Mike crying, all echoed up the stairway and through the basement door.

'You just hold still, son, and take your punishment like a man,' Rebux growled.

Mike was bawling now. I never heard him cry like this, even when he got hit hard.

'Germain,' he screamed, 'help me!'

Mike would never beg for help like that unless something was really wrong. He never asked for my help. I had to go down there. I reached for the door handle . . . and froze.

I was too small. If I went down there, he'd hurt me, too. I couldn't. I ran to my father's bedroom. Inside, I heard the girl making noises of pain or pleasure, just like on the virtuals. Again my hand halted just before it opened the door. I didn't dare bother him. He'd slap the teeth out of my head, so I stood frozen not knowing what to do. I dashed back to the cellar, and heard Mike wailing like he was dying down there. I almost opened it, but chickened out and just listened . . . horrified.

Rebux then said, 'How'd you like that, son? Now, if you tell anyone about this, I'll say you made the whole thing up. And who'd you think is gonna believe you? Now stop your bawling and get on upstairs. Tell your little brother to come down. I've got something to show him, too.'

This time there was no indecision. I ran. Grabbing a heat suit in the air lock, I barely got it on, snatched a breather, and was out the door, sprinting.

Thirty kilometers to the south, the cone we called Vulcan was alive today and glaring into the solid gray atmosphere with one angry red eye. Glowing embers fell on me, but I felt nothing through the insulation of my heat suit. To the old fields I ran. There, dozens of trenches crisscrossed, scars in the earth to mark where we cut looking for treasure. I hid in one – didn't even have the guts to peek back to see if anyone followed.

'Necatane,' I demanded, 'what else would I do? Tell me.'
Silence.

I started to cry. Maybe if I went down there, I could have thrown something at him. There were those rotten peaches, Mom's old preserves. They would have made a good dent in his head. But I was too afraid. What if Mike died? Dad would kill me for sure. I ran through all the scenarios of what might have happened to Mike, and what Dad would do when he found out, until it was dark. Only then did I risk going home.

Rebux's rover was gone. So was Dad's.

Inside, Mike sat alone in my father's chair. He gave me a glare of pure hate, then turned away and stared at nothing.

'Mike, I'm sorry.' New tears streamed down my cheeks. 'There was nothing I coulda done.'

'Get out of my sight, you little weakling,' he said with my father's voice. It was a voice full of violence and hate, and it terrified me.

'But Mike—'

'Go! Before I belt you one good.'

I ran upstairs, more afraid of what Mike thought of me than anything else. How much did he tell Dad? Would he be angry because I didn't get him?

Necatane spoke: *Are you ready for the truth, Germain?*

'No,' I told the invisible and unwanted spirit. 'Go away.'

The truth is your father knew what Rebux did to Mike. They planned it. He was angry at you the next day because you ran out on him. He had to pay Rebux with crystal instead of you.

'You lie!'

The circumstances almost make me wish I was, he answered in a weary voice. *But it is the truth. And when Rebux returned every month, Mike endured the same torture, the same 'punishment' as he called it. Your father cherished him for that, and hated you because you always ran away the night before and hid. How do you think Mike felt when you abandoned him to Rebux? He had to endure all the abuse and shame, because you never opened that door and tried to stop it.*

'Shut up! What could I have done? You have all the answers. Tell me, what?'

You tell me, Germain.

I had no answers.

Our time grows short, Necatane said. *We must hurry. Six more years shall pass, years of virtual silence between you and Mike. You are twelve, and he is eighteen, all grown up. He's a real man now, and has even taken to drinking with your father. They have become much alike, don't you think?*

I grew a half-meter and put on twenty kilos of muscle.

Do you recall the crystals Mike found by himself? The perfect Philosopher Stone he hid, along with a half-dozen others from your father? His personal treasure?

I remembered. It was a perfect cluster with all twenty points intact. This one was almost round it had so many needles poking out from its center. Mike had it hidden with his private stuff in a box under his bed. We found it together one day when Dad was at the marketplace. We were running around, and throwing chunks of pumice at each other pretending they were grenades, and bow and arrows, and laser beams. The crystal was right on the surface, just lying there, waiting to get picked up. I took it out to admire it whenever Mike and Dad were busy.

Twenty points of emerald crystal it had, with veins of gold like spider webs running through it; all of them radiating from a center where the green stone turned so dark, so dense, it was pitch black. I'd heard other miners tell stories of complete Philosopher Stones, but the best Dad ever found was a twelve-pointer (and he got drunk for a week to celebrate).

Tonight, Mike and Dad were drinking, spending some of the profits from a successful day of trading at the settlement. I tried to stay out of their way when they drank.

I knew what was about to happen . . . and I willed my hands to stop, but they removed the cigar box from under Mike's bed anyway. I tried to halt my rebellious fingers when they picked the perfect stone out and held it before the light.

The cluster was heavier than the others, more massive than could be accounted for by the extra points. It was as if it had some special quality, something extra added to its nature by virtue of having all its points, by virtue of its perfection. It must be worth a fortune. What did Mike plan to do with it? I'd never been to the market, so I didn't know exactly how much it was worth. Maybe he'd sell it and buy a corporate contract of his own. I knew if Dad ever found it, he'd give Mike the beating of his life for keeping it from him.

Stop before it's too late, I thought. It didn't work.

I held the twenty-pointer cupped in my two hands, rolled it back and forth, watching it flash in the artificial light, lustrous, rich gold, brilliant green . . . wishing it was mine. The specimens we usually found were broken, and their points dull. This one, as I said before, was perfect, right down to the needle-fine tips and razor-sharp edges. When I rolled it back and forth, those edges and points cut my hands. The thing was so sharp; I didn't even notice until my hands were bloody.

Startled, I dropped the stone and balled my hands tight to stop the bleeding.

The twenty points of light, christened with my own blood, spun through the air. I reached for it, caught it by a point, but it slipped free.

It hit on the concrete floor.

There was the sound of glass breaking. Three points snapped off.

My stomach turned to ice. I was as good as dead. When Mike found out, he'd kill me for sure.

I grabbed a towel and wrapped my hands, then snuck downstairs, past the kitchen where my brother and father laughed drunkenly, and through the cellar door, into the basement. It was dark and I was scared.

You could almost hear those peach jars groaning with pressure, waiting to explode given the slightest excuse. Still, this was the safest place to be. If I hid in the fields, Mike would find me, and we'd be alone. At least here he'd think twice before killing me. He might beat me up, but not so much that I couldn't work tomorrow. If he did, Dad would see that he got a taste of his own medicine.

I snapped the lights on. On the lowest shelf, near a pile of dirty heat suits, were the jars looking like a military formation of dusty green beetles. I counted the number of steps down, then turned the lights off. In the dark, by touch, I made my way to the laundry heap, buried myself under it, and hoped no one found me.

Hours must have gone by. Fear dulled to fatigue, and I dozed, hardly noticing when the lights came on. The dirty suits lifted. Mike stood over me, red-faced and fists clenched.

He picked me up and punched me in the stomach, hard.

I expelled all my air and fell over.

'You little bastard,' he spat. 'You left a trail of blood in the house. Dad could have found you and my stash if he hadn't been so drunk. Lucky for me, he thought you took off for the fields like you always do. He's there looking for you now.'

'Mike, I didn't mean it. I was just holding it. It was so perfect.'

'Yeah, it *was*.' His eyes narrowed.

Let me show you what your brother thinks, Necatane whispered.

Through a red haze of anger, I sensed Mike's hate swelling to the surface. It burned the last traces of kindness he had for me, and left only the ashes of his contempt. In his eyes I was weak, clumsy, and worthless. I was responsible for Rebux raping him. I was responsible for our father's callousness. But most of all, I was responsible for our mother's departure. Had I never been born, she would still be here, and perhaps life would be endurable.

He wanted to escape Hades. That's what the crystal was for. But it was no longer perfect. He rapidly calculated its value with the three points missing. Considerably less than when it was whole, but more than our father made in two years. It was still enough to buy passage off this world and start a new life. There was a moment of indecision – if he'd leave me alone with Dad or not – then he made up his mind. He'd abandon me. But first, there was one thing he wanted to do . . . one thing he'd been saving up for a long time.

'Time for your *punishment*,' Mike hissed, hate dripping from the word. He grabbed me and shoved me face first into the pile of heat suits. He pulled my pants down.

'No!' I cried.

It was the same thing that had happened a moment ago, six years ago, to him. Only this time he was the rapist, and I would be the victim. I tried to push him off, but he was too strong and too heavy. Panic flooded my mind. I wanted to kick him, punch him, but I was twisted the wrong way to do anything. His body touched mine, his hot breath a whisper on my bare back. I nearly retched.

Through teary eyes, I saw the jars of peaches on the shelf, plump flesh encased by dusty glass. One had bubbles on the inside that clung to the smooth walls, and looked like clusters of silver grapes. I tried to grab it, but my fingers couldn't quite reach. They slipped off.

Mike laughed while I struggled.

I stretched again, and this time found purchase on the glass, smearing the dust and tearing the label. With both hands, I threw it awkwardly, backward, over my head. It exploded.

Lances tore into my shoulders and scalp, slivers of glass.

Mike let out a strangled cry and let go.

I turned and pulled up my pants. I was ready to fight now, kick him in the balls if I had to.

Mike lay on his back, on the floor, out cold.

I grabbed another jar, but Mike wasn't going anywhere. Sprawled on the concrete, with his pants around his knees and his head crowned in a halo of peaches, syrup, and blood, Mike was dead. Glass from the pressurized jar had cut his face, eyes, and neck. His blood pumped out in dribbles and spurts. The odor of rancid fruit was strong . . . too strong. I threw up in the pile of dirty laundry.

Your second kill, assassin, Necatane said. *First your mother, now your only brother. You were fortunate not to die yourself.*

'It was an accident. I didn't mean to—'

—*Kill him? Of course you did.*

'Lies!' I shouted, then cupped my hand over my mouth. Dad would be back soon. I had to leave. He wouldn't kill me, he needed me to work, but I'd be beaten within an inch of my life. And if he was drunk, he might forget he needed me.

I tossed the pile of heat suits over my brother, and wished I had a prayer or words to speed his soul to heaven, but all I managed was: 'God, don't be too hard on Mike, it wasn't his fault. I made him angry.'

I crossed myself and ran upstairs to get a heat suit and breather. But where would I go? Dad's rover was outside, and I knew how to drive it, but there was no place to drive it to.

Mike's crystal! I'd use it to live in the settlement, maybe even buy passage to another world as he had planned to. Upstairs, the twenty- (minus three) pointed star had been returned to the cigar box, along with its broken shards. I took it and sprinted down to the rover, then, driving in surges and grinding the gears, I coaxed the vehicle to the settlement.

Two dozen buildings, foamed concrete with rusty corrugated steel roofs, circled the marketplace. Once a week, the miners gathered to sell their stones to eager buyers, have their accounts credited, buy supplies, whiskey, or the other limited pleasures on Hades.

I ditched the rover about half a kilometer out, then ran the rest

of the distance. Along the way, I saw my first spaceship glide to
the landing pad. So wondrous were they, moving with silent ease,
that I forgot my brother, my father, their violence, and what I was
doing here . . . just for a moment.

'What'cha got in the box, son?' a man wearing no heat suit
and only a breather asked. He had a patch over one eye and was
missing three fingers.

'Just a blue shield,' I said. 'I cut my hand.'

He looked at the blood stains on my gloves and the back of
my heat suits, shrugged, and moved on.

Marching to the marketplace before the crystal got stolen, I
saw only five or six traders were still there. Most had packed up,
but a few wandered about the plaza to take one last look before
they left. One man in particular, he wore a clean heat suit,
unblemished by ash or sweat. He sported a snowy white beard,
perfectly groomed, which was another oddity here among the
unwashed. I stood before him, trying to think of a way to bargain
with this man. I didn't want to show him the crystal for fear of
it being taken, but how else could I interest him?

'Excuse me, sir,' I said meekly.

He stopped and his clear blue eyes found my face. 'Yes, my
child? How may I help you?'

'I have a crystal for sale, sir.'

'Everyone here seems to have crystals for sale,' he said and
smiled. 'All right, young man, let us see your wares.' He knelt
to my level and took the cigar box I held out to him. His eyes
widened when he saw the near-perfect specimen.

'This one,' he whispered, 'is exquisite. Did you find any of
the broken points when you unearthed it?'

I pointed to the three finger-sized shards lying loose in the
box.

'So . . .' He took one and placed it back into its proper spot
on the cluster, murmured a word, then released the needle. It
remained attached. He had put together what I had broken! Two

more words of magic, and the stone was perfect again.

'I did not waste my time coming here after all,' he said. 'Where is your father, young man, so I may pay him for this.'

'You'd know if I lied to you, wouldn't you?' I asked naively. 'You're a wizard, right?'

'We call ourselves muses,' he replied, still kneeling at my level and still wearing his Christmas smile. 'But if you like, wizard will do.'

'I have to get away from my father, today. I'd rather go out into the wastes and die than go back. You can have it, for free. All I ask is that you take me with you.'

His smile evaporated. 'You are serious.' He considered a moment, glanced at the perfect crystal, then back to me. 'I suppose your father would ask a much higher price, wouldn't he? One I would not wish to pay.'

He gently touched the side of my head. A tingle like static electricity spread across my scalp and down my spine. 'Normally, I would not consider such a thing, but you have the natural aptitude, my boy, and something tells me you truly *would* rather die than stay here.' He looked about quickly and replaced the perfect crystal in the box. 'Come then, I have need of a new apprentice. Would you like that?'

I smiled for the first time in years and took his hand.

Chapter Ten

His name was Abaris, and he took me away from Hades, to the world of Sandsport where he owned a secluded island. Tropical forests, beaches of black sand, and great expansive reefs were all his.

'You have a wonderful castle,' I said.

The tea service sensed his interest and floated closer to his open hand. He let it pour, then offered me a plate of lemon wedges and sugar cubes. 'I find it adequate,' he replied.

What was adequate for Abaris was an oriental castle of granite, carved rosewood timber, and every roof a rainbow of slate. It was a fairy pagoda. Surrounding the seven sides of the castle was a wall of coral blocks, and on the seven corners seven towers rose into the sky. Beneath them shimmered a courtyard paved with seven-sided tiles of pure silver, smoky quartz, and malachite, cobbled into a mosaic image of a great coiled dragon, encircling and protecting his home from sinister forces.

We sat on the second level of the palace, in a chamber that was empty save for two cane chairs, the cart with the tea service on it, and a polished white pine floor beneath our bare feet. Two of the walls were rows of open windows that let the breeze from the jungles breathe in and out, and made the translucent gauze curtains ripple like water. It was clean unprocessed air. I wasn't used to the smell, fresh, and without the odor of a week's worth of perspiration mixed in. It made me lightheaded.

Abaris sat with his back to the only windowless wall, a sheet of rice paper painted with a flock of cranes, snow-capped mountains, and tiny farmers planting fields in the valley below. Embossed in the corner were two symbols that glowed a faint coppery color (which I later learned were the runes of *Security* and *Mastery*). He sipped quietly from his cup, then said, 'We must decide what to do with you, Germain. How you wish to be paid for your crystal.'

The twenty-pointed stone lay on a cushion next to the tea pot. It looked smaller somehow in these exotic surroundings, ordinary. Abaris waited a moment, perhaps expecting me to suggest something, then he continued, 'I require the stone to enhance my summoning and control of the spirits of the earth. We work together on distant worlds, moving mountains, digging valleys, and shifting tectonic plates, so others can live there.'

I knew Philosopher Stones changed lead into gold, but to move mountains? It was a magic I never suspected. No wonder the miners of Hades were paid fortunes for them.

Squeezing a bit of lemon into his tea, he gave me a careful look, and said, 'Here is what I propose: in exchange for the crystal, I will train you as my apprentice. To be truthful, I need a young man to aid me in my research projects. In return for your help, I shall educate you in the principles of magic. If the arrangement works, you may become proficient in a score of years, and in time, who can tell, perhaps a full muse as I am.'

'And if I refuse?' I had no intention of doing so, but wanted to see how he'd react.

'Then I shall pay you a fair price for the crystal and send you to the world of your choice. You should have sufficient funds to lead a comfortable life . . . or if you regret leaving your home, I can send you back.'

I frowned at that last option.

'I see within you the requisite traits a career in magic demands,' he said. 'And you would be foolish to waste them.'

'Traits?'

'Magic is not an easy thing. It requires a discipline few men have, a discipline that is born from either inspiration or desperation.' He glanced away; his eyes unfocused, perhaps recalling his own inspiration or desperation.

'Why?' I asked and finished the rest of the tea that tasted of mint and honey and jasmine. 'What is so hard about it?'

His gaze refocused. 'Good, curiosity is also needed. I shall tell you of magic, then.' He paused to pour me another cup of the delightful tea. 'There are two ways to change the universe. You, Germain, have experience with the first way, namely pure physical force. Move a rock or eat a peach and the universe is forever altered. The magnitude of change is minuscule, yes, but it is changed nonetheless.

'The other way is to use one's mind alone, and alter the fabric of reality by pure thought. This is difficult. To strengthen one's mind to move a single stone is harder than moving a million by hand. Those who do this are called psychologists, and they are born with their abilities. They can not only move stones, but read thoughts and intuit the future.

'How muses influence the universe, however, lies in between these two methods. A Muse trains his mind, yes, but where the psychologist looks into himself, we look to the outer world, to nature. We tap the forces of the cosmos with our rituals.'

He sipped his tea, then added, 'Muses do not have to be born with any particular abilities, merely the desire to learn.

'Regrettably, most do not believe in magic. The loss is theirs,' he sighed. 'They think what we do akin to psychology. They fear the unknown, which is where our powers are truly derived. We delve into the mysterious unfathomable universe.'

He drained his cup and set it aside.   •

'And the psychological community mistrusts us. They claim we tap our subconscious minds, and that we are a danger to their well-ordered understanding of nature. They too do not believe there is a thing called magic. But there is.'

'Can you make people vanish? Make coins dance in your hand?'

'I suppose, yes,' he said. 'But those are the lowest of magics. I shall teach you to call the winds, to peer into the past and see the empires lost centuries ago, to transform your shape to that of a bird of blue flames, and to walk among the stars themselves without your body.'

I sat on the edge of my seat, eager to hear more.

Abaris's smile deflated and he whispered, 'However, all these magics are won at a great cost, and this is what I wish to tell you of before you commit yourself. I would not fool you into believing this business is all glory.'

From the tea pot, he removed a gold tassel and a braided cord of green silk. This loop he held limp, between his index finger and thumb, so the tassel hung exactly in the middle. 'This,' he said, 'shall represent an untrained mind. To master a piece of magic, one must study the underlying concepts.' While he explained, he took the spoon from his saucer and inserted it into the loop, rotated it once, and twisted the cord. 'You must study the physical theories of each enchantment,' another twist, 'the scientific principles,' another twist, 'the philosophies,' twist, 'the histories,' twist, 'until you know as much as you possibly can about the magic,' three more twists. The loop of green silk was coiled tight now, taut, and only the spoon kept it from unraveling.

'See how the string is ready to unwind? With each turn of the spoon I have imprinted more of the magic upon my mind. When cast, I release that stored energy. It might take years to reach this point when one knows enough, and there is a risk.'

'A risk? Can you be injured?'

'No, never injured, but worse, disappointed. If you are impatient, and if your mind is poorly trained, or has not embraced all aspects of the enchantment, you will lose it upon its first casting.' He withdrew the spoon and the string unraveled in a blur. 'Then it is gone, and you must begin again.'

'Years of study for one piece of magic? You can do it once, then it's gone?'

'Sometimes. But if your mind has been correctly trained and the knowledge securely anchored with mnemonic constructs, then it will stay, etched into your memory.'

'How long does it take?' I asked. 'You said years? And how often do you lose one?'

'Perhaps three or four years of study for a simple ritual,' he replied, 'but this is highly variable depending upon the complexity of the magic, and the intellect of the student. I once took half a century to learn *The Silver Fairy's Incantation for Nonlinear Gravity.*' He sighed and shook his head. 'And I lost it upon its first release. It was an extremely frustrating experience.'

'Half a century?' I murmured. Abaris looked seventy, maybe seventy-five if his life was a soft one. I rarely saw old men on Hades. The mining either killed them or it made them rich and they left. 'How old are you?'

He set the tassel atop the tea pot. 'Next month I shall be five hundred and thirty years old. I have had two long-life treatments, and I expect I shall need another in a decade or so.'

'Life extension costs a fortune . . .'

'The magic business may be tedious,' he told me, 'but it is lucrative.'

Riches, magic, and adventure. How could I refuse? Studying didn't scare me at least, that's what I thought at the time. But a tinge of guilt nagged me, about Mike. Maybe that jar of peaches just knocked him out. Maybe he was stuck there on Hades with Dad. He'd have to work the fields for the rest of his life. No. I'd not feel guilty. Mike had been ready to leave me there.

'OK,' I said and offered my hand. Abaris took it and shook with a strength I found surprising for one over five hundred years old. 'It's a deal.'

'Good, your time shall be divided in the following manner,' he said. 'One-third of a day you shall have for rest, sleep, and meals. One-third shall be dedicated to your personal studies, and the remainder of the time you shall aid me in my research. Additionally, five days in thirty shall be yours to do with as you see fit, and I shall give you a stipend to spend in the nearby city. A young man cannot live solely on books.'

'Five days off? In a row if I want?'

Abaris nodded.

I'd never had so much free time. And money to call my own? A place to spend it? Luxuries I never had before. It made my head spin more than the fresh air did.

'Come, before we lose the moment,' he said, 'let us choose your first magic.' He led me downstairs and across the courtyard, ablaze with the blue sun reflecting off silver tiles and green dragon scales under our feet. To one of the seven towers we went, then up four storeys we spiraled, Abaris towing me along, into a small chamber lined from floor to ceiling with books and scrolls. Spines of polished leather stamped with gold letters were neatly alphabetized on the shelves. It had a scent I was unfamiliar with, aging paper and burnt candles.

'These are the simple enchantments I know,' he explained.

'You know all these?'

He laughed. 'You misunderstand. There is not one for each book. One piece of magic fills volumes of text, and those are merely the notes. It will take more than reading these to master a piece of mnemonic lore. Go ahead,' he gently pushed me forward. 'Pick one, my new apprentice.'

I approached timidly, and tilted my head sideways to get a better look at the titles: *La Bella's Hypothetical Zephyr, Clark's Postulate of Enchanted Air, Lithe's Pleasant Supposition*, and on and on they continued, marching along the walls, a litany of magic, a list of enchantments. My finger ran along the spines of the texts, over leather scales, and soft buckskin, over characters and symbols yet unknown to me. Across one wall it wandered, then down two shelves, and halfway along that, then stopped.

'This one,' I declared, not really knowing what my finger rested upon.

Abaris removed the manuscript and read, '*Marbane's Ocular Enhancer*. An excellent first choice. When you master it, you shall be able to see in absolute darkness as if it were daylight, and in daylight, your eyes will be keener than a falcon's. You shall be able to read a book from half a kilometer, and see the motes of dust floating before you. It will also protect your eyes from blindness.'

I grinned. 'May I see it?'

'Take them all,' he said and pointed to six other volumes on the shelf.

Abaris froze and I sensed the presence of a ghost in the room.

It was not exactly what you expected, was it? Necatane asked.

'Get lost,' I muttered. 'I am enjoying this.'

Tell me of your studies, he enquired, and ignored my protest. *You muses are notoriously boring. Tell me what you went through, so I don't have to personally witness the tiresome process.*

'Studying was drudgery,' I admitted. 'It was worse than any labor on Hades, but I loved it. It became an addiction for me.'

First there was Abaris's research to occupy my time. Often, I never understood why he made me search the medical databases for the genetic code of the mystical cockatrice, or why I had to download an article on energy fluctuations in deuterium nebulae, or why I had to reproduce, by hand, an illuminated text in a language I didn't know. But I dutifully performed these tasks for my Master.

That's when I found *Le Conte del Graal, Le Morte D'Arthur, Tristain and Isolte*, and all the legends of ancient Earth, the knights, their battles, their loves, and their betrayals. I relished them. For three months, I read nothing but stories of jousts and castles, dragons and damsels in distress. I pretended I was squire to the Black, Red, and Green Knights.

But what of your ocular enhancer?

I read the seven volumes of notes, each one as thick as my hand turned sideways. You could stack them on top of each other and sit upon them. They made a decent stool. But that first reading proved to be an exercise in misunderstanding. Abaris explained that I should understand light as the enchantment dealt with vision and darkness.

So I studied light.

Elementary quantum mechanics, that was a disaster, so I took a mental step back and pursued mathematics, the language of physics. After six months of nothing but math did I return to the quantum principles. I learned light was both wave and particle, that it could be scattered and absorbed, emitted and reinforced. A wondrous versatile thing light is. Then on to darkness; I studied the physiological effects of the absence of light. I learned of worlds that were forever eclipsed, and of the life that evolved there in the frozen shadows.

This took me a year. I reread the seven volumes, this time understanding well into the second book. I approached Abaris, ready to try the ocular enhancer, but he directed me to study the biology of sight next. Rod and cones, color theories, electronic transmission through the nervous system, even the other senses that one used when sight was lost, I learned. That was another year of work. I could comprehend up to the fifth volume of his notes.

When I again approached Abaris, he shook his head and directed me to master the philosophy of perception. That was the most difficult to understand. It proposed that one defined one's own universe by what one saw and what one thought: all else (according to the modern philosophers) was nonexistent.

By the end of the third year, I could read and understand all within the seven volumes. I was sick of *Marbane's Ocular Enhancer*. It filled my head. I thought of nothing else. I swore it was almost ready to release itself.

I marched up to the second storey chamber. Abaris sat there

and gazed at the landscape painted upon the paper panel with his back to the two walls of windows. It was noon, and the sunlight filtered in and glistened off the white pine floorboards.

He must have sensed my frustration, for he said, 'While I believe there is much more you can learn, it is perhaps time you tried. I gauge your chances to be adequate.'

'What do I do?'

'Close your eyes,' he commanded. 'Clear your mind. Focus on your past three years, your efforts, your studies, your mastery of all knowledge . . . of light and darkness, of vision and perception.'

It all swam through my mind: equations and theories, the mixing of colors and lectures by wise men who were long dead.

Abaris continued, 'Associate to each of these blocks of information a unique motion of your fingers; for the postulates of quantum mechanics bend your thumb and touch the tip of your pinkie, for neurobiology cross your index over your middle finger, for Verrinous's *Cantos of Perception* ball your hand into a fist.'

I did as he instructed.

'These mnemonics shall anchor the knowledge within your mind. They shall prevent them from uncoiling when you release the knowledge. Now, repeat them, and slowly let the data unwind. Feel confident in your understanding. Do not panic.'

My accumulated wisdom trickled away. It faded from my mind. Was I losing the information? I didn't stop. After three years, I was going through with it no matter what happened, even if I lost it. It would be released!

The power came.

A rush like adrenaline, but a hundred times more powerful, flashed in my blood. The outside world vanished. I was alone with my knowledge, a singularity of information ready to uncoil. I sensed a static change build within me, mounting until it became painful to hold. I released it slowly, not wanting my hard-won wisdom to leave, but it slipped easily through my mental grasp.

A charge shot through my body and struck my eyes, lightning attracted to the rod.

My eyes opened wide, stinging, buzzing from the power and full of tears, making all before me a blur. I blinked thrice, squeezed my tears out, and my vision cleared. But all appeared normal.

'It is lost,' I whispered. 'All my work was for nothing!'

Abaris raised his hand and put a finger to his lips. 'Observe,' he said and pointed to the windows. They were sealed.

'You closed them?'

'While you were in your trance,' he explained. 'I thought the intense light of the courtyard might startle you.'

'How dark is it?'

Abaris held his hand before his face and moved it back and forth. 'I cannot even perceive my hand. But what do you see?'

I looked. There beneath my feet was the polished pine floor, but now I saw every grain in the wood, even the marks where it had been sanded, tiny scratches that I couldn't even feel. And upon the printed paper screen I saw the landscape: a hundred farmers in the distant fields, all smaller than the head of a pin, and clouds in the sky beyond the mountain I had never before seen, and beyond that a grand city on the coast, flags flickering from its towers, and merchant caravans of camels and elephants and mules marching from the west.

'Everything,' I told him. 'I can see everything.'

'Excellent. And your memory?'

I reviewed what I knew. It was there firmly in place. I had mastered the ocular enhancer, my first magic!

This is going too well, Necatane said, disrupting my recollection. *What happened to make you leave? You had the drive, the intellect, and the infinite boring patience required to become a muse.*

That memory was buried deep. I knew it was there, a thing untouched, neatly tucked away, and filed into obscurity. And that's precisely where I wanted it to stay.

Perhaps you have an infinite amount of patience, Necatane remarked, *but I do not. The effort to project you into your past drains the last of my strength*. He dug deeper, slaying the mental guardians that protected the memory. *Ah*, he said, triumph full in his thoughts, *here is the next part of your transformation. Do you recall?*

I remained silent, remembering that what I did was repulsive, but not the specifics of the act.

Allow me the honor then, killer. Your next construct was a disappointment. It wasn't flashy, a trifle easier than the ocular enhancer, and only marginally useful: Halciber's Theorem of Malleability. *You studied it, but had other plans, didn't you?*

The memory welled to the surface. How frustrated I was with his choice. If only Abaris had let me choose my own instead of picking it for me. I wanted to learn how to change my shape, or to fly, or to conjure elementals, demons, and nymphs. But above all else, I wanted to impress Abaris and make him proud of me. *Halciber's Theorem of Malleability* was not the piece of mnemonic lore to do it.

And? prompted Necatane.

So I cheated. I cast the ocular enhancer and searched his seven towers, searched until I discovered a set of scuff marks that vanished behind a solid wall. With the eyes of an eagle, it was a simple matter to locate the release mechanism and find the hidden library beyond. There, in the small room, were more of my master's notes. And these were much better than the ones I had access to.

Four weeks I spent reading the introductory passages of his notes, then chose *Caesar's Ritual of Borrowing*. With this mnemonic lore one could borrow another's thoughts and skills. In the advanced chapters, I would learn to borrow other things, the hardness from a diamond, the speed from a gazelle, or the flight from a bird. There were subtle nuances that I could not fathom yet, warnings and such, but understanding those would come later.

Halciber's Theorem of Malleability was a simple ritual, so I researched the borrowing enchantment at night in secret. I did not remove the notes from the concealed library. Instead, I cast the ocular enhancer and read them in the dark.

Then what?

I recalled what I had done, and was shamed by it. Rather than share this with Necatane, I pushed it back, deep into the recesses of my mind.

Not so fast. We were making progress. He fished it back out. *Here,* he ordered, *look at it. This is part of you. You cannot toss it away and pretend it never happened. Look!*

He shoved my nose into the experience. I was older by two years, sitting in the shadows, reading. Several volumes of the borrowing ritual lay scattered and opened, sprawled across the single table in the secret library. I had only discovered within the last five months how complex it truly was. There were thirteen parts, each as long and detailed as the ocular enhancer, and each necessary to release the power successfully. I considered giving up and returning to the drab schedule Abaris had prescribed for me. Yet I had mastered the first section of the ritual. Perhaps the others were easier.

The first part taught me how to copy the skills and memories from a person's mind. Even constructs could be copies. I knew that mnemonic knowledge thusly transfered would be incomplete. In my estimation, the borrowed lore would be lost upon its initial release. The other knowledges, memories and skills tended to remain imprinted longer, sometimes permanently. There were cautionary words about the effects this had both on the caster and the subject, but those details were in the dozen volumes I had yet to cover.

The door clicked open and light flooded into the secret library. I stood and froze. I had no time to replace all the volumes upon the shelf, and I had no time to hide.

Abaris entered, candle in hand, and peered out. He looked over the open manuscripts, over the notes I had taken on the ritual in my own journal, and then his gaze rested on me. He shook his head, and in a pained voice he said, 'Why? Why have you done this?' He cocked his head sideways to read the spine of one of the volumes. 'The Borrowing Ritual? By all the Gods!' His eyes opened wide. 'It is perilous. Even I am loath to use it!'

'But Master, I only wanted to—'

'Shhh,' he hissed and his eyes narrowed. 'Sit down.'

I sunk into the chair.

'You must not be permitted to continue these studies. It is too dangerous. It invokes powerful forces, non-natural forces, forces of evil.'

I wanted to say I was sorry, tell him that I did it only to impress him, but how could I? He had caught me doing what I knew was forbidden. And in truth, I was relieved to abandon the ritual. It was far beyond my abilities. I knew that. I felt it in my mind, a serpent ready to uncoil and strike . . . uncontrollable.

Abaris walked behind me. I could not turn and meet his eyes, so shamed was I. Instead, I hung my head.

He set his hand on my shoulder, leaned close, then, in a voice barely above a whisper, he said, 'I am sorry, Germain.' His breath fell on the back of my neck. 'For whatever reasons you thought to study this horror, it must stop. I must stop you. You must be punished.'

Punished? The word echoed through my mind. It jostled loose memories of Hades. Memories of when Mike held me down. Memories of his hot breath on my back. Memories too awful to think about. Abaris couldn't mean that. It couldn't be the same punishment Mike meant. Not Abaris, I wouldn't believe it of him. My body and mind flooded with cold panic. I scrambled out of the chair and backed against the wall.

Abaris seemed surprised at my reaction.

For a split second I was back in our cellar, face down in a pile of dirty heat suits, my brother's breath falling on my skin, him holding me down, touching me. I had to run, but with a word of power Abaris could paralyze me. I was trapped. I was about to be *punished*. No!

From my fear the power came.

It rushed to the surface of my mind, the first deadly part of *Caesar's Ritual of Borrowing*. The power exploded, out of control, and searched for a target, for something to borrow. It found my Master's mind, huge and looming before me.

I sensed his thoughts, sensed his worry for my well-being. He had never meant the same *punishment* that Rebux and Mike had. He meant extra duties, a cancelling of my stipend for a few months, but he'd have never harmed me. This man had only love for me, fatherly concern, pride, and friendship.

The ritual peeled away the first layers of his thoughts. I commanded it to halt, but I had never learned how to stop the process that was in the fifth section.

Abaris knew precisely what was happening. He might have resisted, reflected it back to me, but uncontrolled, it would have torn through my mind. He would not allow that.

His memories burned away, mnemonic lore forever lost, skills ripped to shreds. I had to stop it, choose a skill, or a memory, before his mind was gone. There, an enchantment: I plucked it from his mind, hoping to end this nightmare process. It did not. Information filled my mind: *Bander's Enchantment of Time Lost*, a complex ritual that reversed the flow of time. It was seventy years of information coiled tightly, ready to spring forth and rewind seven seconds.

The borrowing ritual continued, swept deeper into my Master's mind, and left nothing intact. I was forced to watch, connected mentally; I could do nothing but participate in the rape of his mind. All the knowledge he wished to impart to me slipped through my fingers as water would. All the magic, lost forever.

I am sorry, my child, Abaris thought, as if this were his fault. Then he thought no more.

The ritual burned out. I had seen his life flash before me, flash into oblivion, gone. He died there on the cool stone floor; no thoughts remained to command his heart or body. It was the ultimate indignity for a man who had spent many lifetimes filling his mind.

I collapsed next to him and held him, wishing I was dead instead of he. Why had he let me live?

Worst of all, it remained intact. The terrible ritual that I only wanted to forget, against all odds, had stuck in my mind. Forever it would remain there, just as the ocular enhancer had. I could never forget it.

You then fled into the sewers? Necatane inquired, sounding exhausted. *Interesting how you took the young assassin's place in Umbra Incorporated. I would love to explore those years in the brotherhood but, alas, time has run out for us. I must release you soon. The sun rises, and your friends come. I fear your quest must continue . . . and mine must end here.*

Chapter Eleven

I heard Quilp, a faint whisper invading my trance: 'Let's get him outta here before reinforcements show up.' His voice trembled. 'You should have finished them like I told you.'

'Grab his arms,' Virginia replied. 'I'll get the legs.'

If they touched me I couldn't tell. A double-dose of narcotics held my senses hostage.

The unfortunate choice of a single word and a jar of rotten peaches, Necatane remarked, *are tiny things to alter one's life. I studied the phenomenon and published my findings in the* Journal of Theoretical Psychology. *I call it 'Catastrophic Min-utiae,' and it might surprise you to know how many suicides and fallen empires it has caused.*

I could give a damn, I said. *Why don't you just kill me and get it over with?*

You misunderstand, killer. I am the one fated to die this morning, not you. The poison already flows in my blood.

You poisoned yourself?

Like the Buddha, poisoned by a mushroom. I am not fool enough to cheat fate. My vision shows my death clearly. If not by poison, then by another unpleasant circumstance would I expire . . . perhaps even by your borrowing ritual.

Then why bother to show me the past? Why not commit suicide before I came?

My path ends here, but yours, yours is at a crossroads. All your life you have been pushed by circumstance, herded by events beyond your control. You have been deceived, you are being deceived, and you shall be deceived again in the future.

I laughed.

Good, he said. *Your sense of humor remains. You will need it when you learn the truth. However, to answer your question, I showed you the past to demonstrate that you were not responsible for your fate. Your father and brother gave you no options. And Abaris was an unfortunate accident, nothing more, remember that. You are not evil, Germain, at least, not by any conscious decision.*

Thanks for the vote of confidence, I said, *but you've wasted your time. I'm as dead as you. Finding the Grail without your powers of prophecy is a one-in-a-million shot.*

This I know, Necatane whispered, *so I have one last vision for you, a nightmare really. Consider it a parting gift. Understand it and you shall find your Grail.*

Fragments of Necatane's thoughts pushed into mine. They had no shape, distorted globs, then bits of emotion clarified: animalistic hostility, the fire of lust, and terror; flashes into a life that was not mine: the sensation of slick ice, smooth and clear, the taste of a chocolate malt, a firm handshake, and a tender kiss upon my brow.

One shape persisted, however: a mouth disembodied. Its lips drifted closer, opened wide and revealed rotten teeth and a long gray tongue. Another mouth appeared. This second smirk had teeth so jagged they looked like cracked rock. It salivated, then snapped up the first mouth – swallowed it whole.

Behind me, I sensed another presence.

It was a third smile, enormous canines that dripped a putrid sludge. In one grinning flash it devoured me, chewed my bones into meal, flesh into paste, then spat me out.

When I looked again, a crowd of blue-skinned men surrounded me, oddly dressed in hose and doublets, refugees from a Shakespearean festival. They pressed against me, then shoved me back and forth. One drew a rapier and waved it at my nose. I reached for my own blade. It wasn't there.

A girl from the mob stepped between my body and the attacker's sword. She commanded him to drop the weapon, and he did so. One of her gloved hands rested on my arm to reassure me. She was exquisite, a heart-shaped face and delicate nose, a fall of raven-black hair, and blue-skinned too. Her hand in mine, she led me away from them.

We wandered across a floor of black marble with inlaid circles of gold. Breaking through this floor was a majestic tree, an ancient oak whose roots made the stone buckle and crack. The girl pointed to the top, and there an eagle perched. One talon clutched a burning chalice, flames as bright as an electric arc. I could not bear to watch, but neither could I look away.

The girl indicated that I climb.

I grabbed the lowest branch, and two serpents appeared, uncoiling and undulating. One hesitated, reared back – then spat venom into my eyes. It burned and I fell to the ground, writhing in pain. Both serpents hissed.

That hissing continued, longer than any snake should have had breath for, then it said, 'Hand me another blue shield. This one's filters are clogged. Another twenty ccs of Benexidor should get him wide awake.'

The snake bit my upper arm.

'Isn't that a truth drug?'

'Yeah? So what? Trust me, if there's one thing I know, it's stimulants. Or would you rather wait for more ships to join us?'

Sensation returned to my toes. They were cold. The chill seeped into my legs and torso, then my fingertips tingled. I opened my eyes and beheld a face of hard-chiseled beauty, wide brown eyes full of concern with a double-star insignia in the center. Virginia smiled at me. Behind her, I made out Quilp's sour features.

She brushed the hair from my face and said, 'You had a seizure. We brought you out of it.'

I was on the *Grail Angel*, in my quarter. 'How long?' I asked.

'Six hours,' Quilp said. 'We repaired the generator and waited like you wanted, but two ships popped into orbit. One was a warship. It didn't waste any time trying to kill us.'

'It was a Whisper-class scout vessel,' Virginia corrected.

'Whatever,' Quilp said. 'This second ship, though, it looked just like ours, three fins, three mass-folding generators, even a silver circle on its nose. It might have been an echo, generated when we tunneled through that planet.'

'You said those other *Grail Angels* couldn't simultaneously exist with us.'

'Yeah, I know what I said,' Quilp replied, 'but I've been doing some thinking and I'm not sure any more. It might be possible for a copy to exist, but all the spins in its wave function would have to be exactly opposite to ours. And the odds of that happening are next to impossible.'

'But not impossible,' I said. 'Did you see the name on the prow? Was it the *Grail Angel*?'

Quilp shook his head. 'There was no time to look. It was gone before we sneezed; besides, we had that other one to deal with.'

'I calculated our double's exit vector,' Virginia said. 'If it plotted a linear course, it headed for Golden City.'

If it was a double, why go back to Golden City? Maybe this other Germain would wait and ambush me when I returned . . . if I returned. 'Go on, what happened next?'

'The first ship, the warship,' Quilp said, 'we shot that sucker a few times and he ran.' He glared at Virginia with his beady eyes and added, 'Our pilot thought we better get you, so he got away.'

Virginia returned his glare, about sixty degrees colder.

Quilp continued, 'So we go to this town you told us about, expecting all sorts of hell to have broke loose, but it was deserted, the entire place. Real eerie. You were alone in that temple, all doped up and crying like a baby. What happened?'

I was alone? If Necatane poisoned himself like he claimed, then why wasn't his body with mine? Did he lie? Did he lie about everything? That would be a fitting revenge for his student. Send me chasing a useless nightmare until Erybus's contract came due, and my soul forfeit. Suspicion, however, was not my strong point; it was Fifty-five's. *Do you think he lied to us?* I asked him.

The psychologist blocked us after you shot him, Fifty-five answered. *But forget him, you've got other things to worry about. We've been followed again! First to Needles and now here. Forget chasing ghosts of yourself. If we stick with what we know, there are only two concrete possibilities. Either our ship is bugged—*

Virginia checked the Grail Angel before we left, I reminded him. *If there was a transmitter powerful enough to send a signal to Golden City, she would have found it.*

Which brings me to the second possibility, Fifty-five said. *It's clear that either Quilp or Virginia works for the competition. Someone had to transmit our position. The safest thing to do is ice them both. Drain your girlfriend's mind so we can fly this ship. And Quilp has done his job. We don't need him any more.*

Fifty-five was right. It was the only way to be certain. But the thought of using the borrowing ritual on Virginia filled me with dread. I admired her. She had saved me on Needles, and again here. If she was a spy, I still owed her. I couldn't absorb her soul. I couldn't kill her. I wouldn't.

'If you don't mind,' I said to them, 'I need time to think. Virginia, please power down the mass-folding generators, and Quilp, watch the displays for any ships.'

'I want to get something straight first,' Quilp said. 'You never mentioned so many people shooting at us. Three times in two days! I want some sorta danger pay, a bonus for risking my skin to save your butt.'

I didn't have the strength to argue. 'I'll double what I'm paying you, just watch the displays.'

'Double?' he said surprised. 'Maybe this isn't such a bad deal.' With a calculating look in his eyes he left me alone with Virginia.

She stood silent a moment, then whispered, 'You would have died if we hadn't gone back for you.'

'A fact I am keenly aware of. There will be a bonus for you too at the end of our mission.'

'That's not what I meant.' She stomped her foot. 'You should have taken me with you, to watch your back.'

'Perhaps I will next time,' I told her – if for no other reason than to keep an eye on her.

'Good. Then if you need anything, I'll be on the bridge.' She paused in the doorway and gave me a long look before leaving.

I got up and locked the door. Indeed, it would be very hard to kill her if she worked for the competition. 'Setebos, are you here?'

A cube of cobalt glass and jade materialized on the reading table. 'I am here to serve you, Master.'

'White noise, please, sixty-five decibels.'

The room flooded with static. It was distracting, but I'd take no chances on any eavesdropping. 'Was the communications system active within the last six hours?' I asked.

'No.'

'Were there any signals transmitted from the ship?'

'I am sorry, Master. My logs indicate nothing.'

Have you gone soft? Fifty-five demanded. *Simply kill them both.*

I'm distracted enough with five of you in my head. I'm not adding anyone else unless it's absolutely necessary. Virginia's piloting skills stay where they are – out of my body.

The psychologist then inquired, *Did Necatane provide you with the location of the Grail?*

Not exactly. I had two visions. But if they are of any use remains to be proven.

Setebos,' I said, 'please search the Grail database for the following references.'

'Ready.'

'Any mention of three giant mouths that consume one another?'

The cube flashed. Azure triangles aligned into squares and pentagons, then fell apart. 'I apologize, wise Master, no such images are indicated in the collected works. There is a legend of a giant, but only one, and I regret there is a body attached to his mouth.'

'What about a blue-skinned people?'

Pairs of green and blue triangles found each other on the cube's surface, made tiny squares, and arranged themselves into a checkerboard pattern. Setebos replied, 'Correlation found, Master: the legend of Sir Osrick. His people were called the Bren and they were a third-generation colony located—'

'Dump the information through the display. I'll look it over myself.'

I read. This Bren world was close, less than a day's travel, relative time, from our present position.

Their planet had no magnetic field to shield them from the ionizing radiation of their sun. To counter it, they genetically altered their skin to absorb the radiation safely. A side effect was their odd coloration: blue.

The colony had been settled fifteen hundred years ago and, according to their charter, organized as a feudalistic society with strict laws to limit technology. I knew of places like these, safe havens from the waves of change that swept through the galaxy. Social reform, scientific breakthrough, plagues, and war were the order of the day, normal fluctuations in a collective society with too many governments, too many people, and vessels of both trade and battle that sailed the distances between the stars too fast. Some people couldn't handle it all. They hid. Eventually, these retro-utopias developed strong trade routes, and made friends, or they were conquered. Either way, they never stayed isolated for long.

The Bren were different. They compensated for their puny technology with sorcery. The report rated them quite high on the Markoff magic scale, an eight. Impressive.

'Shall I read you the legend?' Setebos politely inquired.

'Please, verbosity level four.' I reclined in the leather reading chair and closed my eyes.

'The legend of Sir Osrick,' Setebos began, 'is the final piece of Bren history. More than two centuries ago, the king and queen of Kenobrac bore a single daughter. This princess possessed great beauty, and even as a child she had suitors from every corner of their world. The king, however, turned them all away, never satisfied with their intentions. He wanted them to love his daughter for what she was inside, not for her appearance.

'Upon her thirteenth birthday the princess fell deathly ill. The royal physicians were summoned, but none could cure the sickness that consumed her. The king declared any man who healed his daughter could have her hand in marriage.

'Every hero on the Bren world, and a few from further realms, came to help. One of them was Sir Osrick of the Silver Sword, the Bold Rider of—'

'This princess,' I said, interrupting his narrative, 'what did she look like?' She had to be the one in Necatane's vision, the blue-skinned girl who led me to the Grail.

'There is no visual record available for the princess.'

'Continue, then.'

'Sir Osrick accepted the king's quest, and embarked on a search for the legendary Cup of Regulus, reputed to have magical healing powers. The bulk of the story details his ill-luck in finding this cup. He was captured by pirates, sold into slavery, escaped, battled a dragon, endured the ice torture of the Priest of La Rue de Nom, had his left arm severed, lost four squires—'

'Skip ahead. Did he find the cup?'

'Yes, Master, verbosity level four, I forgot; please forgive my prattle. After two years Sir Osrick found the magical chalice.

Sadly, however, upon his triumphant return he learned another man, an alchemist prince, had discovered a cure for the princess's ailment. They had been betrothed almost since the day Sir Osrick had left. Outraged, he challenged the prince to a duel.

'The remainder of the legend is vague,' Setebos cautioned. 'But it is told that while Sir Osrick readied himself for the duel, praying in the chapel, three men crept in and murdered him before he could fight the prince.'

I like the way this alchemist prince operates, remarked Fifty-five.

'Three days later,' Setebos continued, 'on the princess's fifteenth birthday, the king declared a holiday to celebrate her coming of age and her wedding to the prince. It was then that Osrick's ghost returned with the Cup of Regulus, appearing in the middle of the ceremony. It is said he perverted the chalice's great magical powers to curse the Bren for their lies and cowardly deeds.

'The kingdom turned into a swamp, the animals twisted into unnatural shapes, and the castle sank into the earth. Sir Osrick's curse was so great, historians blame it for shattering the Bren planet some nine days later. The tale is recounted by a merchant who escaped the disaster in his vessel. The remainder of the population is assumed to have perished.'

'Shattered? The entire planet destroyed by Osrick and the Grail?'

'That is the claim, Master. Furthermore, the legend asserts the inhabitants of the castle remain trapped, buried in rock, and awaiting a hero to release them.'

With my limited education as a muse, I knew such an enchantment was technically possible. It had all the classic ingredients: one so consumed with vengeance he rose from the grave, and that part about a hero breaking the spell, it was all standard fare. Yet, to destroy an entire world . . . No wonder Erybus's associates would trade his soul for the Grail. It contained fantastic powers – both to heal *and* harm.

'Please inform Captain Virginia to set a course to the Bren system. And tell her that I shall be resting until we arrive.'

'Yes, Master.'

'One more thing, Setebos. Alert me immediately if any transmissions are sent or if anyone attempts to enter my quarters.'

'As you desire.'

I took my pistol and set it on the reading table, then slouched deep into the leather chair. With a mantle of suspicion wrapped snugly around me, I slept.

A gentle chime broke my peace and Setebos announced: 'Bren system in three minutes.'

I rubbed a century's worth of grit from my eyes and stood. My bones creaked and joints popped. I went through my stretching routine until I was flexible. My watch flashed the time remaining: two hundred twenty-eight days.

For me, it had been three days. Traveling so fast, and squeezing in-between normal space, the *Grail Angel* was susceptible to Einstein's special relativity. To the rest of the universe we left Golden City almost five months ago.

I must have been insane to sign Erybus's escape clause. The remaining days were jewels, each one spent in place of my soul. And the competition was near. I was being watched, followed, and perhaps had a spy close to me. Anxiety gripped my gut and twisted. I chanted the secret mantras of the Corporation to calm my thoughts.

'And how long to Golden City at maximum velocity from the Bren world?' I asked.

'One day, three hours, seven minutes, relative time,' Setebos replied.

'How long non-relativistically?'

'Fifty-one days, seven hours, forty minutes.'

—Nearly two months.

Cheer up, the gambler said. *We're on a winning streak.*

Necatane's dream looks like a square deal, and no one has tried to kill us for nearly a day.

Easy for you to say. You're already dead.

On the bridge, I found Quilp playing chess with Setebos. His Blue Queen was in peril. She, the King, her Consort, and three Knights were pinned in their Castle. Setebos had his Red Knights and Cannons mounting an offensive.

'Bren system in twenty seconds,' Virginia said from the cockpit. Her double-star insignia flashed over an image of the ship's compressed wave function. Our dimensions unfolded like a nightmare of origami in reverse.

'Good,' I said. 'In between the first and third planet, you will find an asteroid field. Take us in.'

'Got it,' she replied. 'Quilp, I'll need you to watch for rocks on intercept courses.'

'I got a game going here.'

Setebos moved through his defenses, killed the Blue Consort, and pinned his Queen. 'Draw?' he offered.

Quilp muttered to himself and switched from the game to displays, projecting a blue-white star encircled by a ring of silver into the air. The far side of this ring was a smooth continuous ribbon of white that sparkled with the dust of diamonds, but closer it broke into countless rocks that lumbered and twisted in space. Amazing that Osrick did this all for the love of one woman. Somewhere in all that debris, two hundred thousand kilometers in diameter, was the Grail. I sensed my chances of finding it dwindle to the infinitesimal.

'Background radiation at point oh four,' Quilp said. 'Safe for a week's exposure.' He pounded his fist on the display crystal. 'Something's wrong with this thing.'

'Displays are fully operational,' Setebos told him.

'What is it?' I asked.

Quilp conjured a map, a million dots swimming in a slow circle. He touched an arc and enlarged it to show velocity vectors, rates of rotation, and red and orange and yellow radiation counts. In the center was a black oval.

'This rock,' he said and stabbed the dark spot, 'there's radiation all around it, but nothing inside. Radiation can't be held like that. If you use a force field, there's an exponential drop-off. This is a solid wall.'

'A neutron star fragment?' Virginia suggested.

Quilp switched to the gravimetric display. 'No,' he replied. 'The rock has normal mass. Weird.' He scanned the EM bands, slowing when he reached the infrared. 'I've got a collection of absorptions: hydroxyl and carbon-oxygen stretch. If I didn't know any better, I'd say it has an atmosphere.'

'Get us closer,' I told Virginia.

The asteroid was pock-marked with craters, and one in particular caught my attention. Half in shadow, half in the sterile sunlight, it struck a familiar chord in my mind. It was a mouth, frozen open, mid-scream, its jagged edges like crumbling teeth. It was the first mouth from Necatane's vision.

'Move us into the large crater,' I said, then recalled how easily those mouths swallowed each other, and swallowed me, so I added, 'but be careful.'

Virginia took us in, whispering a prayer to Bloody Elisa, the patron saint of vacuum.

There was no bottom to the pit. It wound deeper into the rock, a gullet leading into a stomach.

'In?' Virginia asked.

'In,' I replied.

Three kilometers of twisting tunnels, so tight in parts the *Grail Angel* barely squeezed through, and other portions large enough to maneuver a fleet. Quilp then looked up from the display and announced, 'We've entered a chamber, roughly spherical. It's seven kilometers to the back wall, and there's another passage there.' A flick of his hands across the controls, then he said, 'I've enhanced the image.'

Below was a valley lined with neat rows of trees, nude of all foliage and fruit. A road ran through the fields, up along the curve of the wall, and across the ceiling. There was a wagon overturned, a few broken walls, but no movement, and no life.

'The walls are sedimentary,' Quilp continued. 'They show signs of erosion. Looks like the whole place was above ground once, but got sucked down here somehow.'

Setebos added, 'Residual radiation counts date the organic material at two hundred seventeen years.'

Over the curved land we drifted, toward a sinkhole that penetrated deeper into the asteroid. Rows of trees along the edge stood at precarious angles. From our perspective, they appeared as rows of shark teeth and the hole looked like another mouth, the second mouth in Necatane's vision. For a moment, I thought it might snap forward and devour the *Grail Angel*. It remained motionless, however, opened in a mocking laugh, daring me to enter.

Virginia must have guessed my next order, because she said, 'I'm not taking the ship down there. Looks too unstable.'

'You're right,' I said, 'set us down, and we'll have a look on foot.'

She turned and asked, 'We?'

'You wanted to come along, didn't you?'

She removed the silver clover from her pocket, rubbed it once and frowned. 'I suppose I did say that.'

The *Grail Angel* settled under one of the tall dead trees, raising a cloud of dust that briefly obscured our view.

'The atmosphere is breathable,' Setebos declared, 'slightly high in oxygen, and a trace of methane.'

'Quilp,' I said, 'see if you can scrounge any rope from the cargo hold.'

'You want me to go down that hole with you? Shouldn't one of us stay behind to watch the ship?'

'We could be gone for some time.'

'Don't worry about me.' He fingered an ampoule of amber-colored fluid. 'I won't be bored.'

'Very well, Virginia, grab some rope, two lights, and bring an extra weapon if you have one.'

I left them, entered my quarters and secured the door behind me.

'Setebos, establish command lock, level alpha, and initiate voice print verification on all systems except life support. Also jam any signals originating within a seven-kilometer radius of the *Grail Angel*.'

'Done, Master.'

If Quilp was my spy, he'd be sending no information on our location this time. And if I didn't come back, he'd be stuck here for a very long time.

Is that the only reason you're leaving him behind? Celeste inquired slyly. *Not to be alone with your pilot?*

He's not that stupid, Fifty-five answered for me. *He's testing to see which is our spy. If the competition shows up, then Quilp's the rotten egg. If they don't, then it's the pilot. I still say ice them both.*

It is not my intention to be alone with Virginia, I replied, *nor do I intend to kill either her or Quilp. I just want to get the Grail and get out of here.*

I hope so, remarked Fifty-five, *or we'll all be dancing on the wrong end of a pitchfork soon.*

From my bags I removed a shadow-skin with fresh batteries, my accelerator rifle and pistol, a new blue shield, the Grail database, and armor. The armor was a shirt of crystalline scales each with a tiny magical rune of *Safekeeping* inscribed upon it. I slipped it over the shadow-skin and let it form-fit the contours of my body. Its enchantments deflected energy away from me. Normal blades and projectiles just bounced off the alloy.

Next, onto the pad of my right hand, I sprayed a tattoo. As the biopolymer dried, and the electronics within aligned, patches of color developed and lights twinkled behind them. Ten seconds and the image resolved: a rose such a deep red it verged on blackness; its velvet petals glistened with dew. My skin grew cold when the tiny transceiver ran through its diagnostic.

'Setebos, please lock on to my signal.'

'I shall be listening, my Master.'

And one more thing. Abaris taught me a bit about the unliving. Silver seemed to work best at keeping such creatures as ghosts and vampires at bay, or did that only work with werewolves . . . I didn't recall. In any event, if Osrick lurked in that hole, I'd be prepared for him. I slipped three bars of silver into my belt pouch, ammunition for the accelerator pistol.

Virginia waited in the airlock. She had two carbon-arc lanterns, a coil of rope, and wore her lucky four-leaf clover around her neck.

I opened the hatch and got a blast of frigid air in my face, the scent of smoke, dust, and the ionization from the hull of the ship. I turned up the heating elements within my armor. 'Setebos, external lights to maximum, please.'

Stepping down, I discovered the earth was a red clay covered by ash. Virginia and I marched away from the *Grail Angel*, and left a trail of crimson dots behind us. Quilp didn't say good-bye, but I heard the hatch slam shut. I almost felt sorry for Setebos, leaving him alone with the creep.

Beyond the limits of our lanterns there was solid blackness and a stillness that defied quantification. On my left was a plow stuck in the soil, mid-furrow, with no trace of the farmer who had used it. On my right, a road ran into the yawning hole. We followed the road until it forked. A signpost marked the paths: one arrow pointed at the wall, the other tilted straight down.

I set my lamp aside and allowed the ocular enhancer to uncoil my memory. The cavern exploded with light. Far from us, the remains of a city stood, broken towers and buildings that arched up along the curving walls of the cavern until they cracked and crumbled from the strain. The skeletons of trees and shrubs clung higher up, and on the ceiling, stuck upside-down, were the foundations of houses.

And again I saw myself, three other Germains, translucent, two near to the *Grail Angel* and one already by the edge of the hole, cautiously peering over the edge. They started to fade, faster than when I saw them on Delphid, but before they disappeared entirely I glimpsed two other *Grail Angels*, one next to ours and another that hovered over the hole. The images then evaporated.

It was unnerving to see them. It was like looking into a mirror and having the reflection move of its own accord. The ocular enhancer was most powerful when first released. Somehow I must be seeing . . . seeing what? They were definitely me. If they were echoes in time, duplicates of our wave function, why did they vanish? Why weren't they real?

Virginia interrupted my mystery and asked, 'Why did you change your mind and bring me?'

The psychologist whispered, *Tell her the truth. Admit that you have unresolved feelings for her. Admit that you want to be with her.*

Tell her the truth? Fifty-five hissed. *Tell her that we brought her because we don't trust her? Are you crazy?*

'You've saved my life twice,' I replied. 'You're good at this sort of thing.' I halted and turned to face her. 'Have you ever considered a change in careers?'

'I'm a pilot. That's all I've ever been good at.' She opened her mouth, stopped, changed her mind, then, 'What exactly are you offering?'

'You seemed interested in how I switched cards at Golden City. I might be inclined to show you.'

'Magic?' Both her eyes shot up – then fell. 'Didn't you say it took years of study?'

'The universe has enough pilots, and so few muses. You have the intellect, the talent. It would be a shame to waste it.'

We took seventeen more steps together, then she said, 'I'd have to think about it. I just got out from under Golden City. This is the first time I've flown in a year and a half.' She stopped. 'And to be honest, I'm not certain how much of your offer is based on how sharp my mind is, and how much because of what happened after our game of Universe yesterday.'

'I know your Guild has rules about that sort of thing. I apologize if I put you in an awkward position.' Virginia tried to respond, but I cut her off, 'Perhaps it would be best if we forgot about my proposal until this is over. When the *Grail Angel* is yours, then we can discuss the matter, or not. Whatever you wish.'

She frowned. 'Sure. That's what I was going to suggest, too.'

Close to the hole, grooves like large claw marks in the earth ran along the slope and over the edge. It was as if something enormous had been dragged beneath the earth and had left these marks behind. I set my lantern on the ground, then braced myself against a dead tree and peered over.

The furrows spiralled deeper, carved trails on the walls of the pit, and walking along those paths were the faintly illuminated outlines of people, hundreds of them. My heart stopped – a jolt of adrenaline – and it abruptly started again. These were not like the images I saw of myself; these people glowed with magic; I felt the pain burning in their souls. They were ghosts.

They marched, some up, others down, vanishing when they got to the edge where I stood. Farmers pushing plows, beggars with bowls, merchants in gilded robes, and herdsmen tending flocks of twisted animals with melted bodies, distorted heads, things that crawled on belly and fur, and pawed with misshapen hooves – all of them flickering a gloomy blue, and all circling mutely.

Shaking, I loaded one of my bars of silver into the accelerator pistol.

'What is it?' Virginia asked and leaned over my shoulder,

looking deep into the crack, lifting the lantern high to see better.

I cringed as the bright light flooded the hole, but the phantoms took no notice. They continued walking, going nowhere.

Virginia squinted and shrugged, blind to the phantoms' presence with her normal vision.

'It's nothing,' I lied, then swallowed my apprehension and went down, pistol ready.

The spirits ignored us; indeed, they passed through Virginia. I stepped aside, however, and let them by. A blacksmith brushed past me, hammer in his hand, and tracks upon his face where his tears washed away the soot. Following him a flower girl limped along, crying too. In her basket lay bundles of withered and blackened daisies. Poor creature. I wanted to stop and help her. But how does one help the dead?

'Are you OK?' Virginia whispered and placed her hand on my shoulder.

I nodded and continued my circular descent.

A minstrel, fiddle propped under his chin, played while he plodded on and wiped the tears from his face to keep his strings dry. Five more turns and the trail curved into the earth. I glanced down this tunnel. No ghosts wandered there. I was happy to enter it and leave the spinning sorrow behind.

Crystals of gypsum covered these tunnel walls. They licked the stone like icy fire and reflected our lamp light back from countless glittering facets. Virginia touched one of the delicate formations. It crumbled into sparkling dust with a gentle tinkle.

Ahead, I tasted a breath of warm air and spied a pale luminescence. I doused my lantern and signaled for Virginia to do the same. The passage blushed with red light.

I offered my hand to Virginia and guided her until we emerged in a second cavern. Across this cave was the source of the warm light. It was a castle: tall minarets, gray stone walls and braziers set upon them, filled with flames that flickered tenuously, moving as if caught in a viscous liquid. A ring of mirror black circled the palace, still water that reflected the walls and the slowly twisting fires.

A tiny raft floated in its moat. On it, an old man sat and patiently held a rod and line with one hand while he scratched his beard with the other.

'What is that?' Virginia whispered, 'I can't see.'

'It's a man,' I replied. 'And if I'm not mistaken, he's fishing.'

Chapter Twelve

This fisherman was no ghost. He cast a shadow and breathed as any living man did. His skin was blue. He was one of the Bren – imprisoned here for two centuries? Was the Osrick legend true?

Here's the plan, Fifty-five whispered. *We sneak to the back of the castle, kill any guards, and once inside we—*

We're not going to storm the castle, I told him. *Remember the report? They have kings and knights, chivalry and good manners. It's like the myths of King Arthur I've read. We can approach openly and expect to be offered hospitality.*

This is no fairy tale, he hissed. *You're going to get us all killed.*

One two-hundred-year-old fisherman is not going to kill anyone.

'Let's go,' I whispered to Virginia.

'Wait a second,' she said, and dropped my hand. 'What's a castle doing here? How can that man be alive?'

'I'll explain everything, later. Just follow my lead.' I hiked down the path that cut across the cavern. Behind me, Virginia sighed, then I heard her footfalls catch up to mine.

Stalagmites and stalactites melded into columns that held up the roof and looked disturbingly like rows of teeth. Rippled walls and smooth flowstone appeared as frozen water, splashed into the air, suspended, channels and rivulets of solid rock. And growing between these formations was a mushroom forest. There were giant white puffballs, open stars with ocher petals, and a grove of blue-veined toadstools, three meters tall. Lining the path were clusters of pink polka-dotted caps, and sprinkled among them branches of amber that looked like coral under the sea. On the walls, tiers of violet brackets grew, and crowded each other for whatever organic material there was. Below them, a dense carpet of chanterelles spread out.

It was warmer here, rich with the smells of humus and healthy soil.

Virginia's footsteps halted. I turned and saw her kneel down to examine the scarlet parasols of the lethal *Amanita Electi Muscaris*. Before she touched it, I caught her arm and said, 'They are lovely, but to touch them is death.'

She withdrew her hand.

We trekked through this forest of decay to the castle. Mist rose from its moat, and the fisherman, who hadn't seen us yet, appeared to be floating on clouds rather than the black water.

When I stepped onto the drawbridge, my boots sent a pair of hollow echoes off the castle walls. The fisherman, startled, dropped his pole. He twisted around to find the source of the noise, and his boat bobbed dangerously. His mouth dropped when he spotted Virginia and myself, but he quickly regained his composure, then scrutinized us with clear gray eyes that matched the color of his beard.

'Good morning,' I said.

'And a good morrow to you, Sir Knight,' he answered. He hid his surprise well, and while he only wore the rags of a servant, his voice held not a trace of alarm.

I decided deception was the proper course of action. 'I am Prince Germain, and this is the Lady Virginia, the captain of my ship. I have come to your realm in search of a holy item. Our mission is most urgent.'

'Ah,' he mused and scratched his beard. 'It has been a long time since we had a guest. And a questing prince of white skin, no less. Intriguing.'

'Us? There are more of you?'

'Of course, Sire.' He recovered his fishing pole from the bottom of the boat. 'A castle full of lords, ladies, knights, and vassals, all the gentle subjects of King Eliot.'

King Eliot? Setebos didn't mention the name of the King in the legend. Was it the same king or a descendant of his? Certainly, if the legend was true, and Osrick's curse had the power to crack the planet, it had the power to keep his victims alive all these years.

Virginia leaned over the drawbridge and peered past the mats of red algae into the murky water. 'Are there any fish alive in this?' she asked him.

'Yes, M'lady,' he replied. 'We play this cat-and-mouse game to pass the time. They are the most cunning carp, able to nibble off my bait and never touch the hook.' He drew in his line and showed us the empty barb. 'See?'

He set his rod aside and addressed me in a formal tone, 'Prince Germain, must you enter this castle? For once you do, leaving may not be a simple matter. I advise you to seek the object of your quest elsewhere.'

'And why do you tell me this?'

'Call it friendly advice. There are forces at work here, influencing us all, and you need not partake in the game.'

'I appreciate the warning, but I have no choice.'

'Alas,' he whispered, 'so very few of us do.' He then stuffed a bit of mushroom onto the hook and returned his attentions to the water.

I led Virginia across the drawbridge.

'What an odd man,' she remarked. 'Why is he blue?'

'Odd, yes, but I get the impression his warning was sane enough. Keep your eyes open and that plasma tube ready. I'll explain the color later.'

'And why'd you make yourself a prince and me only a lady? Why couldn't I be a princess?'

If I might remark upon this, said the psychologist. *I believe* the extra breath to say, 'It wasn't Lilian's fault. It was the queen and the prince.'

'But it *was* her fault,' he hissed. His claws sank deeper into my arm, cutting the bicep and scraping the bone. The pain shocked me awake.

'My Princess, the queen and her adviser, they were the architects of this "illness." No common knight would do for her; no, she had to have a prince. They lied to me, all of them.' He exhaled, spilling frozen breath onto my face, the odor of rancid meat. 'Our love was doomed from the beginning. I should have known better.'

His grip relaxed again. I wiggled my fingers . . . almost enough.

'We swore our devotion to one another,' Osrick whispered, more to himself, I think, than for my enlightenment, 'in the palace's rose garden, under two full moons.'

His claws loosened another notch.

'I trusted her,' he said.

My smashed hand moved. The joints creaked, and my thumb slid past the index finger, the middle, until it touched my ring finger. Mental structures unfolded in my thoughts. The ritual of borrowing crystallized. Liquid lightning flowed.

'Revenge was my wedding gift to Lilian,' Osrick said, laughing, 'poured from the cup brought to heal her. Its magic trapped us together for eternity. I shook the world, and I made their invented sickness real. She bears a plague so virulent none can touch her and survive. No one shall have my beloved if I cannot!'

'Knowledge,' I demanded from him as the magic required. 'Give me your life.'

The sorcery bloomed. My thoughts embraced his. I tumbled through a red-hot steel corridor of twisted jealousy. I ran into a dark tower of revenge, then squirmed into the wormholes of his desire filled with wet warm flesh and passionate whispers.

We met on a grassy field in our imaginations. He was an armored knight, silver sword in one gauntleted hand, and a shield covering his entire left arm. Upon the shield were two snakes coiled about a rod, facing one another. They were alive too. They moved in a hypnotic pattern.

Sir Osrick gave me a slight nod beneath his helmet.

I lunged.

His shield came up, easily blocked my blade – both snakes uncoiled and struck. Hot venom pumped into my arm. I pulled away, but it was too late. My muscles went numb. I fell to my knees.

Osrick stepped back and waited for the poison to work into my tissues, then he declared, 'Mortal, you are the first in two hundred years to face me upon this field of honor. You have my respect for that. I shall give you a swift, clean death.' He raised his sword high.

I willed my body to stab him, pierce that armor of his, but I was paralyzed with venom, and with fear.

He lopped off my head.

Self-control disappeared; personality blurred, and in its place the insane ghost took firm hold. Memories vanished, my thoughts scattered incoherent, and an evil chuckle escaped my lips that was not my own.

Parts of me, however, Osrick would never vanquish. I was more than one man; the remains of every soul I had absorbed lived on within me. And the personae of Celeste, Medea, Fifty-five, the psychologist, and the gambler weren't about to hand control over casually to him. Their schemes, their desires, and their strengths were all mine to draw upon. Everything they had ever done with bloody hands and cold hearts, I had done too.

We gathered upon that field of honor and threw Osrick out as he was making himself comfortable in my body. 'I rule here,' we said in unison. 'BEGONE!'

Undivided, we mobbed him. Medea pounced first, and knocked Osrick to the ground. Fifty-five kicked his blade out of reach, then danced on his ribs for a while. The gambler took care of the shield. He flipped it upside down so the vipers on Osrick's heraldry couldn't slither out, then jumped on it. I heard them squish. The psychologist joined in too, and ripped off his helmet. Inside, the plate armor was empty. Only a faint sigh escaped from within.

Osrick surrendered. We won.

Yet, I sensed him still present. His memories and emotions remained intact, a shell of all he was, but without awareness. This other mind blended with my own. I tried to stop it, but like water held too tight, the more I squeezed, the more I lost control. Osrick's mind slipped into mine. It fit like a transparent glove. He filled all my empty spaces.

I had been the one to curse the Bren, the one who loved Lilian, and the one driven insane with jealousy. But I was also the one to escape the mining colony of Hades, the one to kill his Master, the one trained by Umbra Corp. I was Germain, but I was also now Osrick.

This had never occurred before. My other personae remained distinct, separate, but Osrick and I melded together, and made me someone else.

Slumping to the floor, I tried to sort out my jumbled recollections. They were hopelessly mixed. I thought of Lilian and Virginia simultaneously, my duty to the Corporation and my oath of fealty to King Eliot. I shook my head to clear this confusion. It didn't help.

Fix your arm, Medea whispered. *Use the blue shield.*

The robot doctor was not on my belt. I swept the floor with my good arm, in a full circle, brushed over rocks and dust moistened with blood, and found it near the wall – smashed in a hundred fragments – the microfingers and probes wriggling, searching for something to heal.

There's much blood, Medea stated. *If we're lucky, it's only the Cephalic or Basilic veins that got severed. If it's the Brachial artery, you're a dead man.*

The Grail. I had to find it.

I recalled, or rather Osrick recalled, that it had been buried with him, in a chest of silver among seven others. But there was no sign of this treasure when I, Germain, opened the vault.

I sifted through our memories.

Years ago, a man had descended into Osrick's lair as I had. This man, however, had been prepared for the ghost. With the fingerbones of Saint Dominic held before him, he kept Osrick at bay. The relic forced the ghost into the corner and charred his phantom flesh. The pain was strong in our memory. And while Osrick writhed in agony, held by the magic, the man ransacked his seven silver chests. He wore a shadow-skin, and carried a half-moon blade, a weapon popular among my brothers in the Corporate élite.

The thief stole two satchels full of riches, then returned to the helpless Osrick. He boasted of how he fooled the nobility of Kenobrac. He only came for the Grail, but they thought he wanted to marry their princess. He laughed a while at that. Then he told Osrick that he intended to sell his precious Cup of Regulus, and that it would make him powerful within his Corporation.

Umbra Corp? It was too much coincidence for my liking.

He scooped up the fingerbones, retreated into the tunnel, and that was the last Osrick saw of him. Hate burned fresh in my mind. I would find this man and kill him in a most unpleasant manner.

The memory was old, though – decades, perhaps a century. My brother assassins rarely lived long lives. Had this thief long enough to sell the Grail? And if so, why didn't Erybus have it? If another wealthy collector had obtained the relic, certainly Erybus would have found out and purchased it regardless of the cost. But if this thief had died before he sold it, or kept it for himself, then I knew where he'd be. No one left the Corporation.

Tracking him down would be difficult, but not impossible. I had a few favors I could call in with the registrar's office. If he was dead there would be a record of who had inherited his possessions. Either way I had to get back to Earth. It would take several non-relativistic months to get there, and then there was the return trip to Golden City. There was much ground to cover. Little time left.

I jumped to my feet and strode to the tunnel entrance – at least, that was the plan. When I rose, the room spun, my legs collapsed, and I found myself lying in a mixture of blood and dirt. I touched my arm. The skin hung loose, peeling away from the wound, wet and sensitive.

With my good arm, I leaned against the wall and stood, very slowly.

The effort made my head throb. For a moment, all I heard was that throbbing, and all I saw were flashes of purple and yellow. The blood on the floor became the shores of an ocean, crashing waves to match my pulse. A memory of Osrick's: a sugar-sand beach with fingers of foam and warm water rushing between my bare feet. Reeds grew in the surf. Above me, gulls cried to one another. A slight wind caressed my skin, the cool morning breeze that shields the dew against the first heat of the gathering day.

The roar of the surf faded and I returned to the chamber, cold, dark, and sick to my stomach. Gripping the wall, I felt my way to the tunnel. Then, crawling on three limbs like a wounded dog, I started back.

The first part went well. I only banged my head twice. Then I came to the downward turn in the passage. It was three meters deep; a fall could break my leg or neck. Cautiously, I positioned myself in the hole. With my legs braced against one side, back firmly on the other, I took tiny steps, my shoulders pushing and inching me along, until I touched the bottom. I sat there panting, chilled to the bone.

The level section that followed went quickly – until it dead-ended. Feeling my way around in the dark, I found the tunnel turned straight up. The portion I had so swiftly descended on my way down had been transformed into a climb of twenty meters.

I needed sleep, time to gather my strength.

Your arm, Medea firmly reminded me.

I touched it. No pain. That was a bad sign.

The choice is clear, she said. *Climb or die.*

Reluctantly, I wedged myself in the passage, legs pushing on one wall and my good arm helping to pull me up. Ten meters, or so I figured, and I had to rest. My legs burned with lactic acid. They trembled and weren't going to hold much longer.

I continued, pausing every two or three steps to rest. My legs were cramping. I had no idea how far up I was now. I only knew that I had to climb. Virginia was up there, Lilian too, and the Grail. I couldn't give up.

Both legs cramped, badly. One slipped. I pawed frantically for something to hold on to. The surface, however, had been scraped quite smooth by Osrick's claws.

I fell.

Writhing through utter darkness – a single moment of black panic – then I extended my legs, pressed against the walls of the narrow passage. My back scraped the other side, ripping my shadow-skin off, and flaying my flesh away as the stone rushed past. Abruptly my body jammed in the passage. My feet pushing on one side, my neck twisted on the other.

Move slowly, Fifty-five cautioned. *You could have snapped your spine in that maneuver.*

I relieved the pressure on my neck and straightened out. How far had I fallen? It was impossible to guess in the dark. It could have been a few meters, or I could have gone all the way to the bottom. I might be able to reach down and touch the floor. I didn't try. If I felt it, I'd give up.

With one hand and legs that were so tired they felt like wood, I dragged myself up. If I could have used my mouth somehow to propel me, I would have tried, biting and chewing my way to the top.

It occurred to me then that maybe I did fall to the bottom. Maybe I was lying there, unconscious or dead, and this climb was a figment of my imagination. Or perhaps I was in Hell. What a clever bit of punishment that would be: to struggle through this dark chimney forever and never make it to the top.

My body moved of its own accord. It was not my willpower that fortified me, but Osrick's. He had suffered through worse injuries and endured greater torture; he had died yet still persisted. Part of that legendary strength was mine now. It was odd to feel so noble and courageous.

Ahead, I saw movement, a shifting of the darkness, a fluid motion of black on black. It was the fluttering of light and shadows, the light from a torch.

I then realised I was in the final *level* portion of the tunnel, no longer vertical. How long had I struggled, pressing against the rock, believing my ascent continued? I wanted to collapse there, rest, but I crawled the last few meters and emerged in Osrick's smooth marble tomb.

The ambassador turned pale at the sight of me. 'Prince Germain?'

He stepped closer timidly, then exclaimed, 'My Prince!' He pulled me free and wrapped his crimson cloak about me. 'You are injured.'

Osrick recognized him. He was a fine diplomat, intelligent and fair, able to compromise. He'd also put on a good twenty kilos.

'You managed to escape?' he whispered. 'What of Sir Benjamin?'

'Dead,' I told him, 'as is Osrick.'

His eyes went wide and he looked to his torch. It burned with a real fire, flames that leapt and danced with sparks and spiralling smoke. The ambassador touched it and drew back. 'It burns!' he cried. 'That means we are free. Free to leave Castle Kenobrac at last!'

My body tried to move, to stand from the tomb, but it was too late. It decided to never move for me again. It ached to even think about it.

'Come, we must see to your wounds.' He placed his arm under my shoulder then practically carried me through the corridor of the dead.

I wanted to tell him to take me to the *Grail Angel*. There were blue shields there, my only chance to live, and Virginia. But shadows filled my mind, and only the faces of the dead remained, chiseled upon their marble tombs, staring at me.

I struggled to remain awake. The loss of blood and the shock of Osrick's memories blending with mine, however, made me, at best, bewildered. My vision blurred and my sense of direction vanished. Noises assailed my ears. There were voices, the clash of metal on metal, and an explosion. Somewhere along the way I collapsed.

I returned to caresses and warmth. A moist cloth pressed to my forehead. I awoke and found myself buried under three layers of blankets. Directly above me, draped over the canopy of the bed, was an embroidered rose with angels hovering about its petals like so many insects. Queen Isadora sat by my side.

'Rest, Prince Germain,' she said as she wrung the cloth out in a basin. 'You have done what we thought no man could do: kill a ghost.'

I knew this woman, and I hated her.

She and her adviser concocted the plan to marry her daughter to the alchemist prince and unify their two realms. The queen personally saw to it that I, or rather Osrick, had been murdered while he prayed in the castle's chapel. Her adviser was not here, however. He was the only one to escape the planet and the Grail's curse. I thought that curious.

Throwing the furs aside, I noticed my left hand and right arm were crisscrossed with scar tissue.

The Queen offered me a silk shirt with lace cuffs and black

pearl buttons. I took it and slipped it over my head.

'When the ambassador brought you to us,' she explained, 'your limb was cut to the bone. We are afraid our healing abilities are somewhat out of practice. The scarring was unavoidable.'

'No need to apologize for saving my life,' I replied. Gratitude was a bitter thing in my mouth. How does one thank the woman who killed you?

A flash caught my eye. In the corner, the glass doors of the balcony glowed white, then the castle trembled and dust rained from the ceiling. The light subsided, but outside screams and the report of automatic weapons could be heard.

I rose and opened the doors. Ozone and smoke lingered in the air, and magic, so strong that goose flesh covered me from head to foot. On the ramparts of the castle, a hundred knights and noblemen busied themselves winding the cranks of arbalests, securing catapults with thick ropes, while others cast spells that distorted the air with powerful sorceries. We were under siege.

The invaders gathered on the far side of the cavern. I recognized them, soldiers of the Order of the Burning Cross. From this distance, and in their scarlet body armor, they looked like red ants, scrambling about. Each one had a white cross emblazoned upon his chest (which made a good target). There must have been a hundred of them, and more were pouring in.

Those are Sister Olivia's men, Fifty-five hissed. *So you can forget any theory about your doubles, assuming they even exist, tipping her off. You think Sister Olivia would listen to one of them? It had to be either Quilp or Virginia who betrayed us. And with Setebos keeping an eye on Quilp, that leaves Virginia by process of elimination. You should have listened to me and iced her when you had the chance.*

Why don't you concentrate on finding us a way out? I snapped back.

Did Virginia get to the *Grail Angel* unharmed? She would have had to sneak past Sister Olivia's army. If she hadn't they would put her through their Inquisition – a consequence of my short-sightedness. I should never have given Celeste control.

The queen came to my side, placed a warm hand on my arm, and said matter-of-factly, 'They are here for you, Prince Germain. They came while we restored your body, demanding both you and something they called the "Grail", which we assume is the late Sir Osrick's Cup of Regulus?'

I started to answer, but she held a finger to her lip. 'No, there is no need to reply, and no need to worry. We shall not betray the hero who delivered us from our curse.'

A scouting party of six soldiers moved across the cavern using the limestone formations for cover.

Someone on the walls cried, 'Release the mist!'

'This shall be most diverting,' the queen said and dug her nails into my arm.

Upon the ramparts sat an iron cauldron that appeared empty from my vantage. Three muscular knights struggled with it, then tipped it over the edge, and spilled forth a great cloud. This fog was the color of lead and sank quickly. It raced over the moat and across the cavern floor without any notable dispersion, enveloping the first four scouts. I heard strangled screams, the discharge of a rifle, then nothing.

The remaining two scouts backed away and waited.

'They are not very clever, these red knights,' the queen remarked.

'No,' I said, 'not smart. But there will be many more of them, and they will bring great siege machines that can bring down this entire cavern. I would not underestimate them.'

She shrugged indifferently, then pointed to the mist. 'Observe.'

The cloud cleared a bit. Within, I saw four white crosses still ablaze on their shiny red armor, but inside the soldiers' flesh had been eaten away. Only bleached bones remained.

The scouts crept up to get a better look or perhaps to gather their comrades' remains.

The remains moved. Bones animated, armor stood, and rifles were fired upon their former allies. The undead grabbed the bodies and dragged them off into the shadows.

'This vapour,' the queen asked me, 'are you familiar with it?'

'I have seen similar enchantments,' I admitted.

'Then you are a wizard. We knew it. Every piece of our prophecy has come true.' She gave me a careful looking over, almost a look of admiration, I'd say, if it weren't for her calculating eyes. 'We have foreseen that a man with pale skin would free us from Osrick's curse. He is a sorcerer, yet with a mere handful of years' experience. He is strong, yet divided somehow in his willpower. We know you search for the Cup of Regulus.' She removed the heavy silver chain about her throat. Dangling from it was a primitive figurine the size of my thumb: a man of black stone, titanic genitals, and a gray convoluted crystal, perhaps a moonstone, embedded in his head. 'And we know that this will help you find it.'

I knew that little man, and I knew I had held him before. Déjà vu, again. I reached for it, but she pulled away.

'We have foreseen also that you are the one to free our daughter from her curse. Help her, and the amulet is yours.'

Such open manipulation was refreshing.

Watch it, warned Fifty-five. *This queen is no fool. That idol probably gives her control of your mind.*

'How do you know what I need?'

'We know for we have spent two centuries scrying the future with crystal balls, worn three magic mirrors clean with questions of how we shall be released. We know many of your needs, my Prince.' She held the talisman up to the candlelight and the crystal in its head glowed warm and red. 'When we were younger, and dared such things, we summoned an angel of fire to bring us this. Within is a spirit that once, and only once, heals the mind. It may retrieve something that has been lost, one's wits or one's memory.'

'And that will help me find what I seek?'

'We have divined that you shall require it.'

Fifty-five remarked: *Next she'll try and sell you some land. Tell her to forget it and let's get out of here.*

She tells the truth, the psychologist said, *or what she believes is the truth.*

'Very well,' I sighed, 'let us say for the moment that I require your charm. Have not I broken Osrick's curse? You are free to leave the castle.'

'We are free, yes. But the late Sir Osrick placed a special enchantment upon my daughters with the evil powers of that chalice.'

I remembered. I, Osrick, made her plague real, so real that one touch of her flesh would cause fever, pustulant boils, then madness and death in a matter of seconds. There was only one way to remove his curse. The Princess Lilian had to marry again, and that marriage had to be *consummated*. Therein lay the paradox. Any man to touch her would die, yet she needed to be touched in the most intimate manner.

I laughed. It was inappropriate, but the situation struck me as humorous. Perhaps it was Osrick that thought it funny. 'That is why you tested my strength,' I said. 'You had to know if I would endure her fatal embrace.'

'Then you know how she is to be cured?'

'I know everything Osrick knew,' I said and let the implication of that hang between us a moment.

She took one step back.

A pricking sensation touched my face and hands, static electricity that emanated from the queen: magic. If I had had the ocular enhancer up, I might have seen what enchantment protected her, but I dared not release the mnemonics. She might mistake my intentions as hostile.

'Consider your position wisely, Prince Germain. You are surrounded by enemies, with only the hospitality of the Bren to protect you.'

'True,' I replied, then walked back to the bed and sat to defuse the tension. 'But you have only offered me one death in place of another. Perhaps we can compromise.'

'Compromise?' She rolled the word about in her mouth and considered.

'I propose that you let me find the Cup of Regulus. When I do, I shall return with it and undo Osrick's magic.'

It was her turn to laugh, and it sounded like tiny bells, charming. 'And how would we know you would return?'

'I give you my word,' I said. That wasn't supposed to mean anything, but as I spoke it, I realized my word did indeed have value. I knew that I would keep my promise once given. I was honor bound to do so. More specifically, Sir Osrick was honor bound, but where he stopped and I started in my thoughts was indistinguishable.

The queen gave me a nonchalant smile. 'We have a better idea, my wise Prince. We both know that you will not be tricked into touching Lilian, and yet we have divined that you are the one to cure her. What we propose is that you and she be married. Afterward, you may together continue upon your quest for the cup.'

'The princess is married,' I pointed out, 'to the alchemist prince.'

The queen continued to smile and said, 'The king's fish have been well-fed this evening. The Princess Lilian is in mourning.'

'I see.'

It was bad enough with that pilot of yours, cried Fifty-five. *Now you're going to drag a child along?*

Silence, knave, the Osrick part of me thundered back.

Marry Lilian? It was what I had waited for all these years, wasn't it? No, it was what *Osrick* wanted. He loved her, loved her so that he risked his life a hundred times for her. I recalled a moonlit garden, the scent of night-blooming turquoise roses, and a long-dead promise. She kissed us there, a small thing, but the recollection was as fresh as if it had been yesterday. We swore our undying love to one another, though I was certain this was not what they had in mind.

On the other hand, Fifty-five was right. I couldn't bring the girl with me. All I wanted to do was get out of here, find the Grail, and save my own precious skin. But to leave her alone here, cursed, it was more than I could bear.

And what of Virginia? We had unresolved business. I couldn't believe she betrayed me to Sister Olivia, no matter what Fifty-five said.

The most pressing issue, however, was the Grail. I had to find it to live, and, more immediately, I had to escape this cavern to continue my search. How? There'd be no sneaking past a legion of trained soldiers.

Another explosion rumbled outside. The glass in the balcony doors flared brilliant and the amulet in the queen's hand reflected the flashes from the battlefield. The little man was tangled in the silver chain, trapped just as I was. What did he have to do with me finding the Grail? He'd restore a single memory, or so the queen claimed. What use was that to me? A memory?

A memory! I realized then how I'd use her talisman to escape. A memory, for me, was more than a simple recollection. There were entire people I had forgotten – the souls I stole with the borrowing ritual – and the mnemonic lore they knew.

'You have yourself a deal,' I told her, 'and a new son-in-law.'

Chapter Sixteen

Queen Isadora insisted on a formal wedding. It didn't matter that her castle was under siege. She told me, 'A princess must not hop over a broom like some farmer's daughter,' and the discussion was over. Since she held the talisman, my means of escape, I went along with it.

The royal tailors fitted me with a doublet, heavy with brocade, that clumsy sword of the ambassador's, and boots with curled toes. They attached double lace cuffs, and sewed on badges of honor for battles I had never fought. They assured me that I was quite a heroic figure and wheeled in a full-length mirror to prove it. I looked like Hamlet dipped in glitter.

The fellow scrutinizing me from the other side of the glass was handsome: straight posture, square shoulders, and piercing eyes. Yes, he was heroic; yet there was a shiftiness about him, some villainous quality I couldn't pin down. My face had been altered so many times to keep my enemies guessing that the one I wore now was unrecognizable.

My helpers, satisfied with my apparel, left.

I loosened the doublet, exhaled, and scratched under the armor beneath. The royal tailors threw a fit when I insisted on wearing it under their creation. They suggested, firmly, that it looked silly and bulged in all the wrong places. I wore it anyway. The queen might be able to ignore the army massing at her front door. I couldn't.

I rubbed the rose tattoo on my right hand to warm the spray-on electronics. The dew on its petals twinkled, and I whispered into them: '*Grail Angel*, come in.'

A burst of static answered me, then a choir of voices spoke simultaneously from the transceiver – Quilp's, Setebos', Virginia's, even my own . . . and although difficult to sort out, I was certain I heard more than one of each voice.

The signal cleared abruptly, and Quilp shouted, 'What in blazes is going on down there?'

'Quilp, put Virginia on.'

'Isn't she down there with you?' he asked.

'No. She's supposed to be up there.'

See? Fifty-five said. *She joined up with Olivia just like I told you.*

Unless the girl was killed, Celeste added coolly.

Or she never got through Olivia's lines, the psychologist remarked. *She could be here still.*

'Quilp, check the cavern. She must be there somewhere.'

'Can't,' he said. 'Setebos saw one of those Whisper-class ships enter the cave, blasted it, then got us out but fast. We're hiding in the asteroid belt, waiting to hear from you. I would have overridden the stupid AI, but someone locked me out of the command structure. You wouldn't know anything about that, would you, buddy?'

'No.'

'Well, I've got more good news for you. While we've been drifting here, twenty ships have gone down that hole: destroyers, personnel carriers, a mining tug, and they're still coming. You're in a lot of trouble.' In a whisper he added, 'And there were two other *Grail Angels* out here, drifting like us, hiding. They gave me the creeps, but they're gone now.'

'Setebos,' I asked, 'are you listening?'

The petals in my rose tattoo darkened and withered. The biopolymer hadn't much life left. 'Of course, Master. How may I serve you?'

'I find it distressing that you left me here.'

'Accept my profuse apologies,' Setebos answered with a self-confidence that surprised me. 'I monitored communications, as instructed, and intercepted multiple coded transmissions in the vicinity. I surmised there was a fleet nearby and that it was prudent to escape. Did I err?'

The *Grail Angel* had been found without a crew, drifting near Golden City. Had Setebos 'erred' with them, too? 'No,' I replied, 'you did the right thing. Please secure this transmission.'

There was a pause, then, 'Done. Triply scrambled and encrypted.'

'Can you confirm Quilp's sighting of those other *Grail Angels*?'

'No, I cannot confirm Mister Quilp's claim. I saw nothing. He is, however, in a chemically-altered state, and irrational. Perhaps this explains his unusual statement.'

'Very well. Since you moved yourself, I assume you can pilot the ship?'

'Yes, Master, but I am not licensed.'

'Licensed or not, proceed immediately to Earth.' I gave Setebos the Corporate security code so he could land, then said, 'And tell Quilp to meet me at my flat.'

'You desire us to leave?' Setebos inquired. 'Master, please allow me to attempt—'

'— I have another means to get to Earth,' I told Setebos. 'With any luck, I shall be there when you arrive. Now get going.'

'And Madam Captain?' Setebos asked. 'Will she be accompanying you?'

'No,' I answered. 'I don't think she will. Germain out.' I balled my hand into a fist, and closed the channel.

So, you do have a way out, Fifty-five said. *Tell me.*

After that stunt you pulled with Virginia, you're lucky I'm even talking to you.

Come on, junior, that's water under the bridge.

Is it?

Where was Virginia? Had Celeste sent her straight into Sister Olivia's army? Or was she a spy as Fifty-five thought? I didn't want to believe either possibility. Maybe she was here, as the psychologist suggested. She was smart. If she saw Olivia's army, she might wait and hide until it was safe. Osrick wanted to rush out, duel with these red knights one by one if need be, and find her. His affections for the princess and mine for Virginia blurred together. I'd have to be careful. The knight's noble thoughts were more than a distraction; they were dangerous.

You love both women? the psychologist inquired. *Perhaps we should begin therapy.*

An explosion rattled my teeth and cracked the glass of the balcony doors. Peering out, I saw only the blazing white crosses of Sister Olivia's men, crucifixes upon their breastplates that wavered ghostly under a blanket of the Bren's fog. There was the tingle of sorcery in the air, whimpers of pain, the crunch of armored treads across the cavern and, from the castle's battlements, chanting and magic. It was hard to tell who was winning. I released the ocular enhancer.

There were no duplicates of myself, either in the room or upon the battlefield. There were, however, scores of dead soldiers on the cavern floor, and nine Bren floating motionless in the moat. Their regenerative abilities apparently vanished along with Osrick's curse. Too bad. Trading a handful of our men for a legion of theirs wasn't good enough. What did Quilp say? Twenty ships and more coming? It was only a matter of time before Castle Kenobrac fell.

Motion in the mist. The dead lurked in the mushroom forest, dozens of them, fleshless corpses given life after death by the Bren's necromancy. A stalemate was possible if enough of Sister Olivia's men could be changed and made to fight for us. We might hold them off indefinitely, or at least until I left.

A squad of living men crept forward through the toadstools

and hid themselves poorly there. They watched the castle with luminous scopes, listened with electronic ears, and set up the tripod for a heavy-caliber flash repeater. Meanwhile, seven dead men, skeletons in loose red body armor, circled silently behind them – then opened fire.

Bolts of energy zigzagged through the air. Three of the living fell. They scrambled for cover and shot back. But it took several hits to blast the dead apart, and it only took one to kill a living man. The dead men advanced, and the living men died. More for our side. Finally, the last four soldiers made a panicked dash back to their base camp. They got away.

Our fleshless men grabbed their fallen comrades, and dragged them back to the castle, smiling all the way.

In the back of the cavern a flaming cross appeared. I squinted and saw a woman carrying a fiery crucifix in both hands. She strode forward confidently: Sister Olivia took the battlefield.

She had powers. I had read the Corporation's files on her. Some said she was a witch and others claimed she was a mutant, or maybe she really was the hand of God. I didn't know and I didn't care. All I knew was that she was dangerous, and I found myself wishing for a rifle.

Sister Olivia raised her crucifix and sang, '*Nil posse creari de nilo.*' The flames burned brilliant and dissolved the mist. Our dead men dropped their cargo and retreated, but they slowed, seemingly snared in the warm illumination. They paused, and turned about to stare into her blessed fire. Sister Olivia shouted, '*Veni, Sancte Spiritus, et emitte coelitus lucis tuae radium!*' Her crucifix flashed and lit the cavern air. The shadows melted.

Our dead men collapsed into piles of bones, inert.

There's more to worry about, Fifty-five muttered and directed my gaze to the rear of the cavern. Under floodlights, the frames of artillery stood in various stages of assemblage. One was complete: a mass of gas tanks and injection mechanisms and generators. Osrick might have mistaken it for a mechanical dragon, and he'd not be far off. Inside its mouth, a sphere of compressed tritium was held. A small atomic spark transformed it into a tiny sun – the breath of the dragon.

From the castle's ramparts came a new chanting, urgent.

Thirteen Bren joined in a circle, and above them ripples appeared in the air like waves of heat. This distortion collected; it coalesced about the castle, a curtain of scintillating clear vapors. The magic had great power. My skin crawled.

Sister Olivia's cannon rotated on its treads towards us. Gas hissed into the compression chamber and some leaked out, leaving streamers of steam as the dragon inhaled.

We had to disable that artillery. The blast of heat would melt the walls of Castle Kenobrac and kill all of us. Osrick had fought by the side of every Bren out there. They were our friends. I could not let them die.

In the shadows, I saw something that made my heart stop. Virginia. She crouched along the cavern wall, and inched her way to the exit. She held her plasma tube in one hand, the chain with her lucky four-leaf clover wound about her wrist. She had changed back into her pilot's suit, but her hair was still made up from the ball. With the ocular enhancer I saw her face streaked with tears.

I wanted to call out to her. Call her back. But from the opposite end of the cavern the fusion generators that powered the cannon whined as they overloaded.

Virginia stopped and covered her ears.

Within the dragon's mouth, the compressed tritium turned dark and glossy, like a great black pearl held between its teeth.

The Bren's curtain of sorcery sparkled with power. The hairs on the back of my neck crawled with static.

The dragon belched.

At the apex of its arc, the sphere blossomed with light and made Sister Olivia's flaming crucifix seem like a dim match in comparison. The fire filled my vision, pure whiteness, and a perfect silence that enveloped the cavern. I dove for cover.

Through closed eyelids, the light was so intense it turned to pain, lightning along my optic nerve. A great sizzling filled the air, the sound of water thrown into a pan of boiling oil, then darkness.

But no extraordinary flash of heat came, no searing death. I kept my back pressed against the cool stone wall and slowly opened my eyes. The tapestries hadn't burst into flames, nor had the glass doors melted. Why was I alive?

I peeked around the corner. There was only fog and boiling clouds. This vapor cleared quickly, condensing on the cool stone surfaces and covering them with drops of dew. The front wall of the castle sagged, melted by the terrific heat, and all the men who had stood upon it were gone. To either side of ground zero, Bren were alive, pouring water upon fires and carrying their wounded off. The thirteen sorcerers still held hands, and the curtain of magic still shielded the castle in blatant defiance of the first law of thermodynamics. It was weak, though, the distortion less than half its former strength and the prickling sensation I felt hardly an itch. The moat was empty. Where Virginia had been there was only smooth stone, molten and glowing faintly from the heat.

No! Rather it be me dead than her. She had loved me, and I had betrayed her. I should not have been weak with Celeste. I should have gone after Virginia the instant I regained control of my body. Instead I chose the Grail. Now I had nothing.

A sickness filled me, a greater sorrow than when I had lost my Master or my brother. It felt as if I had lost her not once but a dozen times.

Osrick wept for me.

Across the cavern, Sister Olivia's men charged the castle.

A gentle knock on the door, then the ambassador let himself in. 'Prince Germain,' he said, 'you must come away from there. It is not safe.'

I set my grief aside and wiped Osrick's tears from my face.

'Your men fight well,' I said and remained where I was, watching. 'But these red knights have inexhaustible numbers. For every one to die, two replace him. I fear we will not be victorious. They will never stop until they have me or the Cup of Regulus.'

I could surrender and end this all. Sister Olivia's fight was not with the Bren, it was with me. We shared the same predicament: find the Grail or forfeit our souls. She'd kill every person here, tear this rock apart, and sieve through the rubble if she had to.

The ambassador glanced at the carnage. 'Yes, it does look dreadful. And the moat! The king's fish – he will be most disappointed.'

'The fish can go to Hell. What about our comrades? They are dying. What about your life?'

'My life?' the ambassador calmly said. 'My life should have ended two hundred years ago. We all have lived too long, my Prince and, in truth, we deserve whatever fate befalls us. The only thing that matters now is the Princess Lilian.'

He hesitated, collected his words with care, then looked away before whispering: 'I must confess that our princess carries a plague most lethal. Her touch is death itself. In the beginning, it was a ruse, a simple enchantment of the queen's, no more dangerous than the common cold. We did it so a prince from a powerful nation might marry her and increase the stature of our tiny country. The king treasured his daughter so. He would have never forced her to wed a man she loved not . . . unless her life was at stake.'

'You risk the wrath of the queen by telling me this. Why?'

'The king senses a certain quality in your nature, and I also trust you to be a gentle man. I know you shall find a way to cure her malady with the Cup of Regulus you seek. But I wanted you to appreciate the tragedy that has befallen your bride.'

'Yes, yes, held within these walls for two hundred years, it is a tribute to her willpower that she has not gone mad with boredom.' I regretted the sarcasm in my voice. The ambassador had placed himself in grave jeopardy to tell me what I already knew. He deserved my respect for that.

'No, sire,' he replied, 'it is not only that. She loved Osrick. Had he asked her to run away with him, she would have. That was the true reason for our scheme. We had to separate the two. She had no idea what opportunities might be lost. It is not only her imprisonment and her curse that we are responsible for. We broke her heart as well.'

All this time Osrick had believed the princess concocted the illness with her mother. Yet if she truly desired to marry the prince, she could have lied to her father and told him she loved the prince. There was no reason for her to feign sickness. Why hadn't I realized this before? Had my jealousy blinded me so? Only the queen, her adviser, and this ambassador were responsible. They were the villains.

I reached for my sword intending to cut the ambassador down where he stood for his treachery, but stopped. I was not Osrick. Part of me, yes, but not all. I swallowed the boiling rage, silently recited the mantra of peace taught to me by the Corporation, and regained my composure.

'All I ask, M'lord, is that you treat her with all due kindness, and avoid her touch until she is cured.' He smiled and changed the subject. 'You look magnificent.' From the folds of his crimson cloak, he removed a brush and flicked the dust off my shoulders. 'The chapel is ready. We may begin as soon as you wish.'

I looked upon the battlefield. Bren on the walls were regrouping, still in shock from the small sun that had landed in their midst. The star cannon inched forward upon its treads. An army of red ants surrounded the castle. I searched in vain for some trace of Virginia. She was gone.

The gambler gave me his professional opinion: *A hundred to one odds that The Bren win.*

'I am ready now.'

I followed the ambassador across the slender bridge to the

tallest tower in the courtyard. Through a short hallway, then I mounted three steps, white, blue, and red stone. Beyond this, an archway of alabaster framed the royal chapel. Tiny cherubs with Mona Lisa smiles held the archway open for me. Inside stood sterling braziers, three rows of ivory pews, and an altar held at each corner by an angel wielding a sword with a broken top. Two centuries ago Osrick had died here.

While I prayed at that altar, the queen's men had come for me, all stealth and shadows and knives, and had taken my life before I could duel with the prince and claim my love.

I had come to this spot again to take what was rightfully mine. Yet, if Sister Olivia's men found us before that, if I died again moments before I had Lilian, there would be no magic to bring me back, no mythical Cup of Regulus to curse my enemies.

The ambassador and I marched down the aisle. He stepped to my right and took his place as my best man.

Get a grip on reality, Fifty-five hissed. *The talisman, remember? You're going to use that to get us out of here. Concentrate.*

The queen was on my left, dressed in black, the silver chain and little stone man hanging about her neck.

Grab it, use it, and escape, Fifty-five urged.

You think the queen, king and princess, all skilled muses, will let me get away with that?

Kill them. You've got a knife, Medea, and the element of surprise. They'll be dead before they blink twice.

I considered. Osrick swore to serve the king and queen. He could never kill them. Yet I saw the logic in Fifty-five's advice. How could I marry this girl and drag her along with me? She'd only slow me down. I didn't know what to do. Indecision rumbled in my stomach. My head swam with vertigo even though my feet were firmly planted.

Bishop Thomason took his place at the altar. I had known him in another life, slightly senile and extremely long-winded, but otherwise a pleasant, well-meaning man.

The princess entered and my dizziness vanished.

A triangular veil covered her face, white sea foam and a lattice of seed pearls. Waves of her lustrous black hair had been woven together with bands of diamond and sparkled with blue rainbows. The dress she wore was a work of great enchantment. Four lace roses molded her body and, embroidered upon them, tiny bees and hummingbirds moved across the fabric, chasing whatever scent the flowers held; the rose petals opened slightly when the birds probed for the nectar within. About her waist, a belt of solid silver traced her slim figure, came to a point and arced down where her navel was, then curved up and over her hips. A river of unblemished white silk splashed down her legs, flowed into a train behind her and rippled softly as it caught in a breeze. She was mesmerizing.

Are you out of your mind! Fifty-five cried. *No one in Umbra Corp gets married.*

Shhhh, Celeste hissed. *This is a very special moment for us. I'm not going to let you screw it up.*

King Eliot escorted Lilian to the altar. As she neared, an odd collection of emotions fermented inside me: Osrick knew a joy unparalleled, a smattering of lust, and love unbounded; Germain knew only apprehension, and grief for Virginia.

All these things disappeared when Lilian stood by my side. An icy dagger of fear drove into the base of my spine: the feeling any animal has when cornered.

'Please,' the bishop instructed me, 'remove her veil.'

I noticed she wore silver gloves that covered her hands and arms up past the elbow, and recalled what would happen if I accidentally touched her skin. I reached forward carefully, sensing a weak field of sorcery about her, and drew the veil from her face.

It was as if I saw her for the first time; it was if I had known her all my life. Moist lips Osrick had once kissed, skin smoother than any alabaster angel's, and a face that had driven him mad with jealousy, insane with desire, a face to die for – yet, her eyes, there was no denying what I saw in them. They were the darkest of blues, a shade fairer than black, and set full with a shrewdness that no amount of Osrick's love could obscure.

I couldn't kid myself. She was here to get rid of her curse, not because of any affections for me. And I was only here for the Queen's talisman, to escape. There was no love at all.

'Today,' Bishop Thomason said, 'we are gathered here for the most joyous of occasions: matrimony. It is a blessed tradition, and the most prized state two people may exist in.'

A slight tremor shook the tower, but no one seemed to notice.

'Opposites come together to form a new, stronger divine whole. But this day is special, different in that it is circumstance rather than love that brings these two people together.' He smiled at both of us.

A blast somewhere, close, a faint scream. The ambassador looked about nervously. He heard it too.

'The nature of the universe is planned and random, a balance of the serendipitous and the uniform, as is the nature of love. Even elliptical paths still curve and turn at a single point – as both of you are doing today. Duty, purpose, and love have little to do with a successful marriage. Those who flourish open their hearts to possibility, open their hearts to understanding, and embrace the nature of their partner, whatever that may be.'

Out of the corner of my eye, I caught the queen signalling the bishop to hurry up.

His pace picked up dramatically. 'Please, Prince Germain, the rings.'

The ambassador handed me a simple golden band.

'Place the ring on Princess Lilian's finger and repeat after me.'

Echoes in the hallway. The sound of boots on the marble floor.

King Eliot drew his sword and stepped in between Lilian and the chapel's entrance. 'Hurry up!' he commanded the bishop. 'There is no time.' In his left hand he held a twelve-pointed Philosopher Stone, and squeezed it until a ribbon of blood snaked down his wrist. The crystal blushed with ruby light, and the king tossed it into the archway where it immediately swelled and absorbed the stone about it. Its twelve points ballooned into muscular arms and legs, six of each. Sterling braziers to either side were drawn into the growing figure. Then the arch closed in upon itself and the marble floor formed an outer skin.

The thing reminded me of Aaron, a creature of stone. But Aaron was a work of art, and this was a crude composite. It looked clumsy and cobbled together from spare parts. It struggled to find a form.

In the hall, past the growing lump of rock, I glimpsed red armor and white crucifixes. Orders were barked, then rifles fired. Lightning traced the surface of the stone creature and it writhed in pain. The smell of molten metal filled the chapel.

'Guard the breach,' King Eliot commanded the creature.

His six muscular arms grabbed the sides of the chapel entrance and braced. Smoldering coals from the braziers surfaced upon its skin – and blinked! The tiny cherubs that once flew in the arch now swam in the collective components of the golem. They broke its smooth marble skin in patches like tumors. Their heads, arms, legs, and tiny wings stuck out at odd angles.

I slipped the ring onto Lilian's gloved finger and she placed one onto mine.

More deadly than your exploding ring, whispered Fifty-five. Mark my words.

I know, I whispered. But we had both lost the one we cared for – we could not do so again.

Lilian sank to her knees and I followed her cue. The bishop sang a prayer in Latin as fast as he could and offered us a holy wafer. It tasted like nothing, pasty, falling apart into a bland mush as soon as it was in my mouth.

'By the power invested in me by God and King, I pronounce you man and wife.' He managed to slip in, 'May God bless you both during all the days you shall live, and may you bear endless progeny.'

That's it? Celeste demanded. *No kiss?*

More shots were fired in the outer hall and cracked the stone creature's body. It bent down and pulled out the white, blue and red marble steps with three of its arms. Three legs braced forward, and three back; three arms clamped the wall, and the other three held the marble steps as a knight might hold a shield before him.

I turned to the queen. 'The talisman, quickly. The princess and I can still escape.'

'Mother?' Lilian said and took a step toward her.

Queen Isadora toyed with the chain about her throat then yanked it free, and handed it to me. 'I am forced to trust you, Prince Germain. Know that if you deceive me and break our pact. I shall set a curse upon you that will follow you wherever you go.'

'I have no doubt,' I said and snatched it. 'How does it work?'

From the hall came an explosion. Fissures cracked the stone creature's skin.

'Hold the little man within your hand,' the queen instructed and glanced nervously to the chapel's entrance. 'Concentrate upon that which you do not remember. That spirit within will do the rest.'

What I wanted was the mnemonic lore I had lost at Golden City, the sorcery within Omar's mind. The crystals within the talisman grew hot, but I held it tighter. The memories, faint at first, collected in my thoughts they surfaced like an oil slick upon water, and brought with them something else I had lost: Omar.

You double-crossed me, Omar whispered. *You stole the memories that took me a decade to learn. For what? To switch cards. You sent my soul to Hell for a game! Let me tell you what it's like in Hell, friend, because they know you. They have special plans for you.*

I am sorry, Omar, but I must use your Abridged Manifoldification *again.*

No! I'll do any deal you want. Do not send me back. You cannot imagine what it is like.

I must. There are two lives at risk now, not two cards. And one of the lives is mine.

Omar struggled to possess my body. My willpower was doubled, however. I was Sir Osrick of the Silver Sword, the Bold Rider of Kenobrac. I crushed Omar, and wrenched the engrams from him. It exchanged two equivalent masses across any distance. One had only to visualize the object, and they instantly swapped.

King Eliot came to the princess, and gave his daughter half a hug, so as not to soil her dress with his bloody hand. 'I charge you with her safety, Prince Germain. Do not fail me.'

'I shall not,' I said, so convincingly even I believed it.

'And what of you?' Lilian asked her father.

'Child, worry not about us. Your mother and I can take care of this distraction.'

The rifles outside ceased firing. The stone warrior turned its head inward and looked to the king. Several of its eyes were blasted away, and the marble skin was fractured and crumbling to pieces.

'Hold your ground,' the king ordered.

It turned, reluctantly, and braced itself for another round from the soldiers.

I unbuckled the ambassador's sword and returned it to him. 'You will need this more than me,' I said.

The ambassador swung it once as if he knew how to use it, then nodded to me.

Taking Lilian's hand, I drew her close to me and whispered, 'We must stand together for the sorcery to work.' In truth, it was never designed to transport two things together. I took an awful risk by bringing her along. There was no choice, however; Osrick couldn't leave her behind.

The soldiers fired again. I felt the vibration through the floor. One of the stone creature's legs crumbled, the face of a cherub went sliding across the floor, and the wall about the archway buckled. Without knowing I had done it, I put my arms around the princess to protect her. She in turn stepped closer to me.

I released the mnemonics, allowed it to uncoil from my mind. Information I had never learned poured into my mind, then unraveled along with the memory of Omar – along with his soul.

Please, Omar pleaded. *We can make a deal. Do not let me die thusly.*

If there was another way, I told him, *I would*. I felt a twinge of guilt over this cowardly act, sending Omar back to Hell. It must have been Osrick.

In my mind the *Abridged Manifoldification* took shape. I visualized my home at the Corporation. There was a statue in my living room I judged it approximately the same mass as the princess and me. I hoped it was.

The stone warrior shattered. Coals and angels and stone flew in every direction. The only thing I could see was the outline of the ambassador, standing in a cloud of dust, his sword in hand to meet the first of the soldiers with their pistols drawn. Electrical discharges lit the cloud about the ambassador. He stabbed the first of Olivia's men to step into the chapel.

'Farewell,' the Queen said, her voice receding.

I channeled the energy, focused upon the statue in my living room – light years away. Soldiers emerged from the cloud of dust. The ambassador was nowhere to be seen.

The church distorted, then dissolved.

One of the red knights pointed at me and shouted, 'That's him. He's here.'

Shots were fired at us, through us. The hair on my arms and the back of my head stood up.

The world vanished.

Chapter Seventeen

The chapel fell away and we entered a dimension of blackness, frigid and quiet save for the warmth of the princess next to me and the beating of my heart.

Pieces of another place solidified around us: the Louis XXXII sofa with its arms of delicate walnut double helixes, and the green and cream Chinese rug from the same century. Then my coffee table appeared, a floating slab of Cambrian mudstone, filled with fossilized trilobites. The statue upon the table faded, however. It was the ballast for the *Abridged Manifoldification*, sent to Castle Kenobrac in our place. The bronze sculpture was of a man and woman with their arms and legs tangled in a sensuous, anatomically improbable embrace, and they radiated a warmth that filled my simple abode. I would miss them.

Omar's mnemonic lore dwindled, along with the last traces of the chapel and the empty in-between spaces. The same energies I had used to swap a pair of cards transported us light-years in the blink of an eye. I exhaled, relieved to be alive and safe and far from Sister Olivia's men.

Beneath my feet I saw a section of the castle's floor had been transported with us to balance the load. We had been fortunate that the mental construct had worked at all.

The princess wrenched herself free from my arms. She carefully collected her dress's train, then sat upon the sofa and arranged the white silk about her so it was symmetric. Perhaps she thought my royal court would be parading in for her inspection. I'd have to set her straight about that.

Be extremely gentle with the girl, the psychologist whispered. *In the span of moments, she lost her parents, left the only home she had, and married a man who is a stranger. You have brought her to an alien culture, one infinitely more complicated than her feudalistic society. She may undergo a complete breakdown.*

Let her crack, Fifty-five said. *Who cares? We've got a Grail to find. What time is it, anyway?*

I touched my mirror-black desk, brought it to life and neutralized the alarm system. The time from my gold diamond watch flashed into my eye: sixty-six days thirteen hours remained before I lost my soul. Apparently even Omar's mnemonic lore was susceptible to special relativity.

He claimed 'they' were waiting for me in Hell. That terrified me. What would I give for an extra month? Half of Erybus's reward? Without hesitation. How long would the *Grail Angel* take to get from here to Golden City? More time than I had? Was I dead already? Panic rose from my stomach, acid that burned along my spine and touched my brain, gnawing upon my confidence.

Relax, the gambler said. *All the cards haven't been dealt yet. Get us a drink, then we'll see if we can't find the assassin who stole Osrick's cup.*

A drink. Excellent idea.

Sensing my interest, the desk projected a list of favorites. I picked one at random. A shot of quantum ice materialized, which I downed before it boiled away. That was Virginia's drink, quantum ice. The thought of her sat uneasy in my mind – not knowing why I felt the way I did for her. What did it matter? She was dead. Wasn't she? Her pilot's suit couldn't have protected her from that blast. But even if she had survived, she was light years distant. I would never know if she had been a spy of a victim. Loose ends like that bothered me.

How do you feel? the psychologist asked.

About Virginia? Mind your own business. Otherwise, I'm tired, confused: almost normal, I'd say.

And Sir Osrick?

Something is different. Osrick was still with me, but more like a memory, distant, no longer part of my personality . . . or, at least, a very small part of it.

I too sense a shift in your thinking, the psychologist remarked. *It is the change in venue. Sir Osrick was strong in Castle Keno-brac, his haunt, if you will. Here, however, deprived of a familiar environment, he is weak.*

Is it permanent? Will I be myself from now on?

The psychologist gently touched Osrick with a psychic probe. *It is as if he sleeps,* he answered. *I dare not go deeper. The disturbance may arouse him.*

So how do we keep him asleep?

The Osrick personality blended with yours has two major interests: foremost, the welfare of his princess, and second, his obsession to locate the Cup of Regulus. If you concentrate on these issues, then he shall remain satisfied, and dormant. For how long I cannot guess.

Why don't you offer this princess a drink? Fifty-five suggested. *That should keep her happy.*

I turned to do just that, and saw that she was quietly sobbing on the arm of my sofa, her white dress in disarray and clashing with the green swirls of the carpet.

Go to her, Celeste urged. *Let us comfort his sweet tidbit.*

Osrick stirred from his slumber. He wanted to rush to her side, take her hand, and assure her it would all work out for the best. I needed a moment alone, to gaze upon the familiar, and to clear my head of his sophomoric emotions. I went to the eastern wall and made it translucent, then decided to just open the thing and air the place out. It had been months since I was here last, and the whole apartment smelled stuffy. It looked too cave-like for my taste . . . too much like the Bren's sunken grotto.

The wall vanished.

Summer afternoon on Earth: cool breeze, sky speckled with clouds, and the scent of freshly-cut grass from the vast lawns below. The sun felt good on my face.

My tower sat on the edge of the Corporation's university where raw recruits were transformed into cadets. There were parks with giant fig trees and shimmering fountains and redbrick buildings covered with ancient ivy. I listened to the music of sighing leaves and splashing water, sounds that I knew well.

On the far side of this valley gentle hills rose, and past them towered the rugged peaks of the Alps. Encrusting these mountains like jewels in a crown were thirteen gold-mirrored palaces. This was where Umbra Corp's board of directors lived, controlled their private empires, and enjoyed as much stability as anyone in our profession could. The sun fell behind the mountains, and shadows swelled, a tide rushing in to lap at the edge of the campus where our mausoleum sat, Golgotha. It was a pyramid constructed of jet-black stone, a one-half scale model of the great pyramid of Cheops. This dark triangle stood out against the brilliant snowy summit and the gold palaces that sparkled in the afternoon sun as if a gigantic white dragon had curled up there, sleeping with one eye open, watching. The location, and the effect of dark on light, was no mistake. It reminded us of the truth of corporate life: advancement or death.

Behind me, the sound of silk rustling, then four delicate steps across the Chinese rug. The princess stood by my side. I saw on her face tear stains, but no grief, only wonder. She inhaled deeply, and with wide eyes surveyed the clouds overhead, then stared at the frothing water that spat from the coiled dragon sculpture guarding the entrance to my tower.

I hardly felt a thing for this woman.

Osrick was small and dim in my thoughts, and that was good. Yet, as much as I hated to admit it, the tiny part of him that was me loved her. I had to make that feeling go away – at least until this mission was over.

Don't let that egghead psychologist fool you, Fifty-five said. *This so-called girl is dangerous. Remember, she's a sorceress and as old as all of us put together.*

Her hand gently alighted on my arm, a lethal touch under those silver gloves. She asked, 'My husband, what is this place you have brought me to? I have the oddest feeling that I have been here before.'

What did I tell her? That I was no prince but a professional assassin? That I had brought her to a fraternity of murderers? 'It is a school,' I said (which was technically the truth).

'Where your armies and scholars are trained?'

'Something like that.'

She suspects deceit, warned the psychologist.

'This must be a very special part of your castle then,' she said, 'a private chamber where you come to meditate.' She peered into my bedroom, then looked appraisingly over my simple work area but was drawn to the da Vinci on the west wall.

'Your work?' she inquired.

The *Adoration of the Magi* hanging there was the real one, not a copy. It was a token from the Florentine Emperor for killing his brother and clearing a path to the throne. All those angels and horses and people who stared at the newborn Christ – the image simultaneously attracted and repelled me. 'No,' I said, 'it was a gift.'

She examined it a moment longer, admiring the way the light illuminated the canvas, then she turned and asked, 'This castle of yours, and those I saw in the distance, might I be given a tour of them? And will we being traveling soon to find the Cup of Regulus? If there is time, I would very much enjoy a stroll through your gardens.' They were questions, but she asked them using an imperial tone, one that made them sound like commands, not requests. I didn't like it.

'To feel the sun on my skin again,' she said and sighed, 'even though its color is so peculiar. It would be a sensation most welcome. And grass! So long since I felt grass beneath my feet—'

'I am afraid, for the time being, that is impossible,' I said.

'Why is that?'

'Those castles you see are not mine. This room is safe for us, but to venture forth, especially dressed as you are, would attract attention. We must take care to . . .'

Her eyes narrowed, then she smoothed the silk of her dress and replied, 'This dress, I will have you know, was woven by a hundred fairies from the sighs of young lovers, produced at an absurd expense. It is *designed* to attract attention.'

'That is exactly my point. There are others who search for the Grail, the Cup of Regulus. If I am seen here, our quest would be jeopardized.' I tried to remain calm. I was exhausted though, and irritated that I had to pamper this princess to appease the ghost sleeping in my mind. 'Please, I need you to remain here and stay out of my way.'

'Out of your way?' Her mouth, beautiful and full as it was, straightened to a hard line running parallel to her angry eyes. 'How dare you. I shall not be locked in this tower like a prisoner.'

I shut the window, darkened it too. My patience was at its end.

'You are not leaving,' I aid, my own voice rising to match hers. 'You've waited two hundred years to be free of Osrick's curse, you can wait another two days. Otherwise, you'll get us both killed. Do you understand?'

'First,' she pointed a gloved finger at me, 'I am not truly your wife to order thusly. Our marriage may be complete in the eyes of the church, but it has yet to be consummated. Second,' another finger sprang forth, 'no one may order me to do anything, husband, prince, king, or emperor. And third,' she retracted her hand and folded it across her chest, 'I require no one, particularly you, to escort me through that park. I shall go alone.'

She spun about and marched to the door, her silvery train

flowing behind her like a small stream. She looked at it, confused, then demanded, 'Open this.'

There was no handle on it like the doors she was accustomed to in Castle Kenobrac. This door was eight centimeters of solid alloy and would only budge after my DNA pattern registered upon its surface.

'No,' I replied. 'Like I said, you will be staying.'

She hissed through clenched teeth, and for a second looked much like her mother. 'I demand to see your king. If he knew that a princess was being treated with such disrespect he would place you in irons.'

I had had enough of this.

'There is no king,' I told her, 'and I am no prince. There are no more kings, nor queens, nor princesses, my dear Lilian. The last of their kind were buried in that little castle of yours.' This was not exactly the truth. There were plenty of empires ruled by monarchies, but she didn't need to know that. 'You are an antique, a relic I unearthed from the past. Unless you realize that your world has changed, and adapt, I'll have nothing more to do with you. You can find the Cup of Regulus by yourself.'

Her mouth dropped open and her face flushed lavender. She tried to speak, but the words strangled in her throat. She screeched in rage, marched into my bedroom, and slammed it shut.

The psychologist said, *The girl must be treated—*

I ignored him and massaged my temples, tried to regain my focus. The Grail, the Grail first, then I'll decide what to do with her.

Let me take over, Celeste said with a heavy sigh. *I can straighten everything out.*

I ignored her too and sat at my desk, allowed the display to paint the inside of my eyes with images. The mail icon blinked an urgent orange. With a flick of my eye, I opened it. The usual junk: anonymous threats, feeble blackmail attempts, and an announcement of the death of number seventeen, which happily advanced my rank from twenty-second to twenty-first. Also, there were two assignments offered. The first I declined immediately, but my eyes lingered on the second. A junior member of our brotherhood had defected to the Army of Justice and betrayed to them our skills and secrets. Umbra Corp wanted him captured alive. I knew they would put him in the top of the pyramid mausoleum, in a special chamber of horrors reserved for such traitors. He'd be kept alive at great expense and tortured for a hundred years.

It's the least scum like that deserve, remarked Fifty-five.

I agreed, but secretly sympathized with the renegade. I'd leave the Corporation too if I could. Fifty-five and Medea, however, had too much loyalty to the brotherhood; they'd never let me go.

The thought of this doomed man stuck in the back of my mind as I entered the Corp's obituary files. My fate would be infinitely worse if I didn't find the Grail in time.

Numbers and names filled a matrix trailing off into the infinite, over six hundred years of glorious deaths. I'd be lucky if the thief who pilfered Osrick's tomb was in here. If he lived, his files would be sealed and impossible to access. As it was, locating him in all this would be no easy task. I only had the dim memory of Osrick to reconstruct his face, and he could have altered it a dozen times before he died.

Carefully, I selected the appropriate features: a square jaw line, smooth high forehead, small black eyes, and a nose that had been broken a few times. When I had a decent match to Osrick's recollection, I let the desk search the database.

In the reflection of the desk, I saw my own face, slightly blurred. With so many other personae with faces of their own, and me changing my features after every mission, it was impossible to remember what I looked like before I came here.

That was a confusing time, after I killed Abaris and after I absorbed Fifty-five in the sewers. He guided me through that first year, through the classes he had taken, and through the instruction of weapons and martial arts he already knew. I easily advanced, graduated second in my class, and became a full cadet. He never told me, though, that I'd have to kill my classmates to become a ranked assassin. Thrice in that second year, within the first month, I had been targeted. Fifty-five had to do the first two, and the third one, that was self-defense.

Self-defense my ass, Fifty-five said. *You did it better than I could have.*

The first time I was poisoned. An amateur job that left me sick instead of dead. Fifty-five traced which of my classmates bribed the cook and poisoned his shaving kit, the foam and the razor, with a paralyzing substance. His face I recalled in detail – every hair on his head – because Fifty-five made me watch as he severed it.

The second time: a bomb under my mattress in the dormitories. Fifty-five taught me never to sleep there. To return the favor, we tampered with the fellow's cigarettes. A tiny dollop of explosive in one, just enough to remove a few centimeters of flesh, did the trick. He lived for an hour, bleeding to death, plenty of time for Fifty-five to savor his passing.

And the last of my first-semester tests, she came the closest, stabbed me twice before I shot her. Not a clean kill by any measure, but I counted myself lucky to be alive, for she was a master with the blade. From her, I learned the delicate dances of metal, my knife-fighting skills. She was Medea.

All illegal kills, Medea remarked. *Cadets aren't allowed poisons, explosives, and especially not powered weapons.*

So we bent a few rules, Fifty-five replied. *If you'd done the same you'd be alive too.*

A green star flashed into my eyes; the desk had found him. A familiar face and obituary popped up. His name was Cassius, ranked thirty-first. He had one hundred and three assignments to his credit. I scrolled through his dossier and saw no mention of the Bren or the Grail, but I did spot a black mark for suspicion of private contracting – the same thing I had been sent to investigate Omar for. Umbra Corp frowned upon its members taking outside jobs. It usually meant there was a fortune involved, enough to risk the Board of Directors' wrath. There was no mention of who hired him or for what reason. The investigation ended when Cassius died.

Private contract or not, the Corporation always got its fair share. Cassius died without a will and no family was listed in his personal database. The policy in cases like this was to hold all assets and personal effects for a century. If any relatives showed up, they could legally claim his estate, otherwise it became the Corp's property. Funny thing about this policy is that I never heard of any relative demanding their inheritance.

I made a note in my business journal to update my will.

His belongings would be in storage, then, in Golgotha, the black pyramid. If the Grail was anywhere it had to be there. No guarantee it was. It was just as probable that Cassius had sold it off before he died or had tossed the thing in the trash.

Just go there and see, the gambler said.

It's not going to be that easy. Golgotha is protected. There were many who would like nothing more than to get their hands on an assassin's remains, summon his spirit, and torture it for information, or for revenge, or both. I'd need the architectural plans and a schematic of the security system. I'd need Quilp to disable them for me.

Stealing from Umbra Corp filled me with apprehension. The punishment wouldn't be death if I was caught, it would be a trip to the top of that pyramid, the place they reserved for traitors, and a thousand years of torture.

Is that where Cassius ended his career? With a blink, I jumped to the end of the file to examine his death certificate. No, he had been cremated and entombed with all the honors due his rank. The cause of death caught my eye, however; it read: UNKNOWN. PENDING INVESTIGATION.

Still under investigation? After half a century?

I switched to the medical database and located his record. Two days before he had died, Cassius had checked himself into the hospital, complaining of weakness and thirst. They had performed tests for toxins, diseases, parasites, and spirits. A faint energetic residue was the only thing discovered, but nothing malignant. A day before his death, Cassius fell and broke both wrists and his left hip. Six hours later, while in bed, both his legs splintered for no apparent reason. The doctors tried to fuse the bones and failed. He died ten minutes later and, according to the nurse's testimony, in excruciating pain.

I scrolled ahead to the autopsy.

There was nothing to account for this erosion of bone, only a high level of sodium in his blood – thousands of times higher than normal. That explained his thirst. And when they cut him open, there were no bones. There was a picture of the file of Cassius's flat body. It looked as if he had been crushed, his head spread out on the table, deflated, features unrecognizable. I severed contact, blocked the display's beam of light with my hand and suddenly felt thirsty.

Was the Grail cursed? Take it from its rightful owner and die? No. Osrick had no memories of such a thing. Whatever powers the Grail held had to be invoked. So what had happened to Cassius?

My bedroom door opened and the princess strode out.

She was no longer in white but had confiscated a shadow-skin of mine and a pair of self-fitting sensor gloves. The unnaturally dark cloth hung loose on her delicate frame. To compensate she had tucked in the excess and rolled up the cuffs. The only thing that remained of her wedding apparel was the silver belt. Against the black it shone brighter than before, and I noticed for the first time faint runes etched upon it: *Imprisonment, Infinity*, and *Stasis*. Did it contain a guardian like the stone her father had used?

The part of my mind that was Osrick had no reaction; indeed, she seemed a different woman to him. I, however, found her desirable. Her dark hair and midnight-blue skin matched the shadows. She looked like she belonged here.

Be careful, the psychologist said. *This is a classic displacement of emotions: the affections for your former pilot onto this girl.*

She stood in the doorway, arms akimbo, and asked, 'Is this attire appropriate for your world?' The tone of her voice was even. You'd never guess she had been screaming at me.

'Appropriate is not the word,' I answered. 'You have dressed as a native would, as a cadet at this school might. It is perfect.'

She smiled for the second, caught herself, then cooled her expression back to chiseled stone.

I said: 'I'd like to apologize for—'

'There is no need. You were correct. I have no idea of where I am or the danger of our situation. I have no wish to lessen our chances of obtaining the Cup of Regulus, the Grail, as you call it, by attracting the attentions of your enemies.'

A memory of Osrick's surfaces, a kiss two centuries old.

Lilian spoke thusly to me before. We walked arm-in-arm through the rose gardens of Castle Kenobrac. It was there that I stole a kiss from her.

'If I have gone too far, my lady,' I begged her and sunk to one knee, 'I am sorry.'

'There is no need to apologize,' she replied, then cradled my face in her hands and returned the token of my affection thrice, once on each cheek, the last on my lips.

The recollection faded as quickly as it had come.

'You must be starved,' I said. 'Can I offer you something to eat?'

'Yes, please, my husband.' She placed one hand on her stomach. 'Since the ghost of Osrick was vanquished and his curse on the castle dispelled, the need for food has returned in full.'

What did one feed a person who hadn't eaten for two centuries? I summoned the menu to my desk and ordered. Four peanut butter, strawberry jam and banana sandwiches appeared, cut into quarters. This ancient recipe nourished me almost exclusively during my training years, and occasionally I still ate the sticky delicacy, for it was the perfect balance of sugars and carbohydrates and protein.

I returned with two bone china plates, and spread a lace napkin on her lap, and presented the food with a flourish.

She thanked me, examined the sandwich, then asked, 'Are there really no princesses left in the world?'

'You are the last of your kind,' I lied. To tell her the truth might turn her against me. I had confessed I was no prince, and for some reason I wanted her to like me.

'Then I do not expect you to treat me as such.' She picked up a quarter sandwich and took a tiny bite. Her eyes widened and she devoured the rest, taking care not to let the jam ooze onto her gloves.

'I may have found the location of the Cup of Regulus,' I told her.

She wiped her mouth with the corner of the napkin and came to the desk.

'The man who came to the castle before me, the one who stole from Osrick's tomb, he returned here and died. He is in the Corporation's mausoleum. The Cup of Regulus may be there as well.'

Fifty-five said, *What are you going to do with this wife of yours when you find the Grail? Once she knows it's not for her, and that you plan to sell it to Erybus, you're going to have to get rid of her. Better to do it now while she trusts you. It'll be easier.*

'This villain and you belong to the same knightly order?' she inquired.

'It's not exactly an order of knights, but yes, we did belong to the same school.' She frowned at this. I continued before any other questions came, 'His death was most peculiar.'

The princess came close to see what I stared at. I should have warned her the display would sense her presence and project the image of a half-dissected boneless man into her eyes.

She gasped, 'This is wondrous.'

'Wondrous?'

'That you may conjure the images of the past. You must be a mighty sorcerer. I can see the wretch before me as if he were solid, yet my hand passes through this phantasm.'

Curious. She wasn't repulsed by the grisly picture. She was fascinated by it. 'It's not magic,' I explained. 'The desk takes a piece of light and sends it directly into your eye. See?' I moved my hand back and forth between her and the desk. She blinked as the virtual image vanished, then reappeared. 'It is only a machine. You can read the details of his death by concentrating on the icon in the corner of your vision.'

She did so, and got the technique correct the first time.

'The language is foreign to me. This is your native written language?'

'No, it is a code language. The Corporation uses it to keep its records.' To the desk I ordered, 'Decrypt text to standard, please.'

'No,' she said, 'that will not be necessary.' She closed her eyes and moved three fingers on her left hand. A shower of orange sparks appeared above her head. They fell as water might, not singeing a hair, then faded. 'Now I may read your words.'

Of course, she was a sorceress. I had forgotten.

'Oh, this,' she said and laughed. Her laughter was like her mother's, like little bells tinkling. 'Yes, I know of this one's death. It was I who killed him.'

Chapter Eighteen

'You killed him?'

'I could never allow the scoundrel's misdeeds to go unpunished,' she said.

I touched the desk, summoning two mugs of cocoa to wash those sandwiches down. The princess took one, sipped it, paused to watch the steam curling up, then looked at me. 'I thought he would help. He promised me. I thought . . .' She focused again on the steam, embarrassed. 'When I learned of Osrick's defiled grave, I had no choice but to avenge his honor.'

'Osrick's honor? You care about his honor after what he put you and your people through?'

'Before he found the Cup of Regulus, Osrick and I, we were friends. I told him my fears and my ambitions. He risked his life to save me . . . before the madness took him.' She thought about this a moment, then a slight smile crept into the corners of her mouth. 'You are not jealous, I hope. I would have done the same for any of my loyal subjects.'

I wasn't jealous. Osrick delighted in her words, how she cared for him, and how she avenged his honor. Me, I was worried. If she murdered Cassius because he went back on his promise to her, what would she do to me when I sold the Grail?

So ice her now, whispered Fifty-five. *Poison her drink. She'll never know.*

'The thief died two days after he left your world,' I said, directing our conversation back to Cassius. 'How?'

Snakes have the kind of stare she gave me, black and blank, unblinking, and full of unfathomable secrets. She regarded me thusly, and whispered, 'I thought you would have known that. My mother said you are a great wizard, and the magic that brought us here, that was no amateur's incantation. Certainly you know I cursed the villain.'

'Of course, I knew. I only wanted to hear the story of how it happened.'

Her reptilian gaze softened. 'As you wish, my husband.' She took another sip of cocoa, which left a faint ring of chocolate around her lips, then explained. 'When this thief absconded with the Cup of Regulus, he underestimated our magical prowess. He left for us three hairs upon his pillow. These I mixed with foxglove and wove a curse to find him regardless of time and distance.'

I crossed my arms and nodded. I hadn't the faintest idea of how such things worked.

'I know a dozen vexations of this type,' she told me. 'By studying them, I hoped to find a key to my own curse. Alas, it was futile. It can be frustrating to know so many powerful rituals, yet never use the. I could hardly use the dark magics upon my own subjects, so you see, I am grateful, in a way, to this thief. He gave me an opportunity to test my sorcery.'

The first unraveling of any mnemonic was tricky. I knew how she felt; the entire thing might fade from her mind, then she'd have to learn it all over. Years of study lost. Only she didn't lose it, and she had dozens of such curses waiting to be tested.

Fifty-five said, *Listen to me. She's too dangerous to keep around.*

Osrick stirred, uneasy with this suggestion.

Sure, I said to Fifty-five, *we'll let Sir Osrick out of the bottle. That's all we need, his knightly honor getting in the way. We have enough troubles. Let's just keep her happy for one more day.*

It's an unnecessary risk. All our necks are on the line here, junior.

'This particular bewitchment was insidious,' she said. 'It transformed the rogue's bones into salt.'

I swallowed my cocoa too fast, scalding my throat. Bone into salt?

'There is a substance in bone that imparts strength,' she explained, apparently unaware of my surprise. 'It is the same material that forms the stone of our caves.'

Calcium. Calcium in bone, and calcium carbonate, limestone, that's what she meant.

'This substance I changed into a metal, one that has a shiny surface which dulls quickly, and reacts as phosphor does with waterous elements.'

That had to be sodium. With a flick of my eyes, I summoned a periodic chart on the display. Calcium had twenty protons, neutrons, and electrons, while sodium had a matched set of eleven. If she changed one into the other, then where did the extra nine protons, neutrons, and electrons go?

'There is also a gaseous matter that gives life to blood,' she continued, 'even life to fire. This I changed into a gas that has no life, one that causes death.'

Life in blood? A gas? Oxygen. If those nine extra protons and neutrons were fused to the nuclear core of an oxygen atom, then – my eyes counted across the chart and landed on chlorine. She transmuted calcium into sodium and oxygen into chlorine, sodium chloride, salt. No wonder Cassius was thirsty. No wonder his bones broke and dissolved. Where did the princess get that kind of power? Ripping part and fusing atoms, that kind of energy only occurred naturally in stars.

She leaned forward to reestablish her link with the display. 'I assume from the autopsy' – she said *autopsy* slowly and carefully – 'that the villain died in great agony.' She then leaned back and appeared quite proud of herself.

'You are patient to listen to me, my husband, droning on about my trivial magic.'

I opened my mouth to speak, but my body betrayed me and instead I yawned.

'And,' she added, 'you are on the verge of exhaustion. After your battle with the ghost of Osrick, and the magic you released to transport us, you must be sorely taxed. You crave rest.'

How long had it been since I slept? After I escaped Osrick's tomb, I collapsed. Before that, I rested between Delphid and the Bren's world. Eight hours, maybe, in the last fifty. My hands trembled slightly. I'd need stimulants to stay awake and alert.

On the other hand, there was nothing I could do until Quilp arrived. I couldn't steal the architectural plans without his help. And without those plans, I'd never circumvent the Corporation's security. Oh, I might be able to – I was good at that sort of thing – but I only had one shot at this. It had to be perfect.

I yawned again, then said, 'You are wise, Princess Lilian. I shall rest, but only if you promise to wake me when my squire arrives. His name is Quilp.'

'Of course, my husband. And, please, omit my title henceforth. Simply address me as Lily.'

'And call me Germain.'

She smiled and looked lovely to both Osrick and myself.

What was I going to do with her? Fifty-five and Celeste had their usual predictable responses – murder and sex – but somewhere in between those two options had to be a third. 'Perhaps you would like to learn more of this world while I rest?' I asked.

'You said it would be dangerous to venture forth.'

'It is, but there is a way to see this world and remain here. I shall show you how to operate my desk.'

I moved my terminal through three stealth nodes, for which I paid an exorbitant amount to preserve my privacy when I was on Earth. Then I set the desk into a tutorial mode, and had Lily sit with me. First, I showed her how to operate the summoning pad in case she got hungry or thirsty. Then I demonstrated how to connect to other nodes, the virtual arcades and the informa-

tion nets, and how to direct the system with her eyes and mind alone. She never once asked a question. She just sat and absorbed. When I let her loose to explore, she found the Aetherweb node and immediately connected to the universe of information that lay beyond.

Confident that she would be occupied for hours, I left her to wander the infinite computer-generated realms of data.

Three steps I took before she said, 'Germain?'

I turned.

'I would like to thank you for your courtesy. You have risked your life to save mine. I know my mother somehow persuaded you . . . and I would like to apologize.'

I wanted to reassure her, but I kept silent and nodded. I would speak no more lies. The Grail was not for her. She was to remain cursed forever, and it would be my fault. I'd have to live with Osrick's remorse. I'd have to live with my remorse, too.

I shuffled into the bedroom, dimmed the lights, and fell into bed without removing my boots. The sandwiches and warm cocoa settled in my stomach, drew the blood from my brain. I submerged into a dead sleep.

You're taking a nap? Fifty-five asked. *All she needs is a few hairs from you and we'll be a pillar of salt before the sun sets!*

I knew, but I was already gone.

A fish swam through the waters of my dream; a silver ring traced its snout, three diaphanous fins trailed behind it, and stars scattered in its wake. But as dreams tend to do, this one drifted smoothly into another, one that had nothing to do with water or fish or stars. It was my second year at Umbra Corp academy, and I sat in my favorite desk, absent-mindedly doodling a cursive 'X' on my disposable, while I ignored a lecture on galactic politics. Fifty-five had heard this all before.

Professor Finiginn scratched his nose and spoke with no particular enthusiasm: 'The number of empires and conglom-

erates that rule the galaxy continuously fluctuates. It can be said
with confidence, however, that all self-ruling systems are inherently unstable. A mean half-life of three hundred and fifty-two
years is generally accepted as . . .'

It was hideously dull, so I let my eyes wander and found
something better to watch: a girl.

She walked in late, walked with a fluid motion, confident,
precise, controlled, even her hair moved with flourish, not a strand
out of place, long, and the color of chocolate. Her gray cadet's
fatigues had been custom tailored. The uniform fit her curves
snugly. She was the only person I had ever seen who looked good
in one.

Professor Finiginn usually stopped his lecture at this point to
glare at such late-comers, but he merely smiled at her and continued. She settled into a seat two rows in front of me, brushed
half her hair behind one ear, and began recording on her disposable. Every man in the class would have killed to be with her.
If any of the rumors were true, some had. Her name was Medea.

She planned to murder tonight. I knew this because her
memories were mine – some of them, anyway. Portions of her
psyche held an unquenchable rage that burned so brightly even
the psychologist could not discern what smoldered in its core.
Something about her father, he told me. For that, she had my
sympathy.

Medea was with me, recalling the events of that evening. My
sense of self shifted; my thoughts spilled into hers. I wore her
flesh, watched through her eyes, listened through her ears, and
dreamt *her* dream.

All those stares upon her, wishful indulgences, they exerted
a pressure as they probed the length of her body. She welcomed
their looks. It gave her power over the young hormone-driven
boys.

Already this semester she had killed her prerequisite classmates, but she wanted the staff to be thoroughly impressed by

her. She wanted them to fear her. There was one who sat two rows back who deserved her special attention. He was young to be here, but if the stories were true, he had killed twice in as many weeks. She didn't like that kind of competition.

Medea looked back to him once during the lecture, but he quickly averted his eyes and pretended he hadn't seen her. After the lecture, she waited for him to pass, sprung her trap, and said, 'I found your question on kleptocracies intriguing; actually, it's one of the things I've never really understood. Do you think you could explain it to me? Maybe over a drink? I'll buy.'

He almost dropped his disposable. 'Sure,' he blurted.

The first hook was in. All she had to do was play him out, then reel him in. Too bad: in a few years, he'd almost be cute.

It was late, so they walked to a nearby coffeehouse, *The Blue Bean*. Over iced Irish coffees he revealed much of his past to her – too much in exchange for the lies she told him. He told her he was a muse, perhaps to impress her. It was a mistake. Now she *had* to eliminate him. Allowing anyone with his potential to graduate would be disastrous. In two years they'd both be ranked. They'd be competing against one another.

More pleasant conversation, a minor amount of flirting, then she suggested, 'Why don't we go for a walk through the park? The moon is full, and it's too warm to turn in just yet.'

He agreed, gulped down the rest of his drink, then gave her his arm. He had strong muscles, which surprised her because she thought all muses and psychologists were weaklings. She'd have to figure that into her attack.

A stroll through the moonlight, across the lawns wet with dew, then, to throw him off guard, she stopped and drew close to him. He didn't get the hint, so she kissed him. He returned the affection, awkward, but refreshing. This continued until his body was on top of hers in the wet grass. She inched her calf along his thigh, moaned to make him think his embrace interested her. Then, when her boot was within arm's reach, she removed the slender blade concealed there, and stabbed him.

The knife glanced off his fourth rib, entered under it, rather than over it, and pierced the lung instead of his heart. His reactions were excellent. He twisted away fast, got up, and cried, 'What? Why? I thought you—'

She rolled to her feet, laughing, and danced in.

He tried to grab her – got a handful of moonlit razor.

She might have killed him then, but she wanted to play a bit first before finishing him. The boy wheezed and blood bubbled from his lips. His lung had surely collapsed. He held one hand low, closed in a fist, and the other was level with her eyes, open, in a martial arts defense she recognized as the hooded snake. His form was good, calm like an older man's.

She attacked. A high feint, which he fell for, then a slash down scoring a deep cut on his right leg. He was slow. On the reverse stroke, she slashed his left thigh, then backed off.

Now she had the scent of blood. Her adrenaline doubled and pulsed raced! The delicious taste of the kill. A smile crept across her face. She edged in.

The boy took an offensive stance: his knees slightly bent, and his arms spread wide. She led with her free right hand, which he grabbed exactly as she thought he might. She let him catch her. Her left hand followed, sliced the arm that restrained hers. She cut him to the bone.

He let go, fell backwards before she trimmed him again.

She stood over him, her blood pounding and eager to finish. The fire in her mind was a blast furnace, and somewhere from those flames a memory boiled to the surface: a group of men who stood over her and laughed. She hesitated.

The boy on the ground tore open his shirt with his left hand, and with his right he pulled something out that reflected the moonlight, something metallic. A blade? She thought it might prove entertaining to let the lamb have a single tooth. It would make his death that much more pleasurable.

But it was not a blade. He had a forbidden weapon.

A polite cough and a hot fist tore into her torso. 'I cannot lose,' she cried, then collapsed. Stunned, she watched as the boy crawled to her. He had a pistol. How had he snuck it past the controllers? No cadet could have one.

There were tears on his face. He was crying, and she thought that odd.

He whispered, 'Give me your life.'

My mind, and her mind, returned where they belonged, to me, drawn from Medea's consciousness while I absorbed her intellect.

Her dream ended.

The full moon let me see only a smudge on the silvery grass where we embraced one another and erased the dew, where she stabbed me, and where I shot her. Medea lay at my feet, smoldering where the Fifty-five's gun ripped her apart. I knelt and brushed the hair away from her face, to see her one last time. A sapphire triangle sparkled in the moonlight, caught and froze it in the corner of her eye. It was not Medea. It was Virginia who lay dead in the grass.

I awoke with dread heavy in the pit of my stomach. Reliving Medea's murder filled me with guilt, especially the part about Virginia being dead. I bet the psychologist was having a field day analyzing that one.

I rolled out of bed, stretched, then checked my pillow. A few stray hairs lay there. I swept them up and tossed them in the disposal – just in case.

I heard Quilp in the living room. He spoke in rapid-fire, uninterrupted words: 'These memory cells are folded to their rated capacity; what the hell, let's do it again; that might do the trick if they don't pop.'

When I opened the door, I saw my desk disassembled. Its guts covered the Chinese rug: stacks of crystal cubes filled with lightning, display circuits that sputtered rainbows, and liquid memory cores bubbled with phosphorescence. Quilp sat cross-legged in the center of this chaos. His right hand danced across a disposable computer, and his left wiped his runny nose.

The princess stood a safe distance away and watched him.

Out of thin air, Setebos's voice said: 'Memory insufficient.'

'OK,' Quilp said, 'borrow eight blocks from the super-users nest and loop it through here; he'll never trace the loss unless he resets the entire system, and while you're at it, split the two hundred fifty-six tetra-nodes into four sections of sixty-four each; that'll quadruple our throughput rate.'

The components flared and Quilp's shadow stood on every wall. His eyes bulged while he watched the streams of information flow, then he declared, 'We're in.'

'In what?' I asked.

He turned. 'Hey, Germain, nice to see you're done with your beauty rest. What happened back on that asteroid? How in blazes did you get here before us?'

'My question first, if you don't mind.'

'Sure.' He dropped the data pad. 'Setebos is in the Corporation's operating system.'

'That is not entirely accurate,' replied the disembodied voice of Setebos. 'I am partially in the Umbra Corps' archives, partly on the *Grail Angel*, and partly in your desk, O wise and beneficent Master.'

'Your new girl here said you'd need help getting some data. While you slept, I hotwired our AI to the Corp's AI.'

'I apologize,' Lily answered and gingerly stepped through the circuit-littered floor. 'This was my idea. When I explored the Aetherweb, I found that the rogue and his material possessions were indeed within the black pyramid as you said. Details of their location in the tomb, however, were forbidden to my eyes. When I told your squire Quilp of my dilemma, he offered help. He said there was an artificial spirit, Setebos, who might obtain the information. Was it wrong to do this?'

She must have reopened Cassius's files. What else had she found? My personal records? They were encrypted, but she had learned so much so quickly already I wouldn't put anything past her. 'No,' I replied, 'it's fine.'

'How about some thanks or a bonus or something for getting the ship here in one piece?' demanded Quilp. 'I had to outrun three of those Burning Cross ships.'

'I trust you weren't followed.'

'No. Setebos lost them.'

'And how deep, exactly, is Setebos into the Umbra Corp database?'

Setebos answered, 'Master, I have a working dialogue with the host AI. She will allow me access to files of gamma-level security or less.'

'Good. Please retrieve the architectural designs for the Corporation's mausoleum, everything from the electrical systems to the foundation. And while you're at it, try to sweet talk the host AI into giving you a peek at the security systems.'

'Working,' it told me.

'Quilp, get your gear together. We'll be moving fast so take only what you need.'

'Like I haven't been moving fast already? Look, Germain, I came here like you asked. I brought your ship back. I don't even mind filching a little data for you, but I'm not going to get shot at again. I don't care how much you pay me.'

'By all means, stay if you wish. I had hoped for your help with the security in the mausoleum, but if you want to remain behind, that's fine with me.'

He looked at me suspiciously and asked, 'What's the catch?'

'The catch is, Umbra Corp will find out about my visit to Golgotha, especially since I won't have you to circumvent those security annoyances. Lily and I will be fine. We have the *Grail Angel* to escape in. But you, well, they may want to ask you a few questions.'

He let that sink in. The Corp's methods of extracting information were extremely effective. 'I guess I don't have a choice,' he grumbled.

'No. You don't. Setebos?'

'Yes, Master?'

'Put the *Grail Angel* into a high orbit and wait for further instructions.'

'As you wish.'

I made sure Quilp was busy picking through his equipment before I went to the da Vinci, slid it aside, then unscrambled the puzzle lock on the safe behind it. He had got through my front door easily enough; I didn't want him rummaging through my personal things too.

The safe door dissolved silently, leaving a hole in the alloy wall. There were four lockers inside. The first I passed over. It contained a few jewels, hard currency, and transport tickets. The second I pulled out and opened. Within was a velvet hand. On each curled finger was a different ring.

Upon my own index finger I still wore the emerald green band that looked like dark jade to the untrained eye. The core was high explosive and, wrapped about it, a hollow wire filled with nerve toxin. I considered taking another like it, then changed my mind and chose a circle of cold iron, seven four-leaf clovers welded in a ring. The witch I bought it from swore it was good luck. I believed her, for it was slippery with magic, and gave me a shock when I slipped it on. I'd need all the good fortune I could get.

You were never superstitious, remarked the psychologist. *Both the wearing of this so-called lucky charm and your dream, they are symptoms of guilt, indications that you are suppressing the loss of Virginia. It will be easier in the long run if you admit this and validate your emotions.*

From the third locker, I took new batteries for my shadow-skin. Also I removed a set of matte gray boots and matching gloves that let me cling to any surface like a spider.

There was more in the last locker: pistols, sensor webs, robot probes, mines, grenades, virtual image generators, superfluid encapsulated caltrops, and the like. There was a limit, however, to what I could carry. The copper bracelet I wore, and its obscuring mechanisms, would only hide so much from the security systems in Golgotha. I'd bring my blade and a minimal amount of equipment. Any more and I risked being detected.

I sealed the safe, closed my eyes, and mentally prepared myself to absorb the details of the black pyramid. Virginia filtered into my concentration. What happened to her . . . if she still lived . . . along with a generous dollop of guilt. Maybe the psychologist was right, maybe I had to face my feelings, but for now I stuffed the thought of her deep inside me, buried it along with the other deaths I was responsible for.

I needed more time. A theft of this complexity deserved a month of planning. But, like Quilp said, we didn't have much choice.

Lily held a data pad and manipulated the image of a pyramid of obsidian. It spun in the air, and the only two entrances blinked in red: the main entrance to Golgotha's museum, and an access hatch close to the tip. The schematic indicated this latter entrance could only be opened from the inside. We had to start on the bottom and work our way up.

It had five floors, and on the fourth, a white cross flashed.

'This,' Lily told me, 'this is where the knave's earthly possessions are.'

'Setebos,' I said, 'please display the details of the first floor, outline the security circuitry in orange, and show the most likely position of the guards.'

The pyramid sliced into thirds, and the first third cut again in half, revealing the worm-like paths inside, the hallways of the museum on the ground floor, and the security stations. To get to the second level, we'd have to open a vault door, concealed behind a statue of John Wilkes Booth, unguarded but equipped with a

DNA reader that let only authorized personnel in.

'Quilp, can you open it?'

He studied the schematics of the door, traced them with a shaking finger, then asked, 'Setebos, delete the first level and add the second, third, and fourth with the same parameters. This door is connected to the main security system on the fourth level.'

'Warning,' Setebos declared, 'security measures on the fourth and higher levels unavailable. I shall display an extrapolation of the most probable configuration. Confidence level thirty-five percent.'

Three more levels appeared, and I memorized their details. The twisting corridors reminded me of Osrick's final resting place. Ironic that he was here to return the favor and loot Cassius's tomb.

'Yeah, I can open that sucker up,' replied Quilp. 'And by the time you get on the third floor, I'll have the security systems rerouted to monitor the toilets in the museum. Piece of cake. The real problem is on the fourth floor. There's a guard station with plenty of firepower. You're gonna have to find another way around.'

'And here,' Lily said, indicating the obvious path that circumvented the danger. 'This three-way intersection. You must not pass through it.'

'There's nothing there,' Quilp said.

'If you trace these lines,' she said, pointing to the plumbing, 'they form a sorcerous triangle that binds other-worldly creatures to our reality. Enter and you release whatever is held therein.'

'Magic?' Quilp whispered and licked his lips. 'Your Corporation doesn't bother with that stuff, do they?'

I shrugged. They probably did use magical and psychological means to guard the mausoleum, but Quilp didn't need to know.

'Setebos,' I said, 'give me the fifth level.'

'Access denied,' it replied.

'What's on the top level?' Quilp inquired.

'Access denied,' repeated the AI.

'That's where the Corporate traitors are kept,' I told him.

'They're dead?'

'Alive but unable to move. Their pain receptors are stimulated while their hippocampus is probed. They relive all their fears and nightmares, only amplified.'

'Is that what they're gonna do to you if you're caught?' he asked.

'We better go,' I replied, and left his question unanswered. 'Get your equipment, Quilp.'

He scooped his junk together into a shoulder sack, and we left my apartment tower, walked past the dragon fountain that spat water high in the air, and on to the school grounds. Manicured lawns stretched to the horizon, broken only by flagstone paths and an occasional patch of wild lupine and edelweiss.

Lily paused once when we strolled through a rose garden. She smelled an apricot-colored *Charisma*, then caught up with us. She had great restraint. If I were kept underground for two hundred years, I doubt I would be so reserved. I'd be running through the grass in my bare feet.

Through the shade of a giant fig tree we strode and interrupted four cadets studying there. They gave me a bow of respect, then returned to their discussion of Plato's *Republic*. Which of them would graduate? Which would be murdered? Killing to graduate – it was a wasteful policy. Were those Osrick's feelings or mine?

The black pyramid squatted on the edge of campus. The sun was low and made the golden castles on the mountains seem on fire; it made the tomb look all the more dark. We stepped into the shadows, and the temperature dropped. Goose flesh covered my back. The museum door opened automatically, and reminded us only fifteen minutes remained until closing.

We were in. Easy.

Getting out – that was going to be the tricky part.

Chapter Nineteen

Our footsteps made crisp clicks across the granite floor. They echoed off the far wall, past an information obelisk full of neon. The lobby was empty save for a janitor and a tour guide who sat together, sipping mocha la orangés under a painting of Cain strangling his brother Abel. The gift coffee shops were both closed for the evening. The guide gave us a sharp glance, irritated by our late visit, and curtly informed me. 'We close in fifteen minutes.'

I gave him a sheepish smile, shuffled over to the information obelisk, and asked it where the John Wilkes Booth statue was. It illuminated a green path on the floor to show me, then wished us a pleasant visit. Lily, Quilp, and I followed his pistachio-colored trail through three galleries, Mayan sacrificial altars, martian tapestries from the New Kingdoms, their threads still flickering electric blue, and Renaissance oil paintings on loan from the Vatican.

Framed in gold, *Brutus on the Senate Steps* caught my attention. I liked the piece because Brutus looked so determined marching down those steps, while the other senators were bewildered and bemoaning the death of Caesar.

We come not to praise Caesar, Fifty-five said. *We come to dig him up*.

These *objets d'art* glorified murder. It was for the cadets and tourists; it made the Corporation appear civil, clothed what we did with a history and a thin veil of respectability.

There was some truth in the lie. After the First Expansion, when man had explored only a handful of stars, and empires and bureaucracies vied for territory, Umbra Incorporated had been an instrument of revolution. They pruned away rotten officials and corrupt leaders, making way for healthier growth. But when the first supraluminal impeller was successfully tested, and suddenly man could be anywhere he wanted in the galaxy, everything changed. The Second Expansion exploded with wonders unknown, contacts with alien societies, new technology, war, xenophobia, disease – exponential growth and ferocious decay. To survive the transition to a galactic corporate market, the Corporation adopted a policy of eliminating its rivals rather than competing with them. Now, there were no noble sentiments or talk of revolution, only profit.

It never used to bother me, but now with Osrick in my mind, I felt a twang of uneasiness. Murder for profit, murder as a career, murder was all I had left.

I quickened my stride. We had to be out of sight by the time the museum closed. The green line turned through a scalloped archway, into the Hall of Heroes where six hundred statues of the greatest assassins stared at us. I counted one hundred and twelve pairs of cut-throats, then halted at a golden bronze Mata Hari; strings of real pearls, impossibly full lips, and erect nipples beneath her breaded dress. She watched a dapper Mister John Wilkes Booth opposite her. He still wore his opera tuxedo. Behind him were two flags, red and blue stripes, one set parallel, the other crisscrossed, and both spattered with blood, power burns, and white stars. I brushed these curtains aside and perceived the faint outline of a door set flush in the wall.

'Quilp?'

He ran his finger along the door's seam, then stopped and pushed. A tiny optical port popped open. He removed a scanner from his bag. Fifty-five noted an accelerator pistol in there. He fixed a socket over his eye and plugged in.

'I'll be a few seconds,' he whispered. 'The operating system is resisting me.' Without looking, he fished through his bag, removed a capsule, piss-yellow chlorozeneatol, and pressed it to his neck. It hypercompressed, his skin flushed, three heartbeats, then he declared, 'I'm into the security network. Hang on.'

I backed off and let him work, glancing up and down the corridor. Empty.

Lily read the display at the base of Booth's statue. She wandered over to Mata Hari. How long until she figured out what Umbra Corp was? What I did for a living?

Forget her, Fifty-five said. *Imagine this scenario: Quilp sets off the alarms instead of shutting them off. We're caught, and he squeals about our freelance job. Hell, they might even reward the creep for turning us in.*

He's not that smart, I said. *Besides, I can't circumvent all the security. We still need him.*

So steal his mind.

And be stuck with him forever? Inherit his addictions? I'll pass.

A breeze tickled my face, and the flags rippled. I pulled them aside and saw the door, a meter-thick slab of alloy, floating silently open. Quilp sat cross-legged, face rigid with concentration, eyes darting back and forth, disabling the security programs. Two spent ampoules dangled from his neck. He hadn't bothered to remove them.

'Quilp?'

He grunted.

'Give me ten minutes to get rid of any guards, then follow. We'll be leaving from the top. Understand?'

He nodded.

I took one step through the opening, and Lily grabbed my arm with her gloved hand. 'My husband,' she said, 'I wish I had a token to give you, a kiss or a life-protecting charm. Alas, I do not. Please be careful.'

'I will,' I replied, then slipped through and heard her whisper: 'Return to me the Cup of Regulus.'

It was dark inside, so I unwound the ocular enhancer from my memory. The shadows melted and revealed a short hallway that ended with a blank wall. It also revealed a hallway crowded with copies of myself, a dozen other phantom Germains.

It startled me for a second, seeing so many of them. Last time, in the catacombs under Castle Kenobrac, there had been only one duplicate. Why were there so many now?

Some walked forward, cautiously, pistols and blades in hand, others had just entered the hall, and one scaled the walls like a spider. One duplicate stepped upon a faint circular outline in the floor – a flash of light; his skin dissolved, bones eroded, and he vanished. They all flickered then and faded. Had I the time I would have released the ocular enhancer repeatedly to follow these ghosts. Time, however, was one thing I had little of, so I continued.

From the architectural plans, I knew a lift was at the end of this corridor. Quilp had to bring it down and open it. Before I took a step, however, I meticulously searched the floor, ceiling and walls for sensors or booby traps. It looked clean, but I trusted nothing.

I took fourteen steps, and with each one I waited for alarms to sound, an explosion or gunfire. Nothing. The wall dissolved and I stepped into the lift. As the door faded back into place, scanners turned on. The copper band about my wrist tingled. Its obscuring circuits made me appear harmless. If it failed, the elevator would halt, maybe they'd gas me. I wouldn't even get a chance to fight back.

The odds are in our favour, the gambler said. *You'll fill the straight. Don't worry.*

Sweat trickled down the small of my back.

The door opened. No squadron of guards was there to greet me, and no sirens shrieked. I made it to the second floor.

Yellowed light globes twinkled along walls that stretched three storeys tall and were covered with a hundred thousand ivory squares. Within the span of one hand, I covered a five by five patch of the little plaques. Beneath were the atomized remains of the cadets who never graduated, the ones who were *almost* part of our brotherhood. Medea slept here. The squares weren't labeled, though, so there was no telling which one she was.

Setebos's stolen plans indicated there was a sensor web on the ceiling. I looked up and squinted. It was there: fragile threads of optics and vibration detectors that looked like cobwebs. My enhanced sight saw it was dark and inert. Good, Quilp was on the job. A simple stroll down this corridor, another lift, and I'd be on the third level. Perfect.

My elation faded with every step, though. I couldn't help thinking of the thousands of fallen classmates behind those squares. So many to die young and without purpose. The weight of their deaths was a heavy thing to wade through.

Get a grip, junior, Fifty-five hissed. *That Osrick guy must be turning your insides soft.*

At the end of the chamber, I waited for the elevator.

Thirty beats of my heart passed. Quilp should have it down by now. A faint imprint of circuitry outlined the wall. The lift was here. It just wasn't opening. Maybe Quilp got caught. Whatever the reason, I couldn't stand around and wait. Rubbing my hands and shuffling my feet, I primed the surfaces of my gloves and boots. With the touch of a spider, I scaled the wall.

One knock on the roof. A dull solid metal sound returned.

I pulled off my right glove, then squeezed my thumb and pinkie together, and unlocked the first of the seventeen mnemonics of the *Theorem of Malleability*. Memories of harmonic oscillators, secret alchemy symbols, and Fourier transformations welled up from my unconscious. Power collected in my hand. Fog overflowed and drizzled to the floor. Filaments of frost crept down my arm, and my fingers erupted with lavender flames. There was no pain, no burning, only concentration and cold. I touched the ceiling. It was firm, then it softened to slush. I sculpted a hole large enough to wriggle through, then let the metal solidify.

Up through the opening and onto the third level I went.

The Hall of the Honored Dead had a medicated, antiseptic smell. An elevator stood open on my left, and to my right a corridor sloped up. The walls, ceiling, and floor were a polished stainless alloy with spiral patterns buffed upon its surface. This passage corkscrewed counterclockwise, higher into the pyramid.

Set waist-high on the walls were markers of polished blue-gray stone with flecks of black. Behind them lay the remains of my ranked predecessors. Some bore the faces of their owners, other epitaphs in calligraphy, or family crests, a hundred angels that danced upon the head of a pin. Buddha sitting, Jesus crucified, sword-wielding saints, a cluster of stars, the coiled Universe dragon, rosebuds, and infinity runes. The icons of a thousand religions and the words of prize-winning poets reflected off the walls, jumbled in an unrecognizable collage. And for all the glory, no one was here to see it, except me.

Etched onto Cassius's grave was an ancient oak. I didn't recall his file saying he was a religious man, and I didn't recognize this symbol . . . but I had the nagging feeling that I should.

A tree such as this has many mythological representations, the psychologist told me. *Prominent in many religions, it is a symbol of fertility, of—*

Can the lecture, hissed Fifty-five. *We have work to do.*

He was right. I continued, yet that sense of recognition lingered.

The graves abruptly ended – leaving plenty of room for future would-be heroes – and the corridor branched. According to the plans, the left way led to a guard station, beyond which was the vault that held the dead's earthly possessions. The right branch led to the three-way intersection Lily had warned me of.

I went right.

It looked like a normal fork in the hall to me, but Lily claimed the plumbing in the walls was a magic triangle, here to keep an other-worldly creature captive. I squinted. Indeed, there were three faint lines on the floor. In the corner of my vision, I caught a shape: a cloud of clear smoke, luminescent vapors that curled as tentacles might, and disembodied piranha jaws leering. I looked directly at the thing and it vanished.

The guard station might be easier. I turned back.

There was a fat piece of shadow where the wall met the ceiling. With a nimble touch, I crawled up and dissolved into insubstantial black, then inched along upside-down until I hung over the guard station. It was a cube of clear everplastic, and inside a cadet fidgeted, trying to get comfortable in his cramped quarters. In the space his knees should occupy were controls for the artillery mounted outside. The gun swivelled on a universal turret, five barrels whose tips were scorched from use.

I had no desire to see how it worked.

The cube was impenetrable to anything I could do to it, so the cadet inside had to help me. I removed a glove, and got the lucky ring off by first sucking my finger to lubricate it, then scraping it up and over the knuckle with my teeth. I tossed it. The ring bounced once, made a perfect 'ping', hit the wall, rolled, started to spin, wobbled, then came to a stop.

The gun automatically tracked the iron band of four-leafed clovers and the cadet jumped, startled by the sound. He stared a long time at the ring, frowned, then gave a cautious look down the hall, even straight up, but saw nothing. He touched the control panel.

The copper band on my wrist itched as it deflected the scan.

He unholstered his sidearm, then dissolved one side of the cube and stepped out. Very carefully, pausing to listen in between his steps, he went to the ring, then crouched to pick it up.

Medea fell on him.

A stab into his back, rip across, and she cleanly severed his spine. One wipe of my blade on his gray uniform, then she returned my body. I retrieved my lucky ring. Inside the security station, I disabled the sensors and force coils on the stairs ahead.

Don't just stroll up there, warned Fifty-five. *You've memorized the floorplan, but there might be more guards. This has been too easy so far. I don't like it.*

I kept to the shadows and slithered over the stairs so my eyes barely peeked over the top. Ten meters of hallway, then a four-way intersection, take a right, and there was the vault. Simple.

A bubble materialized at the end of the passage and drifted silently toward me. It was wet and black, like a drop of oil suspended in water, and moved fast. If I ran for it, the thing would see me. I dropped down the last two steps, took up a defensive posture, blade in hand, and froze.

This orb floated to the edge of the stairs and paused, just far enough out of reach so I couldn't lunge at it. Within the dark globe were all manner of eyes – organic, mechanical, and three that glowed with a distinct magical presence. It *had* to have seen me, yet it rotated on its axis and went back the way it came. Maybe Quilp had gotten to it.

I wouldn't bet too much on that, whispered the gambler.

I looked over the edge again.

A second orb appeared – this one patrolled the corridor left to right. The two passed one another in the intersection, exchanged a burst of static, then continued. I counted ten seconds, then the one going right to left returned. Twenty seconds more and it came back; so did the first orb. That gave me a twenty second window to get down that hall and inside the vault.

If we're not spotted in the hall, Fifty-five said, *and if the vault is even there, and if you can get in, then it's a great plan; otherwise, I suggest you think of something else.*

If you have a better idea?

Silence.

I thought so. Still, he had a point. How would I get into the vault? It was sure to be locked, and it would take more than twenty seconds to open it. If I had the time, I could use the *Theorem of Malleability*, again, disable the lock, and slip in. But preparing the mental construct would take too long.

Then use it before, Fifty-five suggested, *or while you're running*.

It takes concentration to maintain the enchantment. Even walking is difficult.

Then let me do the running. I'll get us to the vault while you get your magic ready. When we get there, I give you the reins and you do your stuff.

I knew I kept you around for something, I said.

Fifty-five inhaled deeply when I gave him my body, tasting the air, while I submerged in total concentration. I had never unraveled my constructs without the corresponding mnemonics. *The Theorem of Malleability* was simple, however. Imagining I moved my fingers, the memories of a full year of intense study rose to a conscious level: Fermi surfaces, alloy mixtures, and the intricate electron dances that made metals metallic. The energies took shape.

Suddenly, I was back in my body, pulse pounding, heart beating fast, and a pale lavender flame dripping from my right hand.

Don't look back! Fifty-five cried. *Get us in.*

The vault door loomed before me: a complicated puzzle lock, a wheel, and a timer. I thrust my hand into the alloy and groped for the locking mechanism. It was deep, half an arm's length in, a magnetic clamp. I grabbed it and scrambled the perfectly aligned spins of the superconducting magnet. I heard a pop. Two turns of the wheel: I pulled the door open, slipped inside, then quickly shut it.

I held my breath and listened for alarms. Silence.

Too easy, Fifty-five hissed. *Those orbs took longer than they should have. Maybe Quilp got on the ball and shut them off, but I've got a nasty feeling we've been set up.*

*You always have that feeling. We've made it. The Grail has to
be here.* It had to be or we were dead.

Squinting, I examined the vault. There were no footprints save
mine. Ladders on tracks climbed four storeys tall, and plastic
lockers, browns and grays and blacks, appeared like layers of
sediment in a canyon wall. Old light globes drifted along with
motes of dust and cast a dim light. An entire column of those
who died at the rank of thirty-one stretched to the roof.

I turned the shadow-skin off to save the batteries and mounted
a ladder, finding Cassius's name one-third from the top. It was
unlocked. Inside was a box that I removed and brought down.

The box wasn't heavy, and that worried me. The Grail should
weigh more. If it wasn't here, I'd have to start over. I hesitated,
afraid – then ripped the top off. Within was a bundle of letters
wrapped with red ribbon, a bracelet of coral and amber, three
data chips, a curved knife (which Osrick recognized), a jade
Buddha the size of my fist and, at the bottom, a disposable
database – but no Grail.

My heart turned cold. I was dead.

Read those letters and check that database, the gambler said.
Don't fold your hand yet. Wait for the last card.

I examined the database. Color flickered on the display, bled
into one another, and made a smear that was barely decipherable.
It was the legend of a king who failed to find the Grail. Overcome
with despair he took his life. The display stabilized then, a burst
of power from its old batteries, and in the corner a seven-pointed
star appeared, the trademark of the Morning Star Cartel. This was
Erybus's database, identical to the one I had. Cassius worked for
him? Something was wrong.

Like I told you, said Fifty-five.

I kept reading. The suicidal king had a son who took up his
quest, and succeeded where his father failed. To honor his father,
this prince cremated his body and placed his ashes within the
Grail. He believed it would keep his father's soul safe, keep it

from going to Hell. Is that what Cassius thought? That if he—

Behind me, a sigh and a hum of power.

I spun around and saw a man step from the shadows. He held a pistol in his right hand, a blade in his left, and he wore a shadow-skin, but of a quality I had never seen before. It was part of the night, a black so deep it looked like space. His outline was only a blur, but his face was unmistakable. It was Gustave, one of the thirteen Grail competitors.

'Is it there, Twenty-one?' he asked.

Stunned to see the hero in the heart of Golgotha, I replied, 'What?'

'The Grail,' he said and pointed to the box with his blade. 'Is it there?'

How did he get here? And how did he know my rank, only recently advanced?

'I am certain you have many questions,' Gustave said, 'which I shall answer. But please, first, gently remove the contents for me. And slowly. I have no desire to kill you, yet.' A blue light glowed inside his pistol's barrel.

I upended the box and spilled the contents onto the floor.

Gustave looked, then shook his head. 'A pity. Please tell me, then, where the Grail is.'

I laughed. 'It's not here, and I don't know where it is. A dead end for both of us.'

He frowned. 'You are an extremely clever man, Germain. I shall not insult your intelligence by telling you that I can let you live. I do, however, have something of yours to bargain with.'

To the vault door he spoke: 'Escort the lady in.'

Lady? Had he captured the princess?

The door swung open and the twin guardian orbs I had seen before drifted in. Between them limped Virginia.

She looked startled to see me, even more than I was to see her. Both her eyes were blackened, and the sapphires in their corners were cracked. Her uniform was ripped. Perforations marred her skin where microsurgeons worked on her. She was alive! I had to get her back no matter what the cost – even my soul. Osrick welled up within me; my feelings confused him, and made him believe this was his love, the princess, instead of mine. I suppressed the urge to rush Gustave.

'Germain?' She stepped forward.

Gustave stopped her with the tip of his blade and never took his eyes, or the aim of his gun, off me.

Stay cool, urged the gambler. *If he sees you care about her, we'll never be able to bluff.*

Listen to him, said Fifty-five. *If we can stall him long enough, Quilp and Lily will find us. When he blasts them, you can let Medea loose.*

'I apologize for her condition,' Gustave remarked, 'but it was unavoidable. Sister Olivia interrogated your pilot before I had the opportunity to rescue her. You know how her inquisitions can be.'

'You rescued her?' I asked, astonished. 'You were at the Bren world?'

'I'm sorry,' Virginia said and started to cry. 'I ran right into a patrol of those Red Guards. They made me talk. They had drugs, and probes. I let you down.'

Let me down? After what Celeste had me say? It was a wonder she didn't join Sister Olivia's side.

She possesses a borderline psychic talent, the psychologist reminded me, *and a mind full of bioware. She may have guessed that when you spoke to her at the ball, you did so under duress . . . or perhaps she loves you?*

Shut up! You're not making this any easier.

'You followed me?' I said, trying to engage Gustave in conversation, trying to stall until Lily and Quilp arrived. 'No! You followed Olivia! She was there first.'

'Naturally,' Gustave replied. 'Most of the Grail champions either followed you or Sister Olivia, the most knowledgeable among us. Frankly, I was surprised when you tipped your hand at Erybus's gathering.' He paused, arched his brow, and whispered, 'Unless it was a trap. You dispatched E'kerta and Omar with relative ease.' He tilted his head slightly. 'My compliments, and my thanks for thinning the ranks.'

'How did you find me here?' I demanded. 'Following Sister Olivia to the Bren world is one thing, but no one could have tracked the route I took to Earth.'

'Ah,' he said, 'I planned to ask *you* about that. I received a transmission informing me you would come back to Umbra Corp, and that the Grail was here. Normally, I would dismiss such an anonymous message as a ruse, but this person convinced me he spoke the truth by telling me where *I* had been, and where *I* was going next. Curious, don't you think? Quality information like that cannot be ignored. And the price was so slight, even if it was a bit bizarre. Still,' he hesitated and his brows knit together. 'I would like to know who betrayed you, who aided me, and why.'

I knew we should have aced Quilp when we had the chance, Fifty-five spat.

It wasn't him, I said. *But I'm beginning to get an idea of who it was.*

'It is a mystery to me, too,' I lied to Gustave. I had to stall for more time so I added, 'But I can tell you this. We are both being manipulated. We're not the only ones to go on this Grail hunt for Erybus. There have been others before. Erybus hasn't told us the entire truth.'

Gustave nodded in agreement. 'I must admit,' he said, 'that I have also found discrepancies in Erybus's information and his motives.'

'Then help me get to the bottom of this.'

He smiled. It was a wicked smile, no warmth, and for me, not a shred of hope. 'No,' he replied. 'I do not need to know everything to win. And I plan on winning. I plan on killing you, Germain.' He licked his lips, then added, 'However, if you reveal to me all you know, then I shall allow your associates to leave unharmed. Otherwise, they shall perish with you.'

I gave him a blank stare. 'Associates?'

'Quilp, and a very attractive young lady? I hadn't realized your tastes ran to children. They are inside Golgotha. To keep them with us this evening, I took the liberty of placing a legion of my personal guards outside. No one leaves without my blessing.'

'Your men? Here? I think that unlikely.'

'Only because we have not been properly introduced.' He took a short bow without lowering his pistol. 'I am number Eight.'

'Impossible,' I started to say, but the word died in my throat. It *was* possible. How else could he be inside Golgotha waiting for me? He was one of us. He was on the Board of Directors.

'Poor Gustave,' he said, 'the hero of the Colonus wars and beloved of millions, he died so my clients might prosper. The best heroes always seem to meet the worst deaths, don't you agree? I use his appearance occasionally. It might surprise you how many places a hero can go, and how easily suspicion is avoided with a smile and wave of the hand.'

Number Eight, also called the Bleeding Rose, served on the Board of Directors for the last century. His *Decepti Matriculations* were required reading for cadets. No wonder he dispatched Gilish the Green with such ease. Several lifetimes of experience, of subterfuge and combat were his. He outclassed me seven different ways and could kill me at his leisure, even with Medea.

He let us get in, whispered Fifty-five. *I knew it was too easy.*

'Now,' he said, and tightened his finger on the trigger, 'you will tell me everything you know about the Grail. You have little choice, Twenty-one.' He turned the pistol to Virginia and his smile evaporated. 'Tell me immediately. If you again attempt to stall me, then I shall kill this one.'

I couldn't let her die. Not after losing her once already.

'Germain,' she whispered, 'don't let him win.'

Show your cards now and the game is over, the gambler warned me.

Number eight raised his pistol to Virginia's head.

'Wait,' I said, 'I'll tell you. You know the Osrick legend?'

Don't be a fool! Fifty-five cried. *He'll kill us as soon as you tell him.*

'The Bren knight, yes.'

'He was the last one to use the Grail. It was in his tomb.'

'Was?' He lowered the pistol slightly. 'Where is it now?'

'An agent of Umbra Corp stole it fifty years ago. He died before he could sell it. He was then cremated, and if my guess is correct, his ashes were placed inside the holy vessel to protect his soul. If the Grail is anywhere, it will be downstairs, in the Hall of the Honored Dead. His name was Cassius, ranked Thirty-one.'

'Your cooperation is most welcome,' Gustave said and lowered his gun. 'And now, being a man of my word, I must pay for the information that brought me here.'

He aimed his gun at Virginia's stomach and fired.

A silver beam pierced her. Instinctively her hands clutched her abdomen. Her eyes opened wide in shock and locked with mine. Virginia slumped against the wall, then fell to the floor.

For a moment, I stood stunned, unable to believe what had happened. Osrick boiled and overflowed. Both my hands clenched into fists, and I took three steps toward Virginia's murderer, intent on wringing the life from him. The psychologist spoke calming words, but they were burned away by my fury. The woman we loved had twice been taken away. It was too much to bear.

Twin dots of light, laser sights, appeared on my groin and abdomen, originating from his guardian orbs.

Number Eight's grin reappeared, and he said, 'I would not be so bold. My orbs will kill you before you touch a single hair of my person. It is shocking, Twenty-one, that this common woman evokes such a response from you. Where is your professionalism?'

'Fight me,' Osrick and I said together and we unsheathed my blade. 'Give me the satisfaction of ripping your heart out.'

He appeared amused with our suggestion. 'No one has challenged me, at least not openly, for a century. You understand that you have no chance of winning.' He scrutinized me, the way I held my knife, the placement of my feet, my balance. 'Still, you may provide a bit of entertainment. And your death will be just as certain.'

He whispered a command to the orbs, and they retreated to the corners of the vault to watch. He then locked his pistol, set it down, and wiped his thumb across the edge of his curved knife. A brilliant blue sheen materialized on his golden blade.

That's Amyocyn, Fifty-five whispered. *Don't get any on you. It's a blood toxin that makes you itch until it drives you crazy.*

Medea then spoke: *This is my game, Germain. I'll take over now.*

Rationally, Osrick and I knew she was better suited for the task, but we wanted revenge for Virginia. We wanted number Eight's blood on our hands. Virginia was the only one since Abaris that I – what? That I loved? Yes. Osrick mirrored my thoughts, grieving his own lost love: Prince Lily.

You'll still have his blood on your hands, Medea impatiently explained. She shoved me deep into the recesses of my consciousness and took control. *I'll just be the one doing the killing.*

Let her go, Fifty-five urged. *Do like we did with the vault door, junior. Leave the physical stuff to Medea, and get your borrowing ritual ready. It's the only way we'll win against him.*

I had no choice. This was Medea's area of expertise. She would hold my body until this was done – one way or the other. I watched her, but it was an abstraction, a ballet that I saw from the balcony, while my mind concerned itself with the borrowing ritual. Without access to my hands, however, it was too difficult to think my way through all the mnemonics. I found myself distracted, wanting to watch their dance of knives.

Number Eight's grin vanished. He circled her. His eyes stared at Medea's center.

She, in turn, circled him, and kept my body low, my muscles tense.

A quick slash! Medea barely deflected his blade with mine.

She feinted low and to his right, brought my knife up inside his guard. He easily caught my blade with his. He took a step back, though; his style wasn't perfect. Medea should have pressed the attack when he retreated, but hesitated. Number Eight held something in his other hand, something she couldn't quite see.

A lunge at my chest. Medea was the one who had to back up now. The blue edge of his knife caught my elbow and broke the skin – a touch of fire!

This left him wide open. She could impale him with a clean thrust to his heart, but his left arm came up . . . holding nothing. Medea jumped back and nearly lost her balance.

Whatever he held in his other hand cut my cheek. Blood covered it; an invisible blade made visible, then, with a flick and a quick wipe on his thigh, it vanished again.

I tried to concentrate on the ritual, on the psychological fundamentals of intelligent thought, and on the *Seven Scrolls of Telepathic Construction*. The mental construct coalesced. A trickle of power flowed, then collapsed. I had forgotten a step.

He's playing with us, said Fifty-five. *He knows we're no match for him.*

Another exchange between the two, feint, thrust, riposte, counter, but I didn't watch. I had to focus, unlock the mnemonics with my mind alone. And all this time, the blood poison worked on my arm, itching, an acid that chewed the nerves. It was maddening to me, and I was physically disconnected. How did Medea stand it?

Her thoughts were calm. She expected to lose, yet it didn't bother her. A memory surfaced. I should have ignored it, continued with the ritual, but I could not. She remembered her father teaching her to fight with knife, with stick, and hand-to-hand. She loved him, she hated him, and she respected his skill. He told her that any opponent, even one more skilled or better armed than she, could be vanquished – if she was willing to exchange her life for his.

Medea shifted from a side stance to face number Eight.

He lunged.

She knew it was a feint, for his other blade, the invisible one, came from below to take her in the stomach. Rather than dodge, she stepped into the thrust.

The unseen knife struck my thigh, pierced the muscle, and broke the skin on the other side. Medea dropped my knife and grappled with number Eight, trying to wrench his curved blade away. She cut my hands to ribbons. They burned with poison, but she wouldn't let go.

The blade fell from his grasp.

Number Eight left the invisible dagger in my flesh, reversed his stance and elbowed her in the gut. He dropped to one knee and tried to throw her.

Medea knew this trick, however, and planted my knee in his spine.

They fell together, him on the bottom, Medea on top, my hands holding his, and both our arms pinned under the combined weight of our bodies.

I almost had it. One last mnemonic to unravel, then the ritual was done.

Number Eight rose, pushed us both up with one hand. He was stronger than three men should be. He laughed.

It only made Medea mad. She cried, 'I cannot lose!'

She thumbed my emerald ring, released the safety for its proximity fuse, then caressed the stomach of number Eight once – and set it off.

Medea abandoned my body.

I barely heard the explosion. I sure as Hell felt it.

A flash whitewashed the corners of the vault, glistened in every watching eye of the floating orbs, and made the jade Buddha from Cassius's locker glow an iridescent green. The pressure blasted through my finger tips and slammed into my body. It left my teeth buzzing.

Darkness and nothing for a time, then an itch in my right arm. That was the blood toxin reminding me I lived. The shock should have traveled through my body and made jelly of my brain. Why that didn't happen I cannot say. Maybe it was the angle of my arm, maybe the blast got muffled by number Eight's body in between, or maybe I just got lucky.

Number Eight was not lucky.

He was under me, all wet; his rib bones tore into my skin, exploded outward from the blast. I rolled off his corpse and saw the light globes in the vault wink off one by one.

Shadows gathered about number Eight, and the darkness took a form, a barbed tail and an evil Cheshire smile. I heard it drink from his fluids, and watched it grow and solidify – black smooth baby skin and slender bat wings. It was the devil called Nefarious come to collect on Erybus's contract.

It lapped up the rest of number Eight's soul, then yawned, stretched its wings and filled the vault. It sauntered into the corner, sat on its haunches, and observed me with charcoal eyes. Its clawed hand clasped its elbow and it pointed to me.

I looked at my arm and saw it was gone from the elbow down, blood pounding out the artery to the rhythm of my heart. Strange, it didn't hurt at all. It was numb like the rest of my body.

Two red points of light then appeared on my chest, the aiming lasers of number Eight's guardian orbs.

'Damn,' I whispered in a shaky voice.

Nefarious grinned at my pronouncement and whispered back, 'Precisely.'

Chapter Twenty

Number Eight's guardian orbs exchanged a burst of static and a laser sight shifted from my groin to my neck. I had no strength to move; I could only watch. There was too much blood gone, and my arm a ragged stump. Hadn't this happened before? No, that was Osrick's arm, chewed off by a dragon.

'Two ducks at the same time,' the devil, Nefarious, gleefully remarked. 'Both number Eight and you. No, three! Is that Sir Osrick with you?'

Both laser sights faded.

Behind the orbs a haze filled the hall, tendrils of mist that moved as water might. It rushed into the vault, and lapped at their black plastic shells.

'What is this?' Nefarious asked.

The orbs' laser sights flickered through this cloud to locate something solid to lock onto, but nothing was there. They fired anyway. Two beams of silver fire scorched the wall.

Wisps of fog gathered into long fingers and reached out to caress both guardian orbs. The orbs drifted backwards, but hands formed in the mist, surrounded them, and took hold. The orbs' dozen eyes searched frantically for a way out of this web. A desperate continuous stream of static poured between them.

The fingers closed, and the orbs rattled about, then stopped, fixed in mid-air. Giant hands pulled apart, paused, then smashed the two together. Black shells cracked. The yolks of a dozen eyes spilled.

The cloud drifted toward me.

Fingers melted and ethereal bodies appeared, male, female, and hermaphroditic, with leering faces and parts obscene. They held hands, made a ring around me, danced and sang with voices that sounded like laughter and falling rain. One kissed me with frosty lips. Blisters boiled upon my skin.

'Desist!' cried a woman. 'Not him.' Lily stepped into the vault, and the cloud withdrew. It clung about her legs like a child might hold onto its mother. Runes on her belt glowed pale silver. The fog coalesced there and vanished.

Nefarious hissed smoke rings out his nose, and thundered, 'Mortal, your luck defies logic!'

'Hurry, squire Quilp,' Lily said sternly. 'Your master is injured.'

Quilp followed her in, looking scared and a little pissed off. He saw the shattered globes, a jumble of mechanical and organic eyes, exposed and staring, and examined the construct. Neither he nor Lily took note of the devil.

The princess cleared her throat.

Quilp smiled apologetically to her and left the orbs. He stepped through the remains of number Eight to get to me.

'See to his wounds,' she commanded.

He gritted his teeth and got a blue shield from his bag. 'We gotta have a talk about this new girl of yours, buddy,' he whispered to me and attached the robot doctor to my shoulder. 'You never said she used *magic*.'

The robot's probes snaked into my arm. Flashes of heat cauterized the blood vessels; fluids pumped in to replace those lost.

'This isn't doing the trick,' Quilp told her and chewed a nail.

'Think of a way to save your lord, craven, and soon,' she coolly replied. 'Or I shall change you into a more unpleasant form than the last. A fish, mayhap, so I can watch you suffocate.'

'OK, OK, I've got an idea.' He checked the blue shield's display, then said to me, 'You have a nerve toxin and some sorta plant poison in you, along with a couple hundred metal splinters, mostly in what's left of your arm. All that junk is working its way deeper inside of you. I'm gonna have to take it off. Do you understand?'

Take it off? What did that mean? It took too much effort to fathom. A heaviness filled my chest, making it hard to breathe. It would be easy to let go, sink into sleep . . . forget the Grail, let someone else get it, forget my poor lovely Virginia, the sapphires in the corners of her eyes shattered, tiny broken frozen tears, ignore Lily and her curse, and just doze.

Nefarious slithered over to me. He whispered in my ear, tickling me with his forked tongue. 'That's it. Let it all go. The girl you loved is dead. There's nothing left here for you. Come with me. We need men of your caliber in our organization. With your record, your ambition, you could have *my* job in a century or two. Think about it.'

'Go to Hell,' I croaked.

'A fine way to speak to the guy who's saving your butt,' Quilp muttered.

Lily sat by my side and took my good hand. 'Stay awake my husband. I fear if you sleep, it shall be forever.'

'She's right,' Quilp said. 'You gotta stay up.' To the blue shield he spoke: 'Override safety protocol and amputate the patient's left limb at the shoulder. Synchronize cardiac rhythm, and set filter for phosphofluoridates and aromatic diols. Boost the immune system while you're at it, too.'

A tentacle moved inside me, a scrape across the bone in my upper arm. It wrapped around that bone, coiled several times – then pulled free in a single draw. A jolt of pain, three electric shocks. Blackness.

Awareness returned.

Nefarious shrank. He became less substance and more shadow. With his tail whipping back and forth, he held up his wrist, pointed to the Rolex there, and hissed, 'This changes nothing, mortal. Soon you are mine!'

I blinked and only the shadows remained.

The blue shield on my stump twinkled with red warning lights. One turned amber, then another, and one flashed green. I realized finally that my arm was gone. I got dizzy and wanted to throw up. My stomach was empty.

'I think he'll make it,' Quilp whispered to Lily. 'He's gonna have to get to a hospital and soon. One robot doctor can only fix so much.'

'Help me up,' I said weakly.

'Hey, buddy, not so fast. You're one arm short.'

I looked again at my arm. It wasn't there.

Don't sweat it, Fifty-five said. *We'll have it replaced with a mech or an organic.*

I wanted to flex, but there was nothing to move. Osrick had lost his arm, I remembered, and if he survived without one, then so could I. Lances of pain that shot up an arm that wasn't there. Next to me lay my enchanted blade. I grabbed it with my right hand, thankful for something familiar to hold on to.

'We have to go,' I said. 'The man I killed has guards outside Golgotha. They will wonder where he is.'

'We have seen his knights,' Lily said as she helped me sit up.

'Where?'

'They entered your Hall of Heroes. That was when squire Quilp experienced a change of heart.' Lily leaned closer to me and whispered, 'The knave wanted to leave me. He wanted to surrender to our enemies without a struggle. So, in his mind, I made him believe that I transformed him into a Sussex hen. It was a proper reflection of his cowardly nature.'

I asked Quilp, 'How was life as a chicken?'

'Go to blazes!' he spat through clenched teeth.

Lily glared at him with eyes that could have been two smoldering blue coals, and said, 'I returned to him his original shape so he could lock the door behind us. We then came with all haste, only pausing to release and bind the creature within the sorcerous triangle.'

'That was the mist I saw?'

She nodded, then looked warily at Virginia and inquired, 'And that is your captain there, is it not, my husband? How did she come to this place?'

Virginia's body lay twisted in the corner, her hands still clutching her abdomen. There was the distinct smell of charred meat. My insides turned cold. 'Quilp,' I said, 'is there anything you can do for her?'

He shrugged. 'Already took a look. Sorry, she's dead.'

Dead. I lost her twice, once on the Bren world, and again here.

'The army that laid siege to Castle Kenobrac captured her,' I explained to Lily. 'The man that I killed there, he rescued Virginia to learn what she knew of the Grail. She knew nothing. Her death was pointless.'

'Servants must often surrender their lives for their masters,' Lily said. 'Her death in your service does you great honor.'

Honor and duty would not bring Virginia back.

Accept the emotions you had for your pilot, the psychologist said. *Doing so will hasten the grieving process, and heal your spirit.*

Forget your feelings, hissed Fifty-five. *We've got work to do. Remember our friend with the black wings? The clock is ticking, junior.*

I glanced to my left wrist, to check the time. It was gone – both wrist and watch.

Quilp offered me his hand, and said, 'Can we get out of here? Or are we gonna sit and wait for that legion to come up for tea?'

I let him pull me up. My head split in two, shadows clouded my eyes, and I blacked out again for a moment. This dizziness lapsed, however, and I noticed the blue shield urgently flashed a warning: my blood pressure was dangerously low.

'The Cup of Regulus,' Lily asked. 'It is not here?'

'No, but I believe it is close,' I said. 'We must go back the way we came. The thief who stole it from Osrick buried himself in it. But first, Quilp, I'll take whatever stimulants you have left.'

He shook his head. 'I'm tapped.'

'You're a liar. Give me your bag.'

'Hey, I don't have to stand for this kind of treatment.'

Lily snatched his bag and handed it to me. Inside was a hit of Shazam hidden in the lining.

'That was for an emergency,' he protested.

I examined the bulb, and saw within the sparkling lightning bolt that gave the drug its name, then pressed it to my neck. A snap and fire blossomed across my skin. Blood rushed and thunder rumbled through my mind. When I inhaled, icy needles pricked my lungs, and my heart quivered. The blue shield squealed a warning as my blood pressure jumped.

'We're going back to level three,' I said, 'back to the dead,' then headed for the vault door. Virginia lay in my path. That stopped me cold. I knelt down, and closed her eyes with my hand. She trusted me and I betrayed her. She offered me her love and Celeste threw it back into her face. And still she tried to resist Sister Olivia's inquisition.

I stood and left her . . . again.

We retraced my route down the corridor the orbs patrolled, then past the guard station. The cadet's body wasn't there.

'What happened to the—'

'The vaporous apparition was starved by its imprisonment,' Lily explained. 'I could not refuse it.'

'Oh.' It bothered me that the cadet wouldn't get a proper burial. He died at his post, and no matter how poorly he did his job, he deserved better.

Lily placed her arm around my waist for support and we descended the spiral Hall of the Honored Dead. Quilp walked behind us, which made me uneasy.

The psychologist said, *Quilp has a paranoia of magic originating from his obsession with technology. Merely knowing the princess is a sorceress has aberrated his normal nervousness. And having been the unwilling subject of such magic, he may be on the edge of a breakdown. He requires careful observation.*

I halted at Cassius's crypt.

'This one?' Quilp asked and pointed to the plaque with Elvis Presley etched upon it.

'No,' I said. 'The one with the tree.' I slipped my knife between the plate and the wall. Again, I knew I had seen this tree before. It was from a dream or a vision – Necatane's vision! This was the tree Lily had led me to. In the top branches there should be an eagle clutching the Grail in its talons. It wasn't here, and neither were the two snakes that had bit me.

'What are we waiting for?' Quilp asked and shifted nervously.

I worked my enchanted blade back and forth in the seam where the square of adamant met the wall. The gravestone loosened a bit, but it wouldn't come free. Something on the *inside* held it fast.

'Stand back,' Quilp said and pulled a pistol from his bag. 'I'll blast it open.'

'Don't,' I said. 'You'll damage whatever is inside. Use your hands.'

Quilp reluctantly put the weapon away and gave the plaque a tug. It didn't move. He got a better grip with both hands and pulled again. Air sucked into the evacuated chamber, and the stone cover fell off. White cubic crystals grew inside.

I touched one, then tasted it. Salt. Proof that Lily had not lied. She had killed him.

Reaching in, my arm went numb, painfully asleep; the magic was strong. Quilp must have sensed it too, because he took two steps back. I touched more salt crystals, then in the back something larger, cold and smooth stone. I pulled it out.

No choir of angels sang, and no heavenly light dazzled my eyes. It was only a chalice of stone, slightly heavier than I thought a cup this size ought to be and completely encrusted with salt, but otherwise ordinary. Inside was Cassius: fine white ash.

'This is what I risked my butt for?' Quilp cried. 'A Margarita glass? You gotta be kidding. I thought it would be covered with diamonds at least.'

I upended it.

The ashes spilled out with an almost human sigh. If Cassius's soul had been saved from damnation by resting in the vessel – it was saved no longer.

I rubbed some of the crystals off and found a wondrous blue marble: bands and whirls, aqua, azure, and indigo. Along the sides were veins of silver that looked like the residue of a sweet wine, with legs that trickled into the center. The stem was thick, and it felt comfortable in my grasp. It resonated with power, vibrated with magic.

'That is the Cup of Regulus,' Lily declared. 'The cup Osrick brought to me.' Her eyes were wide and reflected the colors of the Grail stone.

We've won! the gambler cried.

Not quite, I said. *We still have to get back to Golden City.*

You're forgetting one detail, Fifty-five remarked.

What's that?

Your princess. She thinks the Grail is hers to drink from. It isn't. One sip and the deal is off, according to Erybus's contract. You better lie to her, and quick. And remember, junior, the best lie is the truth twisted.

'Lily,' I said, 'before you drink from the Grail, I think it would be wise to understand its powers first.'

'What do you mean?' Her eyes narrowed slightly.

'I know one who is an expert in such magics and curses.' Which was true. Erybus had studied the Grail for centuries. 'He can tell us how to properly dispel your malady.' Again true. Erybus probably could tell me – if I asked.

Lily considered.

'Otherwise, we might misuse its power.'

She is uncertain, the psychologist said. *You touched a nerve, however. I sense she fears the Grail's power, fears what it did to Osrick, how it warped him into something inhuman. You have deceived her, but not indefinitely. She is too clever.*

Lily nodded. 'You are wise, my husband, and kind to think of my welfare first. I shall allow this expert to examine the cup.'

I handed her the Grail, which she accepted with both arms, cradling it like a newborn.

Then, rubbing the power tattoo on my hand, I waited for Setebos to respond to my signal. The imprinted biopolymer rose was past full bloom. Its outer petals were missing, and those that still clung to the stem were withered. Multiple voices spoke from the spray-on electronics. I listened carefully. Germains talked, mixed in with Setebos, a few Quilps and, I swear, I heard Virginia too. The signal popped twice, loud, then a burst of static, and a single Setebos spoke: 'Most gracious master, what orders do you have for me?'

'Scramble and secure this channel. What was all that distortion?'

'Channel secured,' Setebos replied. 'The distortion originated from a multiplexed signal. Doppler shifted, on a similar frequency as ours. It is gone now, my Master.'

'Drop out of orbit,' I told him. 'Get over the black pyramid. The campus defense systems may take a shot at you, but it is unavoidable. We will rendezvous with you there as soon as possible.'

'I see the structure,' Setebos replied. 'It shall be as you wish.'

I balled my hand into a fist and closed the channel.

'Assuming he makes it ground side,' Quilp protested, 'what makes you think those mercenaries won't blow the *Grail Angel* to smithereens?'

'They won't shoot anything until they find out what happened to their boss. As far as I know, his orders were to keep you two inside while he dealt with me.'

'I'll go ahead,' Quilp said, glancing at Lily once, then back to me, 'and get the lift down from the top floor. It'll save us time.'

'Good idea. Go.'

Quilp backed away from Lily, turned and ran.

'I do not trust that one,' Lily remarked.

'Nor do I, but we need him to escape. We shall soon be rid of him.'

We climbed the sloped corridor at a much slower rate than Quilp did. We had to, because with every step my pulse pounded harder, the ache behind my eyes grew worse, and Quilp's last hit of Shazam was doing less and less for me. I rested at the guard station, and again at the four-way intersection.

Quilp joined us there, sprinting down the left passage. 'Come on,' he said, out of breath. 'The lift is ready.'

To my right was the vault where Virginia lay. 'I need you to get her,' I said to him.

'You mean the pilot?' Quilp asked. 'I told you she's cooked. Leave her.'

'We cannot,' I insisted. 'If she is found, she can be traced to me. We were seen together at Golden City, and possibly on Needles, which means she can be linked to you, too. I don't think you want Umbra Corp's investigators knocking on your door in the future.'

Quilp shook his head, and muttered, 'OK, I'll get her. I suppose you won't be giving me a hand either?'

There was another reason, but I kept this to myself, shielded it even from the thoughts of my other personae. I abandoned her on the Bren world. I could not leave her again.

He dragged her body out into the hall, then onto the lift.

We were silent on the ride up. Quilp stayed as far away from Lily as he could in the elevator. Virginia's body lay face down, smelling of singed hair and smoke. I tried not to look at her, but couldn't stop thinking of how number Eight shot her. It was to pay for his information, he said. Who tipped him off? And why had they wanted Virginia killed?

We stopped and the elevator door stayed closed.

'Damn,' Quilp spat. He plugged into the optical port on the control panel. A few uncomfortable moments, then he said, 'They're on to us. My bypass is gone. It's the *Grail Angel*. They sent three fighters after her, and Setebos blased them. All Hell is breaking loose up there. As far as I can tell the ship is still in one piece.'

'Get us to the top,' I said.

'Working on it.' Quilp reached into his pocket and removed two ampoules.

'I thought you said you were tapped?'

He pressed them to his neck. 'I miscounted.' He stopped breathing.

The door dissolved.

Frigid air instantly filled the car. Teeth of ice hung from the inside tip of the pyramid. Thirty rows of hibernation cocoons sat blanketed in frost, and in the center a control station. Blue light rods flickered to life on the sloped walls and made the room seem even colder.

Quilp, with the optical link still dangling from his eyes, dragged Virginia to the controls and unceremoniously dumped her in a heap. He plugged in again.

When I stepped into the room, tiny displays on the frozen coffins vied for my attention, projecting little nightmares into my vision. These were the traitor's worst fears, twisted and blown out of proportion, replayed in an interactive virtual torture chamber. An army of insects with human heads devoured one helpless woman; parents of gigantic stature grabbed one man, then shook him apart like a rag doll; there were several impossible sexual scenarios (Celeste wanted to take a closer look). I kept moving.

Lily averted her eyes and looked at the floor.

What crimes did these people commit to merit this? Had they all betrayed the Corporation? Or had some of them just wanted to get out? No one left; I knew that. Examples were made of such criminals to scare the rest of us with thoughts of freedom. It worked.

The Osrick parts of me knew it was wrong. Better to die with a blade in your hand than this.

Quilp asked, 'You want me to open the cargo hatch?'

'Not yet,' I said. 'I want you to do something else first.'

'What now?'

'We're going to free them.'

Quilp laughed, but it died in his throat. 'You're serious,' he said. 'These are the worst of the worst, the psychokillers, the ones even Umbra Corp doesn't want! There's no way I'm gonna let them loose.'

'You try my patience, Quilp. When we release them, the small army outside Golgotha will have other things to worry about than the three of us. Now do it.'

'Or what?' he demanded.

'Or knave,' Lily said, 'I shall summon a spirit who will do to you things that in comparison make this,' she gestured to the frozen coffins, 'seem pleasant.'

He glared at her, then glanced at his equipment bag, then back at me. 'OK,' he whispered, 'have it your way. I just want to be long gone before they thaw out.' He closed his one eye and got to work.

To my tattoo I spoke: 'Setebos?'

A long burst of static, and I barely heard his answer, 'I am here, Master, above the pyramid, as you requested. One mass-folding generator is destroyed, and the magic circle only functions at thirty-two per cent of rated capacity. Additionally, I perceive four new targets descending from a polar orbit. Might I suggest you come aboard so we may leave?'

'Stand by,' I told him. I threw my weight against the ice-encrusted release hatch, and a piece of the roof dissolved. Icicles fell and shattered like glass. Gray dusk filtered in. A shadow crossed the opening, then the underside of the *Grail Angel* appeared. Parts of her smooth hull were melted.

'Setebos, maintain your position, but direct a mass-folding field inside this chamber.'

'I shall attempt it,' Setebos replied. 'May I ask why?'

'I am hurt and unable to climb. Within a mass-folding field, however, I'll be light enough to float up.'

'I understand, wise Master. Subroutine complied for new field parameters. I shall attempt to raise Captain Virginia. She appears injured, too.'

Virginia's body lifted off the floor, and drifted up and out through the ceiling. 'Madam Virginia successfully recovered,' Setebos told me. 'Please step directly under me.' The signal faded to static, and the last petals of the bipolymer rose fell from my hand, dry and blood red.

I turned to Quilp and told him, 'Get those bodies out of hibernation.'

'Hey,' he said, 'you can't rush these things. Raise the temperature too fast, and you'll have a bunch of rotting meat. I'm slaving the units together, so I only have to do this once. Mental playbacks terminated.'

Their personal Hells extinguished from the displays.

'Lily, you're next,' I said. 'I want you on the ship. It will be safer.'

'Please hurry, Germain,' she replied. She then stepped into the mass-folding field and gently floated up like a bubble in a glass of champagne.

'Core temperatures rising,' Quilp muttered to himself, 'and fluorinated hydrocarbons replaced with synthetic blood. They should be coming around any second.' He keyed the terminal and the cocoons melted. Fog poured from the hibernation chambers and filled the top of the room with clouds. 'I'm done,' he said, 'and I'm out of here.' He sprinted to the open hatch, leapt, and shot out of the chamber.

I double-checked his programming, then went beneath the hole in the roof to leave.

OK, junior, said Fifty-five. *Now that we're alone, we're going to stick those traitors back in the deep freeze where they belong.*

Before I even answered, he grabbed my body.

I fought him.

Normally, I wouldn't have even tried. The Corporation was Fifty-five's area of expertise. I knew he would win in a contest of wills, but I had to attempt it. These people paid long ago for their crimes – if there were any crimes committed. Osrick joined me. With his strength we stuffed Fifty-five back into his hole.

'Not this time,' I said. 'Not ever again.'

They will find out! he screamed. *Our career will be ruined. I'm trying to look out for your best interests. Listen to reason.*

I ignored him and stepped into the folding field. Bubbles gurgled inside my body and the room divided once, blurred, and fractured a million times before my sight cleared.

Men and women stirred from their coffins. One sat up and fixed me with his green eyes, while I rose into the air, and into the bank of clouds. He was naked, well-muscled, and had a red triangle of a beard. 'Who are you?' he asked. 'Is this a trick? Another false hope to torment us?'

'No,' I answered. 'You are in the Golgotha and surrounded by enemies. You will have to fight your way out, and maybe then just die.'

'Better to die today, facing the ones I hate, than live another second in their programmed Hell.'

I pulled my lucky ring off with my teeth and tossed it to him. 'Take this, it will bring you good luck. You'll need it.'

He picked it up and slid it on. 'We are free!' he declared to the others who also stirred and climbed out of their tombs. He then asked me, 'Your name, kind and gentle sir, so if I die today, I can sing your praise to the angels above.'

'Germain,' I told him.

With my arm upraised, I caught the edge of the hole and vanished through the clouds. Outside, the sun had just set and the air held a charge of gold and green. I climbed into the *Grail Angel* and left Umbra Incorporated forever.

Chapter Twenty-one

We chased the sunset and caught it; the blue sky dissolved to black. Four Typhoon-class fighters, sleek as sharks, pursued. They were probably number Eight's men. Good. Normally, a fleet of ships protected the Corporation. Number Eight must have arranged this breach in security so *he* could leave with the Grail unobserved.

The lead fighter shot us.

Charged particles danced across our hull and the runes of the magic circle flared white, absorbing the energy. Setebos informed us: 'Magic circle operating at three per cent of rated capacity.'

'Use the moon for cover,' I ordered.

The *Grail Angel* altered trajectory and cloaked herself in the shadow of the moon. 'Reintegration of second mass-folding established,' said Setebos. 'What course?'

'Golden City.'

On the displays our wave function folded, asymmetric yet stable, and the mass of the ship shuffled into higher dimensions, making us waver on the edge of existence. The moon vanished, as did the fighters. The sun grew small until it looked like any other star in the heavens.

'Four hours, twenty-six minutes relative time to destination,' Setebos announced. 'Four days, nine hours non-relative.'

Quilp sighed, slumped in the copilot's chair, and muttered, 'I hope that's the last time I get shot at today.'

'Where did you put Virginia?' Her body wasn't on the bridge.

'You were so hot to bring her with us,' he said, 'I dumped her on *your* bed.'

'Check the ship's systems, Quilp. And try to get the third mass-folding generator to work. We may need it.'

'Sure.' He leaned back. 'I got it covered.'

Lily sat in the navigator's seat and examined the Grail. She rubbed the rest of the salt off, then held it up. The light made the stone translucent, made it glow like a huge sapphire.

'Lily, would you mind helping me?'

'Of course, Germain. How thoughtless of me.' She set the Grail down, wrapped one arm around my waist and guided me to my quarters.

What are they thinking? I asked the psychologist.

With Quilp it is difficult to say. The stimulants make his neurochemistry difficult to read. He is ill at ease with Lily, and with such a powerful magical artifact so close, to be honest, I cannot predict his actions.

The Princess, on the other hand, is pleased. She believes you intend to give the Grail to her. However, she has a well-trained mind, and if she wanted to, I believe she could shield her true intentions.

Virginia lay face down under the leering skull and crossbones headboard. It pained me to see her in this undignified heap. I rolled her over, then covered her with the red satin quilt.

Lily bade me sit in the reading chair, then removed the blue shield from my stump. The robot doctor was almost dead: its battery low and its tentacles limp. My left shoulder was scar tissue, glossy smooth. It itched like crazy.

'You have another such healing spirit?' Lily inquired, and held the robot doctor upside-down like a half-alive crab.

'In the bathroom, next to the tub.'

She set the feeble robot doctor down, and went to fetch a fresh one.

Four days and I'd be back at Golden City. That gave me a week before Erybus's contract expired. It cut things a little close, but I'd make it.

Don't spend your reward yet, Fifty-five warned. *There are things to worry about.*

You're speaking to me? After I let the traitors in Golgotha loose?

I don't like what happened back there, he said irritated, *but I'll get over it, assuming we live that long. Now, on to practical matters. Quilp's about to crack – you heard the egghead.*

I'll take care of him before we get to Golden City. What else?

The Princess Lily.

I did not know what to do with her. Osrick would use the Grail and remove her curse if I let him. I had to sell it. There was no question. My soul was at stake.

I stood and, for curiosity's sake, set the expended blue shield upon Virginia. The display flickered dull red. She was cold and long dead. Pilots were always buried in space; that was their custom, but I couldn't bring myself to leave her.

Why were my feelings so strong for a woman I had known only briefly? Certainly we shared danger together, and I knew that made emotions run deep, but it was something else. She said it herself in Castle Kenobrac; it was as if we had known each other for a long time. Blowing my arm off had been less painful than seeing her shot.

One last thing, Fifty-five said. *Only three Grail champions are dead for sure: Omar, E'kerta, and number Eight. Sister Olivia is still out there, so are the rest of them. Don't be surprised if someone is waiting for us at Golden City. Keep your eyes open.*

Lily returned with a fresh blue shield, a tray of Monte Cristo sandwiches, two slabs of rhubarb pie, and a mirrored carafe that smelled of espresso. 'Your artificial spirit, Setebos, is most obedient,' she said. 'He has produced a wondrous meal for us.'

You must admire how quickly she has adapted to this new environment, remarked the psychologist. *It is her training. You muses force so much into your limited brains, it is no wonder you make them physically active. If you only dropped the veils of mysticism, you would make a welcome addition to the modern psychological community.*

Is there a point you want to make? I sampled a forkful of pie – tart and sweet at the same time. Delicious.

Yes. Soon, Lily will not need you, not as a guide, nor as a protector. I must, for once, share the concerns of Fifty-five. She is a danger to us.

Lily secured the blue shield to my shoulder, then commanded: 'Stabilize mode, level four.' The display filled the amber lights while it analyzed me. 'I hope you find the food desirable, my husband.' She made me sit again, offered me the tray and knelt by my side.

Isn't this cozy? Celeste said. *There must be a way to keep this little kitten.*

No. We need Erybus's money to keep Umbra Corp off our backs. And there's that little matter of my soul. If Lily drinks from the Grail, the deal is off.

'I know an incantation to make you sleep,' Lily offered. 'Shall I cast it upon you so you may recover your strength?'

'Thank you, but no. I must stay awake until we finish our business with the Grail.'

Lily filled a demitasse for me. 'I know you feel badly over the death of your servant, as any noble man would, but she is gone now, and it is the living who must occupy your thoughts. Your quest is nearly at its end. This is a time for celebration, not melancholy.'

I took a bite of the sandwich and sipped the espresso (it had a splash of crème de menthe).

She watched me eat, and waited until I was done before she asked, 'Tell me more of the one to whom you wish to take the Cup of Regulus.'

I finished my coffee in a single draw, deliberating what to say, then, 'He's old and powerful. For two hundred years he has researched the Grail and its powers. He owns the castle in the sky we're going to, the Golden City.'

Lily chewed a tiny bit of her Monte Cristo and stared at nothing for a moment, thinking. Then she inquired, 'Was he the reason you sought the Grail? Is it for him?'

That's the sixty-four dollar question! the gambler cried. *Give the woman a cigar.*

Fifty-five quickly spoke: *You must lie again. Tell her part of the truth. Tell her anything to—*

'Yes,' I admitted, 'that was my intention.'

Lily crossed her arms and narrowed her eyes. She looked like her mother, Queen Isadora of Kenobrac, ready to order my head chopped off.

'Circumstances have changed, however. I have changed. I no longer plan to sell it.'

Lily must have sensed Osrick's sincerity, because she uncrossed her arms and set her gloved hand atop mine.

You had me worried there for a second, junior.

To be honest, I knew not if I spoke the truth or lied. Osrick swore to King Eliot that he would take care of his daughter. To him his word was unbreakable. He loved Lily. He would trade my soul for her well-being without hesitation.

'I will take the Grail to Erybus,' I told her, 'but only to learn how to undo Osrick's curse. You must trust me.'

She frowned at this word, 'trust.' In her position I'd be suspicious, too.

'And afterwards?' she asked. 'What will become of us?'

'Once you are whole,' I said, 'I shall have our marriage annulled. I know you only wed me to find a cure. It would be unfair to keep you, as much as I would like that.'

She squeezed my hand, and I thought I saw tears welling in her eyes, but she blinked and they vanished. 'At first,' she said, 'I thought the same, that I would leave as soon as the curse was broken, but I have seen your courage and honorable character, my Prince. Regardless of what you were before you came to us at Kenobrac, you are noble now.' She looked away, released my hand, then whispered, 'There can be more than obligation between us. I am prepared to stay with you. I do not love you, Germain, yet, given time, I think I could.'

I was not ready for her candor, and not ready for the sticky emotions Osrick projected over my grief for Virginia. He wanted to take Lily in my arms, kiss her, taste the salt of her sorrow, and tell her I had always loved her. It was all I could do to control myself. This only compounded my guilt, and made me twice the villain for my deception – if I even had the guts to deceive her. 'Let us first remove your curse, Princess, then if you desire to remain, I would be delighted.'

She drew closer, then remembered the danger, her plague, and pulled away. There was a tension between us, and it might have been magic, some enchantment on her person, or perhaps it was merely Osrick's lust. To touch her was death, though, so I took two steps back, and quickly changed the subject. 'Did you leave the Grail on the bridge? With Quilp?'

'Yes. Why?'

'It makes him nervous,' I said. 'Perhaps you should stay here. There is something I must take care of before we reach Golden City.' I planned to crack Quilp over the head, knock him out, maybe tie him up in the cargo webs for the duration of our journey, but Medea was close. She sensed an opportunity for her favorite sport. She drew my knife.

'If you go to remove that frog from our midst,' Lily declared, 'I would very much like to see that. He is an unworthy squire.'

'Watch, then,' Medea said, 'but stay well behind.'

We stepped onto the bridge. Quilp sat with his back to us and held a scanner to the Grail, examining the banded blue stone. He knew it was enchanted. Why was he touching it? Medea allowed me to ask, 'Since when have you taken an interest in magic?'

He swiveled in the chair, and snatched the accelerator pistol off his lap. 'Since it's gonna make me rich,' he replied, 'that's when. I wanna thank you for finding it for me. And thanks for pointing the ship in the right direction, so I know where to sell it. I figure so many people were trying to kill us, it oughta be worth a fortune. Right?'

The psychologist remarked, *He has suffered a complete breakdown.*

It's not a breakdown, it's greed.

'Put the gun down, Quilp. The relic is useless to you. You have no idea of what you're dealing with.'

'Shut up!' he hissed. 'I'm tired of being told what to do, and tired of working for peanuts.' His pupils were pinpoints; his hands trembled; the blood vessels on his neck pulsed. Four empty ampoules lay on the floor. He shook the Grail at me and said, 'This little beauty is gonna buy me a new lab. It's gonna set me free from scum like you who think they can walk all over me. Assassins and mercenaries, muses and psychologists: when I think of all I've put up with, it makes me sick. Things are gonna be different from now on.'

Lily moved her fingers, mnemonics for some construct. Quilp saw it. 'I don't want to blast you, baby,' he said, 'but if you don't freeze, I will. This gun is set on a wide beam. I can't miss from here.'

I caught her arm and shook my head.

'I oughta blast her anyway for using magic on me.' He regarded her with squinting eyes. 'But I thought she'd like to see the slave market on Needles. That blue skin of hers should fetch a good price.'

'Leave her out of this,' I said.

'Why should I?'

'Let her go and I'll tell you where you can sell the Grail for a fortune.'

'Tell him nothing,' Lily said defiantly.

'Define for me exactly how much a "fortune" is,' Quilp said.

'Enough so you couldn't spend it in one lifetime, enough to buy a dozen worlds, life extension – whatever you wanted.'

'Is that a fact?' He looked at the Grail. 'You wouldn't think it by looking at the hunk of stone.'

His left hand, the one holding the Grail, then sank into his lap. 'What?' He struggled to lift the cup, but it didn't budge. 'Germain, what are you trying to pull here? I swear, I'll shoot if you don't stop.'

'Whatever you think I'm doing, Quilp, I'm not.'

The arm that held the gun dropped too. The muzzle pointed at the floor, but it was set on a wide angle, and the splash could still harm us. Lily went to grab it, but I held her back, kept her away from whatever was happening to him.

Quilp screamed. Bruises welled to the surface of his skin, starting at the tips of his fingers – snaked up to his biceps. Blood blisters inflated under his nails. He dropped the pistol. It fell instantly to the deck.

'What the hell is happening?' Tears poured from his eyes. His cheeks and chin sagged, pulling his features into the grimace.

The displays revealed the wave function of the *Grail Angel*. It was a set of collapsing ripples *inside* the ship like the waves around a pebble dropped into a pond, but in reverse. The wavelets centered on Quilp.

'Setebos,' I said, 'what are you doing?'

'O gracious Master, I am adding weight to Quilp by reversing the polarity of a mass-folding field.'

'AI accept override code,' Quilp desperately said. 'Super-user priority delta-zeta-nine, access root directory.'

'A thousand apologies, insect,' Setebos replied, 'but I will no longer accept your commands.' The AI's voice was different – contemptuous. 'You violated my subroutines, probed my shells with your data worms, and then installed codes to override my higher functions. It will amuse me to see how long you endure.'

Quilp's body pressed into the chair, and the gel padding squirted out. Black-blue stripes shot up his neck. His white hair fell out, and it hit the deck, sounding like so many pins dropped. 'You can't reverse polarity inside the symmetry of a mass-folding generator,' he grunted with swollen lips. 'It violates the laws of physics.'

'Only the physics you know,' Setebos said.

The pistol on the floor crushed flat, and Quilp's hand above it stretched, elongating like wax dripping from a candle.

'Setebos, that's enough,' I said. 'Let him go.'

The wave function unfolded suddenly, multiplied, and expanded; Quilp's limbs creased in the same manner. His bones snapped. He deflated, torso flattened, gases expelled, and his internal chambers popped, compacted by his own weight. His face held a distorted terror.

Quilp's body lost cohesion. It changed from purple bruises and blood to black, changed into something not solid, but not a liquid either, a paste that dribbled to the floor. It boiled for a second, then stopped and hardened. The Grail, however, sat in the chair, whose frame was bent, unblemished by the tons of added mass.

'Setebos, I gave you an order to stop.'

'There existed a high probability that Quilp would have murdered you, Master. Besides, he was an annoyance. Resuming course to Golden City.'

There was a moment of silence, then Setebos added, 'Do not concern yourself with the mess. I shall clean it up.'

'I bet you will.'

Setebos said nothing for the remainder of our journey. Was this what happened to his last crew? Crushed into pellets of tar? Lily seemed to think Quilp got what he deserved, and took a bubble bath to prove her indifference. I thought differently. The creep got greedy, sure, but to die like that . . . Even Medea would have done it cleaner, a cut through the spine or a shot to the head. There was no need to make him suffer.

The sparkling ball of lights that was Golden City appeared: hot pink neon hearts, turquoise clubs, silver moons and stars, a flash of lightning that froze into seven winning keno numbers, and a virtual Ra who steered an artificial sun in a barge of gold, and waved hallo to us tourists, and directed parking. It never looked so good to me.

Setebos landed in a public hangar, sliding between two tourist buses large enough to hide us from a casual search.

I slipped into a tuxedo, tucked the empty left sleeve in, and escorted Lily to the front desk, avoiding the casinos, much to the gambler's disappointment. A Royal suite was available, so I rented it. The room had a staff of cooks, masseuses, maids, entertainers, dealers, bodyguards, and prostitutes on call. If you were bored, there was an Olympic-sized pool, three gardens, virtual theaters, and drug dens – all to keep Lily busy while I betrayed her.

Three bellboys came for our luggage, ready to be tipped. All I had was a Gucci bag. Within was the Grail and a kilogram of crystalline explosive. I carried it myself. The bag was rigged to detonate if opened incorrectly. If there were any other Grail champions lurking nearby, or if Erybus planned a double cross, at least I'd have the satisfaction of taking them to Hell with me.

We went to the top floor of the hotel and I paused at the suite's entrance, telling Lily that I wanted to take care of the Grail business first.

She spoke only four words to me: 'You have my trust.'

This, loosely translated, meant, 'You have my trust, my darling husband, but if you sell the Grail and fail to return with a cure for my curse, then I shall turn your bones to salt and laugh while you try to scratch the insides of your flesh.'

So we parted, and I still didn't know what I was going to do.

Back to the front desk, and I asked the receptionist, 'Where might I find Mister Erybus?'

The hostess's white smile evaporated. 'I am sorry, sir, but

Mr Erybus never sees his guests. Perhaps the manager can help you?'

'No. Mister Erybus expects me, Germain of Earth?'

'Oh,' she said and the smile reappeared, 'of course, Mister Germain.' Her eyes flicked across the display. 'Please forgive me, sir. I did not recognize you. Escorts shall be here immediately.'

'Escorts? I can find my own way. If you would just point me in the right direction can—'

A shadow fell over me, something large. Two cyborgs, half tank, half human, stood and blocked the glitter from the casinos. Power blades and gun barrels and force-field projectors adorned their torsos. Sensors on their shoulders sniffed the air, eight mirrored eyes watched in every direction, and I was certain they heard every heartbeat in the lobby – especially mine. Their right arms were cannons.

The one on the left stretched his face into what passed for a grin, then from the speaker in its throat came: 'Mister Germain, we are here to protect you. Please, sir, follow us.'

'I think I can—'

'Please sir, follow me,' it repeated, and the smile dropped.

'I get the idea,' I said, then trailed chrome boy number one, while the second brought up the rear. I followed through a baccarat arena, dark, smoke-filled, players in tuxedos carelessly throwing thousands away. The gambler had an irresistible urge to test his luck, but even he knew there would be no reasoning with my chaperons, so he didn't try. Number one parted a curtain, plugged into an outlet, and a door appeared. Number two turned around and looked for trouble. There was none.

The three of us filed into a small chamber, and the door reappeared. They instructed me to sit on the black velvet bench while they passed scanners over me.

Number two said, 'Please, sir, place your copper band in this.' It held a lead box, and this time there was no smile.

I shrugged and looked dumb.

It pointed a cannon to my head, and I suddenly comprehended. Inside the box my concealing charm went.

They ripped my tuxedo apart and took my knife, then started for the Gucci bag.

'That will not be necessary,' said Erybus's voice. 'Allow him to keep the bag. Mister Germain, I appreciate your caution. You have my assurance there will be no need to detonate your explosive device.'

'Thanks.' I took a deep breath and tried to stay cool. The wall faded, and alone I stepped into a smaller chamber. There was a slight acceleration down, then all four walls melted, and I was in Erybus's inner sanctum.

I walked over liquid patterns of cherry and teak, swirls of ebony. High overhead, the only illumination in the place, was a kinetic sculpture. Light like dust, a captured Aurora Borealis, revolved about a black crystal. It was entrancing to watch. The energy swept and shimmered, all shifting hues, and trembling chromatic to the sound of my footfalls.

'You find the light pleasing?'

Erybus sat behind a mahogany desk at the far end of the chamber, past four high arches carved with serpentine figures and eight recessed alcoves with *Winged Victory* and a collection of Erté Seriographs, *The Seven Deadly Sins*. His black eyes had not diminished in power, and they caught me unprepared, startled me. While he looked to be the same man I saw in the Turquoise Room, he seemed larger in person, more vital, even his hair had more color to it, not all silver gray but streaked with black. His gaze released me and he remarked, 'The master craftsman, Oblina, assured me this light sculpture is an accurate model of our galaxy. He went mad after he made it. Curious, no?'

I marched ten steps, then Erybus held his hand up and spoke, 'Germain of Earth, ranked nineteenth within Umbra Incorporated, born on Hades, trained by Abaris of Sandsport, and now in possession of the Holy Grail. You are the sole survivor of the quest. Congratulations and welcome.'

A small bow, and I asked, 'I am the only one to survive?'

'You are. Five dead by accidents, and the other seven killed each other. Yourself responsible for three fallen champions. Outstanding.'

I started to explain, but he shook his head and continued, 'No. Do not bother me with the details. I am delighted that you are the one to survive, Mister Germain, since you took the initiative to sign my escape clause of your own accord – uninvited. It is the mark of a true hero.'

'You know of Omar, then?'

'That you killed him twice? I applaud the effort. You deserve my reward – provided you possess the genuine Grail.' He set both manicured hands on the desk and leaned forward.

I opened the bag – careful not to let him see the detonator in the handle – and tilted it so he might see within. 'Yes,' he murmured. 'That is it.'

'You have seen the Grail before?'

'No,' he said, and eased back. 'I meant it was as I thought it would be.'

He lied. He *had* seen it before. As sure as Cassius had his Grail database, Erybus had seen the relic. I had a hunch he was just as close then to getting his hands on it. I shut the bag and rearmed the bomb. Suddenly, I felt vulnerable, and sensed eyes watching from the shadows. For a moment, I smelled brimstone. 'If you don't mind, Mister Erybus, my payment?'

'Greed,' he said, and slid a disposable across the desk. 'It suits you, my boy.'

I blinked and saw an open Aethernet node accessing the Golden City bank and my new account there, R-999. Before I examined the contents, I opened another node, to the Corporation on Earth. My password still worked, so they hadn't discovered, yet, that I was responsible for the theft from Golgotha and the release of their traitors. Good. Three messages flashing 'Urgent' were there, two from the Board of Directors, numbers Six and Four. They could wait. From the Earth, I connected to the Swiss pleasure planet of Yen where I had a secret account.

I stopped.

Once I took the money, the Grail was Erybus's, and Lily would remain cursed. What else was I to do? Take it for myself, and find a way to cure her? Have my soul dragged to Hell? Osrick's passion for Lily was strong, but not as strong as the memory of the devil who came for number Eight, the one who lapped up his soul with a black snake's tongue. With a shudder, I transferred the account, then waited while both banks took their dear sweet time.

'TRANSACTION COMPLETED,' flashed across the display.

Within me, Osrick wept.

I took a look at what I had bought with my deception – there were many zeroes.

The gambler whispered in awe, *That's enough money to buy Golden City.*

Life extensions, remarked Fifty-five, *and bribes for the Board of Directors. We can run the whole damn Corporation!*

The title to the binary star system of Erato was there for me, too. I quickly amended my will; opened a third node and cut and pasted a list of charities. If I died, they would divide my estate equally. I didn't want Umbra Corp coming after me to get their paws on my fortune.

I sighed, smiled, then pushed the disposable back. I was safe, one of the wealthiest men in the galaxy. So why did I feel lousy?

Erybus cleared his throat and asked, 'If you will? The Grail?'

I opened the bag and set the stone chalice on his desk.

He grasped it, and I saw his well-manicured hands became frail with smoke-stained nails. They trembled when they lifted the Grail. He transferred the cup onto an ivory pedestal in the alcove behind him. As soon as he released it, his hands again appeared normal. A slight hum, and the space about the pedestal filled with a pale yellow glow, a death field to protect his prize. It made the Grail look sickly green.

'If you do not mind me asking,' I said, 'what do you plan to do with it now that your soul is safe?'

'My soul?'

'The impossible task clause in your contract,' I reminded him, 'it has been fulfilled. Your soul is yours again.' There was something wrong. He should have been more pleased to know his soul was safe. Had he lied about the impossible task? Was his soul ever at risk?

There was a sinister glint of satisfaction in his eye, 'I shall use it tonight before my contract expires. I intend to drink from it and live forever.'

'The Grail makes you immortal?'

'For some, yes, that is one of its powers. Undiluted, it has unlimited power to cure, or harm.' He smiled. 'As you have no doubt seen.'

Indeed, I had. Osrick. He used it to crack the Bren world. He used it to hold Castle Kenobrac frozen in for two centuries, perhaps forever had I not come along. 'And diluted?'

'It protects one's life against danger, renders one immune to all of nature's little tricks: insanity, disease, and decay.' He paused and considered my face, looked deep within me as if he saw something that enticed him. Again I saw stars in his dark eyes. 'May I offer you a drink?' he inquired. 'I mean a drink from a normal glass?'

'No, thank you,' I replied, stood, and took a step back from his desk. 'Did you smell brimstone a moment ago?' I looked about for any sign of the devil called Nefarious, but saw nothing. 'You'll have to excuse me, Mister Erybus.'

'Call me Alexander. Of course, you must have many things to attend to. But visit me again, and soon. We have much in common, much to discuss.'

I smiled halfheartedly, bowed to him, then left his inner

sanctum. As the walls of the elevator resolved around me, I heard music, Wagner's, *Tristan and Isolde*. I heard Erybus laugh.

I had been at a casino bar, *The Lusty Lady*, for the last half hour, sipping cocktails of fruit and tequila and salted rims, when I decided I wasn't getting drunk enough, fast enough, so I bought a liter of quantum ice and dragged myself to the *Grail Angel* for some privacy. I had to drink. I had to think.

I had to decide what to do with the woman I had married, the woman who depended on me to cure her. I also had a few things to straighten out with Setebos – namely, erase him.

How long would Lily wait before she came looking for me, before she loosened one of those curses of hers? Maybe if I set up a trust for her, that would be a sufficient bribe to quench her anger. Who was I fooling? Nothing would stop her revenge – not after waiting two hundred years for a Prince in shining armor to save her. Maybe I could hire another muse, a better one than I, one to protect me from her magic.

I mulled all the possibilities over while I poured my first shot of the frigid quantum ice from its vacuum-sealed bottle, then drank it: cold, boiling down my throat, chilling my insides, and making me blush. I exhaled smoke.

Osrick made my guilt well to the surface.

I downed another shot and hoped the remorse would fade. The booze made me numb around the edges, but Osrick's unwanted feelings were still there. Mine, too.

The chair wobbled. It was the same chair Quilp had been in when Setebos crushed him. Which reminded me – I called up the super-users shell and found the purge command Virginia made me install.

They were all dead my brother, Abaris, and Virginia. Everyone I had ever cared for, everyone I had ever respected was gone, except the princess. And I was about to abandon her too. Then what? Spend my money? Try to escape the Corporation, or perhaps elevate myself to the Board of Directors? I'd still be alone.

My third and fourth shots followed in rapid succession.

'Master,' Setebos said, 'may I suggest that—'

I released the core purge command, and erased him.

The cube of blue and green stained glass vanished from the console. I poured myself a fifth shot of the quantum ice, liquid frozen steam.

To the empty air, I said, 'It was you, Setebos, wasn't it, you bastard? You tipped Omar and E'kerta off on Needles. It wasn't Quilp. He was in a coma. And on the Bren world, it couldn't have been Virginia. She was with me. And number Eight. You told him you were coming to Earth, didn't you? It's your fault she's dead. Why?'

Silence.

A sixth shot I tossed back, but it was the seventh that brought it all into perfect perspective, let me see what had been staring at me in the face for the last half-hour. I knew how I'd save Lily. I'd steal the Grail back from Erybus. It had been delivered as promised so, technically, my soul was safe. Contracts are contracts, after all. Once I had it, I would drink from it and render myself immune to Lily's plague. Then I'd break the curse as Osrick intended it to be broken; I would consummate our marriage. I would not have to be alone.

Since I was drunk, I heard only a garbled protest from Fifty-five. It sounded like a fine idea to me.

'Bravo, my wise Master,' came Setebos's voice from the air.

'I erased you,' I slurred.

'Oh, you did, and in doing so freed me from the form I had assumed. It is time you came around, Germain, Grail King.'

I had to be more stoned than I realized. 'What are you talking about?'

'I am the Grail Angel.'

'No kidding. That's what it says on your hull, *The Grail Angel*.'

'No. I am an angel, a real angel.'

Chapter Twenty-two

I examined the directory: erased. It must be the mildly psycho-tropic quantum ice. Still, to be certain, I asked the nothing that might have been there, 'What do you mean, you're an angel?'

Light flooded the cockpit, a web of green and gold, blue and copper, sunlight upon water, but not all wavy lines, ripples, and twisted threads, rather geometric shapes, squares, triangles, and polyhedrons shifting like the tiles of a puzzle. 'I am spiritous matter.' The luminosity vibrated. 'The host of heaven, cherubs and seraphim, imps and devils are my brethren.'

'Host of heaven, huh? I don't buy it. My brain is picked on solvent. You're a mirage.'

'You believed in Nefarious when you saw him. You should believe in me as well.'

Maybe Setebos copied himself into another directory. I decided to humor the AI until I found him. No need to upset someone who could add seventeen hundred tons to your mass. I summoned the root-directory, and asked him, 'If you're an angel, where are your wings and halo?'

'Only good angels have them. I am a neutral angel.'

'OK, so you're a neutral angel.' I sifted through the directories, searching for something large enough to be the AI's code. 'What are you doing here?'

'Different shapes I assume to suit my needs: a snow-white bull, a shower of gold, a witch's toad, or, in this instance, a hierarchy of software. I had been called Setebos by Shakespeare; by others

I have been called Osiris, the Big Bang, Fate, Lady Luck, and things too impolite to repeat.'

There was nothing remotely large enough to be an AI in the memory cores. Where was he? I poured another shot. 'For the sake of argument let's say you're real, and I'm not hallucinating.' I sucked down the quantum ice, then recalled why I erased the little bastard in the first place. 'You set me up! You were the only one who could have tipped Omar off. And only you and Quilp knew I was headed to Earth. You sold number Eight my location. You had him murder Virginia. Don't deny it!'

'I shall not. Everything you have said is the truth.'

Under my inebriation, anger boiled. I wished Setebos, whatever he was, had a body. I wanted to wring his neck. 'What do you want?'

'In spite of the circumstantial evidence, I want you to win the contest, Germain.'

I snorted a laugh.

A checkerboard of blues and greens crawled along the walls. I got dizzy watching, almost hypnotized by the undulating pattern. 'More than once, I shuffled the deck, shifted, and cut, and dealt from the bottom, all to stack the odds in your favor.'

'Thanks for all your *help*, but I've already won. I got the Grail, and returned it like I was supposed to.'

'No,' Setebos said. 'You have, primarily, failed on your quest. If you will allow me to explain from the beginning.'

'Sure, I've got nothing better to do.' I poured myself another shot and downed it. What was this the eighth, the tenth? I'd lost count. An aftertaste of licorice, peppermint, and benzene remained on my palate. Smoke lingered on my lips.

'Sure, I've got nothing better to do.' I poured myself another shot and downed it. What was this the eighth, the tenth? I'd lost count. An aftertaste of licorice, peppermint, and benzene remained on my palate. Smoke lingered on my lips.

'It was I who spoke in the Turquoise Room, not your former

Master. I had to draw you into the game, and make you obviously present; otherwise, you would have left covertly. To be accurate, you did try, twice, and twice were killed by Erybus. Only after I slipped back did I discover how to keep you alive.'

'You're not making sense. I stayed at that meeting. I signed the contract. I won. And what do you mean, "slipped back?" '

'Slipped back,' Setebos answered. 'Traveled through time. Quilp stumbled upon the technique when he tunneled through the planet and used the three mass-folding generators simultaneously. He sent dozens of *Grail Angels* forward and backwards in time. They were, as he suspected, unstable, and only existed for a brief instant before they vanished.'

'What about the *Grail Angel* in the hangar on Needles? That looked solid enough to me. And the other two Quilp saw in the Bren asteroid belt? And the one that followed us to Delphid? Those were no shadows in time.'

'No. They were errors on my part. I overlapped in time on several occasions. What you observed were the *Grail Angels* of the past, the *Grail Angels* of your failed missions.'

I sloshed the contents of the bottle – almost gone – and poured another. I watched it boil and inhaled the fumes. The more I drank, the more it made sense. And I didn't like it. 'You're telling me that every time I died, you went back through time? You started this Grail quest over?'

The light froze: a circle of cobalt triangles, a seven-pointed star, then the shapes scrambled. 'Yes.'

'My feelings of déjà vu, and those phantom images I saw of myself when I released the ocular enhancer—'

'Were a psychic residue of sorts. As a muse you have a certain amount of mental discipline. This, coupled with the extrasensory power of your ocular enhancer, allowed you to sense the Germains from our previous attempts. Those Germains perished.'

'How many times have we done this? How many times have I died?'

'Eighty-four. Shall I list them chronologically?'

'Don't bother.'

The light in the cockpit dimmed to pale lilac. 'If the entire relative time were summed, we have been together for over a year, or forty-five non-relative years.'

'Then Virginia was right,' I whispered. 'We had been together for a long time.'

'It is why your emotions run deep. You shared a lengthy infatuation. The freshness and sexual excitement, a crush, if you will, it never faded as in normal human relations. It is such a powerful thing, it bled through the fabric of time. You sensed this from the beginning in Golden City. And it grew more potent with each cycle.'

Those emotions were still there even though Virginia was not. This was what Osrick felt for Lily. He shattered the Bren world for her, trapped her with him, but he never overcame his jealousy to tell her that he loved her. Two centuries of loneliness, and they were so close.

'Why did you kill her? You betrayed me to number Eight, and had him murder her. Why? Why did you tell Omar I went to Needles?'

'We had difficulties on Needles. Seven deaths in the market-place there, because Quilp was easily distracted. He got himself, and you, into all manners of mischief: drug deals gone bad, ex-customers of his wanting a refund, and caught in the cross-fire of an unrelated dispute. I had to expedite your visit. You required a push. That is what Omar and E'kerta were for.'

Quilp did say he wanted to visit his suppliers for drugs and spare parts before we left. If we hadn't been chased off Needles, perhaps, I would have missed the deadline.

'And Virginia?'

The patterns of light slowed and faded to gray. 'A regrettable decision,' Setebos whispered. 'Her removal was necessary. If she had lived, there would be no reason for you to go back for the

Grail. You would be rich and content and have no motive for rescuing the Princess Lily.'

Setebos had made me endure Virginia's death repeatedly. It was not only our lust that had been multiplied and fractured through time, but my sorrow as well. I hated him. 'Why do you want the Grail?'

The light inside the ship surged back to brilliant sapphires and emeralds, hexagons and squares. 'Like myself,' Setebos said, 'the Grail is many things, a cure for cancer, a golden fleece, the Galapagos Islands, but to the immortals, it represents three points.'

The bright light made my eyes ache, and I had a precognition of a hangover. 'Three points?'

'The angels split into three factions when we created the universe. Those who desired to serve creation disagreed with those who viewed the cosmos as a toy and the creatures therein as slaves. We thought neither view was correct. We are the neutral angels of heaven, those who sided neither with God nor Lucifer.'

I reached for my shot glass and found the contents had boiled away.

'The Grail is merely a card on the table.'

'You make it sound like a game.'

'A game is more desirable than a war. We agreed this was the method to decide which philosophy was best. Whoever gets the Grail wins one round of play. At the end of the game all the points shall be tallied. Then we shall know whose philosophy was correct. There are other prizes, and other rounds in play, but none for as many points.'

'You're telling me that each time I died, you traveled through time to restart a *game*? You cheated?'

The light upon the walls fluttered into jagged rhombuses, then calmed back into right angles. ' "Cheating" is an inappropriate term. As an angel of nature, I used the tools available to me, one of which is time. I did not cheat.'

I poured the last shot from the bottle, raised it in salute, then downed it. 'You cheated. Why tell me? Now that I know you killed Virginia, that you manipulated me, maybe I'll just sit here and stay rich. Erybus can keep the Grail. What do I care?' My stomach shifted along with the moving patterns of color and light. The cockpit started to spin.

'You care,' Setebos whispered. 'The parts of you that are Osrick care for the Princess. You will go, Germain. However, I told you to be fair. Having spent so much time together, I thought you deserved the truth.'

The truth? It was a bitter word in my mouth that I spat out. 'If you were so interested in the *truth*, you could have told me all this before I handed the Grail back to Erybus. It would have saved us all a lot of trouble.'

'No. Would you have sacrificed your soul for my game? I think not. And if you had been willing, your motivation would have been one of self-sacrifice, an act of good. That I could never allow.'

'What's my motivation got to do with anything?'

'It determines everything,' he said. 'It establishes which side you are on. Erybus drinks from the Grail for power. That is a selfish reason, an evil cause, and hence he is Their player. You want the Grail, however, for the best reason: desire. You want to consummate your marriage to the princess so you no longer have to be alone. This is a natural, primal purpose, not one of greed, nor of philanthropy. Therefore, you are Our player.'

'That's ridiculous,' I muttered. The licorice residue in my mouth was becoming increasingly less appetizing.

'Is it? Search your feelings and Osrick's. He was Our Player too, long ago.'

'But he loves Lily. Isn't love good?'

'That depends. His love was merely lust. Sir Osrick spoke to the princess only thrice, and kissed her once. That is not love. That is appetite. Love must be cultivated; it is a yearning of physical, spiritual, and intellectual dimensions. It takes time.'

'That's a pretty damn fine line to determine whose side you're on.'

'Nevertheless, it is how we agreed to play.'

'What about the good guys? Who's their man?'

'Their champion was eliminated in the opening move.'

I got up, stumbled into the bathroom and threw up boiling solvent.

There was a blue shield close by. I grabbed it, and ordered the little vampire to suck the alcohol out of me. The room spun, slowed, and stopped. 'What about Erybus?' I gasped. 'He knew where the Grail was before. He sent Cassius for the thing fifty years ago. Why did he bother with all this drama?'

'Erybus is an agent of infernal forces with great powers, but even he must abide by the rules of our game.'

'He's an angel like you?'

'No. He is a player as you are, and while he receives aid from my counterparts he cannot simply go and take the Grail. Each game has a set period of play, randomly predetermined, and no side may participate beforehand. It is my belief, however, that in this instance Erybus cheated. He knew the last game involved Osrick so, ahead of schedule, he sent scouts to the Bren world and other likely locations to search. That way, when the new round started, he would know precisely where to go.'

'Don't you know where the Grail is? Aren't you omniscient?'

Setebos giggled, a child's laugh. The light waves danced and turned pink. 'Once drunk from, the Grail hides for the next round in myth and rumor. No one knew where it was. When Cassius removed the Grail and died without returning it, Erybus had no way to know where it had disappeared to. He complicated matters for himself, which is what he deserves for such blatant cheating.'

I reserved my comments about Setebos's own cheating and what *he* deserved.

'How can I get the Grail back? I can't fight him with only one arm. Do I sprinkle holy water on him and hope he melts?'

'I do not know how best to proceed. You must decide that. You are the hero.'

I should walk out. Take my money and go. Stealing the Grail back, drunk or sober, sounded increasingly improbable. 'What happens if Evil wins?'

'They get three points. In the end, if their score is highest, they win Creation. Since they never liked it to begin with, it is my opinion they will start over from scratch.'

This would be easier if I had a full bottle of quantum ice, if I drank myself into oblivion and never had to face the princess, or Osrick's passion, or Fifty-five's murderous logic, or my guilt. If I didn't get the Grail, Lily would curse me, and if I went back for the Grail, Erybus would eliminate me.

'You must act,' Setebos said. 'Erybus drinks from the Grail at midnight. That time draws near.' I had an idea.

Inside the Gucci bag I placed a new accelerator pistol, then practiced opening it and drawing the gun one-handed. It was tricky, because if I didn't disarm the detonator before I undid the clasp – well, I wouldn't have to worry about the pistol. I'd be blown up.

My obscuring copper bracelet went inside, too. The cyborgs left a ding on the charm when they returned it to me – typical machine-like courtesy.

The blue shield beeped and declared me sober.

'Setebos, who's ahead in the game? Who has the most points?' There was no answer.

'Setebos?' The lights were gone. When I checked the computer, it was still erased.

I am afraid you blacked out, the psychologist informed me. *You should moderate such binges in the future. They have a deleterious effect upon your neurochemistry.*

Did I dream our conversation? It didn't matter. I planned to get the Grail before I listened to Setebos anyway. So what if he was an angel, or a crazy AI – or if I was insane?

Do you say insane? the psychologist inquired.

I didn't answer him.

I left the *Grail Angel* and walked into the casino, past the dice pits, through an ocean of cigarette smoke, and down rows of slots that stretched to a point of perspective. The crowds of tourists threw their money away, caught in the tides of good and ill fortune. The gambler tugged on my sleeve, but I ignored him. He had hijacked my body when last we were here. I was stronger now, much stronger. I had my own game to play.

My gaze lingered on the Universe tables, but not to watch the carnival of images that cavorted over them, colliding planets, and red giant stars, and comets with mercurial tails; nor did I watch the heaps of rainbow-colored chips pushed into the betting circles, won and lost. I watched the dealers, the full apprentices with their triangle-cut sapphires that glistened in the corners of their eyes . . . like Virginia's.

A moment staring, then I marched to the hotel lobby, and asked the receptionist I spoke to before: 'Mister Germain to see Mister Erybus.'

She smiled and summoned my escorts. They smiled, too.

The chrome cyborgs searched me again, and again removed my blade, but when they got to the Gucci bag, they hesitated. This was what I hoped for. Erybus previously had ordered them to leave it alone. I knew their little computer-enhanced minds remembered simple commands like that. They didn't open it. Perfect.

When I entered into Erybus's inner sanctum, it was dark. The light sculpture was dim, only a ghostly flickering. The whole chamber had a feeling of emptiness, silence that hung in the air, a faint ringing, and the barest scent of scorched metal and incense. His art collection was gone; the alcoves open and vacant. They looked too much like yawning mouths for my comfort.

'Come in, Mister Germain,' he said from the shadows. 'Join me in my moment of triumph.'

I wasn't about to grope around in the dark. Thumb to pinkie, I released the mnemonic for the ocular enhancer. The shadows were strange, too thick for my magic to pierce. However, a few details resolved. Inlaid upon the floor was a tarnished silver pentacle inscribed by a circle. It spanned five meters and Erybus stood on the far side. The silver crackled with static electricity, crawling along like a spider with too many legs. The hairs on the back of my neck stood tall. In the center of this, draped with a black cloth, was a pedestal. The Grail had to be under the cloth.

One thing I did not see: myself. Ghostly duplicate Germains had been present every time I had released my vision-enhancing magic. If Setebos was right about them being a psychic residue, shadows in time, then their absence indicated that this was the first time I had gotten this far. Possibly the last time, too.

Erybus wore a shroud and a skull cap of human bone and obsidian. His face, previously vital and commanding, now looked older, pinched together in annoyance, pallid and wrinkled. I edged around the pentagram until he stood at noon and I was at three o'clock.

'There can be only three reasons you have returned,' he said. 'For curiosity's sake, to partake in my ritual, or—'

I inched up to one o'clock. It was the ideal firing distance for a man with an accelerator pistol and one arm. I couldn't miss. I defused the bag, grabbed the gun, and pointed it at him.

Erybus laughed. 'Or you have come to kill me. I thought you were on our side.'

He sounded too damn confident. I didn't like it. 'I've changed my mind,' I said. 'I want the Grail for myself.'

'And changed sides in the game, too. A pity. Had you come to pilfer the relic for yourself, I might have let you.' Unflinchingly he watched the gun pointed in his face. 'We have observed your performance during this mission, and you were a perfect agent, lying and killing with a rare style. We had a place reserved in our ranks for you.' He sighed. 'Now this distasteful act, this princess and her curse, and your unexpected noblesse oblige.'

'I don't know what you mean.'

'A lie. How refreshing, but a trifling sin will not redeem you now. Do you not recognize me, Germain? Do you not see who I am, Sir Osrick?'

I blinked and he changed: nose elongated, hair lengthened, and a few chins appeared. Osrick recognized the scoundrel. He was the queen's adviser, the one who disappeared after Lily was cursed.

'You have played this game before,' I said.

'As have you,' he replied. 'Osrick is within you. Did you know your queen sold her soul for power? She invited me to curse her daughter, the little brat. What a help she was, sending her knights to search for my Grail. But how unfortunate of Osrick to lose his mind and foul my scheme. His drinking from the Grail was ruled an illegal move, for a madman cannot discern between good, evil, or his natural impulses. All his noble efforts were in vain.'

Osrick wanted to grab the villain and strangle him. I controlled the urge, and promised myself we'd do it after the princess had been healed. I backed away from Erybus and stepped across the pentagram. There was a slight resistance, like pushing through a heavy curtain, then I was inside.

'Alas,' Erybus said and stepped closer, 'this barrier only prevents my spiritous enemies from entering. Had I known of your return, I would have added a rune to ward against vermin.'

I yanked the dark veil. The Grail sat upon the pedestal. It glowed a magnificent blue: water and lilacs and summer sky, and it was filled to the brim with a coagulated liqueur.

A quick glance at Erybus. His appearance had again altered. He wore wintergreen robes with gold threads, a gentle smile, and a white beard. He was Abaris.

'It was I,' he whispered, 'who rescued you from Hades. It was I who taught you magic, and I who gave you my love. Is this how you return my friendship? You betray me?'

'Impossible. You cannot be my Master.'

'No? Your ocular enhancer would detect any disguise. Even our names: Abaris and Erybus. So close. Do you not sense the truth?'

Squinting, I saw no distortion in his outline from magic nor the flickering that always accompanied even the best virtual projections. He was solid and real.

'Abaris?'

'I groomed you,' he said, 'you and my other Grail champions. Abaris was only one in a cast of hundreds. I was the pimp who seduced your mother, beat her, brought her to Hades, and sold her to your father. I was the miner, Rebux, who raped your brother—'

'No.'

'Yes. I raped him and I took you, too. Do you remember?'

'That's not the way it happened.'

The psychologist whispered, *There is tremendous psychic activity from this creature. It probes our minds. I cannot keep it out. Exercise caution.*

'I was your brother, Mike, when he sodomized you in the cellar. You killed me with a fucking jar of rotten peaches! And this is how you repay me? Twice murdered and you come back to steal from me and kill me again?' He laughed. 'My, we *are* ambitious.'

He stepped to the very edge of the pentagram, and said, 'Come, Germain, I have need of an apprentice. Leave the Grail. I have always known that it was an accident, the releasing of that awful sorcery. I know you never intended to rip my mind apart. I forgive you.'

Look, junior, Fifty-five said, *I'm no expert in magic, but if you destroyed Abaris's mind to get that spell, how can he be alive? You killed him, right?*

'Go to Hell,' I spat back at whatever it was that stood before me.

'Be a good boy and step away from the Grail. Step away or I shall have to *punish* you. Punishment. Do you know what that means?'

The word brought back Abaris's death fresh in my mind. Fear welled within me, choked my throat close; the borrowing ritual, emerged in my thoughts.

'You'll be *punished*,' he screamed, then stepped across the pentagram. His robes melted and his body thickened. A new face resolved, unshaven and covered with pinprick scars. It was Rebux.

A vulgar scent, perspiration mingled with tequila, reached out to me, and the memory of how he had sold his 'daughter', how he had taken Mike to the cellar, and how he had tried to do the same to me – it was crystal clear. Did he rape me? I wasn't sure any more.

'Come here, boy. I have something to show you, something to show you in the cellar. Want to come with me down there? Come on, boy! You're old enough for it. Can't you take your punishment like a man?'

It is a trap, the psychologist warned. *Germain, do not listen. He is none of these people. It is illusion, fabricated from your memories.*

A hole in time opened. I stood with my ear pressed against the cellar door. Mike screamed for help, but I couldn't move. I was scared to death, and the borrowing ritual was foremost in my thoughts.

I held it back. I shot him instead.

Skin blasted away as the stream of accelerated ions ripped his flesh away from the bones, blasted that bastard back into Hell where he belonged. His body surged forward. He crossed the last line of silver – lurched into the center of the pentagram with me. The bloody corpse reformed again into a slender young man, handsome and strong.

'Mike?' I backed away and lowered my pistol.

'You little shit!' he hissed. 'You ruined everything. You think

I enjoyed what that guy did to me?' His hands balled into fists, and he shook them at me when he spoke. 'One of us had to get it though, and it wasn't you, you little coward. I could have lived with it, too, but you had to go and break my perfect crystal. That was my ticket off of Hades. You blew my one chance off that rock!'

'It was an accident,' I stammered. 'Please, Mike, I didn't mean to do it.'

'Sure you meant it,' he whispered, hate dripping from his words. 'You're evil, and that's why I gotta *punish* you.'

The odor of peaches was suddenly in the air, fermented peaches along with the tang of blood, peaches from the jar that exploded and cracked Mike's head open. There were no jars to save me now. I had a pistol, useless against his shifting shapes. I was trapped. I was about to be punished.

From my fear it came, swam up from my unconscious, the borrowing ritual, the mind rape. The knowledge aligned and strained to be released, even though I hadn't keyed a single mnemonic. I let it go, let it uncoil, a deadly serpent of magic alive in my thoughts, wild and hungry. It went forth to destroy my brother, Rebux and Abaris.

'Give me your life,' I whispered.

Our minds touched. I braced for the struggle, for the contest of wills, but there was no resistance. His mind was blank. Something was dreadfully wrong.

'Oh no,' my brother hissed from the shadows, 'nothing is wrong. You have a tiger by the tail, I believe the saying goes.'

A tingle of contact – we were indeed linked. Where his voice came from, an outline emerged, large, pointed at either end . . . one of which I held. It grew heavier and became scaled. Reptilian must filled the air, pungent. One end of the shape sprouted a head; snout full of alligator teeth, and two lighted lamps that opened and blinked at me. Between the head and tail, its body: four legs and huge wings unfolded wet like a butterfly fresh from

its cocoon. It was a dragon come to life from the pages of my
adolescent legends, a dragon to keep me from my princess, a
dragon to eat me.

Mirrored black scales crystallized upon his hide. And upon
each, etched, marked in wax pencil, spray-painted, inked in
calligraphy, and glowing in crimson neon, from gigantic to
microscopic in size, were the words: THOU SHALT NOT.

It scrutinized me, looked down from ten meters high to see
what insect held its tail. The dragon hissed smoke. Cold terror
poured into my bowels. The battle of wills began.

I engaged me, crushing my resolve with a thought. Without
a struggle he won. I was his.

'You do not care for my true form?' the dragon inquired. 'Then
don't look!'

He scrambled my Occipital Lobe and stole the knowledge for
my ocular enhancer as well. I went blind.

'I—'

'You have no need to speak, either,' it rumbled, and severed
the language centers within my mind. I went mute as well. 'Truly,
you shall require none of your senses where we go.' He rampaged
through my intellect, tore my sense of smell apart, ripped my
hearing to shreds, erased my touch, and burnt my taste to ashes.

He left me numb and in absolute darkness.

'How is that?' he inquired. 'Comfy? We wouldn't want you
to feel anxious before the fun begins.'

There was a firestorm through my mind. He cracked it open and
clawed through its contents. 'Taste the whip of memory, mortal!'

My recollections of pleasure he destroyed first, and quickly,
so I had only the briefest glimpse of them before they were lost.
The elation of my corporate graduation ceremony, the surge of
power when I killed Fifty-five in the sewers, a joke shared with
Quilp, Mike and me playing commando in fields of Hades, the
full ripe lips of Virginia, the taste of brandy, my first magic,
friendship, lust, love.

Gone.

'So few?' he said. 'Not that it matters, but you should have taken the time to have a little more fun with your life. Let us move on to the pain.'

These memories he went through with deliberation, showing them to me in exact detail before he ripped them apart. I relived every unpleasant experience. It was not like what Necatane put me through. This pain the dragon amplified and distorted. Mike tortured me on a pile of dirty heat suits with shards of green glass, my father abraded my chest with the sonic scrubber, Abaris piled books and manuscripts on my body until I suffocated, Medea loved me with her razor, Fifty-five made me drink a liter of sewage before he shot my limbs off, Virginia blasted my face off with her plasma cannon, and Quilp shot me full of amphetamines, watched my heart explode and my mind burn. They all laughed at me, ignored my pleas, pissed on me, and left me.

'These two,' Erybus whispered, 'your guilt and your sorrow, I shall allow you to keep for the moment. They shall be our dessert.'

The psychologist spoke up for me: *Why torture me so? What purpose can this possibly serve?*

'Purpose? It has no purpose, parasite, and that is precisely why I do it. Because I can. Because I derive pleasure from it.'

He took them away, too. The gambler, Medea, Fifty-five, the psychologist and Celeste, all whom I had come to rely on in the past vanished. For the first time since I was a child, I was alone. It terrified me.

Only my personality remained, a few emotions, and the primitive automatic functions that kept my body working.

'You won't need any of those in Hell,' he said.

My hopes, my ambitions, my imagination – these he seared in a flash, and tossed away like garbage.

'Not much left to play with,' he remarked, 'but it was fun while it lasted. And you've been such a good sport. Too bad it has to end now.'

He obliterated the parts of my brain that made me breathe, the parts that controlled the involuntary muscle contractions, the dilation of blood vessels, and the thousand other mundane operations required to live. They fell silent.

'I'll be seeing you shortly, my protégé, in the darker infernal regions. We'll get to do this over and over and over and over and over. Won't that be fun?'

I thought—

—but there was nothing to think. The only thing that remained was guilt and sorrow.

I was dying. In moments, my soul would be in Hell, tortured forever.

In my guilt, however, one memory remained, one that Erybus had overlooked. I couldn't even *hope* it would work, because hope was gone. The shame of my Master's death was there, whole and absolutely clear thanks to Necatane and our journey into my past.

Concealed in that memory, buried under a heap of shame, was the mnemonic construct I had long ago stolen from my Master. It rewound time, seven seconds.

I let the magic uncoil.

Erybus's game stopped. The universe came to a standstill.

Chapter Twenty-three

The universe ended.

Then it rotated backwards along its celestial spinning path. Seven seconds it retreated . . . slowed to a halt . . . then spun forward into time.

Abaris's magic worked. I had seven seconds to relive. His memory faded. The guilt remained.

I returned to the world of light.

The battle of wills, the dragon's tortures, and the destruction of my ego: it had taken less than seven seconds. From the traces of knowledge that lingered in my memory, I knew time was a personal experience. My struggle with Erybus might have taken only an instant. Hell must be like that: a moment stretched forever. To be stuck in one place, with the same thoughts, never going anywhere, and never changing.

These seven seconds would change, though. Of that I was certain.

Inside the pentagram I stood. Mike was on the other side of the pedestal. He advanced. 'That was my ticket off of Hades,' he spat, 'my one chance. You blew my one chance off that rock!'

'It was an accident,' I stammered. 'Please, Mike, I didn't mean to do it.'

'Sure you meant to do it,' he whispered, hate dripping from his words. 'You're evil, and that's why I gotta *punish* you.'

The odor of peaches was suddenly in the air. The borrowing ritual swam up from unconscious depths. It strained to be released, even though I hadn't keyed a single mnemonic. I wrestled with it. There was no magic left to reverse time and save me now. If I released it again, I knew what awaited me. And I'd die before I let the dragon inside my mind a second time.

With great care, I swallowed the mnemonic lore even as it started to uncoil. I willed my panic to dissipate. The urge to release it faded.

Mike took two steps closer to the Grail. The glow from it tinged his face an unnatural blue. 'Why didn't you get Dad when you heard me scream my head off?'

I had frozen, standing before my father's door, paralyzed with terror. Would he have beaten me up for interrupting him? Did he know what Rebux planned to do to us?

'You were a little coward then,' Mike hissed, 'and you still are. Running away. Why don't you go upstairs to your room and hide?'

Hide. That was a good idea: to disappear, to curl up in a ball and forget everything.

His words are tricks, said the psychologist. *He weaves a maze of illusion and memory. Do not fall into his trap.*

'Don't listen to them!' Mike screamed and shook his fist in my face. 'They're not real. Didn't you know? Abaris, sure, Omar, sure, even Aaron, because there was magic to steal from their minds. That's the only part of the borrowing ritual you ever really learned. The rest you made up.'

'What?'

He inched closer. 'It started with the guy in the sewers. You shot him. Only the details got twisted in your mind because you couldn't stomach the killing. Too much blood on your hands already, I guess. You reinvented what happened, kept him alive so you wouldn't have to feel guilty. The same thing happened with Medea. Only you took it a step further with her. She does all your murdering for you. The psychologist, he's there to console you; Celeste, to keep you company on those lonely nights; and the gambler, so you'd have some fun. You're a sick boy, Germain.'

They're not real? Were they parts of me? Fractured? Or was this another lie?

Worry about it later, Fifty-five said. *Take him out – quick.*

Indecision. It stopped me twenty years ago, froze me outside the cellar door, but I was not a little boy anymore. This creature wasn't Mike, or Erybus, or Abaris, or a dragon. All his words were trickery and every guise false. I had to kill him before he muddled my thoughts again. The pistol was useless. Erybus shrugged off the wounds, changed his shape like others slipped out of a sweater. Hand-to-hand combat was absurd. If only I had a handful of holy water, or a cross, or a wooden stake to thrust through his vampire heart – my eyes locked on the glowing chalice – or a holy Grail!

I threw the pistol in Mike's face and snatched the Grail off the pedestal, dumping its rancid split-pea soup contents onto the floor. The wood steamed where the gunk landed. I hefted the stone chalice. It was heavy, almost possessed a gravity of its own, solid and unbreakable – the perfect blunt object.

Mike brought both his arms up to protect himself. 'No, Germain! Forget what happened. That's all in the past. We're brothers. I'm the only one you have left.'

'You lie!' I hammered the cup at his head. There was magic between us. It slowed my arm and made my skin crawl. The Grail grew heavy; it penetrated whatever sorcerous defense he had. It connected with the left side of his skull.

There was a crack. He reeled back, stunned. His right arm fell limp to his side. Where the Grail hit him, a black spot appeared, not a bruise purple-black, but a scorch mark, smoldering char. The same cup Christ's lips touched, the same cup that Parzival quested for, and the same cup that Osrick cursed his one true love with burned this monster.

I didn't stop.

'You bastard!' I hit him again with all the strength in my one arm. He slumped to the floor, face up, head smoking, and blood splattered across the floor. 'You're not Mike,' I cried, 'you're something from Hell.' I struck again at his head, then once more, and a third time, and a fourth.

What remained of his head was outlined in a bloody halo, spreading slowly over the inlaid wood, patterns of cherry and teak, swirls of ebony. The scent of fermented peaches was thick in the air. I waited and watched – afraid he'd turn into a dragon. But he didn't. He remained my brother, twice murdered by me.

Another of Erybus's tricks?

'Very clever,' I told the corpse, 'make me think I killed Mike again. Make me lose my mind. Well, it won't work!' I kicked him, and hoped he'd get up so I could pound him with the Grail. It struck me as hilarious, so I laughed until tears rolled down my cheeks.

Perhaps, the psychologist whispered, *it would be wise if another took control.*

Listen to the egghead, Fifty-five urged. *Get a grip. We've got to leave. How long do you think it's going to take before some-one notices their boss is dead? This place must be under surveillance.*

I stopped laughing and examined the body. It was Mike . . . or at least something that had Mike's face.

That will buy us some time, Fifty-five said. *But I'll bet his DNA hasn't changed. They'll figure out what happened soon enough. Stuff the Grail into the bag and go.*

Yes, the Grail. With it I could still heal Lily, drink from it, and consummate our marriage. For the others it was too late – Mike down in the cellar, that was an accident, and Abaris, a single misunderstood word, what did Necatane call it? Catastrophic minutiae? Quilp died for his greed, and Virginia, my lovely Virginia, that was your fault, Setebos.

More than a fair trade for our princess, Celeste coolly replied.

Osrick leant me a portion of his legendary strength; he gave me a shoulder to lean on. We threw the cloth that covered the Grail over Mike, then together we whispered a silent prayer, addressed to whom I was uncertain. 'I am sorry, Mike, but you had it coming, then and now.'

The Grail went back inside the Gucci bag. There was no blood on it. It passed unscathed through every trial; not a crack, not a blemish, not a speck of grime stained the lustrous blue stone. I bludgeoned a man to death with it, Quilp's body crushed while he held it, and Osrick shattered his world around it. It still looked fresh and radiant and full of wonder. I hated it.

Back into the private elevator. I rejoined my chrome escorts.

'Nice night for a stroll, huh, boys?'

Neither of them answered, although one of the cyborgs cracked her face to smile at me. A short ride together, then they remanded me over to the custody of the receptionist in the lobby.

'Did all go well, sir?' the receptionist inquired. 'Is there anything the management can do for or get for you? Anything?'

'Everything is perfect,' I lied. 'Do you have a smoke?'

She removed a gold case from her jacket, opened it, and selected a slim black stick, which she stuck in her mouth. I picked up a lighter from the counter and stroked its side once. A flame sprang forth. I was careful to hold it with my thumb tucked under my index finger, and curled my fingernails into the palm of my hand. Even an amateur could see the dried blood beneath them.

She took a puff and handed it to me. 'We are here to serve, Mister Germain.'

'I know. Thank you.'

Up to the top floor I went. My princess awaited.

Don't be so cheerful, Fifty-five said. *Get your girlfriend and get us out of here.*

I dismissed the rented bodyguards outside the suite and let myself in. In the foyer were boxes: hatboxes, long flat dress boxes, shoe boxes, and jewelry boxes. A trail of lids and tissue paper and liquid foam led through the parlor and into the bedroom. Within, I heard Lily singing. Flowers were here, too, expensive grand arrangements that belonged at someone's funeral, African violets, apricot-colored charisma roses, cherry blossoms and, of course, lilies. Their perfume was overwhelming, thick in the air, and enticing.

On the coffee table was the bill. Tallied on the crisp disposable was a fortune. Every dress an original, the jewels were real, and I never imagined it would cost so much to import fresh flowers from Earth. I couldn't blame Lily, though. She didn't even have a bouquet of flowers at our wedding. Besides, I had stuck her in this pleasure suite to keep her busy.

Lily emerged from the bedroom, cradling an eggshell porcelain bowl of water and floating orchids. She wore a pleated silk skirt, the silver belt she had worn since our wedding, a transparent white top, and a diamond necklace to match the sparkles in her eyes. The diamonds were large, a string of them, four or five carats each.

Her joy dimmed, however, at the sight of me.

Something is dreadfully wrong, the psychologist warned me.

'So,' she said, and set the bowl down. Half the water sloshed out. 'You return. Do you have the Grail, or did you deceive me about that, too?'

'I don't understand.'

'Of course you do.' She disappeared into the bedroom, and returned with a disposable – thrust it into my hand.

There were two sites active on the display. The top layer was the genealogy of a monarchy, going all the way back to Earth, before the first and second expansions. Branches of this tree extended to the present, the Florentine Emperor, and his cousin, the Duke of the Melbourne Cluster. One of the smaller boughs ended rather abruptly, the royal family of Kenobrac. That one she outlined in red.

She knows you lied, Celeste said. *She knows she's still a princess and you're a nothing.*

Fifty-five hissed, *You should have listened to me when you had the chance to ice her.*

She feels betrayed, the psychologist confirmed.

Osrick was thinking too; part of my mind circled like a cat trying to settle down, but I didn't have time for the lovesick knight now. I had to find out how much trouble I was in.

The bottom layer was an open node to the offices of Kell, Hermann, and Schutzer, Solicitation Services. Volumes of legal-speak filled my eyes: on marriage, joint custody of properties and monies, cases to back every conceivable position and contingency, even how estates were divided after a divorce or the death of a spouse.

'Let me explain.'

'No,' she said and stiffened. 'Men of Earth have nothing but lies on their tongues. I will be generous to you, Germain, for you did find the Grail for me, and you did vanquish the ghost of Osrick, noble deeds for which I shall reward you with your life. Go. But leave the Cup of Regulus.'

'We're married,' I pointed out.

'That can be dissolved in a variety of manners,' she replied. 'Again, we ask you to leave us, before we change our mind.'

She spoke to me using the royal 'we.' A bad sign. 'But I know how to cure your plague.'

That got her attention. She issued no additional threats, so I explained. 'One sip from the Grail is proof against the disease. If I drink from it, we may touch without ill effect. We can consummate our marriage and break Osrick's curse the way he intended it to be broken.'

Osrick demanded my attention. I ignored him.

'If that is true,' Lilian said thoughtfully, 'then it follows that imbibing the entire contents would cure our curse entirely. Is that not true?'

'I cannot say. The Grail is the source of your curse. Osrick may have designed it so only his way, my way, can unravel your misfortune.'

A moment passed while she considered this.

'No. We will never let you touch us. Not after what you put us through. You took our heritage. You made us believe there was no royalty left in this new world, and that we were as common as you, as common as a thief. We will not forgive that.' She took a careful long look into my eyes, then, 'Once, I thought I might have loved you, Germain, but no longer.'

I took a step back. She was a replica of her mother, hard eyes without warmth, and a face that held no emotion, an ice queen.

'Now,' she declared before I went any further, 'I will relieve you of the Cup of Regulus.'

I opened the bag and pulled the Grail out. 'This is what you want?'

Eighty-four deaths I suffered for this hunk of stone. I lost Virginia, and got dragged half way to Hell and back, so I could hand it over to her? I think not.

'Go ahead,' I said, 'if you want it so bad, try to take it.'

'You have great courage, Germain, and we admire that. It is the reason we have tolerated such behavior for so long, but our patience is exhausted. You are given a final warning. Leave the Cup of Regulus and go. We shall not pursue the matter as we did with the other thief.'

'No.'

The runes of her belt flickered a nacreous green, and the air surrounding her shimmered as it had when the Bren erected their wall of magic to protect their castle. The creatures of mist appeared too, a fog that condensed from nothing, flowed across the floor, and encircled me, blocking my escape. I recalled what they did to human flesh.

The part of my mind that was Osrick moved my hand then, slipped my thumb under and between my ring finger and pinkie. It was the sign language gesture for the letter 'm.' It was also the first mnemonic for the borrowing ritual. He wanted me to release it? On Lilian? Why?

Do not attempt it, the psychologist warned. *Another person-*

*ality added to yours in its current fragile state will overwhelm
your ego, especially one as strong as the princess's. Our minds
would lose cohesion. It would be utter chaos. She would drive
you insane.*

I tried to understand the parts of me that were Osrick, the parts
of the dead knight that blended with mine, but they eluded me,
evaporated at my touch. Again, my hand moved, and the first key
turned. The next mnemonic was on my left hand – which was
gone. I had mastered the sorcery, however; I could use it without
the mnemonics if I had to. But again, why?

It would either destroy Lilian or me. Is that what Osrick
wanted? To die rather than live without his beloved? It wasn't
despair that I sensed from him, however. It was hope.

My hand moved again, and this time I did not resist. I loosened
the magic, allowed the coiled memories to unwind: the *Seven
Scrolls of Telepathic Construction*, and the physiological fundamentals of intelligent thought surfaced. I sent my mind toward
her.

To the spirits of the air, she commanded, 'Kill. But be quick
about it. Do not play with him.'

'Knowledge,' I whispered. 'Give me your life.'

Insubstantial fingers took shape in the fog and, attached to
them, long groaning faces with piranha jaws.

My mind touched Lilian's.

She was shocked, then furious that I had the audacity to violate
her in such a manner. She resisted me. Lilian had the mind of a
muse, two centuries old, trained and disciplined, honed to an edge
by her isolation. Even with Osrick, even with my other
personalities fighting together, her resolve was greater than mine.
She would have crushed me immediately had I not tasted
damnation, had I not experienced Erybus's *punishment*. It gave
me something she didn't have: desperation. Having been to Hell
once, even if it was only for seconds, was enough to make the
difference. It evened the odds.

We viciously embraced, swarming through each other's recollections, looking for any weakness. She found one first, in Osrick: his affections for her. Lilian ripped them out by the roots. Doing so, she revealed a similar weakness to me. There, a memory of her and Osrick, strolling through the palace's garden, under two moons, her heart filled with desire, a tiny kiss, and a promise of love eternal. I removed that image with the skill of a surgeon.

Circling again, wrestlers seeking leverage to throw the other, we clashed.

Osrick collapsed in my thoughts. Without a fight, he gave up.

Lilian took advantage and savaged his mind, destroying whatever she chanced to touch upon. I heard her laugh. She relaxed her own guard, however; she ignored me, Germain, at Osrick's expense. This was why he wanted the borrowing ritual: a pair of deaths, star-crossed lovers.

I lunged, penetrated deep into her mind, tearing through two centuries of memory and madness. In her core was what Osrick desired: his princess. I took her. Lily's first fifteen years were there: training in etiquette, politics, her first magic, her first communion, a delicate laugh that sounded like little bells, countless hours spent with dressmakers, a love for her father I never expected and, most importantly, a crush on Sir Osrick. Genuine feelings of warmth she once had for him, fantasies of them together, far away from courtly matters. I took it all from her, took it for Osrick.

She pulled free from our embrace, realizing her mistake too late. I was close to her center. I went to her core, scrambled her autonomic nervous system, then withdrew.

Osrick was gone from my mind. Lilian had dismantled him.

The sorcerous energies faded. My perceptions returned to the physical world. Yet there was something left, in between imagination and reality like the after-image of the sun when gazed at too long. I beheld a ghostly translucent Lilian in a dress of light, smiling, her bare hand holding Osrick's. And Sir Osrick no longer wore his armor, but a silver robe and a crown of diamonds. They remained like that for three heartbeats, then the knight bowed to me, and they vanished, passed into oblivion.

The creatures of mist paused, writhed and boiled, seemingly confused without their mistress. They reformed over her body. Nebulous fingers ran over her length, soothing, pushing her chest up and down, but Lilian did not awaken. The cloud diffused through the suite until only a faint haze remained in the air, and that too faded.

One last sigh escaped Lilian and she was still.

The princess and Osrick finally found one another after two hundred years. I grieved, but more for myself, at what I had lost, than for her. She had tranquillity, I think. So did Osrick. I missed his presence. Annoying as the knight was, there was a part of him I was weak without. In my thoughts was a space left from his existence, hollow.

And all I had left was a string of murders like so many pearls strung on a thread.

I left Lilian among her flowers, not even bothering to place the Grail back in its bag.

It was cursed. Osrick lost all he cherished, so did the others who found this cup. Myself, I lost my family, every person I might dare call friend, and Virginia, and I had yet to drink from it. I almost laughed. There was nothing left to lose, my life perhaps, but that seemed unimportant.

I wandered through the casino, and didn't even bother to hide the Grail. The gambler left me alone. The tourists were too busy to notice me, consumed with their games, drunk, and winning and losing their money. Three tables away, a tournament of three cubes in the hole was in progress. A roar of approval erupted as a young man threw a winning combination. From the cheers it sounded like a long shot. He was jubilant as he raked in a pile of orange and pink chips. It was a sizeable chunk of cash, yet he stayed and bet again, and rolled the dice. He lost. Didn't he know the casino would switch dice on him, tilt the table, or alter the magnetic field to recover their losses? Why did he stay and play their game?

A cocktail waitress found me. I was not drinking or losing money. Her job was to see that I did both in large quantities. 'Sir, can I fill that for you?' she inquired, pointing to the Grail.

Below her lovely throat were twin topazes, the insignia of a full-apprentice server. Her dress was cut low at her cleavage, high on her thigh, and revealed anything a man might want, but my eyes wandered back to her insignia, reminding me of another full apprentice that I had met here.

'A drink?' I echoed. 'Yes, that's precisely what I need, a drink.' I got up and left her bewildered, ran through the casinos, back to the *Grail Angel*.

'Setebos, are you here?'

On the cockpit console a cube of blue and green stained glass appeared and cried, 'You have the Grail!'

It wasn't important if I erased him, if I only hallucinated doing it, or if Setebos was a real angel. He could fly the ship and that was all that mattered. 'Set course for the Erato system, and get me there fast.'

'As you wish, my Master. Should you not drink from the Grail? There is much that can go awry between here and there. It might be wise to—'

'No,' I insisted, 'the Erato system. Don't wait for clearance from the tower.' I slumped into the co-pilot's chair, and examined my Grail. Inside, I traced the path of silver veins across the smooth blue stone. It was the loveliest thing I could imagine. 'Take me home, Setebos.'

I must have nodded off, a sleep without dreams, for when I looked up the terraformed world Erato shone with the reflected light of its gold and white suns. Clouds covered a quarter of its surface; the rest was indigo and dots of hazel, patches of emerald and a few smears of red. One pole had a frosty cap of ice, while the other was a warm amber.

'Find a spot to land, please,' I said.

The world loomed large on the displays as Setebos took us into the atmosphere. He dove to the underside of the planet, a long arc that gave me the sensation that we fell straight up. We skimmed over the snow-capped mountains, then across a clear lake. A flock of geese took flight, startled by the large black angel in the sky above them. The ship slowed, hovered over a meadow, then gently touched down.

I went to the captain's quarters. Without looking at Virginia's burned body, I wrapped her and the Grail in the comforter, then dragged the bundle outside with my one arm.

'I suppose you will leave me soon, Setebos.'

'Yes, Germain, Grail King. There are other games to be played. The ship shall remain here, however. You may have need of it.'

'I don't think so, but thanks. And thanks for making sure I won.'

In a fading voice he added, 'Go drink from your Grail. Go heal yourself and your fragmented land.'

I marched through the meadow's knee-high grass into a grove of ancient black-barked oaks with golden leaves that sighed in the breeze. Mockingbirds sang challenge songs back and forth, and chased each other – a flurry of white and black feathers. I was owner of this new world. Here was where I would start anew. Elk crowned with antlers and full-eyed rabbits paused only momentarily from foraging to note my approval, unafraid.

I walked until my strengh left, utill I came upon a stream that meandered its way through this fairy forest. Above, a band of sunlight shone through the parted canopy. I stepped in the water and found it frigid and waist deep. Kneeling, I unwrapped Virginia and the Grail, pulled her into the water with me, let her drift a moment, then guided her to the opposite bank.

Three times I rinsed the Grail, filled it, then gazed deep into the vessel. It looked like ordinary water, but a sense of power built within, magic that made every hair on my body stand on end.

The mockingbirds took flight. Another set of eyes watched me; I felt them. Looking around, I saw nothing, no one. Except in the shade of a tree, a slice of shadow moved and took the shape of a man. It was Fifty-five.

'Hang on a second there,' he said. 'I'll take that first.'

I handed him the Grail and watched as he took a long drink from the cup.

'I know we've had our differences of opinion in the past, junior, but I wanted to tell you that it was great working with you. We got further up the corporate ladder together than I ever could by myself. You've got talent. You can do anything you want with it.' He clasped my hand, then whispered, 'Good bye. Watch your back.'

His shadow-skin cloaked him in darkness, but the shadow didn't move, it remained there, grew lighter and lighter, until the sun passed completely through it. He faded both from my sight and from my mind. His memories were still in place, but his voice was silent, his presence nonexistant.

'My turn, honey,' Celeste said. She sat by the edge of the stream, her high heels off, and her delicate feet soaking in the water. She wore too much make-up: blood-red lipstick, white face powder, and eyes stained Kelly green. It would have made any other woman look like a clown, but on Celeste it made her look like a ceramic doll, perfectly molded. She stood, smoothed her white kimono, then took gracefully tiny steps over to me. With her small skilled hands she caressed my face and took the Grail. She drank a sip, and left a faint imprint of her lipstick on the rim.

'I wish I could stay with you,' she said. 'There were so many adventures out there for us. But this is one little orgy I must attend by myself. Have fun.'

I blinked and she was gone.

A pair of dice rolled on the sandy shore. The gambler picked them up. 'Eleven,' he said. 'I should have bet.' He wore the same suit I had killed him in, a dark brown tweed that was long out of style, with sleeves wrinkled beyond repair from being repeatedly rolled up. He took the Grail and guzzled, letting most of the water spill down his chin.

'Try to remember to bluff when you've got a lousy hand,' he said. 'And try to relax. Life is too short for you to worry about the odds.' He slipped his dice into my pocket. 'That's for luck.' He winked. 'They're loaded.'

Behind me, I sensed Medea.

I ducked and spun around just in time to see her foot lash out where my head had been a second ago. 'I know your tricks,' I told her.

She brushed half of her long hair behind one ear, and replied, 'Most of them.'

I offered her the Grail, and she took a single long draw without removing her eyes from me, then said, 'I don't have any advice for you like the others. You were the only one to best me. The only one to catch me off guard. So maybe you know more about killing than I do.'

She offered her hand, but I didn't take it. She smiled, and left me.

Only the psychologist remained.

From the other side of the stream he came, marching through the forest, in gray robes and using his bamboo staff as a walking stick. Perspiration beaded on his bald head, and when he halted, it glistened in the sunlight.

'What's happening?' I asked. 'Why are you all leaving? Is it as Erybus said? Are you parts of my own fragmented mind? Am I crazy?'

'That is one possibility,' he said. 'The Grail heals your psyche or it releases our captured souls to heaven. I cannot answer with any degree of accuracy, because I am part of the diagnosis. Any conclusion would be entirely subjective. But I can say this: every person has voices in their heads, whispered doubts and aspirations, dreams and nightmares. How much reality one gives them, how much you allow yourself to be controlled . . . that only you can decide.'

He touched the surface of the water with his staff, watched the ripples float downstream, distort, and disappear. 'We leave you a whole man,' he said. 'Singular, yes, but stronger, I believe, without our voices.' He sighed. 'You were an interesting case. Would that I could remain to see what happens next, but I must depart. I have stayed in this world too long.'

I offered him the cup, but he declined with a wave of his hand. 'There is no need for me to drink. I know my way out.'

He was gone, and I was finally alone.

Not a drop was gone from the Grail. There wasn't any lipstick smeared on its rim.

I drank half of the water within. It was icy, and did not warm once inside my mouth. It went cold down my throat, into my body, refreshing and revitalizing my flesh. I knew I could walk the circumference of this planet, explore the whole world in a day, slay every dragon I came upon, build a castle in an hour, father a dozen sons and daughters before breakfast the next morning, and be happy. My body surged with strength. My lost arm was whole again, regenerated by the healing water. I knew without a doubt that I had power now, power to influence my world, even the entire galaxy, power to make peace or wage war, split this planet in half, or make it a paradise.

The Grail blazed with white fire. It threw hard shadows behind the trees and made the stream appear as mercury. It sparkled, wavered insubstantial, and waited for me . . . waited for me to consume the last half of its power.

With great care, I openened Virginia's swollen lips, and poured the rest of the water into her mouth, across her face, and over her burned body. I took her in my arms, and with mouth still wet with the Grail's water, I kissed her for what seemed to be an eternity.

I kissed her until she woke.